AF609373

FINDING Beauty

ALSO BY ANN PENNY

Capturing Love

Finding Beauty

Saving Soul

FINDING *Beauty*

ANN PENNY

Arndell

FINDING BEAUTY
Copyright © Ann Penny
First Published in 2021 by Ann Penny excluding new content exclusive to this edition.
This edition published by Arndell, an imprint of Keeperton in 2025.
Dharawal Country, 1 / 18 Manning Street, Kiama, NSW, Australia, 2533

10 9 8 7 6 5 4 3 2 1

ISBN 978-1-923232-12-9 (paperback)

Excerpt from Saving Soul Copyright © Ann Penny 2022

The moral right of the author has been asserted

This novel is a work of fiction. Any reference to names, characters, businesses, places, events and incidents are products of the author's imagination or are used in a fictitious manner. Any resemblance to real persons, living or dead, is entirely coincidental.

All rights are reserved. No part of this book may be reproduced or transmitted in any form or by any means, graphic, electronic, or mechanical, including photocopying, recording, taping, or by any information storage retrieval system such as AI, without the express written permission of the Publisher.

Edited by Heather Bosevski Editing Services & Jenn Lockwood Editing
Formatted by Kirby Jones
Cover Design by Christabelle Designs

Printed and bound by CPI Group (UK) Ltd, Croydon, CR0 4YY

Sydney | Washington D.C. | London
www.keeperton.com/arndell

For my husband. Who doesn't read my books,
but supports my writing dreams anyway.

AUTHOR'S NOTE

Thank you for choosing to read **Finding Beauty**. For maximum enjoyment, I strongly advise reading **Capturing Love** before delving into this novel.

* *This full-length, contemporary romance novel contains strong language, sex scenes and sensitive subject matter that could be triggering for some readers. This book is recommended for mature readers.*

Trigger warnings
Major themes: dysfunctional family relationships & miscarriage (backstory).

Minor themes: attempted sexual abuse (backstory) & mental health disorders.

Prologue

Ninety days at New Hope Rehabilitation Center. *Check.*

No alcohol. No drugs. No sex. *Check.*

A newfound sense of confidence. *Fuck.*

I glanced back, waiting for the confidence to Indiana Jones it out the closing doors, but it didn't follow. The brochure lied.

Drawing in a long unsteady breath, I lifted my suitcase and carried it down the stairs. The salty Malibu breeze caressed my face, calming me as I approached my ride. I hadn't seen Grayson since he had brought me here after my self-destructive behavior almost cost him the love of his life. Now, both he and Josie were waiting for me with smiles I didn't deserve.

Although Grayson had kept his distance through my recovery, Josie had called multiple times. After everything I had put her through, she still had the capacity for forgiveness and had turned into an unlikely friend. She is beautiful inside and out, and perfect for Grayson in every way.

My parents hadn't visited once, nor had I expected them to. They were still furious at me for breaking off my *fake* engagement to Grayson and ruining their plans to merge Warren Media with Harlow Corp. I was an embarrassment to the family. A failure. And for the first time in twenty-eight years, I couldn't care less.

With an emotionally and physically absent father and a narcissistic mother, along with years of emotional manipulation, my therapist wasn't surprised my mental health was a shit show. I'd developed depression and a mild dependent personality disorder, and together with my abandonment issues, the anxiety of losing the only person I could truly rely on had sent me spiraling.

Of course, my parents dismissed the diagnosis and refused to support my treatment plan, meaning Grayson had to flip the bill. Ironically, he was the person I was dependent on.

I'd used Grayson as my crutch for so long that I didn't know how to survive without him. I'd done things, terrible things, to keep him beside me, but I'd finally learned to let him go. To let him be happy…without me.

"Do you really expect me to carry my own bags?" I hollered at the two people I cherished the most in the world. Grayson rushed forward to pick up my luggage, but I shoved his hand aside with a laugh. "I got this, Harlow."

Grayson shook his head as he pulled me in for a hug. "Glad to see you haven't lost your sense of humor."

I caught Josie's eye over his shoulder and pushed Grayson off like a sister would a brother. "Hi, Jos," I said, taking a hesitant step toward her.

"Hi, Mel." Josie's mouth curved into a gorgeous smile before she threw her arms around me. "Are you ready to start your new life in the big city?"

Adrenaline filtered through my body. "More than ever."

"Well, jump in the car, or you're going to miss your flight." Grayson snatched my suitcase and threw it into the trunk before opening the door for me.

"I really could've caught a cab," I uttered, sliding into the backseat. I still couldn't believe they had paused their epic honeymoon in Europe just to drive me to the airport.

"Don't be silly," Josie replied, peeking back at me. "We wanted to see you."

Warmth filled my cheeks. "Thank you. It is nice to see some familiar faces."

Grayson caught my eye in the rearview mirror as he started the car. "You still haven't spoken to your parents?"

"No," I said, gazing out the heavily tinted window. "What about you?"

"We're…working on things."

Josie looked across at Grayson with a tight smile before placing her hand over his. "We just need to look forward. We all do."

My heart twinged as I gazed down at their interlocked fingers. I wanted that. Their love was something I never thought possible for people like us, but Grayson had proved me wrong. Their relationship gave me hope. Hope that had gotten me through the last three months.

Apparently, I was a perfect storm of bad parenting and unfortunate experiences. I never realized how damaged I was until I removed all my vices. The drinking, the drugs, and the sex were all my go-to avoidance behaviors. Not even Grayson could fill the inescapable void.

In the downtime I had between therapy sessions, an old love of mine resurfaced—art. I'd studied Art History in college, not to get a job—I didn't need one of those—but to one day fill my house with beauty. I refreshed myself with all the greats... Michelangelo, Van Gogh, Monet, Miro, Dali...and researched new artists I believed had the potential to join them.

"Adrian is so excited to have you join their team," Josie said, breaking the silence that lulled over the car.

My stomach somersaulted. "I am too. Thanks, Josie. I owe you."

"Are you kidding? They practically begged me for your number after my exhibition."

I'd attended many exhibitions at AG Galleries throughout America, but Josie's photography show was my first experience behind the scenes. To my delight and the curator's amazement, her incredible work sold out in just one night.

"I hope it works out," I uttered as the devil on my shoulder started dancing.

"You'll be fine," Grayson said, clearly sensing my apprehension. "You're a natural at this stuff."

Josie reached back and squeezed my hand. "You really are."

For the rest of the drive, we chatted about Grayson and Josie's adventures through Europe. Although I was happy for them, the familiar dread of Grayson disappearing again crept up on me. I closed my eyes and repeated several mantras until the unwelcome feelings subsided. I had to do this without him.

Half an hour later, we arrived at the airport to set off in different directions. Grayson and Josie were heading to Spain—

in a private jet, no doubt—while I spent the last of my savings on a commercial flight to New York.

"Now," Josie said, bracing my forearms. "Amy's moving in with her boyfriend in the same building, so you'll have the apartment to yourself."

"And we're not coming home anytime soon," Grayson said, grinning at his wife. "So there's no need to rush things."

"Thank you, but as soon as I have enough saved for a security deposit, I'll be out of there. You guys have already done more than enough for me."

"I'm so proud of you, Mel," Josie said, throwing her arms around my neck. "You have to send me an email once you're all settled, okay? Oh, and give Luci a big hug for me, will you?"

I scrunched up my nose as we parted. "Who's Luci?"

Grayson slipped his arm around his wife's waist with a deep-chested laugh. "Oh, you'll find out."

"C'mon, he's not that bad," Josie said, nudging him away with her elbow. "He's my dog, but he'll be living with Amy and Reed while we're away."

"Are you sure? I don't mind looking after him. I've always wanted a pet."

Grayson chuckled. "He isn't for beginners."

"Fair enough." I was probably more of a cat person anyway.

"Listen," Grayson uttered as all the humor left his face. "I know you won't accept any help from me, so if you need anything, please ask Josie."

The corner of my mouth lifted. "That's a bit of a loophole, isn't it?"

His stern expression didn't falter. "I mean it. Anything at all."

As I nodded my head, Grayson stepped forward and hugged me. "Show them what you're made of, Warren."

I swallowed back tears as I peered up at the man I didn't need anymore and made sure I was the first to let go. "Goodbye, Gray."

With a warm smile, he grabbed Josie's hand and dragged her away. I expected myself to chase them down and plead with them to come with me, but instead, I remained completely still, relishing the moment. In the midst of the crowded airport, I was completely alone, and for the first time, I was okay with that.

Glancing up to the departure screen, I searched for my home for the foreseeable future. New York City. It was time to live on my terms and finally find out what I was capable of. Feeling lighter and happier than I'd ever been, I took my first step forward.

Chapter 1

11 years earlier

"Hold it right there, young lady!"

My hand froze on the doorknob. "Dammit, Grayson," I murmured, ignoring my mother as I stared out the window at the empty driveway. "Where are you?"

"Melanie?!" Her tone grew sterner.

With a low growl, I followed the sound of chopping blades into the kitchen. "Yes?"

"I knew you'd try to sneak out," she said, running her judgmental gaze over my school uniform. "I wanted to see you before your first day back."

Straightening my posture, I stepped cautiously toward my mother. The five food groups lay scattered across the countertop—the ingredients to her latest dieting fad, no doubt.

"Forget something this morning?" she asked, not even wincing as she whizzed the blender.

"I don't think so..." I didn't have chores.

She poured the liquid breakfast into two cups and tapped her lips with her index finger. "What have I taught you?"

"Never leave the house without lipstick," I droned, reaching into my bag to fish out the red lipstick she bought me, which was three shades brighter than necessary.

"You just keep forgetting these simple rules, don't you?" She chortled. "That's why you need to look your best at all times. A scatter-brain like you will need to find a successful man, and successful men appreciate attractive women."

I pressed my lips together into a tight smile but didn't say a word. It was easier to ride out the storm.

"It also wouldn't hurt to hitch that skirt up a little. You may have to wear that horrendous uniform, but you can still flaunt your best assets."

Peering down at my legs, I ran my hands over the gray skirt that already sat just above my knees. "It's fine, Mom."

"Hmm…I guess you're right. You should probably wait until you lose those extra pounds you put on over summer."

I inwardly pleaded for Grayson to arrive, and praise the Lord, a horn blasted outside. "I've got to go. I'm running late."

"I don't know why you don't get Miguel to drive you. You're putting Grayson out, making him come all the way back to Bel Air after swim practice."

The mention of our driver, aka my mother's lover, made my stomach roil. "I'm not making Grayson do anything, but he wouldn't have to if you'd just let me get my license."

Mom's nose turned up at the suggestion. "Women like us don't drive ourselves, Melanie."

"Bye, Mom," I grumbled, spinning on my heel. I'd already lost that fight a thousand times.

"Wait!"

I closed my eyes and blew all the air from my lungs. I'd almost made it.

Mom sauntered over with a sickly sweet grin and handed me an olive-green concoction. "It's the most important meal of the day."

"In a takeaway cup…" I forced a smile. "How thoughtful."

"This should fill you up for the rest of the day, so there'll be no need to eat any of that dreadful cafeteria food."

I grabbed the drink without complaint, just to get the fuck out of there. "Thanks, Mom."

"Anything for my baby," she said, tilting her head as she reached for my face. I was momentarily surprised by the loving gesture until her fingers pinched the ends of my hair. "You're clearly overdue for a trim. I'll book you in."

The horn blasted again.

"I've got to go. Grayson's waiting." I pulled away from her grasp and strode out of the kitchen before she could insult me any further.

"I'll be out late tonight," Mom called out. "So you'll have to organize your own dinner."

"Got it," I yelled before slamming the front door closed.

My smile grew as I jogged down the stairs toward Grayson's car. I threw open the passenger door and jumped in, careful not to spill the disgusting drink on the leather interior.

Grayson's warm laughter filled the car. "Whoa, since when are you so eager to get to school?"

"Since it means I can spend the next eight hours away from my mom."

"Rough morning?"

I shrugged. "Normal morning."

Grayson accelerated down the long winding driveway and through the iron gates. "There's something in the glove box that may cheer you up."

My gaze flew to the compartment in front of me. "A one-way ticket to Paris?"

He grinned. "Better."

Leaving the hideous drink in the cupholder between us, I opened the glove compartment to discover it full of breakfast bars. Full-fat, full-sugar breakfast bars.

"Oh my god." I grabbed the closest one and tore it open. "Have I told you lately how much I love you?"

Grayson chuckled. "Not since I smuggled you that burger last week."

Settling back into the seat, I relished my first bite. "What would I do without you?"

"Waste away to nothing," he grumbled. Grayson hated the way my mother treated me.

"Thanks, Gray."

"Just don't leave *that* in my car," he said, motioning to the drink between us. "It smells like feet."

"But I made it just for you."

"That's fucked up, Mel. I thought we were friends."

I grinned up at him. "The best."

Grayson always had a way of cheering me up. Ever since we were kids, he was the one person I could count on, and my life would've been a nightmare without him. He understood what my parents were like, because his were no better.

"Are you excited about starting our senior year?" Grayson asked as we grew closer to Summerhill Preparatory School.

"I guess," I muttered, eyeing my latest manicure.

"Wow." Grayson's tone oozed sarcasm. "I've never seen you so pumped."

I gazed out the tinted window as we entered the parking lot. "It's just always the same."

"Have we all become too mundane for the most popular girl in school?"

"I'm not the most popular."

Grayson laughed. "All the girls want to be you, and all the boys want to be in you. I'm pretty sure that's the definition of the most popular."

"Not *all* the boys."

He shot me a sideways glance and nudged my shoulder. "You know I don't count."

I smiled sadly. Life would've been so much easier if Grayson and I were more than friends, but it never felt right. "The boys at this school only want what they can see. They don't care about getting to know me."

"You don't exactly make it easy for them."

"Why bother?" I crossed my arms. "It's not like I'd be allowed to date any of them."

"Your parents would let you date me."

"You don't count, *remember*. Plus, there are *20 billion* reasons why they'd let me date you."

Grayson cleared his throat. "You mean *25 billion*."

"Oh right." I rolled my eyes. "My apologies."

"But Summerhill is full of filthy rich kids. I'm sure your parents wouldn't mind you dating someone like...say...Hank?"

"First, ew. And second, the Townsend fortune is leagues behind ours. Just like everyone else's at this school."

"Well, considering our parents have been planning our wedding since we were kids, I doubt either of us will be allowed to start any serious relationships until we've escaped to college."

"I'm counting the days."

Grayson sighed. "Me too."

I scrunched up the breakfast bar wrapper in my hand and chuckled. "They're going to be so upset with us."

"They sure are," he muttered, turning into the empty car space everyone left open for him because he was…well, Grayson. Summerhill's golden boy.

"I think it's our destiny, though."

Grayson's eyebrows rose as he turned to me. "To marry?"

I snorted. "To disappoint our parents."

Thankfully, Grayson and I shared homeroom, otherwise, we only had one subject together. This suited him, but not me. Grayson took school way too seriously and didn't need the distraction, but I only needed to pass. My parents had the right connections and money to get me into any college I wanted—and I wanted whatever college Grayson was going to.

Grayson was adamant about getting there on his own, spending every waking hour studying. He was expected to follow his older brother into the family business, whereas I was simply expected to find a rich husband.

I lowered myself into the seat in the middle of the back row, while Grayson sat in front, spinning around to face me.

"Schedule swap," he said, holding out his hand.

I handed mine over and took his to peruse. "Ouch, you've got Mr. Dawson *and* Ms. Peters."

"And you've got Mr. West," Grayson uttered, turning serious.

"Ugh, I know." Mr. West was more interested in my legs than my grades.

Grayson's stern eyes met mine. "Make sure you sit in the back row."

"Oh, I will," I said with a shudder. "The farther away the better."

"Harlow!" a deep voice boomed across the room.

I groaned as Grayson turned around with a wide grin.

Hank strutted toward our desks and shoved Zach Freeman, the quiet kid, out of his chair so he could sit beside me.

I offered Zach an apologetic smile as he found a new seat before narrowing my eyes at Hank.

"Looking beautiful as always, Mel," he uttered with a sleazy wink.

"Charming as always, Hank," I replied, dripping with sarcasm.

The corner of Zach's mouth twitched, but he didn't look up.

"How was Paris?" Grayson asked, quick to defuse the growing tension.

Hank and I didn't get along. We merely tolerated each other for Grayson's sake.

Hank chuckled. "Let's just say, French women sure know how to fuck."

I groaned and zoned out of their conversation immediately. Grayson wasn't like Hank, but I still didn't want to hear his friend ramble on about his summer conquests.

Staring down at my schedule, trying to memorize it, I was interrupted by growing murmurs echoing through the room. I lifted my head, wondering what the fuss was about, and then I saw him.

Just like a bad 80's rom-com, he strolled into the classroom in slow motion. A shaggy mop of dark hair, a strong jawline, and the prettiest blue eyes I'd ever seen. And tall…not as tall as Grayson, but taller than me. He had my full attention—along with every other girl in the room.

"What's up with you?" Grayson asked, clearly oblivious to the new arrival.

Warmth traveled up my neck and straight down below.

Grayson followed my gaze to where the newbie stood, searching for an empty seat. With a welcoming smile, he lifted his hand and greeted him with a small wave. "Over here!" Grayson called out before pointing to the seat beside him.

"What are you doing?" I hissed.

"Don't be so rude," he muttered with a knowing twinkle in his eye. He turned back and threw out his hand. "Grayson."

The new guy shook it with an uneasy smile. "Scott."

Scott's gaze flickered to mine, but I quickly lowered my eyes, attempting to slow my racing heart.

Grayson chuckled at my response. "This unusually ill-mannered girl is Melanie, and this is Hank."

Hank shook his hand tightly, undoubtedly trying to size him up. "Welcome to Summerhill."

"So, where do you come from, Scott?" Grayson asked, sending me a curious look that I tried to ignore.

Scott tapered his eyes at our weird exchange as he sat down. "Nowhere in particular. We move around a lot."

Hank's eyebrows drew together. "What's your last name?"

My temper spiked as I glared at Hank. "Does it matter?"

Scott's gaze darted to mine, but I lowered my head again. His eyes were entirely too blue.

"I'm just curious," Hank said, leaning back into his chair and crossing his arms.

"Blackwood," Scott answered, but his gaze still burned into the side of my face.

Hank's head tilted. "I'm not familiar with that name."

"That's probably because we've only just met."

I wiped my hand over my mouth to hide my smile, but Grayson erupted into laughter.

"I like you already," Grayson said, turning to face the teacher as she walked in.

Scott's gaze lingered on me until I looked up. "Front of the room is that way," I said, pointing to the teacher.

Hank sniggered. "Oh, burn."

Scott pursed his lips, but his eyes sparkled. With a quick nod, he turned to the teacher as she began the morning roll call.

"Why did you do that?" I asked, nudging Grayson's side as we exited the room.

Grayson laughed and wrapped his arm around my shoulders as we walked down the crowded corridor. "You like him," he whispered in my ear.

My heart lurched, and I pushed him away. "No, I don't."

That only made him laugh harder. "I've never seen you blush over a boy before."

"Shut up!" I glanced back to make sure Scott wasn't nearby.

"Someone has a crush," he sang, continuing the torment.

I ran my hands down my face. "Oh my god, can you stop?"

His rascally smile made girls swoon as they passed us. "I'm right, aren't I?"

"Argh, I'm going to class." I swiveled on my heel in the opposite direction, desperate to end the conversation.

"I knew it," he called after me.

I lifted my hand to wave but raised my middle finger instead. "I'll see you at lunch, Harlow."

As I walked through the cafeteria with my tray of no more than 300 calories, I spotted Grayson at our usual table, but my steps slowed when I discovered he wasn't alone. I took in the faces surrounding him and groaned. Hank. *Idiot.* Lisa. *Moron.* Miranda. *Okay, I guess.* Sarah. *No thanks.* Randy. *Boring.* And the new guy. *Fuck.*

I usually avoided talking to these people, partly because I hated their sense of entitlement, and partly because I was a bitch. I didn't mean to be. I just had no tolerance for people who annoyed me. And most of the people at Summerhill annoyed me.

Summerhill Preparatory School was where you sent your kids if you had money. *Lots* of money. Only Grayson and I were different. While most of these kids were in line to inherit millions, we were set to inherit *billions.* For one reason or another, everyone wanted to be our friend. Grayson let them. I didn't. No one was genuine in our world, and I hated it.

As if he could feel the daggers shooting from my eyes, Grayson looked up as I approached. "Mel," he said, ignoring my death stare. "I saved you a seat." He grinned mischievously as he tapped the chair between him and the new boy.

"I'm fine over here," I grumbled, changing direction and placing my tray at the opposite end of the table.

Grayson shook his head. "Suit yourself."

My entire body heated as Scott watched me, so I picked at my food until the group continued their conversation. I wasn't used to feeling uncomfortable, and it irritated me.

"You play football?" Randy asked Scott. He had the physique for it.

"I've never really been at a school long enough to join a team," he replied before taking a bite of his sandwich.

Hank threw a tater tot in his mouth. "You an Army brat or something?"

Scott's jaw twitched. "Or something."

His response piqued my curiosity. Most of the kids at our school would've reeled off how much their family was worth, where they lived, and what car they drove by now. But Scott didn't utter a word about himself.

"So, where are you all from?" he asked, cleverly turning the question around to avoid further interrogation.

The table lit up with chatter about their family's fortunes, while Grayson and I remained quiet. We didn't announce our wealth.

"What about you two?" Scott asked, panning his gaze from Grayson to me.

Hank laughed. "I'm surprised you don't already know. These guys are Summerhill royalty."

Scott's brows lifted.

"Heir to Harlow Corp," Hank said, pointing at Grayson. "And sole heiress to Warren Media," he added, turning to me with a smirk. "King and Ice Queen of Summerhill Prep."

"Shut up, Hank," I uttered, glaring across at him.

Hank's smug smile grew larger as the girls around him giggled.

Grayson cleared his throat, drawing everyone's attention effortlessly. "So, what's happening this weekend?" His eyes caught mine, sending me a silent message to calm down.

"I heard there's a party at Rebecca's," Lisa said, squeezing Grayson's bicep.

I rolled my eyes. "Ugh, no thanks."

Lisa glanced around uncomfortably. "Well, I thought if we all went, it would be kind of fun."

"What's this *we* business?" I stared directly at Lisa without blinking. I'd never liked her.

"Sounds fun. Count me in," Scott interjected.

My eyes snapped to his, and he held my gaze in a silent challenge. Not many people were brave enough to take me on, but I decided to cut the new guy some slack. I turned to Grayson. "You may want to give your new friend some advice on how to avoid an STD…he's going to need it."

Scott's face paled as Grayson chuckled.

Lisa's eyes grew wide. "They're just rumors…"

I smirked. "How's that itch, Hank?"

"What the fu…Gray! You told her?!" Hank lunged at him.

Grayson pushed him away with a laugh. "Sorry, man, you know I can't keep anything from her."

Hank sank back into his chair, shaking his head. "You're a bitch," he hissed at me.

"Thank you." I smiled sweetly. "My mother would be so proud."

Scott's judgmental gaze rolled over me, and all the humor drained from my face. For some reason, his opinion of me seemed to matter, and it irked me.

"So, what do you suggest we do this weekend, Melanie?" Grayson asked, clearly annoyed by my behavior.

"Do whatever the fuck you want," I snapped before leaving the table and the remaining 299 calories behind.

"What was with you at lunch today?" Grayson asked as I climbed into his car that afternoon.

My head fell back against the seat. "You know I'm not great with people."

"Come on, it's our senior year. It can't always be just you and me."

I crossed my arms with a huff. "Why not?"

"Because we're going to miss out on all the fun."

I closed my eyes, knowing he was right. "I'll try to be a little nicer."

Grayson glanced across at me with a sad smile. "You don't have to try. You have a good heart. Stop trying to fight it."

"Just don't make me fake it."

Grayson shook his head with a laugh. "Fake is definitely not a word I'd use to describe you."

"What words would you use?"

He grinned. "Annoying…ly beautiful."

I laughed loudly and sank into the leather seat, wishing it could stay like this forever.

Chapter 2

The more I tried to evade Scott, the more he appeared where he wasn't welcome. Every day that week, he was in homeroom, in my classes, at our lunch table, and now, standing in front of my locker.

My step faltered when I saw him, and I lowered my gaze as I grew closer.

"Hey, Melanie," he said quietly, and my heart skipped. My name floated from his mouth way too easily.

"Hi." I refused to meet his problematic eyes and focused on my locker combination instead. I shot him a glance when he cleared his throat. "Did you need something?"

A chuckle left his mouth. "I was just wondering if you've seen Grayson?"

"Nope." I should have elaborated, but my chest tightened, and I couldn't form another word.

Scott hesitated before sighing. "Thanks…I guess," he muttered before pushing himself off the lockers. "I'll see you around."

"Fuck." I screwed up the lock combination a third time as he marched away. My hands were shaking so much I headed to my next class, minus my books.

Arriving at Art History later than usual, I strolled in to find one vacant seat left at the front. I glanced at my neighbor and groaned. This was my favorite subject, and I should've known Scott's presence would ruin it. A hint of a smirk crossed his lips as he followed my gaze to the empty seat beside him.

As I sat down, a voice surprised me from my alternate side. "Hi, Melanie."

I turned to the awkward boy next to me. "Oh, hey, Zach." Everyone gave him a hard time for his nerdy persona, but I found it refreshing. At least he wasn't pretending to be something he wasn't.

His freckled face burned red. "I'm so glad we have Mrs. Weathers this semester."

"Me too." I smiled at him, trying to ease his nerves, but I only made it worse. I hated when the wrong people found me intimidating.

Scott's brows rose as he observed our interaction.

"What?" I asked, tapering my gaze.

He fought off a smile. "Nothing."

I was about to make him elaborate when Mrs. Weathers walked in. "Right, everyone, turn to page ten. We've got a lot to get through this semester."

"Shit," I muttered, dropping my gaze to my empty desk.

"Is there a problem, Miss Warren?" Mrs. Weathers tilted her glasses under her eyes. "Where is your textbook?"

"In my locker," I grumbled. "I…um…forgot the combination."

I sensed Scott eyeing me as the teacher rolled her eyes.

"Not a great start to the year, Melanie," she said, making me feel as stupid as my mother did on a daily basis.

"She's welcome to share mine," Scott announced, drawing the teacher's attention.

My jaw dropped as my head spun to his.

Mrs. Weathers moved her curious gaze to Scott and smiled. "Thank you…?"

"Scott Blackwood," he replied, with a tight smile. "I'm new here."

"Well, thank you, Scott," she said, checking over her class list. "Melanie, shift your chair over to his desk. I want everyone to read pages ten to fourteen and be ready to discuss."

Scott watched me with a peculiar expression as I dragged my chair over and slumped back into it.

"What?" I hissed, growing impatient with his silent stares.

His blue eyes sparkled. "Oh, sorry. I just thought I heard a thank you. My mistake."

"You barely gave me a chance," I muttered, pursing my lips.

With a chuckle, Scott dropped his gaze and began reading. He didn't budge from his book in the slightest, leaving me no choice but to lean in. Between my arm touching his and the smell of whatever God-given body wash he used, my senses were dancing.

By the time the bell rang, my irritation had peaked. Not one word from the lesson had registered in my brain, and it was the only subject I cared about. Without another glance his way, I packed up my things and stormed out of the room to get to my next class.

Walking briskly up the corridor to Sociology, I sensed someone trailing behind. Dropping my shoulders, I stopped and turned to discover Scott not far away. "Let me guess… Sociology?" There was no point hiding my annoyance.

He came to a standstill in front of me. "Are you always like this?"

I let out a grunt and continued on my way.

Scott caught up with a few easy steps. "I don't think you're *always* like this—with me, maybe, but not with Grayson, or that Zach kid. Why's that?"

"I don't know you."

His grin grew. "Do you want to know me?"

"What?" I stopped dead in my tracks. "*No.* Has Grayson said something?"

Scott chuckled, looking entirely puzzled by me. "Why are you so uptight?"

My mouth fell open. "I…I'm not. I'm just—why are you asking so many questions?"

"Because I want to get to know you."

"Why?"

"Do you really want to know?" Scott's dimples deepened with his smile.

Warmth crept up my neck. "I think we should get to class."

His low chuckle followed me into the next classroom. I was relieved to find only two chairs available on opposite sides of the room. Scott offered me the first choice, so I took the seat closest to the window. The only reason I took Sociology was because I'd heard it would be an easy pass. I could spend the next hour staring out the window and dreaming about college. Not for the education, but the freedom it promised me.

After the bell rang, I waited for Scott to leave before returning to my locker to grab my lunch. As I made my way to the cafeteria, a muscular arm slid around my waist, lifting my mood.

"We're all going to that party at Rebecca's Friday night," Grayson said. "I think you should come."

"Seriously," I groaned. "Lisa said she'd give you head, didn't she?"

Grayson chortled. "Well, not as directly as that, but it may have been implied."

"Oh my god, no thanks." I pretended to fight the burn of rising bile.

He poked me in the ribs and whispered in my ear, "Scott will be there."

"So what? Why would I care?"

"Oh, I don't know...but a little bird told me Sarah wants to take him for a test drive."

I screwed up my nose to disguise a surprising twinge of jealously. "You need to warn him about her."

"Why?" Grayson laughed. "The rest of us had to learn the hard way."

I shuddered. Sarah was notoriously clingy.

"Come on," he continued with a sigh. "You're going to miss out on all the fun. It's the first party of the year."

"I'll think about it."

Grayson smirked. "Great, let's go eat."

"Melanie's coming to the party!" Grayson called out as we approached our crowded lunch table.

A few cheers erupted, but I had no idea why. They certainly weren't close friends, nor would they ever be. A small smile played on Scott's lips as he took a bite of his sandwich, and I narrowed my gaze. Why was he tormenting me?

As soon as the bell rang, I rushed out of the cafeteria. Chemistry was the only class I had with Grayson, and I wanted to make sure we were sitting together. After instructing three people to keep moving, Grayson finally dawdled into the room. I attempted to call out, but when Scott trailed in after him, my voice caught.

"Grayson, come sit with me!" Lisa yelled from the back of the room.

I spun around, glaring at Grayson's new love interest.

Grayson grimaced as he slowed at my desk. "Sorry." He turned to Scott. "Can you sit with Mel? I've got to put in a little groundwork for Friday."

I scowled and mouthed the words *Fuck you* as he passed while Scott slid into the chair next to mine.

He laid his books neatly on the table. "It appears we have very similar schedules."

"So it seems," I murmured, realizing I'd have to endure his delicious scent for the next hour.

Mr. Owens closed the door, and the class quieted. No one wanted to be on his bad side. "If you don't already know them, introduce yourself to the person sitting next to you. You're looking at your lab partner for the rest of the semester."

A few moans echoed through the class, including mine. I glanced back at Grayson, who was now paling, and sniggered. Served him right. He had no intention of pursuing Lisa after this weekend, and he knew it.

Fortunately, our first lesson only consisted of note-taking. There should've been a minimal chance of touching, except Scott's broad frame consumed over half the table and made it impossible not to brush shoulders or graze legs. It was infuriating.

By the end of the class, my body was on fire, giving me another reason to get the hell out of there. I had World Literature next, and it was essential I get there before Mr. West.

As I flew around the corner, I ran straight into Cara, sending her books flying across the floor. "Shit!" I cried, eyeing the door up ahead. My shoulders dropped. I needed that seat.

Cara crouched down to gather up her things. "It's okay. You don't have to help."

I knelt beside her. "Of course I'll help you. I did this."

"No really, it's okay. Someone like you shouldn't be…"

My hands paused as I lifted my gaze. "Be what? Helpful?"

Her eyes widened. "I'm sorry," she muttered, pushing a strand of her long dark-brown hair behind her ear. "I just meant…"

"Why are you sorry? I ran into you."

Cara let out a nervous laugh. "You're right, I'm sorry." She closed her eyes tight. "I said it again, didn't I?"

"You shouldn't apol—" My attention was drawn to a piece of paper on the floor. I picked it up for a closer look and encountered the most peculiar illustration. "You drew this?" I asked, gazing down at the surreal image I could only compare to the likes of Salvador Dali.

Her cheeks grew red as she shuffled to her feet. "Um… yeah."

"It's amazing." I'd always loved art. Not creating it, but studying it. Learning the story behind the piece rather than purely appreciating the aesthetic was a passion of mine.

"Thanks," she said, but I knew she didn't believe me.

"I didn't know you were an artist." But then again, I didn't even know her last name.

Cara's mouth fell open before she spoke. "Oh, I'm no artist."

"So, you didn't draw this?" I asked, tilting my head.

"Well, yes…I did…but…" Her gaze lowered to the floor to hide her reddening cheeks.

"So, you *are* an artist."

She laughed and nodded. "I guess so."

"This should be on a wall, not shoved away in a sketchbook," I said, reluctantly handing the drawing back. "Perhaps I could see more someday?"

Cara's eyelashes fluttered. "O…okay."

My grin grew until I remembered where I had to be. "Dammit," I muttered, gazing over at the door to my worst nightmare. "I'm so late."

"I'm sorry. I hope you don't…"

I turned back to her with raised brows.

"Oh right." She winced. "Not sorry."

I smirked. "Better."

Edging over to the closed door, I peeked through the small window. The class had already started with only one empty chair right at the front of the classroom. I was about to retreat when the door flew open.

"Miss Warren. You finally decided to grace us with your presence. Take a seat and see me after class."

Not meeting my teacher's eyes, I swallowed the lump in my throat and slipped into the spare seat. Last semester, I purposefully positioned myself toward the back of the room. It was the only place where it was near impossible for Mr. West to *accidentally* drop his pen in an attempt to peek up my skirt or peer over my shoulder to catch a glimpse of my bra. I immediately crossed my legs and fastened my top button at the disgusting memory.

As much as I had pleaded with my mother, she refused to take me out of Mr. West's class. She believed the teacher's infatuation with me would lead to an easy pass and encouraged me to take advantage of the opportunity.

Drawing a deep breath, I glanced around the room, anywhere to avoid looking at the revolting man who stood before me. My gaze struck Scott's striking profile, and I quickly lowered my eyes before he caught me staring.

I didn't speak a word for the entire lesson. I kept my head down, did my work, and prayed Mr. West would forget about me. No matter how hard I tried to avoid his attention, Mr. West was consistent with his inappropriate behavior. His actions were discreet and purposeful, going unnoticed by the other students. The subtle tilt of his head for a better view of my legs, the slightest graze across my back as he passed, or the way he moistened his lips when he hovered over my desk. It made me nauseated.

Three minutes and twenty-five seconds before the bell rang, Mr. West panned his gaze around the class with a satisfied smirk. "I'm quite happy with the seating arrangements today. Consider these your seats for the rest of the semester."

My chest caved in, and I gasped for air. It was happening again. Lowering my head as my stomach churned, I waited for the bell. Perhaps if I raced out, he'd forget about keeping me back after class.

"Melanie," Mr. West called as soon as I attempted to escape.

I froze in the doorway and slowly turned, standing motionless as the rest of the class filed out.

Scott slowed his pace when he saw my paling face. "Are you okay?" he asked, staring directly into my eyes.

For a fleeting moment, it felt like he was reading my soul. "Nothing I can't handle," I grumbled as I stepped back into the room.

"Close the door on your way out, Scott," Mr. West instructed, not looking up from his desk.

"Yes, sir," he replied and pulled the door shut behind him.

I flinched at the sound. We were alone.

"Please sit," Mr. West said.

Drawing an unsteady breath, I slid back into my seat.

Mr. West pursed his lips and rose from his chair. He sauntered around his desk and rested against it, folding his arms as he observed me. "I'm going to have to keep a closer eye on you this year, aren't I? Wouldn't want you failing this class again." He ambled over to my desk and placed his hand on the back of my chair. "Perhaps I should check over your notes from today. Make sure you're on track."

Without speaking a word, I opened my notebook. His hot breath coated my neck as he leaned over to review my notes. Closing my eyes to block out the discomfort, the door flew open, and Scott marched back into the room.

The teacher jumped backward, bumping into the chair behind him. "Didn't you have to knock at your previous school?" Mr. West uttered, rubbing the back of his neck.

Relief flooded my body.

"Sorry, I thought everyone had left. I forgot my pen." Scott eyed me as he passed.

"Then get it," the teacher bit, returning to the front of the room in a flurry.

Scott searched his desk and then the floor. "I know it's here somewhere."

The teacher grumbled as he rearranged the papers in front of him.

"Oh, there it is," he said, bending over.

My heart dipped. I didn't want him to leave.

Scott proceeded to zip up his pencil case before fumbling, causing all of the contents to spill onto the floor. "Ah, I'm sorry. I'll just be a sec." As he bent over, his eyes met mine. He tipped his head toward the door, silently telling me to go.

"Was there anything else, Mr. West?" I asked, not missing any opportunity to get out of there.

The teacher's face hardened. "No, it's fine. You're free to go. Just make sure you're here on time in the future, or I'll be forced to hold you back again."

With a small nod, I quickly gathered up my things and bolted. I pushed through the crowded corridor and threw open the door of the closest restroom.

"Get out," I said to the petite girl washing her hands.

She spotted me in the mirror and slowly turned. "Are you oka—"

"Just get the fuck out!"

The girl's eyes grew large, and she scampered out of the room with a squeak. Scott witnessing my humiliation was bad enough; I didn't need some junior feeling sorry for me.

I let out a sob as the door swung shut behind her. Why was Mr. West so infatuated with me? I didn't do anything to encourage him. I didn't maintain eye contact. I didn't speak in class. Fuck, I barely even breathed. Yet, he found every reason to ridicule me, hold me back after class, and stare in a way that made my throat clench and stomach tighten. His eyes swirled between hate and lust, and it scared the shit out of me.

Deep breathing did nothing to subdue my anger as I paced the tiled floor. A single tear ran down my face, but I quickly wiped it away. I wasn't going to let him get to me this time. I approached the sink and splashed water on my face, but my anger grew when I caught sight of my reflection. My perfect fucking reflection. The reason for all the torment.

Even with streaked mascara, my face was flawless. Completely symmetrical with crystal-blue eyes, high cheekbones, and perfect red lips. My platinum-blonde hair sat effortlessly straight just above my shoulders, and the subtle curves of my slim body were enhanced by the professionally tailored uniform. I hated all of it.

No one was ever going to look beyond my appearance. No one was ever going to care what laid underneath. As threatening tears burned my eyes and nostrils, rage took hold. I slammed my fist into the mirror, shattering my picture-perfect reflection into shards of glass—some big, some small, and one the perfect size to end it all. Picking up the piece of glass to examine it in my bleeding hand, my mother's voice crept into my head. *"Get your shit together, Melanie. Life is all just a big game. There are winners and losers…and you, my dear, will not embarrass me."*

Straightening my back, I lifted my chin and took a deep breath before side-stepping to the next sink. Turning on the faucet, I washed away the blood spilling from the tiny cuts on my knuckles and prayed I wouldn't have to visit the nurse. While fixing my face with my mother's emergency makeup kit, the door to the restroom opened.

"Holy shit," Sarah said, staring at the floor covered by a blanket of broken glass.

Lisa lifted her wide eyes to mine. "Did you do this?"

I took a step toward them, and they flinched. "Haven't *you* ever had a bad day?" I asked cooly, strolling past them and out the door. I had no intention of explaining myself, and if those girls knew what was good for them, they'd keep their mouths shut.

Chapter 3

I returned to my locker to find Grayson waiting for me. His smile faded as I approached. Even with a fresh face, he could read me.

"What's wrong with you?" he asked as I entered my locker combination.

I shoved my books away. "Nothing."

"This isn't nothing," he said, grabbing my hand to assess the damage.

I pulled away and closed my locker. "Can we just go to lunch now?"

"Mel…"

I stared at him, fighting the tears I wouldn't let fall.

"Okay, but we'll be talking about it later," he said, knowing me well enough not to push. "Will some tater tots brighten your day?"

A small smile played on my lips. "Don't they always?"

By the time we arrived at the cafeteria, the line for food was a mile long. Grayson cut in behind Scott, so I continued to our table. I'd lost my appetite anyway.

As I approached, Sarah whispered something into Lisa's ear. Their eyes darted to mine, making me momentarily pause. Then I remembered I didn't give a fuck what they thought of me and resumed my journey.

"You get into a fight, Mel?" Hank asked, spotting my injured hand as I sat down.

Lisa and Sarah let out a giggle as I quickly slid the evidence under the table. "Not yet," I muttered, staring directly at the girls instead of Hank.

They quickly shut their mouths and continued their

conversation about an upcoming party while I glanced back at Grayson, willing him to hurry up. When he finally arrived at our table, followed by Scott, his usual cheerful demeanor was gone. He slid a plate of tater tots in front of me while he sat beside me with Scott joining his alternate side.

"He's doing it again, isn't he?" Grayson whispered, clearly trying to keep our conversation private.

I glared at Scott. "What did you tell him?"

His jaw tightened. "Just what I saw."

"And what was that?"

He kept his voice low. "He was sleazing all over you."

I was embarrassed and ashamed and couldn't help but project onto him. "Were you spying on me?"

"I just stuck around to make sure you were okay."

"He was just trying to help, Mel," Grayson said, trying to defend his new friend.

I crossed my arms, not looking at either of them. "I can deal with it."

Grayson pulled out my hand and held it tightly. "*This* is not dealing with it."

My cheeks burned as I shook him away, but it was too late. Scott saw the wounds.

"We can report him," Grayson continued, but my focus was on Scott. He was frowning at me, and it was driving me crazy. I didn't need or want his pity.

My gaze traveled back to Grayson. "Can we talk about this later?" Our hushed conversation was starting to draw attention from the rest of the table.

"I saw what happened," Scott said, opening his big mouth again. "I can back up your story."

"Oh my god, will you both just drop it!" Now I had everyone's attention.

"Where are you going?" Grayson asked, grasping my arm as I stood.

I shrugged him off. "Somewhere where I can eat lunch and not be hassled." My head snapped to Lisa and Sarah. "Or be whispered about for five fucking seconds."

Whirling around, I scanned the cafeteria for another table to sit at. My choices were slim. Spying Cara sitting alone in the corner, drawing in her sketchbook, I headed in her direction.

"May I sit here?" I asked, careful not to frighten her. She was so focused on her drawing I doubted she saw my approach.

She lifted her head and began gathering up her paper and pencils. "Yeah…sure. I can sit somewhere else."

I let out a tired laugh. "I meant…*with you*."

Her mouth formed an O shape as she sat back down. "Okay…"

I sat down and nibbled on a tater tot. "What are you drawing?"

"Oh, nothing," she said, sliding the loose sheets back into her sketchbook.

"Why are you sitting alone?" I asked, changing the subject instead of pushing her to elaborate.

Cara shifted uncomfortably in her seat. "I, um…don't really fit in anywhere."

"I feel like that sometimes," I said, gazing around the room at all the stereotypical circles.

A bewildered expression covered Cara's heart-shaped face. "Really? But everyone wants to be friends with you."

I scoffed. "You know that saying about being surrounded by people but feeling totally alone? That's me."

She glanced over to my usual table. "What about Grayson? You guys are inseparable."

I followed her gaze. "Yeah, but he's more like a brother than a friend, if you know what I mean." No matter what, Grayson had always been my person.

"At least you have someone you can talk to," she said softly. The sadness in her voice haunted me.

"You can always sit with us at lunch."

Cara laughed nervously. "Oh, I don't think so."

"Why not?"

"I don't…I'm not…like you. Apart from the new guy, I wouldn't have anything in common."

My interest piqued. "What do you mean 'apart from the new guy'?"

"He's a scholarship student, like me. Normally we can't keep up with people like you, but he seems to be fitting in quite well."

I glanced over to our table. Hank would have a field day if he found out. "People with money are jerks, aren't they?"

"Yep," she agreed before turning bright red. "I mean, not you..."

I laughed. "Don't sweat it. I agree."

We talked about the subjects we had that semester, and I was surprised to find she wasn't taking any art classes, except Art History which didn't require an ounce of artistic ability.

"How is that even possible?" I asked, shocked she wasn't developing her obvious talent.

"My mom doesn't exactly approve."

"Does she know how good you are?"

Cara shook her head and gazed down at her sketchbook. "I don't know what she thinks. She refuses to talk about it."

My eyebrows rose, but I decided to leave it. It was clearly a sensitive topic. "What's this?" I asked, eyeing a small flyer on the table, advertising the Annual West Coast Fine Art Competition.

Cara frowned. "Just some stupid contest."

"It's not stupid," I said, reading over the requirements. "It's perfect. If you win this, your mom will realize how talented you are. Please tell me you're going to enter."

"I want to, but there's an entry fee." She grimaced. "There's no way my mom will give me the money."

I shrugged. "Then I'll pay it."

"What?! No."

"Are you serious? I have that much in my purse right now." I reached for my purse.

"No, no. I'm not comfortable..." she said, shaking her head.

Fair enough. She barely knew me. I'd have to think of another way. "What if I *bought* one of your pieces?"

"I really don't have anything worth...anything."

I lifted the competition flyer. "What if I buy this piece? The one that will win this."

Cara chortled. "I doubt it will win."

"Come on. It's an investment," I said, smiling across at her. "I'll have the first *Cara*...what's your last name again?"

"Deville," she answered with a laugh.

"I'll have the first *Cara Deville* artwork ever sold. It will be priceless one day."

Her eyes narrowed. "Why are you being so nice to me?"

I let out a sigh. "There's clearly more to you than you let on. I'm intrigued."

She appeared even more perplexed. "No one around here has ever bothered to get to know me. Least of all someone like you. I'm not one of those project bets, am I?"

I laughed loudly, and a few people looked my way. "Regardless of what people say, I'm no Regina George. There is more to me than I let on too."

Cara tapped her finger on her sketchbook while staring at the entry form in my hands.

"So, will you let me pay your entry fee?" I asked again, feeling more hopeful.

She lifted her glistening eyes to meet mine and nodded. "Okay."

I reached for my purse, but she held up her hand to stop me.

"Not here," she whispered. "People will assume I'm selling you drugs."

"What? Why?"

"Why else would a girl like you be hanging around a girl like me?"

"Are you selling drugs?"

Cara's eyes bulged in disgust. "*No.*"

"Good. Then I don't see the problem." I handed over the money with a grin.

Cara's blush deepened as she took it from my hand. "Thank you, Melanie. I'll make sure it's worth every cent."

Somehow, I managed to get through the rest of the school day without any further interrogation from Grayson or pity stares from Scott. My anger soon subsided, and when I found Grayson leaning against my locker after the final bell, it faded completely. It was impossible to stay mad at him.

"You still driving me home today?" I asked, trying not to smile.

He crossed his arms as I put away my books. "How else would you get home?"

"I could walk."

"I'd pay money to see that," he uttered with a snort before picking up my bag and throwing it over his shoulder. "How's the hand?"

"It's fine. Hey, can we go home via Nico's? I'm starving."

"I'm not surprised. You barely eat."

"I eat enough...*apparently*," I said, irritated by my mother's obsession with my weight.

"Alright, let's go."

Ten minutes later, we rolled into Nico's Diner. I was not only starving, I was in need of comfort food. A greasy, full-fat, heart-attack-inducing burger. After the day I'd had, I couldn't face going home to celery sticks and hummus.

"You're in a better mood this afternoon," Grayson said as I perused the menu.

My smile grew. "I made a friend today."

"I noticed. Interesting choice."

"What do you mean *'interesting choice'*?"

"Well, she's not exactly who your mother would want you associating with."

"That's probably why I like her."

Grayson shook his head. "She's going to have a fit when she finds out you're hanging out with a scholarship student."

"No more than when your parents find out."

"What are you talking about?"

"Scott's one too, and you guys seem to be getting along just fine."

His eyebrows rose. "Oh, I didn't know that."

"Does it make a difference?"

"Well, no. He's a pretty cool guy."

"Seemingly," I muttered, signaling for the waitress to take our order.

Grayson folded his arms across his chest when the waitress left. "Why are you giving Scott such a hard time? I think he likes you."

My stomach fluttered, and heat traveled to my cheeks. "He told you that?"

Grayson laughed. "No, you idiot, but now I'm *certain* you like him."

Later that night, I sat alone in the kitchen, eating dinner. I wasn't hungry, but I knew my mother would get suspicious if I didn't eat the meal she'd had prepared for me by our chef.

The house was dead silent, but it always was, even when my parents were home. We all lived entirely separate lives, only coming together for social events requiring the appearance of a supportive and loving family unit. My father barely acknowledged my existence due to my lack of male appendage, while my mother's disdain for me only grew stronger after I reached puberty. She didn't like to compete for the attention of men.

As I picked at my minuscule salad, my cell phone lit up.

Grayson: **You need to report Mr. W.**

The memory of Mr. West's breath on my shoulder made me shudder.

Me: **Please drop it. I don't want to go through that again.**

I placed the phone back onto the bench, remembering the last conversation I had with my mom about Mr. West.

"Mom, I'm telling the truth."

"Oh, I'm sure you are," she said, almost laughing. "How could he resist a beautiful girl like you? I had the same problem when I was your age."

"Please, if you won't let me report him, can't you at least get me out of his class?"

"Don't be silly. This will be an easy A for you. Just bat your eyelashes and show him a little leg. He won't do anything else."

"Mom, please. I can't go back to his class."

"You need to get used to this, Melanie. When you look a certain way, men will stare. They'll undress you with their eyes. Hell, they'll even touch themselves when they think about you. What you need to realize is how much power this gives you."

"Power to do what?"

"Make a man do anything you want," she said with a hint of a smile. "How do you think I got your father to marry me?"

"But that's not what I—"

"Well, that's too bad," she snapped. "You're my daughter, and I will not let you waste your perfect genetics."

I never returned to his class after that, so the school had no choice but to fail me. But this year posed a new problem. If I didn't pass his class, I wouldn't graduate.

"You're quiet," Grayson said as we drove through the school gates the next morning. "Everything okay?"

I stared through the windshield in a daze. "Just have a lot on my mind, that's all."

He turned to me with a serious expression as he parked. "You've got him today, don't you?"

"It's only a morning class, so it should be okay. He only holds me back at lunch or at the end of the day when there's no other class to get to."

Grayson's shoulders relaxed. "You know I'm just worried about you, don't you?"

"I know, and I appreciate it," I said, looking up at the only person I trusted. "I'm lucky to have you."

"Don't go all soft on me now, Warren."

I punched his arm. "Shut up, Harlow."

"Ow, that better not bruise," he said, rubbing his arm. "I have a big date tonight."

"Aren't you just meeting Lisa at the party?"

"Yeah, why?"

I chortled. "That's *not* a date."

Grayson's eyebrows drew together. "What would you call it then?"

"A hookup."

His frown curved into a smile. "Even better."

"Just remember who your lab partner is for the rest of the semester."

He ran his hand through his hair with a wince. "Shit."

"Karma's a bitch," I replied smugly. "You shouldn't have chosen her over me."

"Well, I thought I was doing us both a favor."

My mouth fell open. "By putting me next to Scott Blackwood? Hardly." I got out of the car and started walking across the lawn to the main building.

Grayson jogged after me, chuckling to himself. "Come on, admit you like him."

I let out a frustrated growl. "There is nothing to admit. I don't know him." Yeah, he was gorgeous, but I had no idea who he was beneath it all.

Grayson shrugged nonchalantly. "I don't know Lisa either."

"Well, let's see how that pans out first," I said, knowing very well it was going to blow up in his face.

"At least I'm trying to have fun."

I stopped walking and faced him, placing my hands on my hips. "Getting chlamydia isn't my idea of fun."

Grayson groaned. "You need to get laid."

"Shut up." Sometimes I hated the fact that Grayson was privy to my virgin status. "I've got to get to class."

"Scott may be able to help with that..." Grayson sang out as I marched away.

"Bye, loser!"

I made sure I arrived at World Lit class well before Mr. West. Unfortunately, Scott had the same idea, and he was sitting in my chair.

"What are you doing?" I hissed, glancing at the door. "You're going to get me in trouble."

He barely looked my way. "Just take my seat. I've got this."

I hurried across the room and slid into Scott's allocated seat moments before the teacher strolled in. Nausea rolled over me as I waited for Mr. West's reaction. Why would Scott do this to me?

The teacher's pace slowed when he spotted Scott, and he scanned the classroom. *Shit.* I hung my head before his eyes hit mine.

"Melanie, I thought I made myself clear yesterday that the seating arrangement was set."

Panic consumed me as I lifted my gaze.

Scott cleared his throat to divert the teacher's attention. "Sorry, Mr. West. I had to switch with Melanie. My eyes aren't great, and the doc says I need to be closer to the board." He reached into his back pocket and pulled out a piece of paper. "I have a letter..."

Mr. West waved him off. "It's fine," he muttered before approaching his desk with a grumble.

My lungs burned as I filled them with air. I'd been holding my breath the entire time. Now that I was in the middle of the classroom, I could finally let down my guard. As long as Mr. West didn't hold me back, I'd be okay. I blinked away tears as I stared at Scott, whose eyes didn't shift from the front of the room.

When the bell rang, I hugged my books close and hurried away. Scott's eyes trailed after me, but I didn't dare meet them. I couldn't have Mr. West getting suspicious of Scott's obvious lie.

As soon as I reached the crowded hallway, relief flooded my body. Why Scott had taken such a risk for me was a mystery. He didn't even know me. Was he really trying to help, or was he planning to use it against me later? Nobody did these things without wanting something in return.

I rushed to my next class before I'd have to confront Scott about what happened.

"Over here." Cara waved her hand as I entered my Art History lesson.

Smiling in relief, I maneuvered through the tables to sit next to her. Scott walked in moments later, briefly catching my eye before sitting within earshot.

"You okay?" Cara asked, drawing my attention. "You look upset."

"Yeah, I'm fine. I just had an eyelash in my eye, that's all," I muttered, praying Scott wasn't listening.

He threw me a fleeting glance, and my temper spiked. I couldn't let him see how much what he did meant to me. It gave him too much power.

I turned to Cara. "You want to eat lunch together today?"

Her alarmed gaze met mine. "With your friends?"

"No, just us. But if you'd prefer—"

Her blush deepened. "Just us sounds great."

I let out a laugh, which captured Scott's attention, then I immediately shut my mouth.

Cara and I strolled through the cafeteria toward an empty table in the back. Grayson caught my eye as I passed and clutched his chest in a dramatic attempt to look heartbroken. I smiled his way, and he grinned back before returning to his fan club at our usual table.

"Are you sure you don't want to sit with your friends?" Cara asked with a grimace.

"They're Grayson's friends."

"Oh, I didn't realize."

"I just tolerate them for his sake." I dumped my tray on the table and sat down. "Speaking of Grayson's friends...would you like to come to a party with me tonight?"

"A party? I...I can't."

"Why not?"

Cara let out a deep sigh. "My mom's working, so I have to babysit my little sister."

"What about your dad?"

"I doubt he'd be very helpful." Her eyes lowered. "He's been dead for almost four years."

My mouth fell open as dread filled my stomach. "Oh my god. I'm so sorry. I didn't know."

"It's okay." She pressed her lips together in a tight smile. "Not many people do. It happened before I came to Summerhill."

"Where were you before here?"

"Montana. Mom wasn't coping, so she moved us here for a fresh start. I don't know how she got me into this school. I think I'm on some sort of sympathy scholarship, because my grades back home were never that great."

"Perhaps she showed them your artwork? Summerhill has one of the best art programs in the state."

Cara scoffed. "Unlikely. She hates it when I draw."

"Why?"

"She's worried I'll end up like my dad."

I shook my head. "I don't understand. Was he an artist too?"

"Yeah, he was. He was also bi-polar and did his best work off his meds."

My breath caught.

"Of course, Mom thinks I have it too, even though the doctors assured her I don't. She freaks out every time I pick up a pencil, so I only draw here at school."

"What happened to your dad?" I asked, barely finding my voice.

"He, um...disappeared for a few days, which wasn't unusual for him between his highs and lows. But something didn't feel right, so we drove around looking for him. We checked all the usual places, but no one had seen him in days. Then, I remembered this park, about a mile from home, where he used to take me as a kid. He would occasionally pull me out of school and push me on the swing for hours until the sunset or the police came."

She breathed in deeply and continued, "I spotted my dad's car as soon as we arrived and saw him in the driver's seat. Mom called out, but he didn't seem to hear her. His head was slumped, so she banged on the window to wake him. I held my sister while she found a rock and smashed the window, but it was too late. As soon as Mom touched him, she knew. He'd been dead for days."

Tears filled my eyes. "Oh, Cara."

Cara's jaw pulsed as she gathered enough strength to keep speaking. "When Dad went off his meds, he felt everything two-fold. But when he was on them, he felt nothing. He was a zombie. I hated seeing him like that. He had bad days—terrible days—but on the good days, he was amazing. We had so much fun together."

My heart ached for her. "You sound like you were close."

A sad smile played on her lips. "He just got me."

I forced air into my tight chest and lowered my burning eyes.

"Wow, that just got a bit heavy," Cara said, letting out a shaky laugh. "I'm sorry."

"Don't apologize. What you've been through…I can't even imagine…"

"It was pretty shitty. Mom decided a sea change would help us move on, but the darkness followed. Drawing helps me process it all."

"Then keep fucking drawing."

With a laugh, we finally started eating our lunch, even though I'd completely lost my appetite.

"I'm sorry I left it until senior year to get to know you," I said as I played with the remains of my salad. "My parents have made me wary of strangers, so I struggle to make new friends."

Cara looked over to Grayson's table. "How long have you known Grayson?"

"Since birth, I think. Our parents are close."

"And you've never dated?"

I scrunched up my face. "He's not my type." My gaze wandered over to Scott, and his eyes caught mine. Heat traveled up my neck as I quickly looked away. I was certain Cara could hear the hammering of my heart.

"What was that?"

"What was what?" I asked, trying to act casual.

"That look. Is something going on between you and the new guy?"

My jaw dropped. "No."

"Do you want something to?" A cheeky grin covered her face.

"No..." I laughed nervously.

"You're a terrible liar."

I was momentarily insulted before remembering she wasn't my mother.

"We better get to class," I said, trying to deflect. "The bell is about to ring."

Cara followed my lead. "You're not going to tell anyone about my dad, are you?"

I frowned. "Of course not." I wasn't a gossip, but she didn't know that.

"Great, then I won't have to tell anyone who you have the hots for."

I tried my hardest not to smile, but it fought its way to the surface. It appeared I couldn't lie to Cara Deville.

Chapter 4

I knew going to Rebecca's party was a bad idea. Grayson had already disappeared into one of the seven bedrooms with Lisa, leaving me to aimlessly walk around from room to room, dodging drunken hands, dry humping, and bad dancing. I wished Cara had come. At least then I would've had someone to have a decent conversation with.

Instead of socializing, I occupied my time eyeing all the artwork on the walls. A replica of my favorite impressionist painting hung at the end of the hallway, and I paused in front of it. A piece like that deserved to be above a mantelpiece, not between a bathroom and a guest room.

"It's beautiful, isn't it?"

I spun around to face Scott, who threw me a sideways glance before returning his attention to the masterpiece. His arms were folded across his chest, making his pale-blue shirt tighten around his biceps. *Oh my.*

I cleared my throat. "It's one of my favorites."

"Mine too."

My gaze tapered. "You're familiar with Jacque Sinclair?"

"My grandfather took me to his exhibition when it came to Phoenix last year." His eyes blinked rapidly. "I can't believe they own an original."

I scoffed. "Oh no, this is a copy."

He stepped forward, analyzing the work up close. "How do you know?"

"Because the original is in my living room."

His rounded eyes met mine. "Jesus."

"My parents collect art," I said with a casual shrug. "Although, I seem to be the only one who appreciates it."

Scott's name blasted from the living room, but he didn't flinch.

"You're being summoned," I said, hearing his name called a second time.

He rubbed the back of his neck with a grimace. "Do you play pool?"

"I'm not allowed."

"What?"

I tried not to smile. "Seriously. No one will play me."

He grabbed my hand. "Don't be ridiculous." With a small tug, he pulled me into a room full of a dozen other kids from Summerhill.

"No fucking way!" Hank yelled as soon as he saw me.

I pulled my hand away and lifted them both in the air. "I told you."

Scott turned to Hank. "She can't be that bad."

Hank shook his head and handed him both pool cues. "You're welcome to play her, but I'm not making that fucking mistake again."

I smirked at Hank, and his eyes narrowed into slits.

"I guess it's just you and me then," Scott said as he prepared the table.

You and me. My heart quickened at the sound of those words. "Fine," I muttered as he handed me a cue. "You can break."

Word of the match spread through the party, and a crowd gathered around the table. Scott lined up his first shot and managed to pocket two balls. My jaw clenched as a group of girls, including Sarah, squealed in delight. Scott already had his own cheer squad.

Silence filled the room when I finally took my turn. I leaned over, aimed, and did what everyone expected. Missed.

"You want to take that shot again?" Scott asked with a low chuckle. "I can show you how."

Hank patted his back as he passed by. "Yeah, I think you should give her some tips."

Scott came up behind me and slid his arms over mine. I closed my eyes as he positioned my hands on the cue. The warmth of his body ignited my core, and when his face lined up beside mine, I breathed in the subtle mint aroma of his toothpaste.

He brought his mouth to my ear. "You missed that shot deliberately."

My breath caught. "I don't know what you're talking about."

"Don't play games with me," he whispered with a smirk.

I shrugged him off and stepped away from him. "Fine," I grumbled. "A quick game's a good game."

Scott stood back and watched me sink every ball with ease and, consequently, win the game in five minutes.

I shook Scott's hand. "Great game."

He didn't let go. "Want a re-match?"

"Don't you think I've embarrassed you enough?" I asked as I pulled away.

"I'm not afraid of losing a few."

I scoffed. "A few?"

"I'll play with you, Scott," Sarah said, sidling up to him.

My eyebrows rose as her hands slid up and down his arm, waiting for a response, but Scott's eyes never left mine.

"You should play with Sarah," I uttered, handing her the cue. "She might let you win."

I left the room in search of Grayson. I wanted to go home. Storming down the long hallway, I opened doors, not caring who I interrupted, until Lisa's notorious giggles erupted from the room ahead.

I pounded on the door. "Gray, it's time to go!"

"He's busy!" Lisa yelled.

I barged in and stood in front of the bed with my arms crossed.

"Jesus, Melanie," Grayson snapped, launching off the bed to zip up his pants.

Lisa pulled the bedsheet over her torso. "I said he was busy!"

"I wasn't talking to you."

Grayson's hand ran down his face. "Can you just give me a minute? I'm not finished here."

Lisa's face dropped. "A minute?"

His face grew pink. "Half an hour?"

I hung my head back and groaned. "Forget it. I'll find another way home."

"Wait, wait..." Grayson pushed past me and jogged down the hall into the room I'd just come from. Cheers erupted at the sight of his bare chest, but he paid them no attention. Instead, he pulled Scott away from the pool table and whispered something into his ear.

Scott's eyes struck mine in the doorway and offered Grayson a quick nod.

Grayson strode back, slowing as he passed me. "I found you a ride. Now I can go and enjoy mine."

My mouth fell open as he continued down the hall.

"You coming?"

I swung my gaze back to Scott who was standing entirely too close.

"But aren't you in the middle of a game?" I asked, glancing over at Sarah who stood with her arms crossed and mouth pursed, watching us.

"I was, but it wasn't challenging enough."

I bit my lower lip. "You...you don't have to."

"Come on, the car's out front," he said, motioning me to follow.

I momentarily froze before realizing he was my only option.

"Fuck," I muttered, chasing after him.

Cars lined the driveway that spiraled into the property. "Which one's yours?"

He pulled out his keys. "Can you guess?"

I ran my gaze over the cars, looking for something that suited him. I knew he was a scholarship student, but that didn't necessarily mean he had no money. My eyes paused on a beautiful vintage Mustang. Its brilliant turquoise exterior was as alluring as Scott's eyes.

I grinned and pointed.

Scott chuckled. "How did you know?"

"I...um...must've seen it at school," I said, not wanting to admit I found the car as sexy as him.

"Not a chance. She's been in the garage since the start of the semester. I just got the old girl running again."

I pressed my lips together with a shrug. "Lucky guess then."

He opened the passenger door, and I slid inside, silently admiring the original interior while Scott jumped into the driver's seat.

"So, where do you live?"

"Bel Air...you know it?"

He let out a laugh followed by a sigh. "Yeah, I know it."

As we pulled out onto the main road, Scott relaxed into his seat.

"Shouldn't you be wearing glasses?" I asked, holding back a smile. "With all that eye trouble you've been having?"

He grimaced, clearly thinking he'd fooled me too. "Oh, that wasn't true...I..."

My belly filled with laughter.

Scott rolled his eyes and smiled. "Ah, you're fucking with me."

"Did you really forge a note from your doctor?"

"No," he said, running his hand down his face. "It was just a girl's phone number."

My heart dipped. "Well, you didn't have to lie for me, but thank you anyway."

Scott glanced at me then back to the road. "Look, I know you don't want to say anything about Mr. West, but..."

"So, how do you know it's a girl?" I asked, running my hand over the car interior.

His forehead wrinkled. "What?"

"The car. You referred to it as a *she*."

Scott smirked. "Because she's beautiful, powerful, and a pain in my ass."

"Labor of love?"

He nodded. "My grandfather left her to me after he died. It didn't run, so it took a shitload of work to get her back on the road. Now my dad wants me to sell it."

"You can't! She's a piece of art."

Scott smiled. "Don't worry. I have no intention of selling her...ever."

We fell silent for the rest of the drive. It wasn't as awkward as I'd hoped, and I found myself wishing the trip was longer.

Scott's eyes grew wide as he peered up at our iron gates. "This is where you live?"

"Mostly. We have other properties, but I guess you could call this home base."

"Jesus," he murmured. "How do we get in?"

In a bold move, I reached across Scott's lap and typed in the security code through his open window. His whole body stiffened in surprise.

"Sorry," I mumbled, climbing off him. "It's quicker than getting out of the car."

Scott cleared his throat as the grand gates rolled open. "No problem."

If my parents were home, I would've walked from here, but my father was away on business, and my mother was at a spa retreat, leaving me on my own. There was no chance of them seeing Scott, so there was no point in ruining good shoes on the long walk back.

Scott leaned forward as my house materialized in the distance. "And I thought Rebecca's house was big. This is something else."

"It's something else, alright," I muttered, not looking up. *The loneliest place on Earth.*

Once he'd stopped the car beside the steps leading up to the stately entrance, I reached for the door handle, but it wouldn't budge. I feared I'd break it off entirely if I yanked any harder.

"Hang on a sec," Scott said, launching out of the car to let me out. "It only opens from the outside."

Scott placed his hand under my elbow as I stepped out, sending tingles up and down my arm.

"Thanks," I mumbled as heat rose to my neck. I glanced back at the car and chuckled. "She really is a pain in your ass, isn't she?"

Scott's gaze lingered on mine. "All good women are, right?"

The flutter in my stomach traveled up to my heart. "Well, thank you for the ride. I hope you didn't miss too much of the party."

"Oh, I'm not going back. There's no point now."

"I'm sure Sarah will be waiting for you."

Scott cackled. "Then I'm definitely not going back."

I burst out laughing. He was different from the other boys.

"Wow," Scott said, falling back a step.

My laughter faded. "What?"

"You're even prettier when you laugh."

My heart swelled, and I'd never wanted to kiss a boy more in my life.

"I'll see you Monday," he said with a twinkle in his eye.

"Yes...yeah, Monday. I'll...um...see you then." Before he could witness my scorching cheeks, I escaped into the house and fell against the closed door, gasping for air.

The next week, I spent my lunchtimes with Cara. It was safer that way. With Lisa demanding Grayson's undivided attention, I was left making awkward conversation with the boy who I'd been dreaming about all weekend—the type of dreams I thought only boys had.

I'd never been so wound up by a guy before. He turned me into a bumbling mess, and I hated him for it. With a mere glance in my direction, he stripped away my tough exterior and all the power that went along with it—the power my mother instructed I never let go of.

"Good morning, class," my Sociology teacher said as she entered the classroom.

I mumbled a greeting and turned my gaze back out the window. This was the only class I shared with Scott where I could pretend he didn't exist. He sat on the other side of the classroom while twenty-five other students formed a barrier between us.

Mrs. Pearson started rambling on about project partners, drawing my attention. My gaze traveled to the large bowl on the desk, full of folded papers, and my heart raced. "This semester, your partners will be selected at random."

Dropping my head into my hands, I took long deep breaths as

Mrs. Pearson walked around the classroom, asking everyone to dip their hand into their impending doom.

I held my breath as Scott reached into the bowl.

He unfolded the paper and frowned. "Lanie," he read aloud before handing it back to the teacher.

I relaxed back into my chair. I was in the clear.

"Who's Lanie?" someone in the back asked.

The teacher wrinkled up her nose and reread the paper in her hand. "Oh." She laughed. "It must have ripped. It's meant to say Melanie."

I sat up in my chair, wide-eyed. *Fuck.*

Scott tried to hide his amusement while my cheeks burned.

Mrs. Pearson continued to explain the project as she wandered around the room, but I didn't hear a word. I was too busy trying to think of a reason to switch partners.

As if reading my thoughts, the teacher turned to the class. "If for some reason, you wish to switch partners…"

I perked up and listened closely.

"It will not be possible," she added, crumbling all hope.

I slumped back into my chair while Scott pursed his lips.

"I'll give you the rest of the class to get together and go over your game plan."

When I didn't move, Scott shifted his chair to my desk. "Look, I can tell you're not exactly ecstatic over this partnership, but can you please put whatever problem you have with me aside so we can get this project done?"

"I…I don't have a problem."

Scott raised his eyebrows.

"Fine," I growled. "How do you want to do this?"

He pulled out his cell phone. "Perhaps we should exchange numbers and work out a time to meet outside of class?"

I put up my hand. "Excuse me, Mrs. Pearson."

"Yes, Melanie?" the teacher asked impatiently.

"This will all be done in class time, right?"

Her smile was tight. "Sadly, no. You'll have to do a considerable amount in your own time. Oh, and class, this project will account for 60% of your grade."

Scott ran his hand down his face while I grumbled.

"What nights are you free after school?" he asked, growing serious.

"Can't we just halve the workload?"

"Not if we want to do well," he bit out, reading over the outline.

His sharp tone surprised me. "So, how do we pass?"

"I need to do a lot more than pass."

"Why? Because you're a scholarship student?"

His eyes narrowed. "Who told you that?"

I shrugged.

"Is that going to be a problem for you?"

I shook my head with a frown. "No."

"I was hoping the rumors about you weren't true," he muttered as the bell rang.

My mouth went dry as he gathered up his things. "What rumors?"

He stood up and carried his chair back to his desk, completely ignoring my question.

I followed closely behind. "Fine, I'll meet you in the library after school."

With a quick nod, he turned to leave. "See you then... *Lanie*."

"Are there rumors about me?" I asked Cara at lunch.

She looked everywhere but into my eyes. "Um...I mean... I've heard people say things, I guess..."

I lifted my brows. "Like?"

She grimaced and shook her head.

"Spill it."

Cara sighed. "They say you're spoiled."

True.

"A bitch..."

Sometimes.

"Ice queen."

"I wonder who came up with that," I muttered. Hank told everyone I was a frigid bitch when I refused to kiss him at a party a few years back.

"They say you think everyone at this school is beneath you, and you don't waste your time on anyone whose family is worth less than yours. That's why Grayson is your only friend."

"That's not true," I uttered quietly.

"Well, obviously," Cara said with a laugh. "You're sitting with me right now."

I forced a smile. Is that what Scott had heard?

"What brought this up?"

"Just something Scott said."

"Since when are you bothered by what people say about you?"

"Normally, I'm not," I said, gazing across the cafeteria. "But for some reason, everything Scott says bothers me."

Cara smirked. "You know what I think?"

My eyebrows rose. "Go on."

"I think you like him. Like, really like him."

I hung my head back and groaned. "You're as bad as Grayson."

"I just don't think you're ready to admit it yet," she said with a playful smile.

"To Scott?"

Cara chuckled. "To yourself."

Unknown: **Where are you?**

Unknown: **This is Scott. Grayson gave me your number.**

I stared down at the phone, chewing the side of my thumbnail. It was a dick move, but I didn't go to the library after school to meet him. I planned to, but when I found Grayson waiting for me at my locker that afternoon, I panicked and went home instead.

Perhaps Cara was right. Perhaps I did like Scott. And if that was the case, I needed to keep well away from him.

"You stood him up?!" Grayson yelled as I got into his car the next morning.

"It wasn't a date!"

"No, but you still made plans to see him after school. If I'd known, I would've dragged you there myself instead of taking you home."

"And you just had to give him my number."

"He was worried about you," he cried, shaking his head in disbelief.

"He was?"

Grayson ran his hand through his hair. "He's a good guy, Mel. He doesn't deserve to be dicked around. When you didn't show up, he messaged me to see if you were okay."

"And what did you say?"

"Nothing. I'm not making excuses for you. I just gave him your number."

I folded my arms.

"You owe him an apology."

"I know, okay," I uttered, staring out the window. "When I see him next, I will."

Grayson nodded his approval. "Good."

After enduring homeroom with Scott's menacing stare, I managed to avoid him for the rest of the morning. I even skipped Art History to escape confrontation and decided to apologize once he stopped looking like he wanted to murder me.

Before meeting Cara for lunch, I returned to my locker to pack away my books. I hadn't even entered the combination when a hand latched around my elbow and pulled me into the nearby AV room.

Scott let go and slammed the door behind him. "Where the fuck were you last night?"

I looked away from his burning gaze and hugged my books tighter. "I…I had an emergency."

"What? Like a broken nail?"

"No…I…"

"I took the night off work," he growled, stepping closer. "You cost me a hundred bucks."

My chest tightened. "I'm sorry. I'll give you the money."

"I don't want your fucking money!" he yelled, throwing up his hands.

I blinked rapidly. Not many people spoke to me like that.

He took a deep breath in an obvious attempt to calm himself. "Look, I don't care if you hate me, but I need to score well on this project. We're not all leading blessed lives like you and Grayson. Some of us actually have to work for every little fucking thing. So, can you please just take that stick out of your ass and do what's required, then I promise to leave you the fuck alone."

"I…I don't hate you."

"Then why do you look like you're in pain every time I get close to you?"

"Because…" My heart beat rapidly.

His brow furrowed. "Because what?"

Losing my mind, I stepped forward and pressed my lips to his.

A moment later, Scott pulled away. "Jesus," he muttered, staring at me with wide eyes.

"I'm sor—"

Before I could finish my long-awaited apology, Scott slid his hand around my nape and pulled me back to his mouth. My books dropped to the floor as his tongue entwined with mine while his hands ran through my hair. Our kissing became harder and more intense by the second before I pushed him away with a gasp.

We stood there, panting and staring into each other's eyes, not saying a word, until I gathered my senses along with my books and bolted out of the room.

Chapter 5

"Why are you so flushed?" Grayson asked when he found me pacing by Cara's locker. "And why do you still have your books? It's lunchtime."

The heat in my cheeks intensified. "Oh, I was running late to meet Cara."

Grayson made a face. I wasn't a rusher. "Riiight…will you be sitting with us today?"

I spied Cara walking down the hall. "I'm not sure if she's ready for the group thing just yet."

Grayson turned to Cara with a smile, and her cheeks grew pink instantly. He had that effect on girls. "Can you two pleeease join us for lunch?" he asked again, hoping to persuade my new friend.

"Why are you so desperate?" I uttered, giving Cara a chance to compose herself.

"We need more girls at our table."

I narrowed my eyes. "You have girls. Lisa…Rebecca… Sarah…"

"Well, girls who don't give me a headache."

The corner of my mouth rose. "Well, you made your bed, so now…"

"Sounds great," Cara interrupted in the midst of sliding her books away.

"What?" My eyes widened. "Really? Are you sure?" I didn't want to push her to do something she wasn't ready for. Grayson's friends weren't the most welcoming crowd.

Cara rolled her eyes. "Yes, I'm sure."

"But…"

"I'll be fine, Mel. It's about time I start socializing a bit more."

She peered down at my hands and frowned. "Why do you still have your books?"

"Oh…um…my locker was full. Can I leave them with you?"

With a nod, Cara took my books and placed them beside hers while Grayson eyed me curiously. He knew something was off, so I had to distract him quickly.

"Well, I'm starving," I said, linking my arms with theirs and steering them toward the cafeteria. "Let's go eat."

Lisa's eyes tapered as we approached with our lunch trays, and I smirked. Grayson was in trouble. Feeling a pull, my gaze floated to the other side of the table where Scott was sitting beside Hank and Sarah. His eyes caught mine, and I quickly focused on steadying my hands as I placed down my lunch tray.

"Everyone knows Cara, right?" Grayson asked as Lisa pulled him down beside her.

A few nods and reluctant smiles were sent her way, but Scott was the only one who appeared genuinely happy about the new arrival.

"Why is she sitting with us?" Lisa whispered into Grayson's ear, loud enough for everyone to hear.

"Because she was invited," I snapped, glaring at her. "And unlike some people, she's welcome here."

Lisa's mouth fell open, and she poked Grayson in the ribs. "Are you going to let her talk to me that way?"

He rubbed his side before turning to me with a pained expression. "Can you cool it, Mel?"

"Sorry." I pouted. "Did I upset your plaything?"

Lisa sucked in her breath, but Scott's voice drew my attention.

"Is that what you consider us, Lanie?" he said, tilting his head as he searched my eyes. "Playthings?"

My gaze burned into his. "That's not my name."

"Whoa, guys," Grayson said in a calming voice. "Can we all just relax? You're making our new friend uncomfortable."

I turned to Cara, embarrassed by my behavior. "I'm sorry," I whispered, refusing to look at Scott.

She shrugged happily. "It's okay. It's the most excitement I've had all year."

"Mel tells me you're an artist," Grayson said, steering the conversation away from all the drama.

Blush consumed her cheeks. "Oh, it's just a hobby," she said, waving him off.

"You must be good. Melanie has exceptional taste."

My heart warmed. I didn't often get compliments that didn't incorporate my appearance.

Grayson continued to ask Cara questions throughout lunch, much to the annoyance of Lisa, while I kept my head down and shuffled food around my plate to avoid any more conflict.

"I'm heading to class early," I whispered to Cara as I stood up. I'd had enough awkwardness for one day. "You stay and chat with Gray. I'm sure he'd appreciate it."

The moment I stepped out of the cafeteria, someone called out from behind me. I ignored it and continued down the corridor.

"Lanie!" a voice shouted again.

I closed my eyes and turned to find Scott slowing in front of me. "Why do you keep calling me that?"

"I don't know." He took a step closer, threatening my personal space. "I like it. It...softens you."

"I'm not..." I screwed up my nose. "Soft."

The sides of his mouth quirked up. "Your lips are."

With a grimace, I spun around and continued to my locker.

"What the fuck was that?" he whispered, falling into step with me.

I shook my head, wishing I could erase the past. "Nothing... it was nothing."

"It wasn't nothing. It was...*something*."

"Something that should never have happened."

Scott smirked. "But it did happen."

His arrogance made my blood boil. "Look, I've got to get to class."

"Okay," he said, slowing his pace. "We'll talk about it later."

"Unlikely," I muttered under my breath while making a mental note never to be alone with him again for the opportunity to arise.

Midway through my next class, my phone buzzed, and I discreetly read the message.

Scott: **We need to talk.**

I groaned. He wasn't going to let it go.

Me: **It was a brain fade. Don't overthink it.**

Scott: **About our Sociology project.**

Oh.

Me: **Fine. I'll meet you in the library after school.**

Me: **Unless you're working, that is.**

There was a pause, and my heart dipped.

Scott: **I'll be there.**

"Have you at least read the outline?" Scott asked as I sat opposite him in the library after school.

I poked my tongue into the side of my cheek and looked away.

"Jesus," he muttered, running his fingers through his tousled hair.

"I'll get to it," I cried, wondering what the rush was. "It's not due for weeks."

Scott pulled out his planner. "We need to get started on this. With my other subjects and work, I won't have time to do it all myself."

"I don't expect you to do it all. I just haven't had a chance to look at it yet."

Scott's serious gaze penetrated mine. "Look, I can't afford to mess this up. So, if you're not planning on doing your part, tell me now."

"I'll do it, okay? Just email me my section." I wrote my email address on a piece of paper and slid it over.

"Are you *sure* you can handle it?"

My temper spiked. "Oh my god, could you be any more condescending? Of course I can fucking handle it."

Scott's jaw slackened. "I didn't mean to imply—"

"Forget it," I snapped, pulling out my cell and sending Grayson a text to pick me up.

"I didn't mean to upset you."

My phone chimed as I stood up.

"Are you leaving already?" he asked, rising from his chair.

"Yeah, I am. I don't have to take shit from you too." My mother was enough. I picked up my bag and stormed away.

"Come on, Lanie," he called, jogging after me.

I whirled around. "Will you stop calling me that?"

His shoulders dropped. "Can I at least give you a ride home?"

"No. Grayson's on his way," I grumbled, pushing through the library doors.

He paused at the entrance. "Of course he is."

The jealous edge to his voice only pissed me off more. "Just send the email."

"But you have to go," Cara whined on the way to class the next day. "I only said yes because Grayson said you'd be there."

"He did, did he?" I pursed my lips.

Her big brown eyes pleaded with mine. "Please, Melanie? I've never been to a party at Jacob's before."

Jacob had graduated the previous year and was the son of the famous actor, Ian Speers. His parties were legendary at Summerhill, and if you scored an invite, you were doing something right.

"And your mom is okay with it?" From what Cara had told me, I could only assume her mother was protective, especially after what they'd been through.

"Well...I kind of told her I was staying at a friend's place..." She raised her brows in question.

"Reeeally?"

Cara winced. "Is that okay?"

"Of course." I chuckled. "My parents are away, so some company would be nice."

Her face brightened. "So, we're going to the party?"

"Alright."

"Thank you," she squealed, her sweet smile contagious.

"Are you sure you're ready for this?" I asked, knowing how incredibly bitchy the girls could be at these parties.

"No, but I want to go anyway. I'm sick of being on the outside. It's time I had a little fun."

I nodded. She deserved a little fun, and I was determined to make sure she had it. "Have you got something to wear?"

Her face paled. "I didn't think of that. Perhaps I shouldn't go."

"You're not getting out of it now. You can borrow something of mine."

"Really?"

"Of course."

"But we're so different. I'm short and curvy, and you're… you're like a supermodel. Nothing will fit me."

I rolled my eyes and linked my arm with hers. "Trust me. We'll find you the perfect outfit."

I rarely had friends over. With the exception of Grayson, whose house was bigger than mine, I preferred to keep any friends I did make, at school. Summerhill was a level playing field. Once any prospective friend visited my house and literally saw how wealthy my family was, everything changed.

"Wow…" was all Cara could muster as she stepped into the foyer of my 30,000 square foot home. She gazed over the two curved staircases that separated and came back together on the second floor and twirled under the giant chandelier. "You must feel like a princess living here."

"Yeah, with an evil queen and all," I muttered, motioning her to follow. "Come on, my wardrobe awaits."

With a tiny squeal, Cara shadowed me up the staircase, gawking into every room we passed. A gasp escaped her mouth when she stepped into my bedroom.

"Your bedroom is bigger than my entire house," she said, panning her gaze around the large space that was professionally decorated with its own lounge and king-size bed. "And my bedroom could fit in your closet."

"It's a waste of space, if you ask me." My mother always told me to embrace our wealth, but I hated it. Real people couldn't relate and would quickly disappear from my life, leaving me with the fakes and wannabes. I prayed Cara didn't fall under either category.

Leaving Cara wide-eyed and open-mouthed, I walked into my closet to rummage up a few items that would enhance Cara's body type. My legs were much longer than hers, so I stuck with skirts and dresses. Once satisfied, I returned to Cara and dumped the pile on the bed.

"Keep whatever you want," I said, returning to the closet to find something for myself.

Cara picked up the first item in awe. "You don't mean that."

"Oh, please. I have more outfits in my closet than there are days in the year."

She bit her bottom lip. "But…"

"If you don't wear them, no one will." My mother had bought most of the clothing, and I refused to wear them on principle.

Her eyes grew large. "In that case…" She bundled the items into her arms and marched into the dressing room.

A few moments later, Cara strolled out, wearing a short lilac dress that accentuated every curve and perfectly complemented her olive complexion. I'd never seen her in anything other than our school uniform, which, without the right alterations, did nothing for anyone's figure.

"Cara," I gushed. "You look beautiful."

She giggled and ran her hands down the fabric. "I've never felt anything so soft."

"That color suits you," I said as she peered up at me with her endearing doe eyes. "A little bit of make-up and you'll have all the boys chasing you tonight."

Her face burned red. "Shut up."

"I'm not kidding." I laughed. "Every single boy will be looking your way tonight."

"Not every boy," she said with a smirk. "I know one who only has eyes for you."

With a groan, I left her ogling over her dress to fine-tune my outfit.

I settled on a designer dress I'd bought in Italy over the summer. It was white, strapless, fitted, and short—and somehow cost over a thousand dollars. I'd been saving it for a special occasion, but knowing Scott would be at the party, I caved. For some stupid reason, I wanted to get a reaction from him. Good or bad.

Dressing it down with a cropped light denim jacket, I returned to find Cara watching her dress expand while she twirled in circles, and I let out a laugh.

Her mouth fell open when she turned back to me. "Wow."

"Too much?" I asked with a wince.

She shook her head. "I'm guessing you hear this every day, but...have you ever thought of modeling?"

"Mom used to drag me to things when I was little, but once I started getting more attention than her, she stopped taking me." I stepped over to the mirror to review my outfit, first my left side then my right. "I don't have the right physique for it, anyway."

Cara appeared at my side. "Are you kidding?"

"That's what my mom tells me."

"She's wrong, Mel. You could be on the cover of any one of those fashion magazines."

"That's sweet," I said, not believing her in the slightest. "But it never would've worked out."

"Why is that?"

I chortled. "I enjoy eating *way* too much."

Cara's smile grew. "So we *do* have something in common."

With a laugh, I grabbed her hand and pulled her into my en suite bathroom. "Come on, it's time to put on our faces."

I dumped all my makeup onto the counter and proceeded to pick out the perfect colors to match her look. My light foundation didn't suit her skin tone, but her complexion was so perfect she didn't need any. I simply applied some eye shadow and mascara to enhance her warm chocolate eyes and straightened her long brown hair.

"Oh wow," Cara uttered, seeing her reflection for the first time.

"Don't cry. Your mascara will run."

Her eyelashes fluttered. "You're a miracle worker."

"I'm only bringing out the beauty within."

Her gaze met mine in the reflection. "Then you must have an angelic soul."

I rolled my eyes and applied the finishing touches to my makeup. Once I'd set my hair into its usual straight bob, I turned to Cara. "Can you see my split ends?"

"Your what?"

"Mom says I need a haircut."

"Well, I think your mom needs to get her eyes tested," Cara said, sitting on the side of my bed to tie up her Chucks.

"What are you doing?" I cried, staring at her well-worn shoes.

"Well, I doubt any of your shoes will fit me."

"What size are you?"

"Six."

"Wait." I left the room, only to return moments later with a pair of my mother's low heels. "Here, put these on."

"Are they your mom's?"

"Yeah, so?"

Cara's eyes bulged as she stood. "No way. I bet they cost—"

"No more than that dress you're wearing," I said with a laugh.

Her face paled as she gazed down at her outfit. "Oh god."

"Please don't worry about it."

"But what if I spill something on it or rip it?"

I placed my hands on my hips with a sigh. "Do you know how rich we are?"

Her gaze traveled around the room. "Rich, rich?"

"Times that by ten."

Her mouth formed a silent O.

"I don't fucking care what happens to those shoes or that dress. What I do care about is that you have a good time tonight, and that starts with what you're wearing."

Cara drew in a wobbly breath and exhaled. "Okay."

"Now get these shoes on. Grayson will be here soon."

A foreign beep sounded outside while Cara and I were enjoying a glass of my mother's French champagne. With the amount of alcohol she drank, I doubted she would miss a bottle.

Wondering if Grayson had borrowed his dad's car, I peeked out the window.

"Shit," I muttered while Cara peered over my shoulder.

"Grayson has a sweet ride," she said, eyeing the Mustang in the driveway.

"That's not Grayson's car," I grumbled.

"Then who..." She paused when Scott got out of the car before letting out Grayson. "But I thought Grayson was driving."

I pursed my lips. "So did I."

"But isn't this a good thing?"

"No... Yes... I don't know. I just wasn't expecting to see him yet."

Cara giggled. "I've never seen you so flustered."

I grabbed my handbag and marched to the front door. "Let's just go before I back out completely."

Cara hurried through the door as I opened it, and Grayson's mouth dropped at the sight of her.

"Wow, Cara! Looking good," he called out. "You don't scrub up so bad either, Mel."

Scott's gaze passed over Cara and settled on me. Warmth filled my body as his eyes traveled up my legs and over my outfit until he found my eyes, but he didn't utter a word. Instead, he dropped his gaze, opened the car door, and folded back the driver's seat.

As I waited for Cara to climb in, Scott moved to my side. "Did you have fun? Dressing up your little plaything?"

Anger bubbled up inside me. "You're an asshole," I muttered, quiet enough for only him to hear before crawling in after my friend.

With a soft chuckle, Scott flipped back the seat and got in the car.

"What's so funny?" Grayson asked Scott as he started her up.

Scott turned to him with a grin. "Lanie just called me an asshole."

Grayson laughed. "She must like you."

My narrowed gaze shot between the two of them. They were clearly trying to get a reaction out of me, so I was determined to keep my cool.

As we grew closer to Jacob's house, Cara's hand slid over mine. "Promise you won't leave me tonight," she said, losing some of the color in her face.

"Of course." I squeezed her hand and offered her a warm smile. "Unless you want me to, that is."

Cara let out a snort. "I highly doubt it."

Her involuntary nasal function made me laugh. "Come on, you never know what will happen tonight."

Grayson nudged Scott in the front seat. "That's exactly what I told Scott earlier."

Scott's gaze caught mine in the rearview mirror, and my stomach lurched.

"Oh my god, we're here!" Cara's excitement was a welcomed disruption.

I diverted my attention to the ultra-modern Beverly Hills mansion blaring music so loud it was pulsating through the car as we parked.

Scott opened his car door before handing Grayson the keys. "I'm going to go find a drink," he muttered, leaving us trapped in the back as he sauntered away.

"Would you mind letting us out, Gray?" I asked, glaring at Scott as he high-fived some guys from Summerhill at the front door.

Grayson sniggered. "You called him an asshole. What did you expect?"

"Well, clearly he is one."

Also locked in by Scott's malfunctioning passenger door, Grayson shuffled across to the driver's seat and stepped outside before pulling back the seat to let us out. "My ladies..."

As we walked through the house toward the party's epicenter, Grayson hid behind us, clearly trying to avoid Lisa.

"I warned you," I said, turning to Grayson with my hands resting on my hips.

"I know," he whispered, shooting a glance around the room. "I've seen the error of my ways. Now, tell me what to do."

"Just break it off, you idiot."

His eyes widened. "But she's kind of scary."

"Oh, well, I guess you'll just have to marry her then," I said with an eye roll.

"Incoming," Cara murmured under her breath.

We all turned to find Lisa marching in our direction, and I couldn't help but laugh.

"Grayson!" she called. "Where have you been? You were supposed to be here an hour ago."

I linked arms with Cara and pulled her in the opposite direction. "Come on. Let's go find a drink. Grayson has a mess to clean up."

As we walked through the living room, I spotted Scott talking to a group of girls, including Sarah. He turned my way, as if sensing my presence, and I quickened my step toward the kitchen. The way those girls were looking at him irritated me, and I desperately needed a drink to ease my care factor.

Jacob greeted us with a huge smile when we walked through the door. "Ladies," he said, handing us both a beer. "Welcome."

"Thanks, Jacob." I grabbed the bottle and chugged the whole thing down.

His pupils dilated as I wiped the residue from my lips. "Wow. That was the sexiest thing I've ever seen. Want another?"

With my nod, Jacob rummaged through the cooler while Cara prepared herself to follow my lead. She took a deep breath and lifted the beer to her mouth.

"Don't," I whispered, tugging back her arm. "You'll vomit."

Her cheeks grew pink. "Oh, thank god."

"Just take small sips, and don't mix your drinks."

Jacob returned with another beer, making sure to graze my hand as he passed it over. "I'm glad you could make it," he said, not shifting his gaze from mine. "I miss seeing you in the hallways every day."

I smiled, knowing the effect it had on men. "I brought a friend. I hope that's okay."

He ran his gaze over Cara and then back to me. "Does she go to Summerhill too?"

Cara cleared her throat. "Um, yeah. We had World Lit together last year."

"Right," he muttered, but he was clearly clueless. "Hey, Rob," he called to the boy across the room. "Have you met Melanie's friend, Clare?"

Rob's grin grew as he moved closer. "I can't say I've had the pleasure."

Cara blushed as he took her hand in his. "It's Cara."

"Rob's in a band," Jacob said, ignoring her correction. "They're called Jack Knife."

"Oh, I think I've heard of you guys." Cara's eyes brightened. "What do you play?"

"Lead guitar. Some vocals," Rob said, flicking back his shaggy blond hair.

As they delved into music talk, Jacob slid between us, cutting me out of their conversation. "You look fucking amazing tonight, Mel."

"Um…thanks." I glanced over his shoulder to make sure Cara was okay. Rob wasn't from Summerhill, so I didn't know anything about him.

"Excuse me!" Sarah squawked, bumping everyone as she walked past. She only got louder and more obnoxious when she drank.

Jacob took the opportunity to move closer, and my whole body stiffened. My back was now pressed up against the wall, leaving me nowhere to go.

"Jacob, where are the beers?" she asked, scanning the kitchen. "Scott's way too sober."

At the mention of his name, I lifted my gaze to find Scott attached to her hand. His eyes traveled to mine before panning across to Jacob. His jaw twitched on impact.

"He can't drink; he's driving," I said to Sarah, who finally found the cooler.

Sarah groaned dramatically as she handed Scott a beer. "Lighten up, Melanie. You're not the boss of everyone."

"But he isn't supposed to—"

"Relax, will you?" Scott uttered before taking a long sip. "Grayson is driving my car home."

Sarah tugged on his collar and grinned. "And he'll pick you up from my place in the morning, right?"

Scott choked on his beer as a few cheers echoed around the room.

"I need some air," I muttered, edging past Jacob toward the French doors leading outside.

Cara caught the door before it swung shut behind me. "You okay?" she asked, glancing back at Scott and Sarah through the glass.

My smile was entirely fake. "Yeah, I'm fine." I needed to deflect. "That Rob guy is cute."

She lowered her eyes to hide her reddening face. "He is, isn't he?"

"You should go back in there and talk to him," I said, my smile becoming more genuine.

Her nose crinkled. "Are you sure?"

"Of course I'm sure. I think he likes you."

"You really think so?" Cara's large brown eyes twinkled.

"Well, go find out," I said, motioning for her to go back inside. I wasn't going to stop Cara from having fun tonight.

"I'll find you later, okay?" she replied, momentarily pausing before re-entering the house.

"I'll be here if you need me."

With an excited grin, Cara returned to Rob, leaving me standing outside wondering how I was going to avoid Scott for the rest of the night. Sarah was all over him, and I had no doubt they'd disappear into an empty bedroom at some point. I'd just have to wait it out and prepare myself to not crumble when it happened.

For the next hour, I moved from group to group, making small talk, just like my mother taught me. I pretended to be interested in things I didn't give a fuck about and laughed at jokes I didn't find remotely funny. It made for good practice.

Cara moved outside with Rob, meaning only one thing. I was determined not to spoil it for her, so I ventured back into the kitchen in search of another beer. As I fished around the cooler, another hand dove in.

"Having fun?" Scott asked, pulling out two beers.

"You seem to be," I muttered, sighing as I gave up the search.

"Here," he said, handing me one of his drinks. I'd assumed it was for Sarah.

Scott took a sip of his beer and leaned back on the counter. "It's nice to feel wanted sometimes."

"I guess you've got to take what you can get, right?"

Scott's lips pursed as he nodded. "Well, you have a good night, Lanie," he said, straightening his back and placing his half-drunk beer on the counter.

I gnashed my teeth as I watched him walk away. Why did I have to be such a bitch to him?

Realizing I needed to apologize, I followed him into the living room. Cheers exploded, but they weren't for me. Everyone's eyes were on the couple kissing in the middle of the makeshift dancefloor. Pain radiated through my entire body at the sight of Scott's lips pressed against Sarah's, causing my beer to slip through my fingers. It smashed all over the floor, drawing everyone's attention, including Scott's, whose stunned gaze matched my own. I disappeared before anyone could see the tears pricking my eyes.

"Lanie, wait!" Scott's voice only made me move faster.

Taking two steps at a time, I climbed the stairs until I found an empty bathroom. I lowered myself onto the edge of the enormous bathtub and hung my head between my legs. As I took deep breaths to settle the nausea, the door flew open, and Scott barged into the room.

"Jesus, Scott! I could've been on the toilet!" I yelled, rising unsteadily to my feet.

"What was that?" he asked, his chest rising up and down.

"I spilled my drink and probably ruined my shoes. I came up here to see if I could save them."

He stepped closer. "Your shoes are dry."

"Well, I can see that *now*." I tried to move around him, but he blocked the door.

"What made you spill your drink?"

I clenched my teeth. He knew why. He just wanted me to say it. "I…I was just surprised, that's all."

"About what?" His eyes penetrated mine.

Anger surged inside me, but I didn't look away. "By how low your standards are."

"Wow," he said, hanging his head back with a chuckle.

"Wow, what?"

His grin grew until his dimples caved. "You're jealous."

I scoffed. "Don't flatter yourself. I don't care who you kiss."

He folded his arms over his chest, still smiling. "Are you sure about that?"

"Look, I'm sorry if I confused you the other day, but don't be mistaken. It didn't mean anything to me."

"I think it meant more than you're willing to admit."

My hand found my hip. "And how do you figure that?"

"You just don't seem like the type to kiss someone you're not interested in, that's all."

"Is that so?" His arrogant smirk sent me out of the bathroom and down the stairs.

"Hey, where are you going?" Scott asked, jogging down beside me.

"To prove you wrong."

"Lanie…no." He slowed his pace, and I left him behind.

Strolling back into the living room, I marched across the dancefloor until I found a group of boys chatting in the corner. They all turned my way as I approached.

"Hey, Jacob," I said with a huge smile. "You want to dance?"

His eyes grew wide. "Definitely."

As his friends cheered and patted him on the back, I pulled him out onto the floor and wrapped my arms around his neck. Moving in slow circles, I spied Scott on the edge of the dancefloor, watching us. His jaw pulsed as he rubbed the back of his neck, making me shift closer to Jacob.

"Pardon?" I asked, not hearing a word Jacob was saying.

"I just asked if you'd like to go out sometime?"

I played with the tips of his hair. "We don't need to overcomplicate this."

"What do you mean?" he asked, running his hand up and down my back.

"This is what I mean..." I lifted my lips to his and kissed him.

In an attempt to deepen the kiss, Jacob parted my mouth with his tongue, but I jerked away. I glanced in Scott's direction, hoping he hadn't witnessed my adverse reaction, but he was gone. Instead, I found Grayson approaching at speed.

"We have to go," he said, pulling me away from Jacob. He was totally oblivious to what we were doing a moment prior.

I frowned at him. "Why?"

"I just broke it off with Lisa, and she's losing her mind."

I took it as my chance to get away from Jacob. "Okay, I'll go find Cara."

"I'll get Scott, and we'll meet back at the car in five minutes." He turned to Jacob. "Great party as usual, man."

"Yeah, cool," he murmured, watching me as Grayson raced off.

I backed away from Jacob with a grimace. "Sorry, he's my ride."

"Can I call you?"

"Sure," I replied as I entered the mass of gyrating bodies.

"But I don't have your number," he called out.

Ignoring him, I made my way to where I'd last seen Cara talking to Rob. As expected, they were now doing a lot more than talking by the poolside. I cleared my throat to get their attention. Then again, louder.

As Cara's lips parted from Rob to take a breath, she caught a glimpse of me and jumped backward. Her face turned bright red. "Melanie, hi!"

"Hi," I said with a knowing smile. "I'm sorry to do this, but we have to go."

Her eyebrows pulled together. "Is everything okay?"

"Grayson's just getting what he asked for."

Cara laughed. "Okay, I'll just say goodbye."

My gaze shifted to Rob then back to Cara. "Be at the getaway car in three minutes, okay?"

Rob kissed her neck, and she giggled. "Okay."

I made it back to the car moments before Grayson and Scott.

"Where's Cara?" Grayson asked.

"She's just saying goodbye to a boy. Give her a minute."

"Well, I'm hiding in the car. If Lisa comes out, tell her I've already gone home."

Grayson jumped into the driver's seat, leaving Scott and me standing beside the car. He wouldn't even look my way.

"I guess you don't know me very well, after all," I said, filling the silence.

His eyes met mine, but they weren't even angry. They were sad. "Maybe that's a good thing."

My heart twinged. What was wrong with me?

Chapter 6

Grayson's cell chimed as we settled down to watch a movie. Our families had dinner together every few weeks, and while they were drinking in the parlor—planning our futures, no doubt—we escaped to the lounge.

"Um, why is Jacob Speers asking for your number?" Grayson probed, staring at his phone.

I let out a long groan. "Do *not* give it to him."

Grayson laughed as he typed. "Too late."

"Grayson!" I yelled, swinging a cushion around to hit his face.

He knocked it away with a chuckle. "I'm joking…for now. Unless you tell me why he's asking."

"We kissed last night."

"What?!" Grayson's mouth fell open. "How did I not know that?"

"You were too busy with your own problems."

"Wow." He sunk into the couch. "I had no idea you liked Jacob."

"I don't," I muttered, pulling the popcorn onto my lap.

"But you don't kiss anyone you're not into."

My jaw clenched at the familiar opinion. "I guess after a few beers, everyone looks good."

Grayson shook his head in disbelief. "I really thought something was going on between you and Scott."

My heart skipped a beat. "Why would you say that?" Had Scott told Grayson about what happened in the AV room?

"Just a vibe I'm getting."

I threw some popcorn in my mouth. "Well, he's clearly into Sarah."

Grayson burst out laughing. "Are you kidding me? He hasn't taken his eyes off you since the moment you met."

"Then why would he kiss her?"

"She kissed him!" he cried, running his hand down his face. "Someone dared her to. You would've realized that if you hadn't run out of there so—wait, is that why you kissed Jacob?"

I picked up the TV remote and switched it on. "Can we just watch the movie?"

"Jesus, Mel. Scott really likes you."

My gaze tapered. "Why?"

Grayson snatched the popcorn away. "Not everyone has an agenda."

"Everyone in our world has an agenda," I muttered, filling my empty lap with a cushion.

"But he's not in our world, and I think that's why you like him."

"I don't," I grumbled, flipping through the channels.

Grayson's smirk morphed into a grin. "You do."

"So what if I do?" I said, throwing my hands into the air. "It doesn't change anything. My parents won't let me go out with him."

"Have you asked?"

"Are you kidding?" I almost laughed. "Remember when your parents found out you went on a second date with that girl from the country club last year?"

"Yeah, they grounded me for a month."

"And *she* was rich," I added.

"Just not *Harlow* rich." His tone was laced with bitterness.

"Then imagine what they'd do if you wanted to date a scholarship student."

Grayson folded his arms. "Why can't they just let us have a little fun? It's not like we're going to marry someone we meet in high school."

My heart dipped unexpectedly. "I...I know, right."

"My brother has probably screwed half the chicks at college by now, and my parents don't even care. The golden child can do whatever and whomever the fuck he likes, regardless of their pedigree."

"Yeah, but Adam is…Adam. You're the soft target. If anyone is going to settle down and give them grandkids, it's you, and God bless the girl who has to put up with your family."

Grayson ran his fingers through his hair. "She'll have to be pretty fucking amazing, that's for sure."

"Or crazy," I said, turning to him with a grin. As a piece of popcorn flew past my head, I checked the time. "Come on, I want to start this movie. I really don't need another late night. I've got homework to do tomorrow."

"Homework?" Grayson chortled. "You?"

"Scott's pestering me about our Sociology project, so I thought I'd get a start on it."

"Oh…so you *did* get Scott's email. He said you never replied."

"Well, I haven't read it yet," I muttered, annoyed he'd spoken to Grayson about it.

"You're deliberately trying to make him hate you, aren't you?"

I screwed up my nose. "*No…*" It was a complete lie, and Grayson knew it.

"Lanie…"

My gaze snapped to his. "Don't you start."

Grayson held up his hands and laughed. "Alright, I won't use his pet name for you. It feels weird, anyway."

Rolling my eyes, I pointed the remote at the television and pressed play. "Just shut up and watch the movie, Harlow."

Scott's email had laid unopened in my inbox since Thursday night. I should have acknowledged it, but Grayson was right. I *was* trying to piss him off. He'd already made assumptions about the person I was, and it infuriated me. Finally giving in, I clicked open the email.

Hey Lanie,

Here is your half of the workload. We need to have the first part completed by Friday. If you can't manage it, let me know asap. I'll figure something out.

S.

What a jerk.

Opening the attachment, I read over what was required and scoffed. It was all pretty straightforward. With no plans or distractions at home, I got to work. For some reason, I wanted to prove to Scott I wasn't the blonde bimbo he obviously thought I was. So, instead of completing the component due at the end of the following week, I completed all of it.

Just before bed, I responded to his email with two words.

See attached.

Which was much more civilized than the two words I really wanted to say.

"Did you really write this?" Scott asked, materializing at my locker the next morning, holding a printout of my work.

I continued to search for my Sociology book. "Why? Do you think I paid someone to do it for me?"

"No," he said, shaking his head. "Wait, did you?"

"Fuck you." I slammed my locker shut and pushed past him.

He jogged after me. "But how did you have time to do all of this?"

"You mean, between all the shopping and the hair and nail appointments?"

"I'm just surprised, that's all. This would've taken me weeks, and it's good...like, *really* good."

I stopped and turned to him. "Why wouldn't it be?"

"I've noticed how disengaged you are in class. I just assumed you didn't care about your grades."

He wasn't wrong. "Well, I don't…usually."

"So why now?"

"I don't know." Heat rose up my neck and flooded my cheeks. "Can we just get to class?"

Scott didn't budge as I continued down the hallway.

I turned back to find him watching me curiously. "Aren't you coming?"

His brows rose, and he quickened his step to catch up with me. When we walked into class together, I slipped into the seat beside his.

"What are you doing?" he asked, glancing over at my usual place by the window.

"What do you think I'm doing?" I laid my books and stationery across the desk. "I'm getting ready for class."

His eyes widened, and he was about to respond when the teacher entered the classroom.

Toward the end of class, Mrs. Pearson allowed some time to work on our projects. Without hesitation, Scott shifted his chair over to my desk, and my heart raced. Our arms grazed as he settled beside me, and every fiber of my being tingled.

Scott sighed when I edged away. "Look, I'm sorry I made assumptions about you. I just thought…"

"A pretty girl can't have brains as well?"

He scoffed. "Pretty is not a word I'd use to describe you."

My mouth fell open.

"Beautiful, maybe," he said with the hint of a smile on his mesmerizing lips.

Heat seared my cheeks, and I cleared my throat, searching for a distraction. "Are you going to show me what you did over the weekend?"

It was his turn to blush. "I, um….actually haven't started it yet."

"Oh, really…" A condescending grin covered my face. "Well, if you can't manage, please let me know," I said, mimicking his email.

Scott ran his hand through his hair with a chuckle. "I deserved that."

I pressed my lips together with a nod.

"Look, I'm sorry for being a dick about this," he continued. "I've been working a lot lately, so it's been hard to fit in all the schoolwork. I'll stay back and get the first part done this afternoon."

My heart dipped. "It's okay. I'm sure you'll get to it."

"I could use a little help if you're free later?"

"Um..." I shifted in my seat. "I'll have to see if Grayson can wait around after swim practice."

"I can drive you home."

A lump formed in my throat. He eliminated my excuse.

"Come on, I'm not that bad a driver," he said, clearly noticing my hesitation. "What are you afraid of?"

My heart accelerated the moment our eyes collided. I was afraid, but it wasn't because of his driving. "Fine. I'll meet you in the library after school," I said, trying to act like the thought of being alone with him didn't bother me—or my libido.

"Great." I didn't have to look at Scott to know he was smiling.

Scott was impossible to miss in the library. His body loomed over the desk, like an adult sitting at a child's table. I wandered over, taking my time to study him while he was engrossed in his work. His wavy brown hair fell over his face as he chewed on the end of his pen, and I found myself envious. I wanted those lips on me.

He lifted his gaze in surprise as I drew closer. "I wasn't sure if you were going to show."

"I wasn't sure if I was going to come."

"Well, I'm glad you did," he said, patting the seat beside him, "because I'm already stuck on the second question."

I sat as directed but maintained a safe distance. I wouldn't have his touch distracting me. After reading over the first few questions, I explained what I thought it meant, and Scott watched me in awe.

"What?" I asked, pausing mid-sentence.

His mouth curved into a smile as he dropped his pen on the table. "Does anyone else know you're a closet nerd?"

I narrowed my eyes. "No, I'm not."

"Yes, you are." He laughed. "You're ridiculously smart. Why do you hide it?"

"I don't hide it. I just don't need to be." My mother always told me intelligence was a turn-off.

He tilted his head as if he was trying to study me. "What do you mean?"

"My grades don't matter."

"But what about college?" he asked, looking entirely perplexed.

"My parents have already spoken to the admissions board at Stanford. I don't foresee a problem."

"But don't you want to know what you're capable of on your own?"

His question threw me. "Not really, no."

"Why is that?"

"Because I might start wanting something different from what's expected of me."

"And that's a bad thing?"

"In my world, yes." I tapped on the book in front of us impatiently. "Can we just get the rest of this done?"

"Okay," he said, picking up his pen. "Smarty-pants."

I shook my head, but it did nothing to hinder my smile.

After we finished what was required that week, we packed up our things and walked out to the car. As soon as I got in, my whole body tensed. Surely I could last ten minutes in a confined space with this guy…surely.

"Thanks for driving me home," I said, filling the silence that loomed between us as we turned onto the picturesque streets of my neighborhood.

He glanced my way. "I should be thanking you. I never would have gotten through those questions without your help."

I remained quiet for a moment, pondering him. "Why do you work so much?"

Scott's jaw tightened. "To help pay bills."

My gaze lowered to my fingers as they fidgeted in my lap. "Where were you before coming to Summerhill?"

"Living with my grandfather in Phoenix."

I nodded along. "Why did you move?"

Scott's hands tightened around the steering wheel. "He died."

"Oh, I'm sorry."

"He was old. It wasn't unexpected." His casual manner didn't disguise the tremor in his voice.

The innate desire to reach out and touch him overwhelmed me, but I didn't move. "So, where do you live now?" I asked instead.

He let out an exasperated sigh and threw me a sideways glance. "What's with all the questions?"

"I'm sorry." My heart quickened at his sharp tone. I'd stepped over the line. "I just...I don't know much about you, that's all."

"The less you know, the better."

I shook my head in frustration. "Fine."

Pressing the brakes heavier than required, Scott stopped at the red light. "If you must know, I live in a shitty suburb, in a shitty house, with an even shittier dad. I work almost every day after school and most weekends, in a shitty job, just to make sure there's a decent meal on the table for my little brother."

My chest tightened. "You didn't have to tell me that."

"Yeah, but you should probably know."

"Why?"

"Because..." His voice caught when our eyes met, but he quickly returned them to the road. "Because that's the reason I need to ace every subject. I'm not going to college without a full ride."

I grimaced. He must've hated people like me. "What do you want to study at college?"

"Law," he said without blinking.

"Oh, wow. You seem so sure."

"I am." The light turned green, and he accelerated away.

"Is your dad a lawyer?" I asked, wondering if he was expected to follow in his footsteps.

Scott burst out laughing. "No. My dad is *not* a lawyer."

I frowned. As much as I wanted to, I couldn't work him out. "What's so funny?"

"Nothing is funny." The humor in his face vanished. "What about you? What do *you* want to be when you grow up?"

A small smile played on my lips as I pondered the question no one had ever asked me until now. "I'd love to own an art gallery."

"Don't you live in one? You have an original Sinclair."

"My parents own so many pieces, and over half are sitting in storage. It's such a waste. If I had my way, I'd open a public gallery where everyone could experience their greatness."

He glanced across at me with a warm smile. "And what do your parents think of your plan?"

I hugged my waist and averted my gaze out the window. "They don't care about what I want. They're more invested in Grayson's future."

"Why?"

"They expect me to marry him."

Scott's head spun to mine. "But Grayson assured me you were just friends."

"You spoke to Gray about me?" I asked, trying not to smile.

"I tried talking to other people, but no one seems to know you very well."

My cheeks heated. "I guess he knows me better than anyone."

"So, if nothing is going on, why do your parents think you're going to marry him?"

"A couple of years ago, Gray and I overheard our parents planning some big merger between Harlow Corp and Warren Media, but it would only happen if we married." I chortled. "Crazy, right?"

Scott's shoulders lowered. "Yeah, totally."

"Just another way for me to disappoint them."

"No siblings to share the load of expectations?"

"Nope, just me."

Scott pulled up to our iron gates and motioned to the security pad through his open window. "Did you want to…"

"Sure," I precariously reached across his body and entered the security code. While I hovered above him, a low rumble rolled through his chest, lighting up my whole body like we were set to the same frequency. I quickly returned to my seat and watched the gates open. "You can go," I said when the car didn't move.

"Oh, right," he muttered with a shaky breath before driving through.

As we moved along the tree-lined driveway, closer to the ridiculously huge structure I called home, I wondered what Scott was thinking. He'd never seen my house in the daylight, and I was certain it would scare him away.

"So, this castle only houses *three* people?" he asked, scanning the grounds.

"Don't forget the staff."

"You have staff?" His eyes widened. "Living in your house?"

"My *parents* have staff, and they live in separate accommodations on the grounds."

"That's insane."

I laughed. "I know." My smile faded when I spotted the car parked out front. "Fuck."

"What is it?" Scott instinctively took his foot off the accelerator.

My eyes burned unshed tears. "Would you mind if we kept driving for a little while?"

His eyebrows pulled together as he came to a complete stop. "Um...I need to pick up my brother and grab some dinner..."

"Oh, it's okay, don't worry," I interrupted, blinking away the mist. I attempted to get out of the car, but the damn door was jammed again.

"But you can come with, if you want?" he asked, watching me barely hold myself together.

The weight lifted. "Really?"

"Well, yeah. But I'm warning you, where I'm going...it's not a great neighborhood."

I rolled my eyes. "I'll hide my diamonds."

With an endearing smirk, he sped off around the circular bed of red roses and back down the driveway, leaving behind a cloud of dust.

Once we were back on the main road, Scott turned to me. "Are you going to tell me what's going on?"

I kept my eyes on the passing traffic. "My dad's away on business."

"And that car belonged to..."

My throat constricted. "*Not* my dad."

He ran his fingers through his hair. "Jesus, your mom is cheating on your dad...even when you're home?"

My stomach churned. "She thinks she's conditioning me."

"For what?" he spat, flashing me a look of disgust.

"A loveless marriage."

"That's fucked up."

"Just a little." I chortled, but a touch of madness seeped through.

For years, my mother had been having an affair with our driver, Miguel. I wasn't certain my father knew, but she wasn't keeping it a secret from me. She was always consistently clear on her advice. Marry for money and power, *then* fuck whomever you please. And that is exactly what she did.

As we drove farther and farther from Bel Air, the houses became progressively smaller and smaller until we reached a suburb I'd never ventured to before. Old, run-down weatherboard houses with unkempt yards lined the cracked sidewalks while kids played out in the road, dodging traffic.

"Where are their parents?" I asked, seeing a boy sitting on the curb, nursing a grazed knee.

"At work."

I frowned. "So, who's looking after them."

"They look after each other. Most families around here need two incomes to survive, so there's not much left for babysitters."

"Is that why you have to work? Is your mom not around?"

"I haven't seen her in six years. She took off not long after Riley was born. Social services sent us to live with our grandfather a couple of years ago, but now we're back with our dad."

Scott pulled up in front of a little house that was a little neater than the rest. "Wait here. I'll be back in a minute." He jumped out of the car and jogged up to the house, glancing back with a small smile as he knocked on the door.

A moment later, a petite girl, similar in age, appeared in front of him. She stepped toward Scott with bothersome familiarity and smiled up at him adoringly. A twang of jealously shot straight through my body but quickly dissipated when a little boy flew straight through their legs, knocking them both off balance. I silently rejoiced as he ran onto the front lawn, urging Scott to follow.

My gaze floated back to the porch to find that another lady, much older, had joined them. The young girl folded her arms with a scowl while Scott's attention focused on whatever the other lady was saying. He lowered his head and rubbed the back of his neck before calling his brother over. Kneeling to talk to him face to face, his little brother dropped his bottom lip and looked away. He was clearly in trouble.

Returning to his feet, Scott said something that appeared like an apology to the older lady, while the younger girl watched his little brother run to his car. Her eyes struck mine and tapered before snapping back to Scott. "Who's that?" I read her lips.

His gaze followed hers. "A friend," he appeared to say back.

As he waved goodbye to both women, I sank further into the seat, staring out the windshield. The sound of the door opening drew my attention, and a gorgeous little face with shaggy brown hair popped up. His turquoise eyes grew wide when he saw me.

"Hi, there!" I said with a warm smile.

Without a word, he climbed into the backseat and put on his seatbelt.

Scott slid in after him and swung his arm over the seat. "Riley, this is my friend, Lanie. Lanie, this is my little bro, Riley."

"Pleased to meet you, Riley," I said, facing his brother. I decided to let the *Lanie* part slide.

Riley averted his gaze out the window, ignoring both of us.

"Riley, stop being rude and say hello," Scott uttered, his voice taking a sterner tone. "Sorry, he's a bit shy around…well… everyone."

I couldn't help but smile at the boy. He was a mini Scott, only chubbier, with hair a few shades darker. "He just needs to warm up."

"Riley…" Scott repeated through his clenched jaw.

When Riley didn't budge, I reached over and touched Scott's arm. "It's okay. Don't push him."

Scott exhaled his frustration and started the car. "Thanks," he mumbled before pulling away from the curb. He lifted his hand in a brief wave to the girl on the front porch as we set off down the road.

"Who was that?" I asked, trying to sound as casual as possible.

"Mrs. Norris' daughter, Elle. She helps her mom babysit some of the kids in the neighborhood after school."

"I think she likes you."

"She's not my type," he grumbled before looking back at Riley in the rearview mirror. "Hey, Riley, what happened after school today? Mrs. Norris said you were hitting the other kids."

When he didn't answer, Scott continued, "I'm going to have to find a new babysitter if this keeps happening."

My body jerked when Riley kicked the back of the front seat.

"Hey, quit it," Scott snapped, glaring back at him before returning his eyes to the road.

As Riley whimpered, Scott's shoulders lowered. "Rils. Please don't cry."

This only made his brother cry harder.

"Is he okay?" I whispered, unsure of what to do or say.

"This happens all the time. I'm sorry."

"I know what might cheer him up," I said, thinking of the one thing that always brought a smile to my face.

Scott shot me a glance. "What's that?"

With a grin, I turned to his little brother. "Hey, Riley, do you like burgers?"

His eyes widened, and he wiped away his tears as he nodded.

"Oh, Lanie." Scott grimaced. "You don't want to do that."

My breath caught. "Oh, does he have allergies or something?"

"No, he has meltdowns every time we go out. It's a nightmare."

I turned back to Riley. "You're not going to have a meltdown, are you, Riley?

He shook his head.

"See," I said, smiling up at Scott. "No one has meltdowns at Nico's Diner."

He rubbed the sparse stubble along his jaw. "I don't know…"

"Please, Scotty." Riley's timid voice surprised us.

I poked out my bottom lip and used my sweetest voice as I looked up at Scott. "Please, Scotty?"

"Alright." He fought back a smile. "But I warned you."

Riley squealed with delight, and I threw my hand back for a high-five. The slap of Riley's palm against mine filled the car, and my heart warmed.

Once my surroundings became more familiar, I directed Scott to the diner not far from our school, then into the booth Grayson and I shared regularly.

Scott slid in beside me while Riley jumped into the seat opposite. He immediately picked up the salt and pepper shakers, spilling them onto the table.

"Riley," Scott uttered under his breath as a waitress approached our table. "Put them down."

"Are you ready to order?" she asked, taking out her notepad.

"Almost. You wouldn't happen to have some crayons and paper, would you?"

The waitress smiled down at Riley. "I'll see what's in the back."

She returned a moment later with a cup of crayons and a pile of printer paper and placed them on the table. After I thanked her, she took our orders while Riley rummaged through the crayons.

"Do you like to draw?" I asked Riley when he immediately took crayon to paper.

He nodded his head but still no words.

"Maybe you could draw me a picture?"

With a smile, his body relaxed as he began drawing what looked like flowers.

"You're very good," I said, surprised by the detail. "How old are you, Riley?"

"Six," he said, so focused on his drawing he forgot his wariness toward me.

I grinned up at Scott, who was watching our interaction closely. "Six? You're very tall for your age."

Riley puffed out his chest. "Scott reckons I'll be taller than him one day."

"I bet you will be," I said, deciding to push my luck. "Did you have a bad day today?"

He nodded his head with a sigh.

Scott leaned forward. "You want to tell us about it?"

Riley pressed his lips together and shook his head, shutting down again.

"Sometimes it's hard to tell people how we feel," I said, trying to keep my tone casual. "Perhaps you could draw what happened."

Riley's little brow crumpled before taking another piece of paper. "I guess..."

As we watched Riley immerse himself into his drawing, Scott's warm arm pressed against mine. "You're good with kids."

"I always wanted a little brother or sister. You're lucky."

"I wouldn't say I'm lucky, but yeah, Riley's a pretty great kid."

"Pretty awesome, you mean," I said as Riley handed me his completed drawing. "I can't believe you drew this. Are you sure you're only six?"

Scott peered over my shoulder as I ran my gaze over his drawing. He was advanced for his age.

"Who's this?" Scott asked, pointing at the figure that was laughing and pointing.

Riley frowned. "That's Prue."

"Has she been making fun of you?"

Riley nodded. "She's mean to me all the time, but Mrs. Norris never sees."

I peered up at Scott who was obviously planning Prue's demise by the look on his face. "How about we forget Prue and eat some delicious burgers instead...because here they come."

The waitress's timing was perfect, and all was forgotten the moment everyone bit into dinner.

"You should probably get Riley home," I said, watching his brother struggle to hold his head up as he chewed the last of his fries.

"Do you think your mom's *friend* will be gone by now?"

"He should be," I said, signaling for the check. "If not, I'll sleep in the pool house again." I quickly handed my credit card to the waitress before Scott had a chance to open his wallet.

"Lanie..."

"This was my idea. You can pay next time."

His eyebrows lifted. "Next time? So you want to do this again?" he asked as I slid out of the booth.

Riley's head smashed onto the table, and he let out a sleepy yelp.

"Come on." I laughed. "You need to get Riley to bed."

"Okay, but this conversation's not over."

Scott picked up Riley and bundled him into the car before driving me home. After a few minutes, I glanced back to check on him. He was adorable.

"He likes you," Scott said, meeting my gaze. "I've never seen him warm up to anyone so quickly, let alone *talk* to them."

"I like him too. He's a really sweet kid."

"I wish Mrs. Norris thought so. I can't afford to lose her as a babysitter if he keeps getting into fights."

"Maybe he's frustrated," I said with a shrug. "Perhaps he fights because he can't express how he feels through his words."

"Like us?"

My mouth twitched when he threw me a sideways glance.

"Encourage him to draw. It may help," I said, trying to stay on topic. Cara used art to express her feelings. Perhaps Riley could too.

"Thanks for the tip. I will." He slowed at the gate and wound down his window.

My face burned when I realized I'd have to climb over him again. "Perhaps I should just give you the code."

"I'd rather not know."

I tried to hide my smile. "Fine," I muttered before reaching over him.

As I typed in the code, his warm breath blew through my hair, exposing my neck to his mouth. A shiver rolled through my entire body, causing me to push the wrong button and sound an alarm. "Can you stop it? I can't concentrate when you're doing that."

Scott leaned forward, hovering his mouth over my ear. "Doing what?"

My core pulsed, and I quickly sat back down. "869432," I blurted, still trying to find my breath.

Scott laughed. "What?"

"That's the code. 869432."

Shaking his head with a chuckle, Scott entered the code into the security system and drove through the opening gates. Once we reached the house, he jumped out to open my door.

"Can you tell Riley I said goodbye?" I asked as I stepped out of the car.

Scott slipped his hands into his pockets and rocked on his feet. "Of course."

I lifted my school bag onto my shoulder. "Thanks for letting me hang out with you guys tonight. I really appreciate it."

"Anytime."

My heart raced as I stood there like an idiot. "Well, I better go…"

"Lanie…" Scott called before I'd barely taken a step. "Can I take you out sometime? Maybe without my little brother in tow?"

My chest constricted. I desperately wanted to say yes, but I knew it was a bad idea. I glanced back at my house, praying my mother had already retired for the night. "I…I can't."

"Why not?"

"Because you're…you're not…" I grimaced. He wouldn't understand.

"The heir to some fortune?" His lips pursed. "I heard that's your preference."

My fingernails cut into the palms of my hands. "I guess it must be true then."

Scott's brow furrowed as he stepped forward, reaching for my wrist.

I flinched at his touch and fell back a step. "Goodnight, Scott."

"Lanie…"

Without faltering, I jogged up the stairs and into my house before falling back on the door in tears.

Chapter 7

My back stiffened as soon as he walked into homeroom. Scott's eyes found mine in a matter of moments, and he marched straight to my desk.

"Lanie," he greeted as he sat down beside me.

I turned away. If he was so eager to believe the rumors about me, I couldn't see any point in being polite.

He leaned over and lowered his voice so no one would hear. "I want to talk about how things ended las—"

Hank's obnoxious laughter filled the room, drowning out Scott's voice, and Grayson trailed in behind him. They sauntered over to where Scott and I sat and threw their books onto the tables in front of us.

"Are you guys going to Randy's party this weekend?" Grayson asked, panning his gaze between us.

"I don't know," Scott said, turning to face me. "Are we?"

My eyes widened. What the fuck was he doing? "I'm going with Cara."

Scott turned back to Grayson. "Then I guess I'll be there too."

I narrowed my gaze at his profile, but he didn't face me.

Grayson smirked as he motioned to the two of us. "What's going on here?"

"Nothing," I muttered, but my cheeks were already burning.

Scott finally met my stare. "It's not nothing. I'm trying to get Lanie here to go out with me."

Hank scoffed as Grayson chuckled, and I gritted my teeth.

"And how's that working for you?" Grayson asked with a knowing smirk.

Scott shrugged nonchalantly. "Still working on it."

"Good luck," Hank huffed, folding his arms as he turned to the front.

Grayson's smile seeped through his composure, but he didn't say anything.

"Shut up, Gray," I muttered, reading his thoughts.

He snickered as the teacher entered the room. "I didn't say anything."

It was going to be a long day.

Knowing Scott shared the next class with me, I jumped out of my seat as soon as the bell rang and flew out of the room.

He caught up with me with little effort. "So, if it's not a money thing, then what is it?" he asked, continuing our conversation like it had never ended the night prior.

"Can you drop it?" I hugged my books closer to my chest.

"No. I just want to know why you won't go on a date with me?"

"Maybe I just don't like you that way."

"Oh…" he said, slowing his step before shaking his head with a chuckle. "No, that's not it. I'll just have to keep trying."

And he did. Every day that week, he asked me out—in homeroom, in class, at lunch—until I was so wound up I could barely think straight. I wanted to say yes, and he must've known, because he made every minute together torture. He'd sit unnecessarily close to me in class, accidentally-on-purpose let his leg graze against mine under the table, or just stare at me until my body was on fire.

"Can you get him to stop?" I asked Grayson on Friday at lunch.

"Why would I? It's refreshing seeing you squirm for once."

I blew out an angry breath. "Maybe I should ask Lisa to join us for lunch then."

Grayson's face paled as he searched the cafeteria for the girl he'd been avoiding since Jacob's party.

"Then tell him to back off."

"Just go on a date with him," he uttered, throwing up his hands. "What's the harm in one date?"

I filled my mouth with salad. "Wanting another," I grumbled.

Grayson's expression softened. "Why don't you just ask your mom? She might surprise you."

I shot him a look that translated to *Are you kidding?*

"Or don't. It's not like she'd find out, even if you did go out with him."

Saturday afternoon, Mom called me into the living room. She was hosting a charity gala in a couple of weeks and was busy making decisions on the finer details.

"What do you think about these?" she asked, standing beside three elaborate floral arrangements. "I'm tossing up between these two."

She was testing me. "What color are you wearing?"

"It's a rose-colored dress, why?"

"Well, you don't want your outfit clashing with the décor, so I'd choose the white one."

Mom raised her brows. "I've taught you well," she said, signaling for her assistant to note the decision. "While you're here, will you fix these bows?" She scowled at the tiny boxes scattered over our dining table. "Nina has made a mess of them."

"Sure," I said, glancing over at my mother's paling assistant. It was a rare opportunity to get into my mother's good graces, so I took it.

While Mom fussed around with linen and glassware samples, I proceeded to re-tie each ribbon I knew didn't reach my mother's expectation of perfection.

"Where's Dad today?" I asked, trying to fill the mundane silence.

"In his study, preparing his speech for the gala tonight."

I nodded my head. "Silly me," I mumbled quietly. My father rarely left his study when he was home, which was seldom. Heaven forbid he spent time with his daughter.

After Nina left to run some errands for my mom, I decided it was the perfect opportunity to ask about Scott.

"Mom?" I tried to sound as casual as possible.

"Yes..."

"Would I be allowed to go on a date?"

Her face lit up. "With Grayson?"

"Um...no." I grimaced. "Someone else."

She frowned and shook her head. "But you and Grayson are perfect together."

"But I don't..."

"Don't what? Think of him that way? How can you not? He's gorgeous."

"I know," I groaned. "You keep telling me."

Her eyes narrowed. "Then who?"

I moved my focus back to the ribbon in my fingers. "Just someone from school."

"Well, does he have a name? Who are his parents?"

Panic flooded me. "You know what, it doesn't matter."

"Well, good. High school boys will only cause you unnecessary heartache, not to mention ruin your untarnished reputation."

I pulled the last bow so tight it almost snapped in my fingers.

Unfortunately, my mother continued. "If you want to date someone *other* than Grayson, your father and I will find a suitable match after graduation."

"I'm perfectly capable of finding my own dates, Mom."

"Of course you are. But I expect you to set your sights much higher than the boys at Summerhill. Apart from Grayson, I doubt any of them are worthy of your attention—not until you have a suitable ring on your finger, at least."

I almost laughed. Apparently, I wasn't allowed to sleep around until after I was married. "Thanks for the advice," I uttered, wondering if she caught my obvious sarcasm. I stood up to leave, needing to get away from the absurd conversation as quickly as possible. "I better go. I'm heading to a party tonight."

"Will Grayson be there?"

"Yes."

"Good. Make sure you wear that new dress I bought you."

"Sure thing." *Not a chance.*

Shortly after my parents left for dinner, Cara picked me up. Her mom let her borrow the car, provided she came home early.

"Wow, you look great," I said, impressed by her combination of clothes and makeup.

Her cheeks grew pink. "Thank you for lending it to me. Do you think Rob will like it?"

"I think he'll *love* who's in it," I said, giving her a nudge before grabbing my handbag.

Her giggle faded when she caught sight of my dress. "Wow, you look *amazing*."

"Thanks," I muttered, gazing down at the outfit I changed into after my parents left. It still showed off my legs, but it softened my features, giving the illusion of curves. My mother preferred I wore fitted numbers with bold lines, but I never felt comfortable in the so-called power dresses she filled my wardrobe with.

"Scott's going to lose his mind."

"I'm not wearing it for him."

"Oh really?" She chuckled. "For Jacob, then?"

"Let's go," I grumbled. "You don't want to keep Rob waiting, do you?"

Her eyes sparkled. "No, I do not."

All heads turned our way when we entered Randy's house. I was used to the attention. Cara was not.

"Why is everyone staring at us?" she said, peeking up at me. "Is there something on my face?"

I laughed. "No, there is nothing on your face, except Rob's lips as soon as he sees you."

As if on cue, Rob appeared with a gigantic grin spread across his face. His disheveled hair and his tall, lanky build gave him a slightly goofy appearance, but he seemed smitten with Cara, and that pleased me.

"I'll see you later," I whispered into her ear, wanting to give them some space.

Her eyes grew large. "Are you sure?"

"I'll find someone to talk to."

"I think they just found you," she said, waving at whomever was approaching from behind me.

By the smirk on her face, I knew who it was. "Let me guess." My heartbeat accelerated as I turned. It took all my strength not to let Scott's gorgeous smile turn my insides into mush. "No, I will not go out with you," I said, not waiting for him to ask the question he had pestered me with daily at school.

"I was just going to ask if you wanted a drink," he said, holding out a red cup.

Heat traveled up my neck. "Oh, um…okay, thanks." I took it from his hand with an uneasy smile and looked away when our fingers grazed.

Scott's eyes didn't budge from my profile. "You look really pretty tonight."

I squeezed my eyes shut. "Don't start."

He dipped his head. "Okay then," he said, shoving his hands into his pockets before strolling away.

Exhaling the breath I didn't know I was holding, I walked in the opposite direction to find someone else to talk to. Someone who didn't make me feel so…*so much*.

No matter what group I joined or person I spoke to, I could feel Scott's eyes on me. I was used to being watched by men, but this was different. There was something deeper about the way he looked at me. It wasn't just lust. He wanted more than my body…and that was what scared me.

"Have you been avoiding me?" A voice startled me as I wandered outside. Jacob's eyes traveled down my body and back up before he took a long drag of his cigarette.

"Um…no…" I hadn't even noticed he was there.

"Did you have fun at my party last week?" he asked, moving closer.

My smile was tight. "Yeah, it was great."

"Want to have a little more fun at this one?"

His smoky breath made me grimace, and I turned my face away. "I don't think so."

Jacob tucked a strand of my hair behind my ear then whispered into it. "Why not? Most girls would do anything to be in your shoes."

"Well, I'm not most girls, so if you don't mind…" I attempted to push past him, but he grabbed my wrist.

"You really are an ice queen, aren't you?" he hissed.

"Is there a problem here?" Scott asked, materializing behind Jacob.

Jacob loosened his grip and turned around. "Mind your own business."

"Let her go, and I will." Scott's death glare didn't falter.

After a silent standoff, Jacob mumbled something under his breath as he stamped out his cigarette and stormed back into the house. Scott's jaw pulsed as he eyed my reddening wrist.

"I didn't need you to save me." I covered my wrist from his view as tears pricked my eyes.

His gaze met mine and softened, making it so much worse.

"Just leave me alone," I snapped before escaping into the house. I refused to break down in front of him.

With the guest bathroom occupied, I snuck into the vacant bedroom opposite, desperate for privacy. Leaving the lights off, I dropped onto the bed and cradled my head in my hands.

I wasn't supposed to show any weakness around men, but lately, I'd been failing miserably. I allowed stupid rumors to get to me, I tolerated Mr. West's harassment, I let Jacob hurt me, and worst of all, Scott had witnessed all of it.

Light streamed through the door as it creaked open.

"Lanie?" Scott called, squinting into the darkness.

I stood up and quickly wiped the tears from my face. "I'm fine, okay? You didn't need to follow me."

"You're not fine," he said, stepping into the room. "What did Jacob say to you out there?"

"Nothing everyone else isn't saying."

"I can go back out there and punch him if you want. Just say the word."

I started laughing before remembering how much he bothered me. "Can you stop?"

"Stop what?"

I lifted my gaze to his face, half-lit by the hallway light. "Quit being so nice to me, okay?"

His face scrunched up. "Huh?"

"I'm being an absolute bitch to you, and you're treating me like…"

"Like what?"

My frustration spiked. "Argh, just stop it."

"No," he said, crossing his arms.

My eyes widened. "*No?*"

"I guess girls like you aren't familiar with that word."

I took slow, purposeful steps toward Scott until my finger pressed up against his hard chest. "That's better."

Before I could leave, he grasped my hand. "What's your problem with me?"

I should've pulled away, but his touch was nothing like Jacob's. It was tender and goosebump-inducing. "Just because you're hot, and charming, and smart, doesn't mean every girl is going to fall to their knees around you."

His mouth curled upwards. "You think I'm hot?"

I growled as I attempted to yank my hand away, but he pulled me closer.

"Go out with me."

"No."

"Give me one good reason."

I shoved him, but he barely moved. "Because I'm not allowed!"

"What?"

"Everyone thinks I'm a frigid bitch who refuses to date anyone from Summerhill, but it has nothing to do with my high expectations." I blinked back tears. "It's my parents. They control everything I do…and I was totally fine with that until you came along."

"So, you *do* want to date me?"

I shook my head. "That's irrelevant."

Scott's warm breath grazed my neck. "It's very relevant."

Each hair on my body stood to attention. "What are you doing?" I whispered, barely finding my voice.

His eyes fell to my mouth, but he said nothing.

Anticipation and fear stirred through my body. "Sco…"

His lips closed over mine, stealing the last letters of his name. As I breathed him in, I opened my mouth, allowing his tongue to test the waters. When I didn't resist, his fingers dove through my hair, taking my nape into his calloused hands. He angled my head upwards and kissed me harder and deeper until a moan escaped my mouth. Our lips parted, but our eyes remained millimeters apart, staring into each other's souls.

"You want to get out of here?" Scott asked as his chest rose and fell in quick succession.

I nodded without hesitation. I couldn't think of anything I wanted more.

Slipping his hand around mine, he led me out of the room, down the hallway, and through the crowded living room.

Grayson saw us and grinned when he spotted our interlocked fingers. "You finally wore her down," he said to Scott, grasping his shoulder.

Scott rubbed the back of his neck. "We're going to head out. Are you okay to get home?"

Grayson raised his eyebrows at me and chuckled. "Yeah, I'll find a ride."

I punched his shoulder. "Can you let Cara know? She's a little busy right now."

"No problem."

I glanced back as Scott tugged me along. "Thanks, Gray."

"Have fun…" Grayson sang with a corny wink.

Once we were in the car, neither of us spoke until we passed the sign noting a notorious make-out spot along Mulholland Drive.

"I'm not going to ask how you already know where the local hook-up spots are."

"Ha-ha, Grayson gave me the intel," he said, pulling into a secluded parking spot. "I promise you, I've never been here before."

I sighed. "Neither have I."

"You sound disappointed about that." Scott took off his seat belt and rested his arm over the back of the seat.

I stared out the windshield at the beautiful view. "I am."

"Why is that? Never seen the city lights before?"

I turned my gaze to his and drew in a shaky breath, along with a dose of courage. "No, because I've never been able to do this…" Unbuckling my seat belt, I climbed over Scott and straddled his legs, pressing my lips to his before he had a chance to speak. As the kiss intensified, I reached down to unfasten his jeans.

"Whoa, Lanie, slow down."

My fingers paused. "Why?"

"Because I don't want this to be a one-night thing."

"But this is all it can be," I said, tucking my hair behind my ears as I lowered my gaze.

Scott's hands tightened around my thighs. "No. I want more," he said, tipping my face up with his finger. "And I think you do too."

"It doesn't matter what *we* want. My parents will never let me go out with you."

His lips found my neck, causing a moan to float from my lips. "Tell me what *you* want, Lanie," he whispered between kisses. "Right here, right now." Scott's hands slid up and down my thighs, inching up the hem of my dress.

My panties grazed over the denim barrier between us. "I want you to touch me."

A deep growl rumbled through his chest. "Lanie…"

"Please?" My throat tightened. "I'm not an ice queen."

"I never thought you were," he said, cupping my cheeks in his hands.

My eyes welled. "But don't you want to?"

"God, yes," he said, pressing his forehead to mine. "But you have nothing to prove to me."

I closed my eyes, willing the tears away. "I'm sorry."

"You don't have to apologize. I just want you to really want this."

"But I do," I said, meeting his deep blues.

Scott's hands traveled down my arms as he pondered me. "Have you ever…"

I drew back. "Does it matter?"

His eyes softened. "Yeah…it does."

"Oh." I attempted to shuffle away, but his firm grasp held me in place.

"Hey, hey, I'm not saying I don't want to…I fucking want to…just not like this." Scott pushed my hair back and laid a kiss on my exposed shoulder, clearly sensing my disappointment. "There are plenty of other things we can do until then, though."

My smile grew. "Like…"

He dragged his lips up my neck and kissed me under my ear. "Like this."

I pretended to look disinterested, but my heart raced.

"Or this," he said as his teeth grazed my ear lobe.

My girlish giggle shocked me more than Scott.

"You like that?" he asked, squeezing my thighs.

His hardness twitched below, making my core ache. "I like *that*."

He did it again, and I pressed myself against him, wanting more.

"Lanie…" he uttered in warning.

My mouth found his as I rocked into him. "Say it again," I whispered over his lips.

"What?" he asked in a lustful haze.

"My name."

He chuckled as he kissed me. "So you like it now?"

I bit my bottom lip as I nodded, and he slid his hands further up my dress. Needing more, I parted my legs wider and pushed myself closer while Scott shifted his hand to my inner thigh. My legs clenched over his when his fingers ran over my panties, and when he pulled them aside, I gasped. No one had ever touched me like that.

"Lanie…" Scott repeated my name like a prayer.

"More," I rasped.

He slid his finger in effortlessly, and I cried out. My temperature rose as I rode the waves of ecstasy while perspiration slid down my spine. I'd never been so intimate with someone before, and I could only imagine how good the real thing would be. With his hands on me—in me—and his tongue tracing every curve of my neck, I was moments from losing control.

With one last whisper of my name, I shuddered over his hand and collapsed into his arms.

The next three hours were spent in the backseat of Scott's car, making out, and by the time he pulled up at my security gate, my lips were swollen and red. I would've spent the entire night with him, but Scott had to work the next day, and I didn't want to be the reason for him losing his job.

"I'll get out here," I said reluctantly, staring at the lips I wanted back on mine.

Scott frowned as he entered the security code. "Are you sure? I can drive you closer."

"No, my parents are home, so..."

He pursed his lips.

"I just don't want them to—"

Scott reached out and squeezed my hand. "It's okay. We'll figure it out."

My heart warmed at his touch. "Okay."

As the iron gates opened, Scott got out of the car to open my door.

"Thanks," I said, reluctantly climbing out. I didn't want the night to end.

He ran his hand down my cheek. "Goodnight, Lanie."

"Goodnight." I gave him a sleepy smile before backstepping through the gates as they closed.

He followed me until the iron bars forced him back. "You forgot something," he said, reaching out for my hand.

With a laugh, I let him pull me back. "I thought it would be safer this way."

"It'll take more than an iron gate to keep me from kissing you," he said, leveling his face with mine.

Our noses touched, and my smile mirrored his. "Just one more?"

His dimples deepened as he grazed my lips. "I'll try."

Chapter 8

As soon as my cell phone chimed on Sunday afternoon, I launched across my bed and read the message.

Cara: **You and Scott???!!! Tell me everything!**

My heartbeat slowed. I'd been waiting for a call or text from Scott all day.

Me: **You first...**

Cara: **Rob and I got a little carried away.**

Me: **How carried away?**

Cara: **All the way.**

My mouth fell open.

Me: **Oh my god. How was it?**

Cara: **You know...**

I slumped into my pillows with a huff.

Me: **I don't, actually.**

Cara: **What?! You haven't...**

Me: **I tried last night, but Scott wants to wait.**

Cara: **That's sweet.**

Me: **Tell that to my libido.**

Cara: **Well, I missed my curfew, and I'm grounded for two weeks.**

Me: **I don't even know who you are anymore ;)**

Cara: **I'll tell you everything tomorrow.**

Me: **Fine. I'm used to waiting :P**

With a twinge of envy, I tossed my cell back on the bed and thought about the previous night. Scott wasn't like the other boys at Summerhill. They were so focused on 'thawing out the ice queen' that they did not attempt to get to know me. I was merely a stepping stone to popularity.

Until now, Grayson was the only boy who didn't want anything from me. I could trust him with my secrets and cry on his shoulder, and he'd never judge or ridicule me. The only part missing for us was what I saw in Scott's eyes. Desire. Just the thought of Scott's supple lips on mine, or his hungry hands, induced an ache only he could relieve. I was desperate to see him again, but I would happily settle for his voice.

Knowing Scott had to work all day and probably couldn't call me until he got home, I decided to do something unheard of. I sprawled my school books over my bed and studied.

Hours later, after a rare dinner with both parents, I returned to my bedroom in a foul mood. Scott still hadn't called. Perhaps what had happened between us meant more to me than it did to him. Perhaps it was just a hook-up. Doubt tumbled around my mind until I lost all self-control. I picked up my phone, typed a message, and was about to press send when it chimed loudly.

"Fuck," I muttered when it fumbled out of my hands. As I gazed down at the screen, the crushing weight lifted off my chest at the sight of his name.

Scott: **Sweet dreams, Lanie. x**

His three simple words made my heart swell, and it took all my strength not to text him back. It was his turn to wait for me.

Cara's face grew bright red when I appeared at her locker the next morning. I'd arrived earlier than usual, hoping to see Scott before school started, but he hadn't shown up.

"You're glowing..." I sang as she rummaged through her locker, trying not to make eye contact.

Cara laughed while repositioning an array of pencils and paintbrushes to fit in with her books. "Melanie, stop," she said, quickly checking to see if anyone had heard me.

"Sorry, but I need the distraction."

"Why? Where's Scott? I thought he'd have you well and truly distracted."

"He's not here," I grumbled.

Cara checked her watch and frowned. “Homeroom is about to start. Can we talk at lunch? Oh shoot, I can’t. Mrs. Weathers said I could use the art room to work on my competition piece.”

“Argh, the suspense is killing me,” I said, hanging back my head. “But I guess it’s for a good cause. How *is* my masterpiece going?”

Cara’s grin grew. “Mrs. Weathers thinks I have a real shot at winning.”

I placed my hands on my hips. “I’m pretty sure I told you that already.”

“But you haven’t even seen it yet,” she said, giving me a soft nudge. “And I don’t want you to until I know the result.”

“Well, I’m sure it will be amazing. Mrs. Weathers knows what she’s talking about.”

“And if I do win…I have a really good chance of getting a scholarship.”

My mouth dropped. “You’re applying to art school?”

Cara nodded, barely containing her excitement. “Mrs. Weathers wants me to start building a portfolio, so I’ll be working through lunch most days. She’s even going to call in a few favors. Can you believe it?”

“This is perfect for you,” I said, squeezing her arm. “But what about your mom? Does she know?”

“No way.” The light in her eyes dulled. “She freaks out when she finds a paintbrush in our house. Imagine what she’d do if she found out about this?”

I bit the inside of my cheek. “Well, I hear Stanford has a great art program.”

“I know, but it’s not far enough away. I need to put some distance between me and my mom. She’s only getting worse.”

A short laugh escaped my mouth. “I get that.”

“Well, I should go. I’ll call you after school to answer all your burning questions, okay?”

“You better.”

Scott missed homeroom and didn’t appear at school until midway through Chemistry. He walked into class, handed the teacher a note, and slid into the seat beside me. As he opened his textbook, his arm grazed across mine, and our gazes collided.

I wanted to ask him where he'd been and why he hadn't called since we kissed, but I bit my tongue. The room was entirely too quiet to expose my desperation.

When I lowered my eyes, he tore the corner off his worksheet and wrote something down. Once the teacher's back was turned, he slid it across the desk.

Meet me in the AV room after class.

My body heated instantly. His eyes burned into my profile while I reread the note three times before hiding it between the pages of my book. As much as I wanted to, I didn't turn his way. I loathed how revoltingly needy he was making me feel.

After class, I fought every urge to sprint to the AV room and hung back to speak to the teacher about extra credit. I needed to stall. I needed Scott to doubt whether I'd meet him. I needed the control back.

Once Scott packed up his books, he edged past and discreetly dragged his finger across my lower back, sending shivers throughout my body. With a casual glimpse over his shoulder, he strolled out of the classroom, beckoning me to follow.

Although I had every intention of making Scott wait, minutes later I found myself standing in front of the AV room, reaching for the handle. Before I had a chance to turn it, a hand flew out and pulled me in, spinning me around until I was pressed up against the metal shelving.

"Hi...Lanie," Scott drawled my name in a deliberate attempt to arouse me.

My cheeks flushed. I was already there. "Hi."

"Where wer—" was all I could mutter before Scott devoured my lips.

"You were saying?" he asked when we came up for air.

My heart thumped against Scott's chest as I cleared my throat. "Where were you this morning?"

"Dad slept in, so I had to get Riley to school."

"Oh."

Scott stepped back and grinned. "You miss me or something?"

"No," I grumbled, crossing my arms.

"Liar." He hooked his finger into the waist of my skirt and pulled me toward him.

I said nothing but couldn't help but smile.

"So...when can I see you?" he asked, laying a gentle kiss on my neck.

"You're seeing me right now."

"No..." He ran his thumb over my lips. "When can I see *more* of you?"

Without taking my eyes off his, I began unfastening the buttons of my shirt.

"Whoa, mind out of the gutter, Lanie," he said with a laugh. "I meant...when can I take you out...on a date?"

I refastened my buttons in a huff. "I told you...we can't."

"How would your parents even find out? I won't tell, if you don't."

Perhaps he was right. My parents hadn't a clue what I did with my spare time, and they didn't associate with anyone from Summerhill except Grayson's family, so the risk of them finding out was minimal. "Alright, pick me up on Saturday. No earlier than seven...and don't plan anything fancy."

He chuckled. "Don't worry, my budget won't take us anywhere where we'll run into your parents."

"It has nothing to with my parents...I just hate fancy."

His brows rose. "Noted," he said, reaching for the door as the bell rang.

I pulled his hand away from the handle. "Can't we just skip class? I'd much rather do more of this." I dragged his tie down until his lips met mine.

Scott moaned. "As much as I want to, I won't give Mr. West any reason to hold you back."

The mood dissipated immediately, and I dropped my hands. "But he hasn't done anything since we switched chairs."

Scott's gaze darkened. "That doesn't mean he won't."

I sighed. "Fine."

"I'll wait for you after class," he said, encircling his hand around my nape. "No matter what, okay?"

I offered him an uneasy smile. "Okay."

With one last kiss, we snuck out of the room and walked to our next class, our hands grazing with each step.

After a week of stolen kisses and seductive grazes, I was finally getting ready for our first date. I ran my gaze over my bedroom, wanting everything to be perfect. Scott may have wanted to wait, but I wasn't going to make it easy for him. My parents were away, and I planned on bringing him home after our night out.

Sitting at the bottom of our grand staircase, fiddling with the hem of my favorite dress, I checked my phone for the twentieth time. It was almost eight, and he hadn't shown, nor had he called to tell me he was running late.

Me: **Where are you?**

I cringed at how pathetic I sounded. When another half hour passed, I pondered calling him until I remembered my mother's words: *A woman must never chase a man.*

By nine-thirty, I gave up on him entirely. I threw my shoes across the floor, stripped off my dress and crawled under my freshly changed bed sheets before bursting into tears. Perhaps my mom had a point about high school boys, because this heartache was bullshit.

"What's wrong with you?" Grayson asked when I threw my school bag onto the backseat with more force than necessary.

"Nothing," I grumbled.

Grayson glanced up at the house before accelerating away. "Your mom?"

"Surprisingly, no," I said, taking a breakfast bar from the glovebox and tearing it open. "I had a date with Scott."

His mouth dropped. Perhaps Scott didn't tell him everything. "And it didn't go well?"

"It didn't *go* at all."

"What?"

"He didn't show." I took a large bite to hide my emotion. "Nor did he call *or* send me a fucking text to tell me why."

"Something must have come up," he said, shaking his head. "I don't think he would've—"

"What? Played me?"

"Come on, he's not like that."

I scoffed. "Isn't he?"

"Just hear him out, okay?"

I let my head fall back onto the seat. "So he can humiliate me some more?"

Grayson glanced my way. "Mel…"

"I don't want to talk about it," I said, turning my gaze out the window. "I'm embarrassed enough."

"Fine," Grayson muttered before turning up the radio for the rest of the drive to Summerhill.

As soon as we pulled into the parking lot, I saw him. Pacing beside Grayson's usual space, Scott looked up as we drove in and rushed to open my door when we stopped.

"Lanie, I'm so sorr—"

"Save it," I bit, pushing past him as I climbed out.

Grayson winced and quickly moved away to give us privacy.

"I need to explain," he said, following me toward the main building.

I spun around. "Was this all just a game to you? Make me agree to a date so you can stand me up the first chance you get?"

Scott recoiled. "No, I wouldn't do that."

"Then where were you?" My eyes burned.

"Riley got sick, and I couldn't leave him."

My anger waned momentarily. "Then you should've called me."

"I know," he said, threading his fingers through his tousled hair. "But I ran out of credit."

I scrunched up my nose. "Credit?"

Scott looked away. "We don't all have unlimited access to our daddy's bank account."

The pressure on my chest returned. "Fuck you," I spat and marched away.

"I didn't mean that…" Scott sighed before jogging after me. "I wanted to message you. Fuck, I've wanted to ask what you've been doing every minute of the day, but I can't right now, and I hate it."

Blinking away my tears, I turned to him, meeting his eyes dead-on. There was no flicker of uncertainty or hint of a lie, only remorse, and I knew, in my gut, he was telling the truth. "Then let me give you some money."

"No." His serious expression left no room to negotiate. "I'll sort it out."

I looked away with pursed lips. He was as stubborn as I was.

Scott's thumb grazed my cheek, coaxing my eyes back to his. "I'd really like to try again."

My anger dispersed under his touch. "Is Riley okay now?"

"Yeah." He smiled. "He's fine."

"Good."

"So…" His gaze pierced mine as he took my hand. "Will you give me another chance?"

"Maybe."

He chuckled. "Maybe?"

My mouth twitched. "I'll have to check my schedule."

"Your schedule?" His eyes twinkled in amusement.

"I'm very popular. Didn't you know?"

"Oh, I know," he said, squeezing my fingers. "There are about ten guys throwing daggers at me right now, and I'm only touching your hand."

I glanced around the grounds and noted a few faces quickly turning away. "I wonder what they'd do if you kissed me right now."

Scott stepped forward and slid his hand around my lower back, pressing his body to mine. "Let's find out."

Saturday couldn't come fast enough. Scott arrived moments after my parents left for a charity ball, and I couldn't help but feel relieved when I saw his Mustang coming down the drive.

As the car slowed out front, I checked my face in the hallway mirror with lipstick in hand. My makeup was subtle and soft—so different from my usual look—and I liked it. So, instead of applying the deep-red hue to my mouth, I dropped the lipstick back into my bag.

Tilting my head as I walked outside, I wondered why Scott was taking so long to get out of his car. He sat motionless, staring out the windshield with his hands tense on the steering wheel. I strolled over to the door and opened it before sliding in.

Scott jumped. "Lanie, I was going to come up and get you."

"Well, I beat you to it," I said with a smile before it faded. "You okay?"

He rubbed the back of his neck. "I had a fight with my dad, so I'm a little wound up."

"Want to talk about it?"

"No." Scott exhaled as he leaned back into his seat. "I just want to take my girlfriend to the movies."

"Oh, are we picking her up on the way?"

His gaze whipped to mine. "No, I meant—"

My smirk gave me away.

"Fuck, Lanie," he said, chuckling as he shook his head.

The sight of his smile warmed my heart. "So, what are we seeing?"

Scott ran his hand around my nape and pulled me toward him. "Does it matter?"

"Not really," I said with a giggle.

He pressed his lips to mine. "Then we better not be late."

The moment the lights dimmed and the movie began, we were all over each other. Two hours later, a red-faced usher tapped my shoulder to alert us to the empty cinema. After apologizing profusely, we ran out laughing.

"This is *way* more comfortable than the movies," I said, cuddling up to him in the back of his car as we gazed over the city lights. I angled my face up to kiss him and slipped my hand over his upper thigh.

Scott closed his eyes as it crept a little higher. "When's your curfew?"

"I don't have a curfew," I whispered into his ear.

His growing smile was replaced with a grimace. "Shit, I'm sorry. I have to get home. The babysitter can only stay till eleven."

"You paid for a babysitter? Where's your dad?"

"He had to work, and I didn't pay. Elle's watching him as a favor."

Her name lit a fire inside. "You should have told me. We could've postponed."

"I wasn't going to blow another chance with you."

"Or we could've hung out at your place."

Scott scoffed. "Definitely not."

"Why? I don't mind. I'd love to see Riley again."

"You're not coming to my house," he snapped.

My back straightened at his harsh tone. "But it's okay for Elle?"

"That's…different."

"How?"

"Because she's…she's not…"

"Forget it. Just take me home." I climbed back into the front seat. "You don't want to keep your *babysitter* waiting."

Scott shook his head and returned to the driver's side, clearly agitated.

After an uncomfortably quiet drive home, I noticed the parlor light on as we approached the house down the long driveway. Scott stopped the car out front, and my heart leaped when he reached for his door handle to get out.

"I've got it," I blurted, winding down my window and opening the jammed door from the outside.

His shoulders slumped as I climbed out. "I'll text you tomorrow, okay?"

I leaned down to the window as I closed the door. "You're out of credit, remember? I'll see you Monday."

Scott hesitated for a moment before restarting the car and speeding back down the driveway. Before the dust had time to settle, the front door opened.

My mother stood before me, nursing a nightcap. "You're home early."

"So are you." I edged past her, making a beeline for the stairs.

"Your father has an early flight tomorrow, so we had to leave." She took a sip to mask her displeasure. My mother loved to socialize, but my father loathed it. If it didn't make him money, it wasn't worth his time.

"Well, I better get to bed too." I ascended two steps before she dropped the question I was hoping to avoid.

"Who drove you home?"

Turning slowly, I tried to come up with an acceptable answer. "Grayson…why?"

"But that wasn't Grayson's car."

My voice caught. She must've been watching through the window. "He's…um…into classics at the moment."

Mom rolled her eyes as she downed the remains of her drink. "Well, hopefully that won't last."

"I doubt it will," I said softly and resumed my climb.

I spent the next morning dozing in bed. Sleep eased my uncertainty, so I welcomed it. Why would Scott allow Elle into his home and not me? Was there more to their story? She clearly knew him better than I did, and it bothered me.

"Melanie!" my mother hollered from somewhere downstairs.

I dragged myself out of my warm blankets and swung open the bedroom door. "What?!"

"There's someone here to see you!"

Wrapping a robe around my body, I crept through the hallway and paused at the top of the staircase. I peeked down into the foyer, praying it wasn't Scott.

Cara stood at the bottom, smiling tightly with a mysterious paper bag in her hand.

"For God's sake, Melanie, get dressed. It's after midday," my mother snapped, spotting me instantly. Mom always looked immaculate, no matter what time of day, and she expected the same from her daughter.

I tightened my robe and stepped out of the shadows. "We're about to give each other facials, and I didn't want to ruin my clothes."

Cara's eyes widened, and I almost laughed.

"Well, that sounds like a sensible idea," Mom said, eyeing Cara curiously as she climbed the stairs. "You've been looking very washed out lately."

I motioned Cara to follow me down the hallway. She offered me a smile, but it didn't reach her eyes. Something was wrong.

"What's going on?" I asked as I closed the bedroom door behind her.

She peered up at me through glistening eyes. "I missed my period."

"You what?!"

"It was supposed to come earlier this week, and it hasn't."

"Alright, don't freak out. It may just be late. Have you done a test?"

"No," she whimpered, dropping her head as she held up the bag. "Not yet, anyway."

I took the bag and led her to my bathroom. "Then I guess we better find out."

After she peed on the stick, I set the timer and held her hand as it counted down.

"I'm such an idiot," she uttered, wiping a tear from her cheek. "We were so caught up in the moment that I didn't even realize until it was too late."

I groaned inwardly, but I didn't have the necessary experience to lecture her. "Have you told him?"

"I haven't told anyone. Oh god, my mom is going to lose her mind."

"Just calm down, let's see what we're dealing with first, then we'll work out what to do next."

"Thank you, Melanie," she said, squeezing my hand. "I couldn't have done this alone."

"No matter the result, I'll be here for you."

An uneasy silence fell over us as the timer ran down.

"How's the painting going?" I asked, trying to ease the tension in the air.

"I…um…" Cara blinked a few times, resurfacing from her drowning thoughts. "I sent it off yesterday."

"Good. That's good. I can't wait to find out how it goes."

"Oh god, what have I done?" she cried, dropping her face into her hands. "I won't be able to go to art school, even if I do win the stupid competition and get a scholarship."

I ran my hand over her hair. "Everything will work out."

When the timer rang, Cara's fearful gaze shot to mine. "I can't look. Can you just tell me?"

Swallowing the lump in my throat, I picked up the stick and peered down at the tiny screen. My smile grew as I ran my gaze over the single line. "You're not pregnant."

"Oh, thank God," she cried, clutching her chest. "How accurate is that thing?"

I picked up the instructions. "99%, but there's a spare test if you want to try again."

"Let's wait a week, and if I still haven't gotten my period, I'll do the other."

"Great plan."

"Can I hide it here until then? Mom will send me to a nunnery if she finds it."

"Well, you don't have to worry about that here," I said, slipping the box deep within my bathroom cabinet. The only reason my mom ever came into my room was to complain about something I'd done or to borrow my makeup.

"Would you mind if I hung around for a bit?" Cara grimaced. "I told my mom I was coming here to study."

"Sure, I've got no plans. What do you want to do?"

Her eyes lit up. "Well, you had a pretty good idea earlier…"

"You want a facial?"

"Well, I've never had one before."

My mouth fell open. With skin like hers, I assumed she'd had many. "Well, you're in for a treat. But first, I think we need ice cream."

Chapter 9

Scott was leaning against my locker when I arrived at school on Monday.

"Hey," he said warily, stepping aside to let me through.

I opened my locker but didn't look his way. "Hey."

"I'm sorry about Saturday night. I shouldn't have snapped at you like that."

I shuffled my books around until I realized I wasn't achieving anything. "I was just trying to help. I don't mind spending time with Riley if it means I get to spend more time with you."

He picked up my hand and laced his fingers through mine. "I get that, but I don't want you seeing where I live, that's all. It's hard enough seeing where you live."

"You know I don't care about that stuff."

"Well, you should. You deserve better."

I pulled my hand away and slammed my locker closed. "You don't need to spoil me."

"But I want to."

"Don't you get it? I don't expect you to take me to fancy restaurants or drive a flashy car or buy me expensive gifts. I just want someone to see who I really am, beyond all that superficial bullshit."

He curled a strand of hair around my ear. "I see you, Lanie," he said, cupping his hand over my cheek. My heart thumped at his touch and almost burst when he pressed his mouth to mine.

Murmurs and giggles echoed through the halls, pulling us out of our intoxicated trance. My cheeks seared when I found most of the student body watching us.

"I guess our secret is out," I said, hiding my face against his warm chest.

Scott's chest vibrated with his chuckle. "Your secret, you mean?"

"What?" My wide eyes glared up at his irritatingly gorgeous smirk.

"Because, Lanie..." he whispered, sending tingles straight to my core. "Everyone already knows I'm crazy about you."

We didn't bother hiding our affection after that. Partly because we couldn't keep our hands off each other, but also because I wanted to deter other girls from hitting on him. He was oblivious to how gorgeous he was, and it drove me crazy.

Cara nudged my side as she slid into the seat next to me in the cafeteria. Scott, Grayson, and Hank were heavily absorbed in a discussion about an upcoming football game while I sat there, bored shitless.

My face brightened instantly. "I thought you were working on your portfolio today?"

"I'm meant to be, but I've decided to celebrate instead."

"Oh, what are we celebrating?"

"The arrival of..."—she panned her gaze around the table, making sure the boys weren't listening—"a special friend."

Lines formed across my brow.

"You know? The one who visits once a month?"

My eyes grew wide. "Really?"

"I'm so relieved," she said as her deep brown eyes glistened.

I wrapped my arms around her and squeezed. "Have you told Rob? I think he needs to know what you've been going through."

"Yeah, I will, but after Saturday night. He's super stressed and excited about their upcoming gig, and I don't want to put a damper on it. It's their biggest show yet."

"Are you going?"

Cara picked at her lunch. "I want to, but there's no way my mom will let me stay out that late."

"Stay at my place—or just say you are. I don't mind."

Hank left the table, and the boys' conversation quieted while they ate.

"I don't know..." Cara mused. "It's really not my scene, and I've never been to a gig at Cherry before."

"Then I'll come with you." I loved live music.

Scott's chewing slowed. "You're not going to that club by yourselves."

His protective side was cute. "Then you'll have to come too," I said before turning to Grayson. "What about you?"

Grayson shook his head. "Count me out. Adam's in town for the weekend, and Mom's planned a family dinner."

I winced. Grayson's mom doted on his older brother. "Oh, that sucks."

"Tell me about it," he muttered before taking an angry bite out of his sandwich.

I turned back to Cara. "So, are we doing this?"

Her eyes were bigger and brighter than ever. "Yes, thank you. You're amazing."

After lunch, I strolled back to my locker with Scott to collect my books for our next class.

"It's okay if you can't go Saturday," I said, peeking up at him. "I know it's difficult with Riley."

He ran his hand down my back. "I'll make it work."

I leaned into him and kissed his cheek before whispering in his ear, "There's a good chance Cara won't be spending the night at my place...so I was thinking...perhaps you would like to keep me company instead?"

"What about your parents?"

"They're in New York for the weekend, so we'll have the place to ourselves."

His cheeks grew pink as he chuckled. "You're going to be the death of me, Lanie Warren."

Scott, Cara, and I arrived at the venue midway through Jack Knife's first set. Rob had been begging Cara to come to one of their gigs, so she wanted to surprise him. We stood in the shadows until they took a break then pushed ourselves through the crowd toward the backstage door.

"Not a chance, buddy," the bouncer uttered as Scott approached.

Before Scott could react and ruin all hope of getting through, I pulled him aside. "Just wait here, okay?" I knew how this worked.

"Fine," he grumbled, crossing his arms as he leaned back on the graffitied wall of the nightclub.

Returning to the burly man blocking the doorway, I offered him my most alluring smile. Before I had a chance to speak, he grinned and opened the door without hesitation, letting us both through.

We made our way down a long, dingy corridor, dodging roadies tuning guitars and groupies adjusting their push-up bras until we found the door marked *Jack Knife*. Music blared from within, so I didn't bother knocking. With one push, the door swung open. The room was empty, except for Rob, who was standing with his back to us, with a girl kneeling in front of him.

He spun around at Cara's gasp, and his eyes went round as he scrambled to zip up his fly. "Cara!"

Cara's paling face triggered an onslaught of rage inside me. "Do you know who my father is?" I asked, taking a step toward Rob. Venom dripped off every word.

His chest rose up and down as he swallowed. "Y…yes."

"So, you're aware he controls most radio stations, magazines, and newspapers across the West Coast?"

The blood drained from his face, giving me the answer I'd hoped for. He peered down at Cara as sweat beads gathered across his forehead. "I'm so sorry, Cara. I nev—"

"Save it," I said, blocking his view of her. "If you ever go near my best friend again, I will ruin you."

The girl beside him tried to latch onto Rob's arm, but he shook her off angrily.

"I want to go," Cara said, pulling me away.

With one last menacing glare at Rob, I spun around and followed Cara down the hallway.

"What the fuck just happened?" Scott asked after Cara marched straight past him toward the exit.

"We just walked in on Rob getting a blowjob from some girl he probably just met."

He ran his palm down his face. "Fuck."

"Yep," I muttered, picking up my pace. I didn't want to lose sight of Cara. "Can you drive us back to my place? I don't want her to be alone right now."

He reached into his back pocket for his car keys. "Of course."

Once Cara was safely in the backseat of Scott's car, I turned to him with a sigh. "Rain check?"

His eyes twinkled in the moonlight. "There's no rush," he said, grazing his thumb across my cheek. "Another time."

With a nod, I climbed in after Cara.

"How could he do that?" Her lower lip quivered as Scott started the car.

"He's a jerk. A big fucking jerk."

A sob burst from her mouth. "I thought he liked me."

"Oh, he does," I said, wrapping my arm around her. "But some guys can't keep their dick in their pants."

"Some guys," Scott uttered, catching my eye in the rearview mirror. "We're not all like that. I promise."

Cara ignored him. "I can't believe he almost got me pregnant."

Scott swerved the car, and my eyes shot up to his in the rearview mirror.

He cleared his throat. "Sorry…there was…a cat."

"Right," I said, smirking at his wide eyes.

"I really thought…he could be…you know…"

My heart dipped. "The one?"

"No." She wiped her nose. "My way out."

I sucked in my breath at her devastation and held tighter. Perhaps Cara's home life was worse than I thought.

When we arrived back at my place, I guided Cara through the front door and directed her up the stairs. "Head to my room. I'll go fetch some ice cream."

Scott waited in the doorway like a vampire without permission to enter.

"You can come in," I said with a chuckle. "My parents aren't home, remember?"

Scott smirked. "That's exactly why I'm not coming in. Cara needs you. My *needs* can wait."

Making my way back to where Scott stood, I encircled my arms around his neck. "I'm sorry."

"This isn't your fault." His jaw twitched. "Rob, however…"

"Don't worry about Rob. I've already sorted him out."

"I have no doubt," Scott said, squeezing my hips. "You're a good friend." He pulled me close until his forehead rested upon mine. "Goodnight, Lanie."

My whole body lit up when our lips met, and it took all my strength to push him away. "Goodnight, Scott."

"Maybe we should have day dates," I said, snuggling closer to Scott's side at the lunch table. "You could bring Riley so you won't need a babysitter."

"I really don't want to share your attention with a six-year-old. Plus, Elle said she doesn't mind looking after Riley, so I don't see the problem."

I folded my arms. "Of course she doesn't."

"You don't need to be jealous of her," he said, poking my ribs.

"Don't I?" I asked, nudging him away. "She's been to your house, she knows your family, and she clearly has the hots for you."

Scott nuzzled his face into my hair. "Well, that's a shame, because I have the hots for you," he said, nipping my neck.

I cried out then giggled when he kissed it better.

Grayson made gagging noises as he approached, announcing his arrival. "You're not going to be like this *all* the time, are you?"

Scott slipped his hand under the table and over my leg as he grinned up at him. "No promises."

"Is Cara in the art room today?" Grayson asked, panning his gaze to the empty seat opposite us.

My shoulders fell. "No, she's at home. Heartbroken."

"Scott filled me in. What a fucking prick." Grayson placed down a full tray of food and passed over his tater tots. Our usual routine.

"I never should have encouraged her to go out with him," I said. "He's in a band, for Christ's sake."

Grayson's expression softened. "You didn't know, Mel."

Scott's jaw tightened as I lifted a tater tot to my mouth.

"What?" I asked Scott, sensing something was wrong.

He shook his head with a sigh. "Nothing. Grayson's right. This isn't your fault."

As I walked to my next class, I pulled out my phone to check in with Cara.

Me: **We're missing you at school.**

Cara: **I just need some time to process.**

Me: **I hope you're okay...**

Cara: **Mom's at work, so I'm painting :)**

Me: **Do whatever makes you happy :)**

Over the next month, Scott and his little brother took me on all kinds of adventures. Picnic lunches at parks, swimming at the beach, free art exhibitions, and I loved every minute of it. Scott managed to keep at least one day free on the weekend for our day dates and planned activities that cost almost nothing except the cost of gas to get us there.

Riley had a new drawing for me every time I saw him, and he was only getting better.

"His illustrations are amazing for his age," I said, leaning into Scott as we lay on the picnic blanket while Riley ran around the playground.

"He's been communicating through his art, just like you said, *and* it's keeping him out of trouble with Mrs. Norris and at school."

"I'm so glad. He deserves to be heard, even if it's in a picture."

"You're pretty amazing, Lanie," Scott said, pressing his lips to my cheek.

My face warmed at his touch. "You're pretty amazing yourself. Riley is lucky to have you."

We lay there quietly amongst the fallen leaves, watching Riley's unsuccessful attempts to run up the slide. When he finally gave up, he sprinted over and ninja-rolled back onto the picnic rug.

"So, what crazy adventure do you boys have planned for me next weekend?" I asked as Riley scarfed down the remaining strawberries I'd packed.

"We may have to skip next week," Scott said with a mysterious smirk. "Riley has to preserve his energy."

"I'm going to Jordan's sleepover party," Riley mumbled through his full mouth. "There's going to be cake, and games, and chocolate. I can't wait. Oh, and popcorn! I love popcorn."

Scott chuckled as his brother jumped up and rocketed back to the swings. "He's pretty excited about it."

"I can tell." I laughed as my heart galloped away with the possibilities of what that meant. "I don't blame him, though. Sleepovers are fun."

Scott's breath tickled my ear. "Maybe we should have a sleepover of our own."

My core pulsed at the suggestion. "With cake, and games, and chocolate?"

"I can arrange that." He chuckled before kissing my shoulder. "There's a hotel nearby. Nothing fancy, but it's clean, and I doubt we'd need anything but a bed."

"Why bother with a hotel when my house is empty? My parents will be away until Sunday afternoon."

Scott's eyebrows rose. "That's definitely better than any hotel I can afford."

"I just don't want you wasting your money."

"Nothing is a waste on you," he said, running his fingertips up and down my arm. "I just wish I could give you more."

I closed my eyes and melted into him. "You have no idea how much you have given me already."

Chapter 10

I rarely saw Cara after her breakup with Rob because she spent every spare minute in the art room. It was where she was happiest, so I let her be. When I spotted a familiar girl with long brown hair ambling down the hallway, I bounded toward her like an excited puppy. I'd been in a great mood since Saturday, and I was desperate to tell Cara about the upcoming weekend.

She forced a smile. "Hey."

"I've been trying to call you, but…" My excitement faded when I met her vacant eyes.

"Mom took away my phone."

"What? Why?"

"I wouldn't tell her why I've been so upset lately, so she confiscated it. Then, she searched my room while I was taking Poppy to dance class."

"And…"

"She found my sketchbooks, including all the preliminary sketches for my portfolio."

My stomach plummeted. "What did she do?"

Her lips formed a white line as she tried to hold it together. "She destroyed everything."

"No…"

"Then she made an appointment for me to see her psychiatrist."

I shook my head. "You're heartbroken, not crazy. Can't you just tell her about Rob?"

"I want to, but I'm worried it will only get me into more trouble. She doesn't want me anywhere near boys, let alone dating one."

Guilt gnawed at me. "I'm sorry, Cara. I never should've encouraged you to—"

"Have fun? Follow my dreams? Mel, this isn't your fault. You're the only person who has ever believed in me. And *that* is something you should never apologize for."

I blinked back tears. "So, what are you going to do now?"

"To be honest, I'm tired of fighting her. If she wants me to see a doctor and express my deepest darkest secrets, then I will."

"What about your portfolio?"

"There's no way I'll get it done in time now. I'll just tell Mrs. Weathers I've decided to focus on my other studies."

"But—"

"Please, Mel, I can't do this right now."

"Okay, but if you ever need to talk, you know I'm here for you."

She held my hand and squeezed. "I know."

"Jesus, Lanie. The other half don't even live like this," Scott said after I'd given him the grand tour of the Warren mansion.

I waved him off. "It's just a lot of empty rooms. You hungry?"

The left side of his mouth quirked up as his eyes traveled up my body. "Starving."

Warmth filled my cheeks. "Come on, we need to eat something."

He grabbed my hand and pulled me into him. "I intend to."

"Scott!"

"Alright." He chuckled. "We'll eat first and play later."

I tried my hardest not to smile. "I'll go order us a pizza."

Twenty minutes later, I buzzed in the delivery guy and met him at the front door.

"Hey, Melanie," he said, handing over my favorite pizza.

"Hey, Paul. Thanks for getting here so quick." I smiled at him, knowing his face would turn bright red. It always did.

"Well, we don't want to keep our VIP waiting."

I tilted my head as I handed over his tip. "Aww, that's sweet."

Paul's face fell when he caught Scott watching our exchange. "I'll, um…see you next time," he said, quickly backing out of the house.

"Okay, thanks." I closed the door and turned to Scott's scrutinizing gaze. Ignoring him, I continued to the kitchen with our dinner.

"Do you always do that?" he asked, following closely behind.

"Do what?"

"Flirt with the pizza delivery guy?"

I slid the pizza onto the counter. "It gets my dinner here quicker, so yeah."

Scott shook his head with a laugh. "You're supposed to use your superpowers for good, not evil."

"Superpowers?"

He ran his hand through his hair. "What man wouldn't fall to his knees around you?"

"You're an idiot," I said, rolling my eyes.

Scott panned his gaze around the huge kitchen. "Why do you get food delivered anyway? I assumed you'd have your own chef."

"We do, but I let all the staff go home when my parents are away."

"Why?"

I lowered my eyes before Scott could see the emotion lurking behind them. "I'd prefer to be alone than with people who are paid to stay."

"Well, you won't be alone tonight."

We ate in silence, sitting side by side at the island, throwing each other sideways glances until each slice disappeared.

"Now it's time to burn the evidence," I said, grabbing the empty pizza box and taking it to the living room where a fire already burned.

Scott trailed after me. "What are you doing?"

I threw the cardboard into the flames and poked it until it lit up. "Mom has me on a strict meal plan, so I can't let her find this here. She's adamant I need to drop a size."

"What? You're kidding."

I shrugged. "She's probably right."

"That's bullshit. Your body is smokin' hot."

I scoffed.

"I'm serious. Anyone who says otherwise is crazy…or jealous."

"My mom isn't jealous of me," I said, thinking of all the ways I disappointed her and all the flaws she so willingly highlighted.

Scott fell into the couch. "If you say so."

After the remains of the box turned to ash, I turned back to Scott and smiled. "So, what do you want to do now?" I asked, resting my hands on my hips as I stood in front of him. "We have a pretty good movie selection."

Scott reached for my hand and pulled me toward him until I fell in his lap. "I have you for an entire night, and I'm not wasting one second of it on a movie."

"I'm sure we can think of something else to do." My body ignited as he kissed my neck. "Want to see my bedroom instead?"

His tongue ran over my earlobe. "I want to see more than your bedroom."

"Let's stop wasting time then," I said, rising to my feet.

As he stood up to follow, I took off for the stairs, giggling as he chased after me.

He slowed at the entrance of my bedroom and panned his gaze around the room. "This is better than any hotel I could afford."

I ran my hand down his cheek. "It wouldn't matter if we were in the fanciest hotel or the backseat of your car…I just want to be with you. The rest is just background noise."

His shimmering eyes met mine as I took his hand and pulled him toward my king-size bed. Before he could change his mind, I grabbed the hem of his tee and tugged it over his head, smiling at the sight before me. He wasn't a jock, but he had the body of one. Defined muscles carved his chest, seemingly as a result of hard work rather than any sports training.

With a knowing smirk, he ran both hands around my waist and lifted my top until it fell to the floor. I shuffled out of my jeans, waiting for him to follow, but he didn't.

His chest expanded, but the rest of his body remained still. Was he changing his mind?

I wrapped one arm around my bare stomach and peered up at him. "Why aren't you touching me?"

"You're just so…so fucking beautiful." His blue eyes electrified. "I don't feel worthy."

Annoyance bubbled up inside. "If you don't touch me in the next five sec—"

Scott launched forward and pressed his mouth to mine. His hands threaded through my hair and grabbed the nape of my neck, deepening the kiss until we fell onto the bed. The heat of his skin seared mine, causing a shiver to filter through my body.

"You're nervous," he said, running his fingers over my goosebump-covered arms.

"A little, I guess."

His hands traced over my shoulders. "We don't have to rush this."

"Just go slow, okay?"

"Oh, I intend to." His grin grew as he slid down my body, taking my panties with him. As they fell to the floor, he parted my legs to each side and ran his hands up and down my thighs. His breath touched my core before his mouth, and I fell back onto the bed, giving in to desire.

As my moans morphed into a whimper, Scott grasped my hips and steadied my body as I rose off the bed with each movement of his tongue. A moment later, I seized the bedsheets into my tight fists as a shudder rolled over my body. My first taste of heaven.

A trail of kisses ran up my inner thigh and over my stomach until Scott's face was level with mine. The bulge in his jeans pressed against my throbbing core as he searched my eyes for permission.

With my nod, he reached into his back pocket and pulled out a condom. Shifting to one side, he removed his pants, slid on the condom, and crawled back over me. I gasped when his tip settled at my seam.

"Are you sure?" he asked, his jaw tight as he waited for my response.

I nodded again, still entirely speechless from my orgasm.

His gaze penetrated mine as his long length pushed inside.

I let out a gasp as the initial burn subsided. "More," I rasped, finally finding my voice.

Pausing momentarily, Scott cupped my face as he slid in entirely. Pleasure soon outweighed discomfort as he began to rock with gentle thrusts until our skin glistened with perspiration.

Taking a more animalistic turn, our rhythm quickened as we drew closer to something bigger than I'd ever anticipated. While our bodies moved in unison, Scott's heated gaze never left mine until my eyes rolled back and he squeezed his shut on release.

I always thought my first time would be with some college frat boy who'd be too drunk to realize he took my virginity. But *this*... this was perfect. Scott was everything I didn't know I wanted, and now he owned a part of me that could never be returned.

The sing-song voice of my mother calling out my name stirred me awake. My eyes shot open, but the weight of Scott's arm draped across my stomach held me in place.

"Get up, get up, get up!" I hissed, tapping him relentlessly until his eyelids flickered.

A sleepy smile formed on his lips as he squeezed my side. "Again?"

My name sounded once more, only this time, closer.

Scott sat up in bed, now wide awake. "I thought you said—"

"I know what I said," I bit, shoving him out of the bed. "Bathroom. Go!"

As soon as Scott's naked ass dashed across the bedroom and into the bathroom, my mom sauntered in.

"Mom!" I gathered the sheets around my naked chest. "I didn't expect you back until later tonight."

"Your father had some business to attend to, so I arranged an earlier flight so I wouldn't miss Sunday brunch with the ladies. Oh, that reminds me, have you seen my pearl earrings? I'd ask Marie, but I can't find her anywhere."

"Perhaps you left them by the pool again," I said, hoping the gentle reminder would spark her into action.

"Well, if that's the case, Marie should have found them by now."

I wanted to defend our housemaid, but I needed my mother gone.

She huffed. "I guess the diamonds will have to do. If I don't leave now, I'll be beyond fashionably late."

Relief flooded my body when she turned to leave, but a loud clash stopped her mid-step.

"Is someone here?" she asked, staring in the direction of the noise.

I winced as she took a step toward my bathroom. "Mom, please don't."

"Why?" she asked, crossing her arms. "Who's in there?"

Panic filled my body. "It's, um…Grayson."

Mom's face brightened. "Oh, yes, of course. I saw his new car out front. What is he doi…" Her voice faded as she took in my bare shoulders and the clothing strewn across the floor. "Oh my goodness," she uttered, her eyes sparkling in delight.

I groaned. "Please don't make a big deal out of this. It's… new."

"We always knew it would happen eventually," she said, clapping her hands.

"Alright, you can leave now. This is really embarrassing…for the both of us."

My mother's grin turned into a full-blown smile. "Don't be embarrassed, darling. This is wonderful news." She stepped closer to the bed and whispered, "If you ever need any advice…I'm very experienced in how to keep a man happy in the bedroom."

Bile rose to my throat, and I pointed to the door. "Go!"

"Okay…" She laughed. "But I want to hear all about it when I get home. We'll have a special dinner tonight to celebrate." Her smile warmed. "I'm proud of you, Melanie."

As soon as she disappeared, my head crashed down onto the pillow, and I squeezed my eyes shut. "Fuck." A moment later, I opened them to find Scott gathering his clothes off the floor. "I'm guessing you heard all that?"

His jaw tightened as he stepped into his jeans. "Yep."

"I'm sorry." I grimaced.

He shoved his arms and head through the holes of his tee. "I'm Grayson? Really?"

"I freaked out, okay?" I reached for my robe to cover my body. "What was I supposed to tell her?"

"The truth, perhaps."

"You know I can't do that."

Scott ran his fingers through his disheveled hair. "Why not?"

"Because they'd never let me be with you."

"I never took you for a pushover," he muttered, lowering his eyes from mine.

"I'm not a pushover."

"Do you always do what your parents want?"

"If it makes my life easier around here…yeah, I do."

"Life isn't always easy, Lanie. You may not realize it, but some of us have to fight for what we want."

"I…I know," I said, climbing off the bed. "But you don't know what it's like living here."

He glanced around the room and chuckled. "Yeah, it must be really tough."

"I may have more money than you, but I still have problems."

"These aren't real problems, Lanie," he said, picking up his shoes. "They're not even fucking close." He stormed toward the door, shaking his head.

Every molecule in my body didn't want him to leave. "Scott…"

His steps slowed, but he didn't look back. "Don't you mean *Grayson*?"

Chapter 11

Luckily, I managed to speak to Grayson before the news got back to him, so he was able to back up my story. My mother had been brunching with his mom after *the incident*, and there was no doubt her discovery would've dominated their conversation. Unfortunately, Grayson found the whole situation hilarious.

"Hey, girlfriend," Grayson sang as I entered homeroom Monday morning. Swim practice went longer than expected, so to my disgust, Miguel had to drive me to school.

My step faltered when I found Scott sitting beside him. He hadn't returned any of my calls or texts since he walked out of my bedroom the morning prior and was clearly still angry with me.

"Gray…" My warning tone only encouraged him.

"Or should I call you babe or honey…"

Scott's scowl drew my attention, but he dropped his gaze before our eyes collided. He'd always been uncomfortable with my close relationship with Grayson, and this was only making matters worse.

I smacked Grayson's arm as I sat down. "Quit it, will you?"

"Does this mean I have to take you to the winter formal now?"

"Will you shut up?" I hissed, glaring at him while motioning to Scott.

Grayson's smile faded when he turned his way. "Hey, sorry, man. I'm only joking."

Scott's jaw twitched. "Don't sweat it."

There was an awkward silence before Grayson opened his big mouth again. "But seriously, what are we doing for the winter formal?"

"I figured we could make it a group thing," I said, hoping a change of subject would lift Scott's mood. "Cara's never been before, and after the Rob fiasco, I doubt she'll want to couple up with anyone."

Grayson hummed. "Yeah, but if you plan to keep up this façade of yours, our parents are going to insist we do it properly. Matching attire, corsages, limo…not to mention professional photos. Maybe we should pick up Scott and Cara on the way and save them the torture."

Scott collected his books and stormed out of the room.

"Scott," I called after him, but he didn't slow. With a frustrated sigh, I chased him into the hallway and blocked his path. "Are you seriously still mad at me?"

"Do you seriously intend to keep lying to your parents about us?"

"It's less complicated this way," I said, moving closer. "And Grayson's fine with it."

He stepped back, avoiding my touch. "Oh, so if Grayson's fine with it, I'm just expected to play along, right?" When I didn't say anything, he shook his head and continued up the hallway.

My temper sparked, but I didn't follow. "It's not like you've told your dad about me."

His body stiffened. "He doesn't need to know about you."

"Oh, wow. Thanks."

"That's not what I meant," he said, hanging his head back in frustration. "It's just that…he's not…" He pressed his lips together until they turned white. "The less he knows about you the better."

I took slow steps toward him while narrowing my gaze. "What do you think is going to happen when my father finds out about you? Do you think he'll welcome you with open arms?"

Scott's eyes burned into mine before turning away. "Well, maybe he won't have to."

"What?" I recoiled like he slapped me. "What are you saying?"

"You know what I'm saying."

My chest tightened while the world around me stilled. "Are you breaking up with me?" I blinked back tears as my anger grew. "Are you fucking breaking up with me?" I bit into my lower lip, desperately trying to hold it together.

Without meeting my eyes, he took off down the corridor toward the exit, slamming the double doors open before disappearing into the daylight.

Struggling to breathe, I dashed into the AV room before doubling over. This couldn't have been happening. All of the air I forced into my lungs expelled in a sob, followed by many more. It was ugly. Too ugly for anyone to witness. I sank to the cold concrete floor, hugging my legs in an effort to control the tremors rippling through my body.

Hours passed, but I didn't move. Bells rang, footsteps scurried by, but I stayed hidden amongst the AV equipment. My tear-streaked face was a billboard for heartbreak, and I refused to admit to the student body how stupidly pathetic I was. So, I waited.

My gaze shot to the door as the light from the hallway filtered into the small room. I remained completely still as Zach, the unthreatening boy who shared a few of my classes, stepped into the room. He rummaged through the shelves, entirely oblivious to my presence, until he knocked over a pile of DVDs.

"Ow," I yelped, lifting my hands to protect my head from the falling discs.

"Oh shit, I didn't see you there." His eyes grew wide. "Melanie?"

I peered up at him with a grimace. "Hey, Zach." The raspy voice sounded nothing like my own.

"What are you doing in here?" His ginger eyebrows pulled together as he searched my face. "Are you okay?"

I chortled. "Peachy."

"Did something happen between you and Scott? Neither of you came back to homeroom this morning."

I swallowed past the lump in my throat. "We…um…had an argument."

Zach offered me a sad smile. "I'm sure you'll work it out."

"I doubt it," I said, shaking my head. "We're just…too different."

He crouched down beside me to gather the DVDs. "Maybe you're too similar."

I screwed up my face but was too tired to think of his meaning. "Why does everything have to be so complicated?" I asked, letting my head fall back on the shelf.

"I guess if everything were easy, we wouldn't appreciate anything."

"You're a very wise man, Zach." I tilted my head to get a better view of his kind face. "Why don't you have a girlfriend?"

His freckles disappeared into his deep blush. "The girl I like doesn't know I exist."

"I doubt that. Have you spoken to her?"

"No…not really. She's just so smart and funny and so ridiculously talented…I'm completely intimidated by her."

"Wow." I chuckled in surprise. "You didn't even comment on her appearance."

"My feelings have nothing to do with her looks…although she does have the most amazing brown eyes," he said with a dreamy grin.

I smiled. Zach was a breath of fresh air. Perhaps some boys did look beyond the surface. "You should ask her out."

He rubbed the back of his neck and winced. "I don't think I'm her type."

"You never know. She might surprise you."

"To be honest," he said as he stood, "I don't think I could handle the rejection."

"Yeah." I laughed back tears. "It does suck."

Zach's jaw slackened. "Scott rejected you? That makes no sense. Everyone knows how much he loves you."

My head jerked back. *Love?*

"He won't even let another guy near you—except Grayson, of course. I'd hate to think what he'd do if he caught me in this confined space with you now."

"That's absurd," I said with a forced laugh. "Plus, he went home ages ago."

"Well, he must've come back, because I just saw him run into Mr. West's class."

"Mr. West?" My heart lurched. "Shit, what period is this?" I rose to my feet and brushed the dust from my skirt.

"Fourth, why?"

I squeezed my swollen eyes shut. "No, no, no." My next class was World Literature, and if I didn't run, there was no chance of making it on time. "I've gotta go." I pushed past Zach, uttering a quick goodbye, and launched out of the room.

Mr. West smirked as I entered the classroom moments too late. "See me after class, Miss Warren."

I closed my eyes and nodded. I didn't need to worry about tears. There weren't any left.

Not daring to glance in Scott's direction, I opened my textbook and stared blankly at the pages before me. My peripheral vision confirmed my senses. Scott was watching my every move, only making me angrier with each passing minute.

The bell signaled the end of class, and the students filed out, leaving Scott lingering in the doorway before disappearing completely.

"Is everything okay, Melanie?" Mr. West asked before approaching my desk.

"Everything is fine."

"You seem off. Are you worried about passing this class?"

"Should I be?" I asked, nervous about the prospect of not graduating.

Mr. West ran his tongue over his bottom lip as he walked around my desk. "I'm sure we can work something out."

My stomach churned at his unspoken suggestion. "No, thank you. I'll manage."

His hand slid over my shoulder before squeezing it. "I wouldn't want you failing this subject again."

"Was there anything else?" I asked, gathering my books as I stood up. "I have an appointment with the guidance counselor." My heart hammered in my chest. I'd used this tactic a few times already.

Mr. West's back straightened as he dropped his arm. "Oh, well, you better get going, then."

Without looking back, I scurried out the door and down the corridor toward the guidance counselor's office. I didn't have an appointment, but I couldn't risk Mr. West checking up on me.

As I lingered outside, trying to catch my breath, I pretended to read the notice board full of college posters until a gentle tap on my shoulder startled me.

"Whoa, are you okay?" Scott lifted his hands as I spun around. It wasn't Mr. West, but his presence made me just as furious. He stepped forward and lowered his voice. "I was trying to think of an excuse to come back into the classroom when you ran out of there. If he did something, I want to know."

"Why?" I glared at him. "I don't have *real* problems… remember?"

Scott's shoulders slumped. "Come on, Lanie."

I pointed my finger at him as rage flooded my body. "You don't get to call me that anymore."

The door to the guidance counselor's office creaked open. "I thought I heard voices out here. Did you need to see me, Melanie?"

"Um… Yes. Yes, I do," I said, flustered, before rushing into her office. "I was hoping to go over my college options with you."

She chuckled. "Again?"

"I just can't decide." My hard gaze struck Scott's tortured eyes as the door closed behind me.

The guidance counselor's smile was warm—caring, even. The kind my own mother deprived me of. "Why don't you take a seat?"

With a deep breath, I sank into the chair, preparing myself to listen to all the opportunities I'd never be allowed to take.

The days leading up to Thanksgiving were tense. Both Scott and I refused to give up our mutual friend, and Grayson refused to take sides. Thankfully, Cara was around more, and Scott upgraded his friendship with Hank, meaning our interaction outside class was minimal. Lunchtimes were spent on opposite sides of the table, with Grayson in between, playing the buffer.

Cara had become progressively quieter over the last couple of weeks, so I dominated the conversation. She politely nodded as I talked about the dress I'd bought for the winter ball and proceeded to talk her through all the options I had for her in my closet. I thought she'd be excited by this, but her eyes remained dull and her voice flat. Something was off.

"Have you been drawing lately?" I asked quietly while the boys were distracted.

Cara shrugged. "No, not really."

"You could always keep your art supplies at my place and come over whenever you need."

"There's no point." She lowered her eyes. "I'm grounded."

"Until when?"

"Indefinitely."

"But what about the winter ball? It's in three weeks."

"I'm waiting for a good time to ask. Dad's family is coming over for Thanksgiving, so Mom's super stressed and emotional right now. I don't want to make it any worse for her."

I winced. "It must be hard. Seeing his family."

"My uncle looks so much like my dad. Mom can't even talk to him without bursting into tears." Cara's eyes glazed over. "So yeah, it's pretty tough."

"If you weren't grounded, I'd ask you to spend the afternoon at Grayson's house with me."

Scott's irritated gaze flickered to mine from across the table.

I didn't meet his eyes, but my words were for him. "Our families have been spending Thanksgiving together since before we were born. Once our parents slip into food comas, we begin our annual board game tournament. It's a tradition."

Grayson's ears pricked up. "Invitation is open to everyone. I could use some better competition."

I threw a piece of lettuce at him. Grayson knew very well I was undefeated for three years running.

"You keen, Hank?" Grayson asked, glancing at his bulky friend who had just shoved an entire sandwich into his mouth.

Hank shook his head as he chewed. "There's no way. Mom's for lunch and Dad's for dinner. Joys of having divorced parents."

"Fair enough." He turned to Scott. "What about you? You can bring Riley if you want."

My breath caught.

"We're having dinner with the neighbors, so I'll probably hang there afterwards."

"Of course," I murmured as jealously filtered through my body.

Scott grabbed his half-eaten lunch as he stood. "But you guys have fun," he said before stomping out of the cafeteria.

Chemistry was straight after lunch, and I was dreading it. Scott sat down beside me and laid his books on the desk without speaking a word. Unlike before, he was careful to keep his body from touching mine, making it microscopically easier on my senses.

With a glance his way, my composure wavered. "So, you're spending Thanksgiving with Elle?" The noise in the teacher-less classroom hid my pathetic words from the other students.

Scott opened his textbook and flicked through the pages. "I'm spending it with Mrs. Norris and her family, yes."

"Figures," I muttered, tapping my pen on the desk.

"You're spending Thanksgiving with your betrothed. I may as well succumb to my reality."

A sharp pain radiated across my chest. "If she's your reality, why did you bother with me at all?"

His eyes burned into my profile, but I refused to turn. He had stripped me of my power the night I slept with him and left me disgustingly vulnerable. I couldn't let him see that.

"Because I…" He swallowed back his unspoken words. "Because I stupidly thought we could make it work."

I wiped away a lone tear as it trailed down my cheek, but I didn't look up. "Yeah, me too."

Scott went quiet, and not just because the teacher walked in. For the rest of the lesson, he remained lost in his thoughts while I watched the clock. I only had one class left before home time, and I was desperate for something greasy to mop up my bleeding heart.

Once I'd packed my books into my locker at the end of the day, I pulled out my cell phone and messaged Grayson.

Me: **Pit stop at Nico's please :)**

Grayson: **Meet me at the car.**

With a shrug, I picked up my bag, threw it over my shoulder, and wandered out of the school building. As I approached Grayson's usual parking space, my steps slowed. A turquoise Mustang sat in its place with Scott pacing in front of it. When he saw me, he froze momentarily before moving my way.

"Where's Grayson?" I asked, scanning the parking lot.

"He's gone." His jaw tightened as his Adam's apple bobbed up and down. "I said I'd take you home."

My eyes shot to his. "What? Why?"

Scott's hand brushed over my lower back as he guided me toward the car. "I want to show you something."

"Scott, I don't thin—"

He opened the passenger door. "Lanie, please."

With a growl, I slid into the front seat and crossed my arms. "Fine, where are you taking me?"

"To a place I never wanted you to see."

Scott turned down the radio as he pulled into the gravel driveway of a tiny, dilapidated house, not much bigger than a campervan. The surrounding earth was dry and lifeless, and I was almost convinced it was abandoned until Riley burst out the front door.

My mouth went dry. "Is this…. Is this your house?"

"Home sweet home," Scott murmured before getting out of the car.

Riley wrapped his arms around Scott's legs with a smile that only grew when he saw me. "Lanie!" he squealed, racing to the passenger door.

Scott helped him tug it open, and Riley threw his arms around me as soon as I stepped out.

"Hey, buddy," I said, giving him a little squeeze. "How was school today?"

Before Riley could answer, a girl ran outside, yelling his name. She spotted Scott's car and exhaled in relief. "Riley, you can't just run outside without asking."

My blood ran cold.

"Elle, it's fine," Scott said, pushing my door shut. "Thanks for picking him up today."

"Anytime." Her feline eyes traveled to mine and narrowed before returning to Scott.

"Is your mom all ready for Thanksgiving?"

Her sweet laughter matched her smile. "Hopefully. She's been baking all week. I helped her make your favorite."

Scott cleared his throat and glanced my way. "Lanie. This is my neighbor, Elle. Elle, this is Lanie. We, um…go to Summerhill together."

Elle dragged her gaze over my uniform. "I figured."

"It's nice to meet you," I said, pushing past my instant hatred.

Her pressed lips paled. "Well, I should get back and help Mom," she said, speaking directly to Scott. "Looking forward to seeing you tomorrow."

As they said their goodbyes, Riley tugged on my arm. "Come inside, I want to show you my room."

Not wanting to witness another moment of their familiarity, I let Riley pull me into their world. I barely had a chance to take in the tiny living room and kitchenette before I was standing in the doorway of a room just large enough to fit a dresser, two twin beds, and a makeshift desk between them. One side was messy, with crumpled sheets and colorful drawings stuck haphazardly to the walls, while the other was incredibly neat. Bed made, neatly piled books, and a sole picture frame facing the bed.

"This is our room," Riley remarked, puffing out his chest in pride.

I cautiously stepped inside. "You're lucky to share with your brother."

"He gets grumpy sometimes, but I think it's the best!" He climbed onto his bed and jumped around with a giggle.

Assuming the picture frame housed a photo of his mother, I edged closer, curious to see what she looked like. Did she share Scott's brilliant blue eyes or his thick brown hair? Or were those features simply a gift from God? I guessed the latter.

Tilting the frame around, I discovered it wasn't a photograph at all. It was a drawing.

I glanced up at Riley then back at the image of a girl with yellow hair, sitting under a tree surrounded by flowers and butterflies. "Did you draw this?"

His cheeks grew pink as he nodded. "It's you."

"Oh." Warmth flooded my body.

"It's Scotty's favorite, so my teacher helped me frame it for his birthday."

"When was his birthday?"

"A couple of weeks ago," he said, rummaging under his bed. "Want to see some more drawings?"

With my nod, Riley pulled out his frayed sketchbook and sat beside me while I made a mental note to buy him a new one.

"You're very talented," I said, taking in every detail of his artwork. My gaze settled on the dark figure looming in the background of a few of his pieces, and my heart dipped. "Who's this?"

Riley's innocent smile faded. "That's my dad."

Scott cleared his throat as he rested against the doorframe. I wasn't sure how long he'd been watching us.

"You didn't tell me it was your birthday," I said, feeling horrible for not knowing. "I would have given you something."

The corner of his mouth rose. "You did."

Heat filled my cheeks. I guess I did.

Riley's eyes lit up. "What did she give you?!"

Our nervous laughter faded as the front door closed.

"Dad's home," Riley whispered, peering up at Scott. "Do you think he's in a good mood?"

Scott closed his eyes in visible pain before drawing his shoulders back and reaching for my hand. "I'll find out."

He led me down the narrow hallway and into the living room, where a dark-haired man wearing a well-worn leather jacket walked out of the kitchen, opening a beer. He threw the bottle top onto the coffee table, but it slid to the floor, joining the others.

As he relished his first sip, his gaze caught mine, and he lowered his drink. "Well, hello there," he said, licking the beer off his lips as his eyes traveled over me.

"Dad, this is my friend, Lanie."

"Your *girlfriend*, you mean," Riley said, pushing past to get the toy cars scattered over the shabby carpet.

His dad chuckled. "You seem entirely too pretty to be with this guy." He held out his hand. "Kurt."

I shook it, but his dad held on a fraction longer than I was comfortable with.

"You go to that fancy school too, I see," he continued before taking another swig of his beer. "What's its name again?"

"Summerhill," I said as Scott glared at his father's profile. Surely he knew which school his son went to—the prestigious school he had earned a *scholarship* for.

Kurt chortled as he slumped into his armchair and turned on the television. I got the impression he knew—he just didn't care.

"Where are your manners, boy? Get the girl a drink," Kurt said, lighting up a cigarette. "There's beer in the fridge."

I winced. "Um…it's okay…"

"Don't sweat it, sweetness." He grinned. "I won't tell your parents."

"I'll get you some water." Scott grazed my back as he moved to the kitchen only a few feet away.

"Have a seat," his father said, motioning to the ragged chair opposite.

Glancing Scott's way, I sat on the edge of the seat, not knowing what he expected me to do or how long he wanted to stay. I'd never felt so uncomfortable.

Kurt blew out a mouthful of smoke. "Are you one of those scholarship students too?"

"Um, no…I…"

"Dad..." Scott's tone lowered in warning.

Kurt met Scott's dark gaze with a chuckle. "What? I'm just making sure my son is hanging out with the right crowd, that's all.

Scott mumbled something under his breath as he returned with my drink.

"Your parents must have pretty good jobs to send you to a school like that," Kurt continued, unfazed by his son's clear warning.

Instead of handing me the glass, Scott scooped up my arm. "Alright, time to get you home."

"And where might home be?"

"Lanie lives in a castle in Bel Air," Riley blurted excitedly.

"Bel Air, huh?" Kurt's underlying smirk sent shivers down my spine. "Impressive."

"I knew this was a bad idea." Scott placed the glass on the table as he directed me to the front door. "I'll see you later."

Kurt took a long drag of his cigarette. "Take the kid, will you? I've got shit to do."

Scott's jaw pulsed as he inhaled a long breath. "Riley! Let's go!"

Riley leaped up and followed us outside like a well-trained puppy.

With a sheepish glance my way, Scott started the car and flew out of the drive. Riley played quietly in the backseat, running his matching toy Mustang over the interior while we said nothing. My agitation grew as a million questions rolled around my mind, not one I wanted his brother to hear the answer to.

Scott slowed at the gate and typed in the security code. "Are they home?"

I shook my head. It was our usual routine. If my parents were home, we'd say our goodbyes at the gate. "Mom's out for dinner, and Dad's working late. You want to come in?"

Riley appeared between us. "Please, Scotty? I want to see inside."

"Alright. Just for a little bit."

As soon as Riley walked through the front door, his eyes bulged.

"Go explore," I said, smiling at his wonderment.

With a delighted squeal, he disappeared into the parlor while Scott followed me into the kitchen.

Once Riley was out of earshot, I spun around. "Why would you spring that on me?"

"I thought you wanted to meet my dad."

"No…I trusted you had reasons for not wanting me to meet him. Just like you should trust me about my family."

"I'm sorry." He ran his hand down his face. "I haven't been thinking straight since I left you Sunday morning, and now I've probably made things worse."

"With me or your dad?"

Riley charged through the kitchen until his face squished up against the glass of the French doors. "Wow! There's a swimming pool *and* a tennis court!" He found the latch and sprinted outside.

"Maybe he could come over for a swim one day," I said, smiling as he attempted handstands and clumsy cartwheels across the vast lawn.

Scott winced. "I don't think that's a good idea."

"Oh, right, we're not togeth—"

"No, no…" he said, grabbing my hand. "Because he can't swim." Scott squeezed my fingers until I looked up at him. "And we *are*."

My vision blurred as his words sunk in.

"I'm sorry, Lanie. I've been a jerk." His eyes glistened. "I don't want to break up. I…I never want to break up. I lo—"

"Melanie!" Mom's voice echoed through the hallways. "Why is there a strange child running across the back lawn? You didn't let the staff bring their children to work again, did you?"

Scott's gaze shot to mine. "You said she was out."

"I thought she was," I hissed—although twenty people could live in this house and never cross paths.

Our hands parted seconds before Mom waltzed into the kitchen. "Grayson, I wasn't expecting to see you unt—wait…" She paused and pointed her manicured finger at Scott. "You're not Grayson."

I drew in an unsteady breath, preparing to admit who he really was to me. "Mom, this is Scott. We're..."

"Working on a sociology project together," he interrupted. "And that's my little brother running around. I hope that's okay. I couldn't find a babysitter."

"But I thought I saw Grayson's car out front."

"My car's in the shop," Scott said quickly. "Grayson generously loaned me his until it's fixed."

Her face brightened. "Oh, you're a friend of Grayson? Would I know your parents?"

"Mom, we really have to get this project done, so..."

"You should come to our little Christmas party were having in a couple of weeks," Mom continued. "I'm sure Grayson would appreciate the company of another male his age." She turned to me. "And I suppose you can bring that bug-eyed girl if you want."

I groaned. "She has a name, Mom."

"I'm sure she does, Melanie," she uttered while checking her nails. "Just not one I need to remember."

Heat rose to my neck as a small sound emitted from Scott's throat.

"Well, don't work too late. You need to look your best for the Harlows tomorrow." With one last lingering look at Scott, she sauntered out of the kitchen with an extra sway to her hips.

"Are you always left alone like this?" Scott asked once my mother was gone.

"It doesn't bother me so much anymore."

He frowned. "It bothers me."

"Then why don't you and Riley stay for dinner?"

Scott glanced out the window at his brother. "I think Riley would love that." His sparkling eyes moved to mine. "I would too."

After dinner, Riley settled in the living room to watch a movie while Scott and I finished off the lasagna I had our chef make and hide in the fridge a few days earlier.

"Your mom doesn't seem so bad," Scott said, running his finger over my hand.

"Neither does your dad."

He dropped his head with a chuckle. "Point taken."

"She's always charming to strangers. But once she realizes you have nothing to offer her, she treats you like…like…"

"Like what?"

"Like me," I said with a half-smile. "You know, she's actually been bearable this week since I'm now one step closer to becoming a Harlow. I'm finally fulfilling my parents' dream."

"Then we'll keep up the act."

"Are you sure?"

He threaded his fingers through mine. "If it means she'll ease up on you, then yeah. I'm sure."

Warmth flooded my body and consumed my heart. He was willing to put his pride aside to make me happier. My gaze traveled to his lips, and my breath staggered. I wanted to thank him in so many ways.

Scott cleared his throat, clearly sensing my desire. "I really should get Riley home."

My cheeks burned. "Of course."

He stood and pulled me up with him. "We'll get together this weekend, okay?"

"Are you sure you can't come to Grayson's after dinner tomorrow? I promise to let you win a game or two."

He drew me close and encircled his muscular arms around my waist. "Will there be a prize?"

"I'm sure I could arrange something," I said, pressing my pelvis into his.

A low growl escaped his mouth. "Then I'll bring my A-game," he murmured before crashing his lips down onto mine.

We reluctantly drew apart and wandered into the living room, still holding hands. Riley was fast asleep as the credits rolled down the screen, so we stood there quietly while Scott's thumb ran delicate circles over my hand. With a deep breath, he finally let go and scooped up his brother.

I followed them out to the car and helped Scott place Riley in the backseat. As he closed the passenger door, our profiles lit up. We both turned to find the headlights of my mother's chauffeur-driven car traveling down the driveway, and any chance of a goodnight kiss evaporated.

"Happy Thanksgiving, Lanie." His longing gaze was more intimate than any kiss.

"You too."

With a polite wave to my mom, Scott jumped into the driver's seat and sped away.

"Do all of Grayson's friends look like that?" Mom asked as I followed her inside.

"I don't know what you're talking about."

"Oh, come on." She giggled. "Don't pretend like you haven't noticed. He's cute." She'd clearly had a few drinks with dinner. "If he were a few years older, I'd—"

"I'm going to bed."

Chapter 12

"They're going to be so angry when they find out," Grayson uttered while setting up the first board game. We'd just endured a multi-course dinner with our families combined and desperately needed time away from their mutual excitement for our *developing* relationship.

As soon as his older brother had gone away to college, Grayson moved into the pool house. It was twice the size of Scott's entire house, and it had everything he needed, meaning he could avoid his overbearing parents for days.

I grimaced. "Are you sure you want to go along with it?"

"Are you serious? Dad's already promised to buy me a new car." He chuckled. "We should have started this fake relationship years ago."

A throat cleared behind us, and we both spun around.

Grayson stilled. "Fuck, Adam. How long have you been standing there?"

His brother smirked as he stepped through the front door. "Long enough."

"Please don't say anything," I pleaded. "It's only temporary."

Adam folded his arms as he gazed around the room that used to be his domain. "And burst their ridiculous dream of the Harlow-Warren empire? Yeah, no thanks."

Grayson and I exhaled simultaneously.

"We won't even need that merger once *I'm* running the show," Adam continued, knowing it was a sure way of riling up his younger brother.

Grayson rolled his eyes. It was always the same argument with them. For years, their father had purposely played them against each other to find out which son was worthy of taking over the reign of Harlow Corp. My bet was on Adam. Grayson was incredibly smart and had amazing people skills, but Adam was a force of nature when it came to business. Every summer and spring break, his brother shadowed their father, learning every aspect of the business instead of partying with his classmates. His sole focus was success, and everything else was deemed an unnecessary distraction.

With a satisfied grin, Adam dropped onto the chair opposite. "So, why all the lies?" When neither of us answered, he tilted his head for a better view of my burning cheeks. "Now I'm even more intrigued."

"Melanie's seeing someone," Grayson blurted. "Someone who's not exactly...like us. So, she needs the cover."

Adam turned his gaze back to Grayson. "And what's in it for you?"

"Breathing room," he muttered. "Since you left for college, Mom and Dad have been on my case about everything. I don't know what else I can do to prove myself."

His brother rubbed his chiseled jawline. "You need to be harder on them, or they'll walk all over you."

"Easy to say when you don't live here anymore."

"Well, how long do you plan on keeping up this charade?"

Grayson and I exchanged looks. It all happened so fast that we hadn't had a chance to discuss the finer details.

Adam leaned forward. "I suggest breaking the news once you've moved away to college, or things are going to get a lot worse for you around here. Dad doesn't tolerate liars. You know that."

Grayson grumbled before rolling the dice. "I better make the most of it, then."

A phone rang, and I launched for mine, expecting a call from Scott at any moment.

Adam slid his phone from his pocket. "Sorry, Smelly. It's mine," he said, standing up. "Have fun, kids. I have a...meeting."

Grayson scoffed. "Don't you mean a date?"

"No, a date would mean I'm meeting a girl with the intention of starting a relationship. And, well...that's absurd." With a deep rumbling chuckle, he strolled out of the pool house and answered the phone.

Adam had a multitude of desperate women on call, each vying for a chance to be the future Mrs. Harlow. I had no doubt Grayson would be just as popular once college started, and my heart dipped at the thought of having to share his attention.

"When's Scott getting here?" Grayson asked midway through the game.

"I'm not sure." I glanced at my phone, willing it to light up. I'd messaged him three times already, and he still hadn't replied. "I'm waiting for him to call me."

"Well, call *him*."

I scrunched up my nose. "No."

"Are you following your mom's stupid rules? It is possible to call a guy and not appear desperate."

"That's not why I'm not calli—fine!" I grabbed my cell phone off the coffee table and dialed his number. It rang and rang, and just as I was about to hang up, my heart lit up.

"Lanie, hey," Scott uttered just above a whisper.

"Hey, are you still coming over?"

There was a moment's pause before he spoke. "Yeah, look, things haven't exactly gone as planned. Can we talk later?"

"Is everything okay?" I asked as muffled yelling sounded in the background.

"I've gotta go."

The line went dead, and I dropped the phone from my ear.

"What's going on?" Grayson asked, lifting his gaze to mine.

"He's not coming."

"You okay?"

"Yeah, I think so," I said, trying to hide my disappointment.

Grayson's eyes softened. "Come on, don't get stuck in that head of yours. Sit down and play so I can beat your ass."

I smiled past the forming tears and sank down next to the only person I could truly depend on. "Unlikely," I said with a laugh. "You haven't beaten me at this game since third grade."

Scott: **You awake?**

Me: **No.**

Scott: **I'm outside.**

What?! Shooting out of bed, I threw on my robe and ran down the stairs, grasping the bannister with each careless step. I inched open the front door to discover Scott waiting by the stairs, hands in pockets and face semi-hidden under the hood of his sweatshirt.

A shiver ran over me as I stepped out, and I hugged my robe a little tighter to stay warm. "What are you doing here?" I glanced up and down the empty driveway. "And where's your car?"

"I walked from the gate so I wouldn't wake your parents."

"After the amount they drank at dinner, I doubt they'd hear a tornado." I forced a laugh. "Why don't you come inside? It's freezing out here."

"No, I can't stay," he said, keeping his head lowered. "I just wanted to see you."

My brow furrowed as I tried to catch his gaze. "I wanted to see you too." I stepped toward him. "What happened today?"

As he lifted his head, the moonlight lit up his face, highlighting the freshly dried blood along his bottom lip.

I sucked in my breath as I reached out. "Scott..."

He flinched away from my touch. "I had a fight with my dad after I dropped you home last night. Then, he turned up at Mrs. Norris' Thanksgiving dinner, so I had to stay to make sure Riley was safe."

My heart quickened. "Where's Riley now?"

"Sleeping over at Mrs. Norris'. She knows what my dad is like when he drinks."

Another puzzle piece fell into place. His father was a drinker. "Then you should stay here tonight." I offered him a small smile. "I'll lock the door this time."

His blue eyes radiated desire, but he shook it away. "No...I have to get back. If I'm gone before he wakes, it'll only make things worse."

"I don't understand. Why is he so angry with you?"

Scott rubbed his tired eyes. "He thinks I should be providing more for our family."

"But you work almost every day." I shook my head. "What are you supposed to do…quit school?"

Scott's despondent gaze met mine. "We don't exactly see eye to eye on the importance of education."

My mouth fell open. "But you're on a scholarship. At *Summerhill*. Doesn't he know how incredible that is?"

"He thinks Summerhill only offered me a place to fulfill some diversity requirement."

"Surely he knows how smart you are? You're going to have every college in America offering you a full ride."

"If only that was enough."

"What do you mean?"

Scott looked away, his jaw tense as he held in the truth. "The less you know the better."

I moved closer. "But I could help…"

"You *are* helping," he said, lifting his hands to my face. His palms held my cheeks like fine bone china. "Every time I see you…touch you…" He rubbed his cold nose against my warm one. "You make me believe I can do anything."

I pressed my forehead to his and closed my eyes. "Because you can."

With a low growl, Scott pushed away. "I have to go."

"Will I see you this weekend?" I asked, keeping hold of his hand.

"I'm going to take on some extra shifts at the garage to get my dad off my back, so I won't be able to see you outside of school for a while."

"Oh." I lowered my gaze as disappointment consumed me.

"There's always the AV room," he said, squeezing my hand.

I offered him a half-smile. "I guess so."

"And I can come to your parents' Christmas party if you want me to…"

My spark returned. "And the winter formal? I'm not going without you."

"I'll make it work," he said, laying his soft lips on mine. "I'll see you Monday, Lanie."

"In the AV room?"

His smile grew as he stepped away. "In the AV room."

He jogged down the road leading to the iron gates, and I sank to the step below, waiting for the distant hum of his Mustang. Once it faded away, toward the home he didn't belong in, I stood up and walked back into mine.

I'd barely had a chance to put my books into my locker before Scott flew past, pulling me along with him. His lips were on mine before the AV room door closed, and his hands struggled to find a place to settle on my body. My face, my breasts, my hips, my thighs…my…*oh my.*

"How far do you think we can go in here?" he asked breathlessly.

"As far as you want," I murmured, keeping my lips on his.

His mouth moved down to my neck, and I moaned, springing his pants to life. The pressure against my pelvis sent waves of anticipation through my body, and I wanted more.

As he lifted me onto the small desk, the bell tore through the room.

"Shit," Scott growled, trying to readjust his…situation.

I winced. "Sorry."

"You go," he said, pushing me out the door. "Tell the teacher I had to go to the office."

Trying not to laugh as he mumbled repeatedly about naked old people, I crept out and ran to homeroom.

Grayson chuckled as I sat down. "You might want to wear a scarf or something."

"What? Why?"

"Nice hickey, Warren," Hank blurted as he slid into the seat beside Grayson. "Who would've thought you could draw blood from ice."

My hand flew over the spot on my neck still tingling from Scott's lips, and my face burned.

"Chill out, Mel," Grayson said with a laugh. "It's not…that bad."

As I lifted my collar and positioned my hair over the evidence, I rummaged through my bag for the emergency makeup kit my mother gave me junior year. Once I had it in hand, I held it tightly until the next bell rang, and I bolted to the nearest restroom.

While endeavoring to conceal the mortifying love bite, Lisa and Rebecca waltzed through the door.

"Who did that?" Rebecca said, pausing mid-step.

"Isn't it obvious?" Scott and I weren't exactly discreet about our relationship at school.

The girls looked at each other and snickered.

"Well, after reading about you and Grayson in the paper the other day, we figured you and Scott broke up." Rebecca glanced at Lisa with a smirk. "Or we hoped."

"What paper?" I asked, ignoring their infatuation with my boyfriend.

"Um…*your* paper…"

I squeezed my eyes shut. Of course my mother would tell the world about Grayson and me. "You shouldn't believe everything you read."

Lisa stepped forward, meeting my reflected gaze. "Why would a Warren Media publication lie about the company's sole heiress?"

"Anything to sell papers, right?" My teeth gnashed behind my smile.

"But it doesn't make sense," she said, pulling her eyebrows together. "You and *Scott*? I mean, he's not worth…*anything*. And well, Grayson is set to inherit billions. How could you possibly choose Scott over Grayson?"

My head ached. "I didn't choose…"

Rebecca's eyes widened. "So, you're dating both of them?"

"No!" These girls were incredible—incredibly stupid.

"Well, this just got a little more interesting," Rebecca said, grinning at Lisa.

Apparently, I needed to spell it out for them. "I'm not with Grayson. We're just friends."

Lisa's nose crinkled. "Then why did he tell me he was in love with you?"

"Sorry?!" I asked, hoping I'd heard wrong.

"When he broke it off with me, he said…"

My groan concealed the rest of her sentence. I didn't need to hear it. Grayson had used me as an excuse.

"So, are you in some kind of open relationship?"

"Oh my god…" Before I slammed my head *or theirs* into the mirror, I quickly fixed my hair, quadruple-checked my neck, and marched out of the restroom, leaving their idiotic brains to generate more stupid rumors about my love life.

I dug my fingernails into Grayson's arm as soon as I saw him in the hallway at lunchtime. "You told Lisa you were *in love* with me?"

Grayson winced. "It was my only way out. She wouldn't believe anything else."

"Gray…" I groaned.

"You weren't with Scott then. I didn't think it would matter."

I pinched the bridge of my nose. "This is getting too messy. I think we need to tell our parents the truth."

Grayson's eyes bulged. "Are you joking? They'll kill me. My brother's right. We need to play this out until we leave for college."

"But that's months away."

"Please, Mel," he begged. "Dad's already talking about an internship over spring break, not to mention the new car I'm getting for Christmas. If we tell them now, my father will never trust me enough to take over the company."

I grimaced, knowing how much his father's approval meant to him.

"Look, don't worry about the rumors," Grayson continued. "Even if they get back to our parents, they wouldn't believe them."

Muscular arms slid around my waist, and a chin rested on my shoulder. When Scott's voice breathed past my ear, my entire body lit up. "Believe what?"

"Mel's having second thoughts about our…arrangement. She wants to come clean to our parents."

Scott turned my hips until we were face to face. "Won't they be furious?"

"I don't care anymore. I'm sick of lying. I want to go on proper dates with you. I want to invite you over for dinner—as painful as my parents may be—and I want my dress to match *your* suit for the winter formal. You know…normal couple stuff."

Grayson ran his fingers through his hair as tension distorted his perfect features.

Scott's gaze panned from Grayson's to mine. "Fuck normal. Normal is for boring people, and you are far from boring."

"So, you don't mind all the rumors?"

"Yeah, I mind…but I figure it's only short term." His finger grazed my cheek. "I have you in my long-term plan."

My heart fluttered. "Long term, huh?"

"As long as you want me," he said, staring at my lips as I moistened them.

Grayson cleared his throat, breaking our trance. "So, we're still on the same page?"

"I guess so."

"Thank God." Grayson's shoulders relaxed. "Now, are you guys coming to lunch, or are you just going to stare longingly into each other's eyes all day?"

"Actually…" Scott's hand engulfed mine. "Mel and I…have an important project to work on."

Grayson laughed. "I'm sure you do. One you'll both score very highly on, I'd imagine."

Scott held back his smile as he pulled me away. "That's the plan."

"Where are we going?" I asked mid-laugh, knowing very well we were heading to the AV room. "I can't be long. Cara will be waiting for me."

"I just want a few minutes alone with you first."

"What could we possibly achieve in a few minutes?"

He ran his finger over my makeup-covered neck. "Well, I achieved this in a matter of minutes…"

My gaze narrowed as I pointed at him like a naughty puppy. "No more. Do you know how embarrassing this is?"

"I'll have to find somewhere else to put my mouth then." His eyes traveled downward.

Heat filled my body. "Oh."

Making sure the coast was clear, Scott opened the AV room and ushered me inside. Once the door closed, he tugged me close until I was almost swallowed whole into his arms. His lips found mine, and when our tongues intertwined, his length once again rose to the occasion.

Scott's head pressed against mine as we peered down. "He's got a mind of his own."

"Maybe I could help with that…" I said, unlatching his belt buckle.

Scott's pupils dilated as I unzipped his fly and slid my hand inside his pants. His eyes rolled back in ecstasy when my fingers curled around his hardness and began to stroke. A surge of excitement rushed through me as Scott moaned. The power was intoxicating. I knew, in that moment, Scott would do anything for me, yet all I craved was his pleasure. With one last kiss to his lips, I sank to my knees and took him into my mouth.

Scott's knees buckled as he grasped the shelf above me. His other hand threaded through my hair, guiding me back and forth. "Lanie…" he growled, trying to pull away. With his strength depleted, I held him in place as he spilled into my mouth with one last deep-chested groan. "Fuck, that was hot," he uttered in a husky voice. "You didn't have to…"

I rose between his arms, feeling like I'd won a war. "I know."

"No one has ever…"

A small smile crept over my lips, happy I could give him a first.

Drunk on desire, he leaned in to kiss me but jerked away when the door swung open.

A voice I knew well filled the room. "What on earth?!"

Scott grimaced as he quickly zipped up his pants and turned around, carefully hiding me from view.

"This room is off limits, and I'm guessing no one gave you permission to make out in here, am I correct?"

"Sorry, Mr. West," Scott said, refusing to budge as I cowered behind him, burying my face into his back.

"Well, get out of here unless you want detention," the teacher snapped.

With a sigh, Scott took cautious steps out of the room. My gaze struck Mr. West's as I followed, and all the power I had felt before evaporated in an instant.

"Miss Warren. I thought you'd be spending your spare time more wisely since you almost failed your last assignment."

With a sharp nod, I quickened my pace to meet Scott in the hallway. We didn't say a word until we were safely around the corner.

Scott ran his hand down his face. "That was close."

"Too close," I mumbled, wondering what punishment was coming later.

"What happened with your assignment?" Scott asked as he stood in front of me, arms folded. "I saw your work, and there's no way you almost failed."

I lowered my gaze. "I guess he expects more from me." It wasn't a lie.

Scott lifted my chin with his finger. "Don't let him mess with you."

"Okay," I said as my stomach churned. I couldn't tell whether it was from dread or hunger. "Can we go have lunch now?"

His eyes twinkled. "Didn't you just eat?"

"What? Oh my god." I choked back laughter and bumped his side.

Scott kissed my scorching cheek. "I'm sorry, but it's going to take me a while to recover from that."

"So, no round two after school?" I asked, dropping my bottom lip.

"I can't," Scott groaned. "I have to go straight to the garage."

"Do you have to work every afternoon, *as well* as weekends?"

"If I want to keep my dad off my back, then yeah, I do," he said, taking my hand as we strolled toward the cafeteria. "I'm still coming to your parents' Christmas party, though."

My heart dipped. "Are you sure you want to? Cara's still a maybe, and I'll have to spend most of the night with Grayson to appease my parents."

"As long as I'm close to you, I'm happy."

"I'm sure I could find a moment to slip away undetected," I said with a grin.

He pulled me to his side and brought his mouth to my ear. "I'll make it worth your while."

As my eyebrows lifted, Scott pushed open the door of the cafeteria and ushered me through.

"Where's Cara?" I asked once we arrived at our table. Grayson, Hank, and Randy were already there, plus another girl I didn't know—Hank's latest conquest, I suspected, going by her hand caressing Hank's thigh.

Grayson shrugged. "I assumed she was in the art room."

My heart lit up. Maybe she was reconsidering her portfolio. I squeezed Scott's bicep as he sat down. "I'm going to go find her. I'll see you later in class."

With a quick peck on his cheek, I made my way to the art room. I poked my head inside to find the teacher hovering over the basin, washing brushes, but the rest of the room was empty. "Excuse me, Mrs. Weathers. Have you seen Cara today?"

The teacher's eyelashes fluttered under her glasses. "Unfortunately, no. I've just been informed that Cara won't be returning to Summerhill."

My stomach fell to the floor. "What?"

"Moving to another state, apparently." Mrs. Weathers sighed. "It's such a shame."

"I can't believe it," I muttered in a daze. Cara never mentioned any of this.

"Neither can I. That girl has so much potential, even more so after winning the West Coast Fine Art competition."

"She won?!"

"Yes. They released the results this morning. If you speak to Cara, please congratulate her for me. I've tried to call, but their home phone appears to be disconnected."

With a small nod, I retreated from the room and pulled out my cell phone. Perhaps Mrs. Weathers was mistaken. I paced the hallway while the phone rang with no answer, then I sent a message begging for her to call me.

My afternoon classes dragged by. I checked my cell phone every few minutes, hoping for a reply, but there was nothing. So, when the final bell rang, I ran to Grayson's locker and begged him to drive me to Cara's house.

We pulled up in front of a little house, not much bigger than Scott's but in a seemingly nicer neighborhood. Two cars filled the driveway, one I recognized as Cara's mother's, but the other unknown.

"Want me to come with?" Grayson asked, turning off the engine.

"You better stay here. Cara's mom doesn't like her associating with boys."

"But moms love me."

"Not this one," I muttered, getting out of the car.

I walked along the slate pathway toward the house where a pile of empty boxes lay waiting to be filled beside the entrance. Before my knuckles collided with the front door, I glanced back at Grayson. With his encouraging smile and nod, I breathed in a dose of courage and knocked.

Moments later, the door opened, and an older lady stood before me. Her curly, graying hair and blue eyes led me to believe I was at the wrong house. There was no way she was Cara's mother.

"May I help you?" she asked when I couldn't utter a word.

"Um...hi. Is this Cara Deville's house?"

Her face lit up. "Oh, you're a friend of Cara? She's in her bedroom. I'll go get her."

As she wandered down the hallway, I lowered my gaze to my twiddling thumbs.

"How dare you?"

I jerked back in surprise. A woman with long dark hair and striking brown eyes glared at me from the doorway—undoubtedly Cara's mother.

"Excuse me?"

Her eyes narrowed into slits. "You have no idea what you've done."

"I'm…I'm sorry…I don't know what you're talking about."

"Of course you don't," she spat, running her eyes over my body in judgment. "You don't care about anyone but yourself. You, with all your money. No wonder you're so careless." Her eyes glistened as she pointed her finger at me. "I won't let you push her down the same path as her father. I refuse to go through that again."

"I never meant to—"

"Mom! Stop!" Cara ran down the hallway and tried to pull her away. "Aunt Sylvia!"

Her mother shook her off. "No! You can't talk to this horrible girl anymore! She doesn't care about you."

The other lady rushed back, wrapping her arm around Cara's mother as she faced me. "Forgive my sister-in-law. She's due for her medication." She steered her in the opposite direction until all I could hear were muffled wails from another room.

"I'm sorry you had to see that," Cara said, hugging her stomach. She looked smaller today, even more fragile than normal. "She's…um…had a mental breakdown."

My heart sank. "I'm so sorry…"

"I guess it's been building for a while, but Thanksgiving pushed her over the edge. Luckily, my aunt and uncle were here when she lost it entirely. They're taking us back to Montana to live with them while Mom gets the help she needs."

"I had no idea how bad it was."

"To be honest, neither did I. I thought she was just being overprotective until I caught her lacing my food with antidepressants."

I gasped. "Why would she do that?"

"She thinks my drawings are a symptom. That I'm going to end up like my dad if she doesn't intervene."

"Oh my god…and she blames me for encouraging your art?"

"She blames everyone," she said, stepping forward. "Trust me, you've been my savior through all this."

I believed her, but guilt slipped through regardless.

"Please don't worry about me. My aunt and uncle have a great school close by with an amazing arts program. I probably won't graduate this year, but now I'll have plenty of time to work on my portfolio."

"That's great," I said, forcing myself to smile. "Maybe you'll win some more awards."

Cara's brows pulled together. "What do you mean?"

"Haven't you heard? You won the West Coast Fine Art Competition."

Her eyes bulged. "I won?"

"Of course you won. Mrs. Weathers asked me to pass on her congratulations."

A new light appeared in her eyes. "I can't believe it! Wait right here." Cara bolted down the hall, returning seconds later with a large rectangular package. "I was going to drop this off on our way to Montana, but since you're here…"

My mouth parted as she passed it over. "Is this…your painting?"

"No, it's *your* painting," she replied, shifting her weight from side to side as she bit her lower lip. "Don't open it yet."

Emotion bubbled up inside. "Thank you, Cara. I have no doubt I will love it."

"Please don't cry. I've only just stopped."

I placed the package carefully at my feet. "I'm sorry. It just… it just sucks," I said, wiping away the first tears to fall. "I feel like I've only just gotten to know you, and now…"

"We can still talk on the phone every day. It's going to take me *at least* a few years to make a decent friend anyway." Her sad laughter reminded me of the lonely girl I had met at the start of the semester.

"Don't shut yourself off from the world, okay? You're an amazing person. I'm the one who'll struggle."

"You have Scott and Grayson…and whoever else you decide to let in."

She knew me better than most. "I'm going to miss you."

"Me too." Cara wrapped her arms around me and squeezed. I wasn't used to affection, but she broke through the awkwardness until I hugged her back.

After we said our final goodbyes, I returned to Grayson's car in a daze.

"So, she's really leaving?" Grayson asked as we drove away.

With a quick nod, I stared out the windshield until everything was a blur.

"You okay?"

My jaw clenched so tight I thought I'd break a tooth. "Yep."

When Grayson's hand slid over mine, I broke. A sob erupted from my chest followed by a waterfall of tears. I already missed her.

"Want to go to Nico's?" Grayson asked in an effort to cheer me up.

"Thanks, but I just want to go home."

"Sure thing."

Not another word was spoken until we rolled to a stop behind my mother's chauffeur-driven car in the driveway. I thanked Grayson for the ride, grabbed my things, and stepped out, following the steps leading to my own version of hell. If only I had relatives to save me from *my* mother.

I pushed open the front door, rubbing my puffy eyes. Unfortunately, it was too late for a cold compress or cucumber slice, because my mother stood frozen in the foyer, staring at me like a terrified chihuahua.

She grasped her chest. "What's wrong? Did Grayson break up with you?!"

"What?" It took a moment for my mind to catch up. "No."

"Did you have a fight?"

I screwed up my nose. "No…"

"Then why on earth does your face look like that?!"

I groaned. "This has nothing to do with Grayson, Mom."

"Oh, thank god," she gasped. "Everyone is expecting to see you two together at our Christmas party. You would've humiliated me."

I waited for her to delve into the real reason why I was upset, but alas, she didn't.

Instead, she grabbed her handbag and threw open the door. "Well, I'm off to dinner now. Ciao!"

As the door closed, I almost laughed at her complete lack of empathy. "Unbelievable," I muttered as I stomped up the stairs.

I made my way to my bedroom window and sunk into my loveseat, nursing Cara's artwork. I hadn't even seen it yet, and it was already the most precious thing I owned. Finding a loose edge, I tore at the brown paper until the back was exposed along with a small note.

Dear Melanie,

Well, here it is. Your world-famous Cara Deville original, as promised. Winner or not, I hope you like it. Either way, you're stuck with it.

It's titled 'Finding Beauty' because even in our darkest moments, there is still beauty within. Sometimes we just need a little help to find it.

Thank you for being my light.

Your best friend,

Cara

With a deep breath, I spun the painting around and took a step back.

The artwork was divided into three layers, reminding me of a babushka doll. The outer layer was dark and full of shadowy demons reaching inward. The middle layer depicted an angelic light projecting from a feminine figure whose body encircled the final element of the painting—a delicate yellow rose.

I'd never seen anything more beautiful.

Chapter 13

My gaze shot straight to Scott as he sauntered through my parents' annual Christmas party with Grayson. They arrived together, and by the look of his outfit, he'd raided Grayson's wardrobe. I'd never seen Scott look so dapper, and wow, did it suit him. Even though he was the only guest not wearing a tie, no one would question where he came from. My mom's friends ogled, and my first instinct was to stab their eyes out.

Warmth filled my body as they approached, but my eyes were glued to Scott. "You look…"

"Like me?" Grayson interrupted with a grin.

I smiled up at Scott, whose gaze was tracing the curves of my body. "Better."

"Whatever." Grayson scoffed. "I'm going to go find some food. I'm starving."

"You look…wow." Scott kept his distance, but his hand was twitching. He wanted to touch me as much as I wanted him to.

My mother chose my dress. It was deep red, tight, and short. My dad's friends were certainly appreciative, so I knew Scott would lose his mind.

"You're going to make this hard for me, aren't you?" Scott said, clearing his throat.

"No." I ran my gaze down to his waist. "Not yet, anyway."

He threaded his hand through his slicked-back hair. "Jesus. I need a drink."

With a laugh, I signaled to the waiter, who walked over with a tray of options. Knowing Scott was driving, I offered him a soda while I chose something stronger. I was going to need it. My parents weren't concerned about underage drinking as long as I didn't embarrass them and remained in full control. Thankfully, Grayson's parents had the same philosophy, which made these events so much more bearable.

We took slow sips, eyeing each other until my name was called.

I closed my eyes. "I'll find you later, okay?"

With a quick wink, he wandered away.

"Where's that boyfriend of yours?" my mother asked as she pulled me toward Grayson's parents. "I promised Caroline we'd get a photo of the two of you."

"Here I am, Victoria," Grayson said, appearing behind me. He gave me a peck on the cheek, and a few sighs echoed around us.

My smile was forced as I straightened my posture for the photo.

"Just relax," the photographer said. "Grayson, why don't you whisper something funny into Melanie's ear."

Grayson leaned in, but he didn't need to say anything. Gazing past the camera, I found Scott watching me with an amused smirk. He crossed his eyes and poked out his tongue, making me burst with laughter.

"Perfect!" The photographer smiled down at his camera.

'Come on, you two lovebirds." My mom squeezed herself between us and hooked her arms into ours. "I want to show you off."

This continued over the next two hours. Mom flaunted our relationship in front of my father's colleagues and friends, relishing the attention. We were, in their eyes, the ultimate power couple…or we would be once we were married.

I watched Scott from afar, eating hors d'oeuvres, sipping water, and unsuccessfully avoiding the advances of desperate housewives. When one lady ran her hand down Scott's bicep, I almost broke the champagne glass in my hand. I couldn't take it anymore.

"Excuse me. I need to go to the ladies' room," I said before leaning into Grayson's ear. "Keep them distracted for a little while, will you?"

With his nod, I sauntered over to the bar, making sure Scott was watching. I placed my glass on the table and continued over to where he stood, surrounded by women. As I walked past, I ran my finger across his back, hoping he would take the hint and follow.

I snuck into the empty pool house, leaving the door ajar for Scott to enter.

Within moments, Scott's arms were around my waist, pulling me into his hard chest. "Finally," he whispered as his lips grazed my neck.

I turned in his embrace and circled my arms around his neck, pulling his lips down to mine. "I'm sorry, this must be awful for you," I murmured, barely pulling away to breathe, let alone speak.

"Are you kidding?" His dimples deepened. "I've been propositioned at least twelve times already. It's been great for my self-esteem."

I whacked his chest as I laughed. "Stop it."

"Seriously, these women are forward. I'm pretty sure I got assaulted leaving the restroom before." His eyes sparkled down at me. "I'm going to have nightmares."

"Poor baby," I said, running my hand over his cheek. "Is there anything I can do to ease your trauma?"

"Well, we could start with this…" Scott leaned in to kiss me again. "Then we could…"

Nearing voices sounded from outside, and my eyes grew wide. "Shit," I muttered, glancing around the room. "We need to hide." I grabbed Scott's hand and pulled him into the closet. It wasn't a great hiding place with the louvered doors, but if we stood still, they wouldn't notice us.

My mom's distant giggles grew louder as she entered the pool house, and a friend of hers followed.

"That's the one!" Scott whispered, pointing to my mother's friend, Lacy, through the slits in the door.

I covered my mouth to stifle my laughter. Lacy was a train wreck. She was on her fourth husband, her seventh playboy, and I'm pretty sure that wasn't her face anymore. Scott had every right to be scared of her.

"This should tide us over until he gets here." Lacy handed something to my mother and proceeded to shuffle items around the coffee table. "Are you using that new contact I gave you?"

"Yes, and he assured me someone was coming." Mom spilled white powder onto the glass and divided it into long, thin lines. "I don't know what's taking so long."

Scott's entire body tensed. He was clearly surprised by the recreational habits of my mother. I slid my hand around his and squeezed. I'd seen it all before.

"Perhaps he didn't get past security," Lacy said, rolling a dollar note in her hand.

"It shouldn't be a problem. His pseudonym is on the guest list."

Lacy walked over to the window and panned her gaze through the crowd. "Do you know what he looks like?"

"Apparently, he's clean-looking, tall, dark hair…oh, and wearing a red, white, and blue tie."

Scott's hand clammed up, and he pulled it away to wipe it against his pants.

"God bless America." Lacy snickered. "A hideous tie like that shouldn't be hard to find." She wandered back to the coffee table and knelt beside it, snorting up the first line.

"If he doesn't show himself soon, I'm going to call his boss and tell him I'm taking my business elsewhere." She joined Lacy on the floor and chuckled. "Even drug dealers can't find decent help these days."

I lowered my eyes as they proceeded to consume the rest of the cocaine through their upgraded noses. It was too humiliating to watch.

Scott's hands curled into fists by his side while he took slow, steady breaths. Perhaps he was claustrophobic.

Once they floated out of the room, I pushed open the closet doors and stepped out. "Well, that was a new low point in my life," I said, trying to make light of the situation.

Scott's jaw pulsed as he stared out the window. "I've gotta go."

"What? Now? But we've finally found some time to be alone."

He paced the room. "I know, but I…I shouldn't be here."

"Then I'll come with you. We'll drop Grayson at home and go for a drive or something."

"No, you need to stay. I have some stuff to sort out."

My brow furrowed. "What stuff?"

He shook his head in frustration. "I don't have time to explain. I'll see you at school."

Before I had time to process his words, he'd slipped out of the pool house and into the crowd.

My flaring temper had me chasing after him, but the moment I stepped out of the pool house, I met my mother's glare from the other side of the pool. Her tapering gaze panned to Scott as he disappeared into the house then back to me. A friend of hers latched onto her arm, distracting her enough to look away, so I bolted. I'd deal with my mother and her assumptions later.

Just as the valet handed over Scott's keys, I caught up with him. "Can you slow down?"

"I'm sorry. I have to go." He continued to his car, taking long determined strides.

I pulled back his arm, forcing him to stop. "Not until you tell me what's going on."

"I'll explain everything later," he said, shrugging me off.

I blinked a few times at his abrupt dismissal before panning my gaze through the window of his car. A long piece of fabric lay on the passenger seat, blaring the undeniable colors of our country. A shiver rolled over me. "What's that?"

Scott followed my gaze and stilled.

"It's you." My lower lip trembled as I peered up at Scott, praying for him to deny it. "You're the guy they're looking for."

"It's not what it looks like."

Tears blurred my vision. "Are you…dealing drugs?"

"No, Lanie. I despise that shit," he said, running both hands through his hair. "My dad wanted me to sell some to your mom's friends tonight, but I flushed everything before I got here. I planned to give him the money I had saved from the garage as payment." He clenched his fists. "I didn't know he'd already made a deal with your mom. I swear. He's going to kill me when he finds out what I've done."

I stared up at him in disbelief. I knew his dad was bad news. I just didn't know what type of bad. "Scott, you need to go to the police."

He shook his head. "You don't understand. If my dad gets arrested, Riley and I are fucked. We don't have anywhere else to go. No family, nothing. I'll lose any chance I have of a college scholarship, and Riley will be thrown into the foster system. I can't do that to him." Scott grasped my hands as tears flooded my eyes. "That's why I've been working my ass off at the garage. I'm trying to save money for a shitty lawyer to give me some options."

Pain radiated through my chest. "Why didn't you tell me?"

"What was I supposed to say? 'My dad's a fucking low-life who deals drugs out of the trunk of his car…oh and hey, will you go out with me?'"

"I can handle the truth."

"You wouldn't have gone anywhere near me if you knew the truth."

"You don't know that."

He raised his brows.

Anger consumed me. "Fuck you. You don't know that!"

"Then why are you so upset right now?"

My mouth parted, but nothing came out. Before I could find my voice, Scott jogged around the car, jumped in, and took off down the driveway, leaving me standing alone in a cloud of confusion.

I had no idea how long I'd been there, staring at the empty driveway, until Grayson's voice pulled me out of my trance.

"Did Scott leave?"

"He, um…" I cleared my throat. "He had to get home."

"Shit, he was my ride," Grayson said, rubbing his jawline. "Now I'm going to have to wait for my parents…" He threw me a sideways glance. "You okay? Too much champagne?"

"Not enough," I muttered, determined not to cry.

"You and Scott have another fight?"

"I'm not entirely sure what just happened." There was no way I could tell Grayson about this.

Grayson was silent as he gazed back at the house. "Want to sneak upstairs and watch a movie? This party kinda sucks."

"Yeah, it really does."

"I'll rummage up some snacks and meet you in five." Grayson reached for my hand and squeezed. "Don't worry, Warren. You and Scott will sort it out."

My heart dipped. I couldn't see how.

Scott wasn't at school Monday or Tuesday. He'd barely missed a day since the start of the semester, and I was concerned. I'd called and sent messages, but they went unanswered. I walked the hallways in a haze of worry and prayed Scott and Riley were okay.

"Hold on a minute, Melanie," Mr. West called as I attempted to sneak out with the rest of the class after the final bell rang.

He closed the door behind the last student. "You seem distracted today."

I glanced at Scott's empty chair while my chest caved in.

Mr. West returned to his desk. "I thought I'd have your full attention with your boyfriend away."

"I'm pretty sure I'm up to date with everything, so..." I moved closer to the door.

He picked up a novel from his desk and flicked through the pages. "I'm concerned about your comprehension. I want you to read this so we can go through it together."

"I don't think that's necessary," I said, eyeing the time and the dark clouds outside, echoing the impending threat. The hallways would be empty soon.

"I wouldn't want to have to tell the principal how you prefer to spend your time." His smirk sent chills down my spine. "Like, on your knees in the AV room."

Fear consumed me. I couldn't let my relationship with Scott get back to my parents—especially now. "Fine," I muttered, snatching the book and returning to my desk. I glanced at the title as I sat down. "Wait, this isn't on the reading list."

“Read it anyway.” Mr. West sauntered back to his desk. “Chapter eight. Don’t rush.”

Relief washed over me as he sat down. He couldn’t touch me from there. Perhaps he really was intending to help. Perhaps I was being ridiculous. I turned to chapter eight, cleared my throat, and started to read.

Instead of stopping me in intervals to talk about the text, he let me read. After a few minutes, I heard the distinct sound of a zipper, and a long sigh escaped my teacher’s mouth. My voice caught as the words before me delved into a sex scene.

“Keep reading.” Mr. West’s voice was low and raspy.

My fingers turned white as I endeavored to keep the book still in my hands. I threw up a glance and found him watching me, jaw clenched, while his arm rocked back and forth.

I dropped my gaze as bile burned my throat. His deep grunts confirmed my suspicions. He was touching himself. The words in front of me lost all meaning, yet I continued to read, afraid of what would happen if I stopped. Tears stung my eyes, but I fought them, knowing how much he’d enjoy them.

On his release, my voice faltered.

“You can go,” he muttered while adjusting his pants.

My head grew light, and my stomach roiled while I gathered up my things and dashed out of the room. A few people still scattered the halls, but I couldn’t see their faces. As the fog grew heavier, I pushed open the door to the closest restroom and ran into a stall, where the entire contents of my lunch spilled into the toilet.

Thankfully, Grayson was in the midst of a conversation with a member of his swim team when I finally exited the school building. No amount of makeup could hide my blotchy face or bloodshot eyes from him.

“Where have you been?” he asked, glancing my way as I approached his car.

I lowered my gaze and swung my bag into the backseat. “I got held up.”

Grayson continued talking to his friend while I sank into the passenger seat, wanting to disappear. As if sensing my despair, his eyes collided with mine through the glass and softened. He muttered something to his friend before joining me in the car.

Instead of starting the engine, he shifted his body toward mine. "Have you been crying?"

"It's just…um…allergies."

"Bullshit," he spat. "This is about Scott. He hasn't contacted you yet, has he? I told him to call you."

"You spoke to him?" I asked, irritated that Scott had contacted Grayson and not me. "Is he okay?"

"He's having some trouble with his dad and needed some time off. I'm sure he'll be back at school tomorrow."

My body shook until tears erupted from deep within my chest. "But I needed him here *today*."

"Whoa, Mel." Grayson reached for my hand. "What happened?"

His gentle touch only made me cry harder.

"Wait…" Grayson's face dropped. "You just had Mr. West, didn't you?" The anger in his voice was undeniable. "Whatever he is doing, you need to report him."

My eyes pleaded with his. "No, my mom doesn't want me to make an issue out of it. It'll only embarrass her."

"Embarrass her?!" he cried. "This is crazy. He can't keep doing this. Look at you."

I wiped the tears from my eyes and took a deep breath. "I'm fine, Gray. He didn't touch me…I'm fine."

He lowered his eyes. "I'm sorry I wasn't there for you."

"It's okay, Gray. I'm not your responsibility."

"You kinda are."

I threw him a funny look. "That's ludicrous."

"Apparently, I have to 'protect my investments'," Grayson said, mimicking his father's voice.

I rolled my eyes. That was all I was to the Harlows. An asset to generate more income. "So, what do they do when their investments go bad?"

A small smile played on his lips. “I guess we’ll have to wait and see.”

With a soft chuckle, I closed my eyes, relieving the ache in my head.

“You hungry?” Grayson asked, sliding the key in the ignition.

“Always.”

“Nico’s?”

“As long as we order it to go. My face is a mess.”

When the car didn’t start, I opened my eyes to find Grayson on his cell phone. “Who are you texting?” I asked, wondering which girl he had his eye on now.

“I’m…just letting Mom know I’ll be home late.”

I snorted. “That’s a first.”

With a shrug, he sheepishly slid his phone back into his pocket and started the engine.

As we neared Nico’s diner, my eyes were drawn to the familiar blue-green hue of Scott’s Mustang in the parking lot. With his cap sitting low, Scott leaned against the hood, clearly waiting for someone.

My eyes tapered as I turned to Grayson. “I knew you weren’t messaging your mom.”

Grayson pulled into the space beside Scott and wound down his window. “You guys need to talk.”

Scott’s back straightened when he saw me through the windshield. “Fuck, Gray. You said it was urgent.” He slammed his hand against the roof of his car as he turned away. “She can’t see me like this.”

I jumped out and circled the car, grabbing his arm before he had a chance to leave. “Like what?”

He shook his head as he reluctantly faced me. His eyes remained hidden behind dark sunglasses.

My mouth fell open at the sight of his bruised cheekbone and swollen nose. “Scott…” I cried. “Did your dad do that?”

Ignoring my question, he stepped toward me and grazed my cheek with his thumb. “Have you been crying?”

“It’s nothing.” My problems were minuscule compared to his.

Grayson growled from the car window. "If you're not going to tell me, at least tell *him* what's going on."

Scott ripped off his sunglasses, revealing the extent of his beating. "What happened?"

"You're supposed to protect her from that scumbag teacher," Grayson uttered when I didn't answer straight away.

"Gray, it's okay..." My heart warmed at his overprotectiveness, but it wasn't helping.

"No, it isn't. I thought you'd be safe with Scott, but clearly you're not." Grayson panned his gaze to Scott, assessing his injuries. "Whatever you're into, man, keep her out of it. She's got enough to worry about."

"Lanie..." Scott's face paled. "Did Mr. West—"

"He didn't touch me!" I bit, fighting a fresh batch of tears.

Grayson blew out a lungful of air, clearly frustrated. "Mel..."

"Go home, Grayson," Scott's voice grew low and authoritative. "I'll take it from here."

Grayson's gaze met mine, and I offered him a quick nod. "It's okay."

"Fine." Grayson shot Scott an unspoken threat before reversing his car out of the space and driving away.

Scott eyed the parking lot before opening the passenger door. "We can't talk here. I think my dad has one of his guys following me."

"Why would he do that?"

"Because I told him we broke up, and my guess is, he doesn't believe me."

My chest tightened. "Have we?"

"No," he said with a sigh. "When he found out who you were, he decided I was his ticket into the Bel Air market. If he thinks we've split up, he'll move on. I'll explain more later, but first, you need to tell me what happened today."

"I'm going to fucking kill him." Scott's hands clenched the steering wheel as he pulled into a secluded park we'd often take Riley to on our day dates. The threatening rain clouds must have been keeping the crowds away, because the place was deserted.

"I won't let you lose your scholarship over this. If it gets any worse, I promise I'll go to the police."

Scott checked his mirrors before climbing into the backseat and guiding me after. "I'm so sorry I wasn't there for you. I've been working extra hours at the garage to pay back what I owe my dad, and I let you down in the process."

"You can't exactly show up to Summerhill looking like that, either," I said, lowering my eyes.

He rubbed his jaw. "A few bruises won't keep me away."

I peered up at his battered face, almost unrecognizable except for his brilliant blues that would forever be imprinted into my memory. "I wish you'd let me help you."

He turned his gaze away, hiding the emotion trickling through. "The only way you could help is by staying the hell away from me."

My heart sank.

Scott's head dropped with an enduring sigh. "If only I could stay the hell away from you." His jaw tightened as he lifted his eyes to mine. "I've never met anyone like you, and I have no idea how to make this work."

My fingers crawled over his. "We'll figure it out."

"There's no way I'll get into Stanford, Lanie. I don't know where we can go from here."

"Then I'll go wherever you go."

"And you think your parents will allow that?"

"I don't care," I said, climbing over him until I was straddling his legs. I needed to be closer to his eyes. "I want to be with you."

"When they find out who I am, who my father is...they'll—"

"I don't fucking care." I took Scott's broken face into my palms. "I love you, and nothing they say or do will change the way I feel."

His eyes twinkled as his dimples unfurled. "You love me, huh?"

"At least I have the balls to say it," I said, poking his chest as the first droplets of rain drummed against the roof of the car.

With a deep-chested laugh, he flipped me onto the bench seat. "I fucking love you, too," he said, lowering his lips onto mine.

What started as a sweet and tender kiss soon turned into a feverish wrestle. Our arms and legs entangled as we unfastened our clothes, craving the heat from our yearning bodies.

Scott's hands crept up my skirt and grazed along my panties. "Jesus, Lanie…" he rasped, running his finger over the dampness.

My core pulsed at his touch. "Don't stop."

He hooked onto the edges of my underwear and pulled them over my legs. A giggle escaped my mouth as he threw them onto the front seat and dove, headfirst, under my pleated skirt. When his tongue weaved over my seam, my eyes rolled back in pure pleasure. "Oh, my g—" My words were drowned by liquid fire flooding my body.

As the rain grew heavier and the condensation thicker, I squirmed and shuddered until my mind muted everything except his touch. At that moment, I could believe we were the only two people in existence, and everything was perfect. "That was amazing…" I said huskily as he resurfaced with a satisfied grin.

Scott climbed over me until his hardness pressed against my aching center. "Do you want me to stop?"

"Don't you dare."

With a drunken smile, he eased his way in then quickly jerked away. "Shit…" he muttered, pushing himself upright. "I almost forgot."

"Please tell me you have something," I moaned, not caring at that point. At least Scott had some sense left in him.

His eyes flickered around his car and settled on his glovebox. "C'mon, c'mon, c'mon…" he chanted as he stretched over the front seat to rummage through the contents. "Thank fuck," he uttered, waving a foil packet in the air. "I don't even remember putting it there."

After sliding it on, his hands ran over my body, tugging open my shirt to expose my lacy bra. He lowered his mouth to my breasts and grazed his teeth over the delicate fabric.

"Please, Scott..." My core throbbed, begging for attention.

With a chuckle, Scott yanked the thin material aside and sucked on my breast, making me cry out. As his tongue trailed from my neck to my earlobe, he pushed himself in, and I gasped at the fullness.

His dilated pupils bored into mine. "I can go slower if you need."

"Don't even think about it," I said, rolling my hips into his.

Scott closed his eyes and pressed deeper, increasing the pressure with every stroke. I grasped his biceps as each thrust pushed my problems further and further away until all I saw were his beautiful eyes and the promise of our future together.

Chapter 14

"You want to take Elle to our winter formal?!" I fell back against the lockers with my arms crossed.

With softening eyes, Scott reached out and squeezed my tense shoulders. "No. I want to take *you*, but since my dad thinks we're broken up, he's asked me to take her as a thank you."

"For what?!"

"He said it was for all the babysitting she's been doing lately."

"Wow, your dad's so thoughtful."

"Come on, Lanie. She can use Cara's ticket." He closed the distance between us until I had to tilt my head upward to see him. "If I can endure seeing your parents taking happy snaps of you and Grayson, I think you can tolerate me escorting Elle to the formal." He smiled tightly. "Plus, Dad's already told her, and she's really excited about it."

"I bet," I muttered, looking away.

"She's never been to a formal before. Her school can't afford them."

I narrowed my gaze at him, but his eyes confirmed he wasn't joking. Rolling my tongue around my cheeks, I felt myself caving. "Does she even have a dress?"

"I'm...not sure."

"I guess I can lend her something," I grumbled under my breath.

Scott pulled me into an embrace and kissed the top of my head. "You've got a beautiful heart, Lanie."

"Shhh." I quickly spun my head around. "Someone might hear you."

"You won't be able to hide it forever," he said, tugging a lock of my hair.

I tried not to smile. "But if she tries anything on you, I'll break her."

"You have nothing to worry about. She knows we're still together."

Panic surged through me. "Won't she tell your dad?"

"She's a friend, Lanie. I trust her."

I pushed past the ache in my heart. "Does this mean your dad will call off his minions?"

"I hope so," Scott uttered with a scowl. "I swear I was followed to school again today."

"But it's been weeks since my parents' party."

"I know, but we still need to be careful. He's been trying to infiltrate the Bel Air crowd for years, and if he finds out we're still together, he'll..."

I touched his cheekbone where the purple bruising had faded to yellow. "He won't find out. I'm not risking you getting hurt again."

"I'm not worried about me. I'm worried about Riley."

My blood ran cold. "He'd hurt him?"

"I don't think so, but he'd use him to get to me if it meant more money in his pocket."

"Scott..." I swallowed back tears.

"It'll be okay. In a few weeks, I'll have enough money to start working with this lawyer who specializes in situations like mine."

I closed my eyes to hide my frustration. "Can you *please* just let me pa..."

"I need to be able to handle this, Lanie," he said, taking my hands. "I need to prove that I can look after Riley on my own, and that includes financially."

"Okay." I sighed. "I'm sorry. I'm just so worried about you."

"Don't be. This will all be over soon."

A week later, I was shoved up against Grayson, standing in front of our mantelpiece for the hundredth photo that evening.

Mom clicked her fingers at the photographer. "Okay, now one by the chaise."

Both our mothers fussed around like it was our wedding day, while our dads smoked cigars and drank whiskey in the parlor.

"Mom," I whined. "Our limo will be here soon."

"Your limo can wait."

I glanced at Grayson, and he shrugged. All the photos were supposed to be done before Scott and Elle's arrival, but my mother kept pressing for the perfect picture. Even Grayson's mother was tiring.

Moments later, our butler escorted Scott and Elle inside. Grayson introduced them to everyone, but my parents barely looked their way.

My gaze caught Scott's, and my whole heart lit up. He looked so drop-dead gorgeous in his suit I had to force myself to look away. The pink in his freshly shaven cheeks mirrored the heat in mine until my eyes caught sight of the pretty blonde girl beside him.

Elle stood there, wide-eyed, wearing my dress and standing beside the guy I loved. I hated it. Our butler offered her a soda, and she took slow slips as she wandered around the room, gawking at all the fixtures. Scott's presence drew my gaze, and I found his eyes hadn't left my dress. He clearly liked what he saw, and I couldn't help but smile.

"I'd like one more photo, Melanie," my mother snapped, glaring at me then Scott. She pulled me toward Grayson, making me wince as her grip pinched my arm. "Aren't they a beautiful couple?" she asked, motioning the photographer to start snapping. "Come on, get closer." Once we were uncomfortably close, my mother grinned. "Now kiss."

I glanced up at Grayson with wide eyes, and his jaw tensed. With a deep breath, he leaned down and pressed his mouth to mine, holding it there for what felt like an eternity. It wasn't awful, but it didn't induce the rush I craved since the moment Scott's lips touched mine.

Once we pulled away, I sheepishly lifted my gaze to Scott but found him studying our art collection while sculling the entire contents of his glass.

"This one will do," my mother said to the photographer. "Just add a little more spark to her eyes, will you?"

I grabbed my clutch and followed the others outside and into the waiting limo.

"Well, that was torture," Grayson said once we'd settled inside.

Scott stared out the tinted window at my parents. "Tell me about it."

Elle pulled a champagne bottle from her oversized bag with a huge grin. "Who wants some champagne?!"

"Definitely me." Grayson chuckled.

She proceeded to open the bottle. "Scotty, can you pass me the glasses?"

Scott's eyes struck mine, and my eyebrows rose. *Scotty?*

Instead of waiting for *Scotty* to reach across for the glasses, I did it instead. "Here," I said, holding them out, one by one.

"Thanks for lending me this amazing dress," Elle said, leaning closer to Scott than I was comfortable with. "I've never worn anything like it."

I smiled tightly as I ran my gaze over her outfit. "Want me to run back inside and grab you a clutch?" I should've realized she wouldn't have had anything to match.

Elle clung to her tattered bag like a life preserver. "Oh no, it's fine. I like this one."

"O...kay," I muttered before calling out to the driver. "Let's go."

Once we passed the gates, Scott motioned to Grayson to swap places.

"No problem at all," Grayson said, smiling at Elle as he slid over. He was clearly interested.

While Grayson flirted and Elle giggled, Scott whispered in my ear, "You look amazing, Lanie."

I leaned on his shoulder and closed my eyes, breathing him in. "I know it's just pretend, but I hate seeing you with her."

"Then you know how it feels," he said, finding my hand and threading his fingers through mine.

I was so tired of pretending. "Just one more hurdle until you're mine for the night."

Our limo pulled up in front of our school hall where a white carpet laid, guiding us to our winter formal. Sparkling snowflakes floated above the entrance with hanging wreaths entangled with fairy lights, all alluding to the winter wonderland inside.

Grayson took my hand and led me to the official photo station by the ice-sculpted Christmas tree. I glanced back at Scott, whose arm was linked with Elle's, and frowned. I'd promised my mother an official winter formal photo, and this was the price: watching Scott get his taken with Elle.

A shiver ran over my body as I waited in line, not from the cold, but from the prying eyes of the teacher patroling the entrance. Grayson maneuvered his body to shield me from Mr. West's view, but it was too late. His eyes struck mine, and I froze.

Grayson nudged me forward. "It's our turn."

Mr. West observed our poses then panned his gaze to Scott waiting next in line with Elle. By the smirk on his face, he must've assumed we'd broken up.

As soon as our picture was taken, Grayson quickly steered me into the hall. Whether he was protecting me from Mr. West or saving me from witnessing Scott place his arm around Elle for the photo, I didn't know, but I appreciated it.

"Thank you," I said to Grayson before panning my gaze around the hall.

The winter formal decorations were incredible. Falling snow, Christmas trees, mistletoe, giant presents, and a DJ dressed up as Santa Claus mixing classic songs with Christmas carols. I wasn't surprised. Not a cent was spared for Summerhill events.

"Oh…my…god." Elle appeared beside me, mouth hanging open as she absorbed the room.

Grayson tugged her hand. "Let's go get a drink, and I'll introduce you to a few people."

Exhaling in relief, I watched Grayson disappear into the

crowd with Elle. As much as I wanted to dislike her, she was so naively sweet even I felt warmth toward her.

Scott's breath on my neck sent tingles through my body. "Wanna dance?"

I melted into him. "That's one of the things I want to do with you tonight."

With a soft chuckle, Scott led me onto the packed dance floor. "There'll be plenty of time for that."

"But I've barely seen you outside of school, and I want to make the most of it."

"We have the entire Christmas break to make up for lost time."

"But don't you have to work?"

"The garage is closing for the holidays. I have the next two weeks off."

Fireworks exploded through my heart. "Oh my god." I lifted my arms around his neck while he encircled my waist, leaning his head down to mine. "It's a Christmas miracle."

Scott's smile grew wide and adorable. "You're my miracle, Lanie."

I ran my hand over his smooth jawline before pulling his lips down to mine. I'd never been happier.

Most of our time was spent on the dance floor, lost in the crowd, where I didn't have to worry about Mr. West. Occasionally we were joined by Grayson and Elle, but the only person I wanted to see was standing in front of me.

Toward the end of the night, I scanned the room for Elle, but she was nowhere to be seen.

I tapped Grayson's shoulder while he danced with a few overly eager girls. "Where's Elle?"

"She seems keener to socialize than dance, so I left her to it."

Lines formed on Scott's brow as he searched the room.

"She's probably gone to the restroom," I said, knowing Scott felt responsible for her. "I'll go check."

I made my way to the ladies' restroom and peered under stalls, but Elle wasn't there. Thinking she may have decided to give herself a tour of the school, I wandered the deserted hallways until I heard voices up ahead.

"Please," a female voice whimpered. "I'll do anything..."

As I peeked around the corner, I found Elle backed up against a wall with Mr. West in front of her.

I darted forward. "Elle! What's going on? Are you okay?"

She glanced at me with eyes full of fear, then back at the teacher. "I'm fine, Lanie."

"I caught your ex-boyfriend's date dealing drugs in the hallway."

My eyes shot to Elle. "What's he talking about?"

Mr. West smirked. "Imagine what's going to happen when the principal finds out Scott brought a drug dealer onto school grounds."

"Elle?!" I gasped. "Is it true?"

Elle wept as she nodded.

Fear laced every breath as I watched her cower before him. "What will it take to make this go away?" A sentence I'd only heard my father speak.

Mr. West laughed. "You think you can buy your way out of anything, don't you?"

"Because I can." My father taught me everyone had a price.

"Very well." He turned to Elle. "You're lucky you have rich friends."

Elle ran toward me, tears streaming down her cheeks as she hugged me.

"Find Scott," I whispered into her hair before pushing her away.

Once she'd disappeared around the corner, Mr. West sauntered toward me. "The problem is...I don't want your money."

When he invaded my personal space, I shoved his chest hard, and he stumbled backwards. "You make me sick."

With a snarl, he flew forward, grabbing my arms as he pushed me against the wall. "I always imagined you'd like it rough," he uttered, pressing his prickly cheek to mine.

I tried to struggle and call out, but he clamped his hand over my mouth. "I know you want this."

Tears filled my eyes as he hitched up my dress before all the air was knocked out of me. Gasping, I spun around to find Scott sprawled on the floor with Mr. West underneath him.

"Don't you fucking touch her, you piece of shit!" Scott's fist crunched into his face over and over while I stood there frozen.

Mr. West's cries brought teachers running. "Call the police," one yelled while the others grabbed Scott and pulled him away.

"Let go of him!" I yelled. "He was protecting me."

Elle stood to the side, doing nothing, saying nothing.

Mr. West rose from the floor, wiping blood from his nose. "I caught Scott's date dealing drugs, and then he attacked me."

Mr. Owens, our chemistry teacher, turned to Scott. "Is this true?"

"What?! No!" Scott shook his head vigorously. "He was attacking Melanie!"

Mr. Owens frowned. "That's a serious allegation."

"It's true," I said, wrapping my arms around my waist. "He assaulted me."

Mr. West growled. "You're going to believe this stuck-up princess and drop-beat kid over me? I've been teaching here for twelve years." He pointed at Elle. "Check her bag, then you'll know."

Elle paled as the teacher grabbed her bag and rummaged through the contents. When he pulled out a bag of pills, my stomach plummeted.

"What the fuck, Elle?!" Scott glared at her.

Her lower lip trembled. "Your dad said he'd give me $100 if I sold..."

"No..." he cried, covering his face with his bloodied hands. "How could you be so stupid?"

"I...I'm sorry, but I really needed the money."

Mr. Owens opened the door to an empty classroom. "You three wait in here while I call your parents. Mr. West, follow me."

Once the door closed, Elle huddled in the corner of the room while I wrapped my arms around Scott. "I'll tell them everything. They'll understand why you hit him."

"It won't matter," he said, unmoving.

"But surely when they find out what he did, what he's been doing to me..."

"Lanie…it's not just that. The police are coming. When they find the drugs, they're going to arrest my dad."

Fear washed over me. Scott closed his eyes as I brought his forehead down to mine. "It'll be okay. When my father finds out you were protecting me, he'll make sure you and Riley are taken care of. He has money and power and a whole team of lawyers… he'll make it okay." I wasn't sure if I was trying to convince him or myself.

With a kiss to my forehead, Scott pulled me into his arms and held me until the principal walked in.

"Melanie, your parents would like a word in private. Scott, you and your friend are required in my office."

"It'll be okay," I whispered again, giving him one last embrace.

His mouth pricked up at the sides, but his eyes were dead. He attempted to speak, but nothing came out. Instead, he turned and followed Elle out the door.

Seconds later, my parents walked in.

"Are we going to the police station?" I asked, picking up my handbag.

"Good god, no." Mom shook her head in disgust. "The situation has been sorted. Now, let's go home."

"What do you mean *sorted*? I want to press charges against Mr. West. They need to know—"

"No one needs to know about this, Melanie!" she snapped. "We don't need this sort of attention on our family."

"But Mr. West—"

"Will no longer be teaching at this school…happy?"

"Happy?! He attacked me, Mom! I'm not happy! I'm terrified!" I turned to my dad, but he looked away, void of emotion.

"Oh, stop being so melodramatic," she said, grabbing my arm. "Let's go."

I shook her off. "Not until I know if Scott's okay."

My father spun around. "That boy is none of our concern!"

"He was trying to protect me!" I latched onto his arm. "Dad, please…we have to help him."

"And why would we help the son of a known criminal?"

I froze the moment I saw my mother's lips purse.

"We've had a private investigator trailing him for weeks," she said, enjoying my reaction. "We know *everything* about him."

"Why..." I gasped. "Why would you do that?"

"You're the sole heir to our fortune. Who you're *associating* with is our business."

"Then you know..."

"That you're cheating on Grayson? Of course we do." Mom stepped between me and my father. "How dare you jeopardize everything we've worked for, for some drug-dealing trailer trash."

"Scott's not a drug dealer!"

"Just because his date was holding them doesn't mean he had nothing to do with it. And you were *this* close to getting caught up in it. You're lucky we turned up before the police did and convinced them to overlook your involvement."

My mouth parted, but I couldn't draw a breath. "Scott is nothing like his father. He's amazingly smart and driven, and he's working so hard to give himself and his brother a better life than the one they were dealt. He has so much potential, but if Summerhill expels him, he won't get a college scholarship, and if they arrest his dad, his little brother will grow up in a foster home. This will ruin everything." For a slim moment, my father's stern expression faltered. "He can't afford a lawyer, Dad...but *we* can. Please. He protected me tonight. We need to protect him too. I'll do anything."

My parents exchanged a look I couldn't decipher before my father turned to me. "I'll make a call on one condition."

Shit.

"Your ridiculous infatuation with this boy ends now. Your future is with Grayson."

Chapter 15

I needed to ride it out. After Mom confiscated my cell phone and laptop and grounded me to the confines of our property, I had no choice but to wait. Although I'd promised to end my relationship with Scott, it was only temporary. Once we were in college, away from my controlling parents, we'd be together whether they approved or not.

My father had called his lawyers the night of the formal, and a few days later, he told me the matter was sorted and refused to discuss it any further.

Without access to my phone, I had to wait until Christmas before I could speak to anyone other than my parents. We were due to have dinner with the Harlows, so it was the perfect opportunity to find out through Grayson if Scott was okay.

The Harlows usually spent the Christmas holiday in The Hamptons, but Grayson's father had recently acquired a new business, so they had to postpone their trip a few days. I knew Grayson would've been disappointed, but I was ecstatic. I didn't have to endure another dinner with my parents in an uneasy silence.

Mom scowled as I descended the staircase. "I told you to wear stilettos with that dress. Your legs look ghastly in low heels."

"But they hurt my feet, and this dress is already giving me hives."

"There is no beauty without pain, my dear." Her hand flapped toward the stairs. "Go change."

With a puff of air, I turned and marched back up the stairs. If the sky-high stilettos meant I'd get my freedom back. I'd wear the fucking stilettos.

The scarlet material felt like sandpaper against my skin as we approached the front door of the Harlows' mansion. As I shifted uncomfortably, trying to relieve pressure by switching from foot to foot, my gaze caught sight of a shiny new convertible parked in the driveway. Grayson evidently got his new wheels.

Their butler welcomed us into their home and escorted my parents to the drawing room, while I scampered off to the pool house to find Grayson.

"Wow, nice dress," he said, barely glancing up from his video game. "You seeing Scott later?"

I slumped into the chair next to him and kicked off my shoes. "No, I'm grounded. How's he doing?"

"I don't know," he said, frowning when he lost the game. "I haven't heard from either of you since you all ditched me at the formal." He threw the controller on the coffee table and turned to me. "You feeling any better? Your mom told my mom you went home sick."

"What? That's not what happened…" Fear bubbled up inside. "You mean you haven't spoken to Scott since the formal?"

"No, I figured you'd shared your germs with him, hence the radio silence."

My chest constricted. "Where's your phone?" I asked, frantically searching the table and couch. "I need to call him."

"It's Christmas Eve. He's probably busy with his family." He shuffled his phone from his pocket and passed it over. "Did you lose your cell?"

Ignoring him, I stood up and dialed Scott's number. It rang and rang as I paced the floor.

"I told you he was busy," Grayson muttered on my second attempt.

On my third try, Grayson rose from the chair and approached me. The V between his eyebrows deepened with each step. "What's going on? You're making me nervous."

"Something's not right, Gray," I muttered, mentally trying to rationalize why I couldn't get through.

"Look, I don't know what's going on, but if he's into something bad…then maybe…" He grimaced. "Maybe you should stay away."

"You know him, Grayson. He's a good guy." I swallowed the lump in my throat. "But his father is a drug dealer, and I'm pretty sure he got arrested the night of our school dance."

Grayson's eyes grew large. "Holy shit."

"I convinced my dad to get his lawyers to help Scott and his brother, but he won't tell me any more. And I haven't been able to contact him because my fucking mother confiscated my fucking phone."

"Your dad is helping Scott?" he asked, rightfully suspicious.

"It's a long story." I swiped his car keys off the table. "I'll fill you in once we're on the road."

"We can't go now. Dinner will be ready soon."

"I need to know if he's okay, then we'll come straight back. Just tell our parents you're taking your *girlfriend* for a spin in your new car." I dangled the keys in front of him.

Grayson's eyes lit up as he grabbed them out of my hand. "That'll work. Let's go."

I explained everything to Grayson on the way to Scott's house, including my parents' ridiculous idea that I was cheating on him with Scott. He thanked me for not coming clean, but at the same time, he was disgusted by my parents' ultimatum.

Once we turned into Scott's empty driveway, I burst out of the car and sprinted to the front door on my bare feet, dodging broken glass, cigarette butts, and bottle caps. Ripping away the *Do Not Enter* tape, I banged on the door. When no one answered, I wandered to the window and peered through, praying for movement.

"They're gone."

I spun around to find Elle standing in the middle of Scott's barren front yard.

"What do you mean they're gone?" I glared at the girl who had set the ball rolling.

Her eyes dropped to the dust piling around her well-worn shoes. "The police raided their house after the formal and arrested Kurt."

"Where are Scott and Riley?"

"I…I don't know." She lifted her glistening gaze. "After they got back from the station, they packed up all their things and left."

"Like…to a hotel or something?"

"I'm sorry, Lanie…but I don't think he's coming back."

I stared at her. She was obviously mistaken.

Grayson appeared next to me and placed his hand on my shoulder. "Maybe he's just waiting until things settle down."

Elle shook her head. "My mom called the police station because she was worried about Riley's welfare. Apparently, some private arrangement was made, but they weren't allowed to disclose any details."

I hunched over like she'd punched me in the stomach. I would've fallen to the ground if Grayson hadn't been there to catch me.

"I think we should go," Grayson said, nodding to Elle as he guided me back to the car.

"He wouldn't…just leave," I stammered as the car took off down the road.

"Mel, his dad just got arrested. I'm sure he'll be back once the dust settles."

The pain in my chest eased. Grayson had a good point. "I'm overreacting again, aren't I?"

"No…" He sighed, knowing my mother regularly accused me of overreacting. "But I think a lot is going on here that you don't know about." His hands tightened on the steering wheel. "How long is your mom keeping your phone hostage for?"

"If I'm on my best behavior tonight, I should have it back tomorrow."

"Okay." He breathed. "Let's go home, have dinner, and pretend everything is okay. Then tomorrow, when you get your cell back, call him again. It's Christmas. Wherever he is, I'm sure he'll take your call."

"And if he doesn't?"

"Ask your dad again. I'm assuming this private arrangement involved his lawyers." Grayson flashed me a comforting smile.

"Just wait until he's on his fifth whiskey. That's what I do when I have to talk to my dad."

With a strained laugh, I sank back into the seat as we drove home, preparing myself to be the best daughter/dream daughter-in-law I could be. I needed my cell phone back.

"What is this?" I asked, staring at a brand-new cell phone in a sparkling red case, nestled in a Christmas gift box.

"You were due for an upgrade, so we got you that new cell phone everyone is raving about. Grayson has the same one, I believe."

I turned it on, and my heart hammered as the little apple icon loaded onto the screen. With a trembling finger, I scanned the display until I found my contacts and tapped into them. The list was never a long one, but it housed the details of the most important people in my life.

My eyes darted over the few names that appeared. Mom, Dad, Grayson… "Where are the rest of my contacts?"

Mom scoffed as she turned to my father. "Typical. She's more concerned about her social life than her gift."

"The essential ones are still there," Dad muttered, turning back to the Christmas tree to pull out another gift for my mother.

My stomach plummeted as I lifted my panicked gaze. "Please tell me I have the same phone number."

Mom and Dad threw each other a sideways glance, answering my question.

"How could you?!" I yelled, rising to my feet.

"It's just a number, Melanie," my father snapped as he matched my stance. "Maybe you'll be more careful with this one."

"What's that supposed to mean?"

"We are in the business of information. Legal or not, phones are tapped, emails are hacked, and messages are intercepted." He stepped closer until he towered over me. "If your *relationship* with this drug dealer's son gets leaked to a competitor, they'd use it against our family. Do you understand?"

Tears burned my eyes. "I…I'm sorry, but I just need to know if he's okay."

"He's fine."

"Dad, please…" I slipped my fingers over his. "You said you'd look after—"

"And I did!" He pulled his hand away and turned to the fireplace. "Now, no more questions."

"You can't do this!" I cried, demanding his attention. "Dad, please! I love him!"

Mom chuckled. "Well, he clearly doesn't love you as much as your father's checkbook."

My blood ran cold as my gaze panned between them. "What are you talking about?"

"We offered him an opportunity, and he took it," she said, barely hiding her smirk. "He's much smarter than we thought."

"He wouldn't do that," I cried, but my heart faltered. *Maybe he would.* I gritted my teeth as I stared them down. "How could you?!"

"How could I what? Look after your future? Our *family's* future?"

Rage rippled through my body. "Fuck this family!"

I heard the slap of my mother's palm against my cheek before I felt the pain.

"You ungrateful little bitch," she spat. "Go to your room."

The knot in my stomach pulled so tight I could almost hear the fibers breaking. "With pleasure."

As soon as my bedroom door slammed shut behind me, I dialed Grayson's number.

"Hello?" My best friend's voice instantly calmed my soul.

"I need you to send me Scott's number, and Cara's too, if you have it."

"Merry Christmas to you too, Mel." He chuckled. "Why are you calling on a different number? Did you buy a burner phone or something?"

"My super thoughtful parents bought me a new phone for Christmas and deleted all my contacts."

"Geez…well, I don't have Cara's, but I'll send Scott's over now."

"Thanks." I exhaled in relief. "And Merry Christmas, Gray." I hung up before he had a chance to respond and anxiously waited for Scott's details to come through.

When my phone buzzed, I dialed the number and waited.

This number has been disconnected.

The words doused my body in ice. I glared at my phone and furiously dialed again.

This number has been disconnected.

FUCK!

Frantically trying to figure out another way of contacting him, I opened my laptop—which had reappeared in my bedroom—to email him. However, hope quickly faded when I realized I only had his Summerhill email address, and my email bounced back immediately.

After about a thousand more attempts to call him, I collapsed onto my bed in tears. Had he really taken my parents' money and left? Without even saying goodbye? It didn't feel right. This wasn't the Scott I knew. This wasn't the Scott who loved me and wanted a future with me…*was it?*

The one person who'd understand this heartache was Cara, but her number was gone too. My parents had eliminated her from my life, just like they had Scott, leaving only Grayson—the only person they'd ever approve of.

"He's not coming back." My raspy voice barely reached a whisper after hours of crying through the night. "My dad…he…he paid him off."

The line was silent for a moment. "Fuck, Mel," Grayson said. "I'm sorry. I really thought…"

"He was better than that? Clearly we were both wrong."

"Maybe he was more involved in his dad's *business* than you thought?"

"No. There's no way. He promised he wasn't."

"What else did he promise you?"

My lower lip trembled. "What are you trying to say?"

"Maybe it's better this way…before it got too serious."

"Too serious?" I laughed through my tears. "I loved him, Gray."

"I know, but do you really think it would've worked out? Our parents are relentless. They never would've allowed you to stay together." There was a pause before he continued. "Maybe once we're in college, we'll be free to choose who we go out with, but until then, we should be having a little fun, not starting any long-term commitments."

My irritation surfaced. "I wasn't planning to meet anyone like him. I wasn't even looking for a boyfriend. You know that."

"Yeah, I know…but you'll get through this, Mel. You'll be okay."

I squeezed my eyes shut. He didn't understand. How could he? "I'm gonna go, Gray."

"Look, I know I'm not Cara, but I'm here if you ever need to talk, okay?"

"I know."

"Look after yourself, Warren."

For the remainder of the holidays, I did exactly the opposite. I barely left my bed because sleep was the only relief from the heartache. The blankets were my cave, and I never wanted to come out. Every time I attempted to face the day, grief overwhelmed my soul and nausea sent me running for the bathroom. I'd had a weak stomach since I was a kid, and every time something overwhelmed me, I'd vomit. Grayson thought it was hilarious, but this wasn't funny at all.

After losing the contents of my stomach for the second time that day, I stared into the mirror at the unrecognizable girl gaping back at me. Her face was gaunt, dark circles surrounded her lifeless eyes, and all her color was gone, except for her flushed cheeks and chafed nose. I'd lost my best friend and boyfriend in the space of a few weeks, and I was on the verge of losing myself.

"I've had enough of this nonsense," my mother barked as she marched in my room and drew the curtains.

Sunshine blasted through the windows, offending my eyes. "Just leave me alone," I cried, smothering my face with a pillow.

"You've been sulking in this bedroom for two weeks now. It's time to get on with things. Not only does school start back tomorrow, but we also have the Harlows coming over for dinner tonight to celebrate our children's early acceptance into Stanford. I won't have them see you like this. It's pathetic."

I gazed over at my desk where I'd left a couple of envelopes to gather dust, but they were now gone. My parents obviously thought it was okay to open my mail, because I had no idea about Stanford, but then, I didn't care.

"I'm not well enough," I murmured, pulling up the bedsheets.

"Is it cramps? Because I can give you something for that."

"I've had enough of your pills, Mom." She had an artificial cure for everything, but nothing could ease this pain.

"Then suffer in silence. I want you downstairs in two hours, looking your best." She examined my pale face. "So you better start now."

I wasn't lying. I felt terrible. I lay there for the next hour, wondering if it was my period, but that wasn't due until…fuck. It was due at Christmas! That was almost two weeks ago! Had all the stress and despair screwed with my timeline? I've heard about it happening but never experienced it, but I'd also never had my heart broken before. Anxiety consumed me as I counted back the weeks since Scott and I had sex.

Launching from my bed, I flew into my bathroom and rummaged through the drawers until I found the spare pregnancy test Cara had left behind. My hands shook as I slipped it out. It wasn't possible…surely.

After peeing on the little stick, I left it on the counter and set the timer on my phone.

"Mel?" Grayson's voice sounded from my bedroom.

My heart leaped. He was early. I shoved the test back in the drawer and met Grayson outside my bathroom. "Hey!" My voice was unnaturally high.

"Hey…" Grayson said, trying to read my face. "You okay?"

I glanced back into the bathroom with a wince.

"Ignore that," he continued. "That was a stupid question. Of course you're not okay."

Grayson had been amazingly supportive. He called me from the Hamptons at least once a day to check in and tried his hardest to pull me out of this funk with little success.

I pressed my lips together as my eyes stung.

"Hey, please don't cry. I hate it when you cry."

My body vibrated with a sob as he put his arm around me. "You must think I'm pathetic."

"No…I don't. I think you're heartbroken."

"How could he just leave like that?" The question was set to repeat every day since Scott disappeared without a word.

"I don't know. I'm just as clueless." He loosened his embrace and held me at arm's length. "I considered him a friend, and to just up and leave like that…" He shook his head. "To leave *you* like that…it's unforgivable."

My phone's timer sang from the bathroom, reminding me of another issue entirely—one I didn't want to burden Grayson with just yet.

Grayson frowned. "What's that?"

"I, um…have a treatment in my hair. I better go wash it out."

He looked quizzically at my bone-dry hair and shrugged. "I'll wait for you downstairs. But don't take too long. I can't handle the four of them on my own."

The side of my mouth tugged upward. "I'll be there soon."

When Grayson left, my heart pounded against my rib cage as I returned to the bathroom to learn my fate. With a silent prayer, I closed my eyes, opened the drawer, and fished out the stick of doom. I lifted my gaze to my reflection, not daring to look down. "How much have you fucked up this time, Melanie?" I swallowed the bile creeping up my throat and dropped my gaze to another punch in the gut. My parents would be so proud.

I slid into the chair beside Grayson at the long mahogany table in our formal dining room.

Once the first course was served, my father lifted his glass. "To new beginnings."

The champagne caught in my throat as a laugh erupted from my mouth. Everyone turned to me as I eased the crystal back onto the table. I probably shouldn't have been drinking anyway.

"Is something funny, Melanie?" my mother asked, glancing anxiously at our dinner guests.

My smile grew big and tight. "Oh nothing, I'm just excited about...life, I guess."

Mom tapered her gaze. "Someone's spirits have picked up, I see."

"Glad to see you're up and about," Caroline said, smiling at me. "The flu is a terrible thing, isn't it?"

I turned to my mother. The liar. "It's the worst."

"So, Melanie," she continued. "Have you decided if you'll pledge? Your mother and I have the best memories from that house."

"Oh, I'm not sure they'll want me." I filled my mouth with soup, hoping they'd do the same.

"You're a legacy," my mother blurted. "Of course they'll want you."

"We'll see." I couldn't imagine a sorority wanting a heavily pregnant freshman in their midst.

"Grayson will be pledging, of course." William's chest puffed out. "Much of our business has come from fellow Stanford alumni. Adam is already making the right connections."

The lentil soup churned in my stomach. "Excuse me, I...I just can't stomach this right now." The food or the conversation.

Caroline's eyes softened as I stood up. "You are looking pale," she said, turning to her son. "Grayson, help Melanie back to bed. We can't have her missing school tomorrow."

My mother cleared her throat, undoubtedly annoyed. "Yes, go rest, Melanie. I'll have some supper brought up to you later."

"Thank you," I said, knowing it would never come.

Grayson followed me up the stairs and into my bedroom, lifting my blankets as I crawled under them. The bed lowered as he leaned over to tuck me in.

"Can you stay up here for a bit?" I asked, not wanting to be alone with my thoughts.

Grayson eased back onto a mountain of unnecessary pillows. "I'll stay as long as you need me too."

I nuzzled into his side and closed my eyes, breathing in his scent, which was as familiar to me as home. "I don't know what I'd do without you."

His chest rose and fell. Always constant. Always predictable. Always safe. "I'm not going anywhere. I promise."

My bed and stomach were empty when I woke later that night, but my mind was full of anguish. I tossed and turned until I gave up on sleep altogether and ventured downstairs to the kitchen to find some food. Surely there were leftovers from my mother's elaborate spread to impress the Harlows.

The light of the refrigerator lit up the dark room as I rummaged through the contents. Settling on the only food warranted in my situation, I grabbed the tub of ice cream, tossed it on the kitchen counter, and fetched a spoon from the drawer.

"You're going to get fat."

The spoon dropped from my hand and clattered onto the floor. "I thought everyone was in bed," I said, eyeing my mother as I rescued the spoon and dropped it into the sink.

"Clearly," she muttered, taking a sip of scotch as she watched me return the ice cream to the fridge. "You need to make better choices."

"I was only going to eat a little bi—"

Her hand slammed down onto the kitchen counter, along with my positive pregnancy test, and all the blood drained from my face. I couldn't form a word, let alone an excuse.

"You stupid *stupid* girl. Is this why you're so desperate to see that boy again?"

"N...no." I shook my head vigorously. "I had no idea until today."

"Is it his?"

"Yes."

"Does anyone else know about this?"

"No…no one."

"Well, keep it that way." The entire contents of her glass slid down her throat. "I'll book you into a discreet clinic first thing Monday."

"I'm not making any decisions until I've spoken to Scott," I said, panicky.

Mom rolled her eyes. "He's not coming back, Melanie."

"He will…" My voice wavered. "If he knew—"

"You're so naïve! Can't you see he was using you?"

"He wasn't! He loved me."

"He loved what you could do for him. Just like everyone else you'll meet in your lifetime. They'll either want your money or your body, and that boy won the jackpot with you."

Her words stung. "He's not like that."

"Then how was it so easy to convince him to leave?"

That exact question had haunted me for weeks. I wanted to believe he was biding his time before returning, but with no contact, not even a letter or a message, I was skeptical. If you loved someone, wouldn't you fight for them? Wouldn't you do whatever it took to be with them? Maybe my mother was right. Maybe his feelings weren't as deep as mine. Maybe he had traded them in for a better life.

"Are you going to risk everything we've worked for? For some fairy-tale notion that he'll return someday? What could he possibly offer you? Life in a trailer park?" She placed her empty glass on the counter and stepped closer. "You're an heiress, Melanie. You'll never be like him. The way I see it, you have two choices: abort this baby…or convince everyone it's Grayson's."

I sucked in my breath. "But Grayson and I…we…" I paused, needing to figure out a way to protect Grayson. "We haven't slept together yet."

Mom pursed her lips. "Well, your eighteenth birthday is next week. We'll throw you a big party, get everyone drunk, and the rest is up to you. We'll slip something into his drink if we have to."

"I can't do that to him."

"Melanie, this is your opportunity to push all of our plans forward. Grayson is an honorable man. If he believes this child is his, he'll look after you." She took my hands into hers as her eyes lit up. "Once you marry, we'll finally be able to unite Warren Media with Harlow Corp. and become the most powerful media company in America, if not the world. It's a little earlier than expected, but it's nothing we can't handle."

The noise in my head amplified. Everything my parents wanted was dependent on my decision. As much as I despised them, I was also desperate for their love and approval.

My mother lowered her eyes. "We weren't blessed with a son, so one day, the responsibility of this company will fall on your shoulders. And when that time comes, you'll need a capable man to run the show. Grayson is perfect for you."

"But I want to marry for love...not because it's a good business decision."

Her gaze hardened. "As an heiress, you don't have that luxury, and with an illegitimate child, your options will be slim. No one of any worth will want you after this." She let go of my hands. "I'd hate to think about how your father will handle the news. After all his hard work, I doubt his heart will take it."

Tears welled in my eyes as I recalled my father's heart attack a few years prior. "Please don't tell him yet. I need time to think."

"Well, we need to move swiftly," she said, spinning on her heel. "You have until morning." And with that, she was gone.

This number has been disconnected.

This number has been disconnected.

This number has been disconnected.

It was the definition of insanity, but I kept trying, praying to hear Scott's voice.

This number has been disconnected.

I thumped the cell phone into my pillow, over and over, until I crumbled on top of it in tears. He wasn't coming back. I knew it deep within my soul. Whatever arrangement was made, it was worth more to him than our relationship, and it crushed me. My heart would never recover.

Hours after my sobs had subsided, I endeavored to rationalize my thoughts and process my options.

If I terminated the pregnancy, the memory of the love Scott and I shared would die along with it. My life would continue as though we had never met. I'd go to college, marry a boy my parents approved of, and settle for a loveless life. Grayson would eventually meet the girl of his dreams and drift away, leaving me desperately alone.

If I kept the baby and decided to raise it by myself, the humiliation would be too much for my parents to bear. They'd send me away—if not disown me—and then I'd have nothing. No college degree, no security, and no one to share the responsibility. Grayson wouldn't hang around for long. He'd have the whole world waiting for him.

The final option made my skin crawl, stomach churn, and head spin. What if the baby *was* Grayson's? He, or she, would have an incredible father, doting grandparents, and opportunities many only dreamed of. Our company would expand and thrive, my father could retire and focus on his health, and my parents would finally be proud of me. My friendship with Grayson could eventually grow into love. Maybe not what I had with Scott, but we could get close. All I had to do was sell my soul to the devil.

But what worth was a soul when you were already in hell?

The next morning brought something unexpected. Complete numbness. There were no tears, no heartache, nothing. It was like my brain had switched frequencies, and I could finally think clearly. I absolved my parents of any wrongdoing and shifted the blame onto Scott. *He* was the one responsible for my situation. *He* was the one who ruined my heart. It was *him.* And from that day forward, I was determined to make him a mere blip on my radar.

Welcoming my new state of existence, I climbed out of bed and proceeded to dress for school. An hour later, Grayson's horn blasted outside, and my heart leaped. I raced downstairs, not wanting to keep him waiting, but paused in front of the hallway mirror. I had to look perfect.

My freshly pressed uniform fit my body flawlessly, the skirt had been taken up an inch as per my mother's request, and my dead-straight hair hovered exactly one inch above my shoulders. Foundation disguised my blotchy face, eyeshadow highlighted my unusually pale blue eyes, and mascara accentuated my long lashes. Only one feature remained untouched. As I dipped my hand into my bag to find my lipstick, my mother materialized behind me, breakfast smoothie in hand.

"So..." She waited until my gaze met hers in the reflection. "Have you made a decision?"

With an almost unnoticeable tremor, I coated my lips in the brilliant red hue as I pushed away the last thread of my morality. "Looks like we have a party to plan," I said without a second glance in her direction. Before she could process my words or show her elation, I sauntered through the front door and slammed it shut behind me, preparing my most dazzling smile for the future father of my unborn child.

Chapter 16

Present Day

My first real job. I couldn't believe it. It should've been waiting tables at Nico's Diner at sixteen, like every other teenage kid, or suffering unpaid internships like my sorority sisters, but instead, I had wasted all those years being a spoiled brat.

Working for *Maude* magazine didn't count. I hadn't done anything of substance there, and everyone knew it. The only skills I had—thanks to my mother—were planning parties and buying artwork, which surprisingly made me the perfect fit for AG Galleries.

With a glance up and down the street, I lowered my gaze and stepped through the doors of the little art gallery in SoHo. I was so grateful for the opportunity, but the shame of needing to work ran deep. My mother's disapproval was ingrained in my soul.

A chime filled the room, announcing my arrival.

"Lanie!" a lady called from the mezzanine floor above.

I peered up to the immaculately dressed, caramel-skinned woman swaying her hips as she sauntered down the stairs. I recognized her instantly from my online interview. "Faye, hi!"

"Welcome to AG Galleries. We're so excited to have you onboard," she said as she moved closer. "Your reputation in the art community speaks for itself."

Heat rose into my cheeks as I shook her hand. "I don't know about that."

"You've had the power to make or break artists in the past. Josie is the perfect example."

"I'm not exactly in the same position I was back then," I said, hoping she wasn't just after my social media following. "I hope that doesn't affect things."

"I didn't hire you for your social status. I hired you for your incredible eye. You have remarkable taste, and I plan to abuse it." Her eyes twinkled playfully as she motioned for the stairs. "Let's get you started. I already have a pile of clients awaiting your expertise."

"Great," I uttered, mustering up a smile. I'd never felt so nervous.

The staircase rose to a mezzanine level overlooking the gallery. I peeked over the edge as I followed Faye down the corridor and grinned. It was a beautiful outlook. Each office donned a glass wall, filling the space with natural light and a panoramic view of the latest art installation below. Who needed windows?

"This will be your office," Faye said, ushering me into the stark-white room at the end of the hall. "Mine is at the other end, next to the kitchen and meeting room, and Adrian is right next door. We're a small team, but we're efficient. Everyone has their expertise, but we all pitch in and help when required."

"That sounds great," I said, panning my gaze around the room. It was equipped with an ergonomic chair, a long slim desk, a laptop, cell phone, and a small meeting table off to one side.

"We have casual staff for events, of course," Faye continued. "But I'll get Adrian to run through those details once he gets back from his client meeting." She edged back to the door. "We haven't been the most profitable gallery under the AG Galleries umbrella, but we're finally getting somewhere. After Josie's exhibition, we've had numerous high-flyers come back for more. They want something fresh. Something they haven't seen before. And now we finally have the manpower." She stopped. "Correction. *Wo*-manpower to find what they're looking for. Alfie Gibbs was on the verge of cutting us loose before Josie contacted us, and your efforts to promote her show...well, they saved our ass."

"I...I had no idea," I said, surprised by her admission.

Faye's smile tightened. "Alfie's son will be keeping a close eye on us over the next few months, so we have a lot of work to do."

My gaze shot to hers. "Do you mean Nicholas Gibbs?"

"Oh, you know him?"

I wished I didn't. "We...um...went to college together."

"Wonderful." Her face brightened. "Then he might go easy on us."

I lowered my face to hide my grimace. "Yeah, hopefully."

"Well, I'll leave you to settle in," she said, fluttering her hand around the room. "Feel free to decorate however you like."

"Thanks," I called out, already conjuring up possibilities, but my shoulders lowered when I remembered I had no money to fund my desired décor.

As disappointment rolled over me, I slumped into my desk chair and picked up my employment contract. On paper, the job was perfect. The role required me to organize exhibitions and sell artwork, along with private home and business consultations to assess their artwork needs. It was something I'd been doing for years, except now I was going to get paid for it.

Although the salary wasn't great, I'd receive a commission from every piece of artwork sold, so I was going to have to work extra hard to save for a place of my own. Josie refused to charge me rent, but I insisted on paying the bills, meaning there wasn't much left over. I'd given up my frivolous life to gain something more substantial. Independence. And I was determined to succeed.

A passing figure captured my attention, and I spun my head to the stylish man posing in the doorway.

"Melanie Warren," Adrian said, waltzing in with more swagger than Faye. "We meet again."

I smiled at the curator of Josie's exhibition. "I go by Lanie now."

His eyebrows rose. "Oh, I see. Keeping a low profile, are we?"

"Something like that."

A snigger emitted from his mouth. "I doubt that will work."

"Why not?"

"Because you're too damn gorgeous, that's why," he said, resting his hand on his hip. "You may not be as recognizable here on the East Coast, but people are going to notice you. *Men* are going to notice you. Hell, you're going to steal all the eye candy."

"Pardon?" I asked, perplexed about his meaning.

"Our clients? The men who come in here…" He fanned his hand over his face. "Even the queer ones are going to want to work with you."

"I highly doubt that," I said, running my gaze over the most impeccably put-together man I'd ever met. "But you're welcome to screen the clients before we delegate."

"Perfect!" He dumped a pile of files on my desk. "Because that is exactly what I've done."

With a laugh, I flipped open the first folder to find a client brief, numerous room photos, and artwork style examples enclosed. My heart lit up.

"You look like a kid at Christmas," Adrian said, clearly amused.

"No…" My smile grew. "This is better."

"Well, clearly my childhood was better than yours," he muttered with a chuckle.

My mind ignited with possibilities as I stared at the images in my hand. "I can do this," I whispered under my breath.

"I'm glad you think so," Adrian said on his way out the door. "I'm excited to see what you're capable of, Lanie."

I drew in a deep breath and exhaled my nerves. "So am I."

Exhausted after my first day, I dragged myself back to Josie's apartment and fell onto the couch I'd slept on the night before. I'd barely had time to assess my new living quarters after the six-hour turbulent flight from LA and didn't have the know-how or energy to make the bed at one in the morning, so I'd opted for the familiar warmth of Grayson's couch.

Finally drawing enough energy to explore, I changed into some comfy clothes and ambled around the open-plan apartment like a voyeur into Josie's life. Packing boxes piled the floor with Grayson's name scrawled over them, while the rest of the apartment laid almost empty. The exposed brick walls donned beautiful photographs, but the minimal furniture barely did them justice.

I wandered into the bedroom to discover a modest queen-size bed—a far cry from the California King I was accustomed to—and grimaced. A pile of fresh linens laid neatly folded on top, and I wished I'd paid more attention to Maria, our old housemaid. She would've shown me how to make a bed, if only I'd asked.

A whole string of swear words erupted from my mouth as I attempted what looked to be a fitted sheet. The elastic ends bounced back from each opposing corner as I jumped from side to side, trying to solve the seemingly unsolvable puzzle. Once I'd finally secured the last corner—while stretched across the bed like a contortionist—the bed leg gave way, sending me tumbling to the floor.

"Fuck," I muttered, staring at the ceiling while I waited for the pain. When nothing arose but mere embarrassment, I scrambled back onto my feet, then jumped when loud banging sounded at the front door.

"Melanie? Is that you?"

Amy's voice lifted my spirits instantly. I quickly brushed the dust from my black yoga pants and ran my fingers through my disheveled mop on my way to welcome her. The door swung open before I reached it, and a mass of wiry hair bounded into the apartment and charged through the living area.

My eyes grew wide. "What the fu—"

"Oh, phew," Amy cried as she marched inside. "I thought someone was robbing the place." She continued on to the terrace door and shooed the beast outside. "I heard lots of banging—and not the good kind, if you know what I mean."

"I was…um…trying to make the bed, and it…ur…broke."

"Again?!" Amy's cheeks grew pink. "Grayson and Josie really need to invest in sturdier furniture."

My eyes were glued to the horse-size creature peeing on the small strip of artificial grass which, until now, served no purpose. "I'm sorry, what the hell is that?"

"Oh, that's Luci! Josie's dog."

"*That's* Josie's dog?" I turned to Amy with wide eyes. I was *definitely* a cat person.

"He'll be living with us until the newlyweds return. Reed adores him."

"When do you think they'll be back?" If anyone knew, Amy would.

She giggled. "Sooner than they expected…" Her eyes shot to mine. "But don't worry. They're not going to kick you out."

"I know…but I was hoping to have my own place by then."

"I get it. There's nothing like having your own place…" A dreamy glaze coated her eyes. "Until you find your soul mate, that is."

Envy nipped at my heart. "So…you and the guy downstairs… it must be getting serious if you're living together."

"We'll see how it goes. I'll keep paying rent at my old place until I know for certain. My sister is adamant I have a backup plan. I don't want to end up having to move back home with my dad like she did. Cheap rent is hard to find around here."

"I know how you feel." I'd rather sleep on the streets than live with my parents again.

"Speaking of fragile sleeping arrangements," she said, peering into the bedroom. "Let's fix this bed."

Amy marched toward the stack of Grayson's moving boxes and ran her finger along the cardboard until she reached the one marked *books*. Tearing it open, she slipped out ten large hardbacks and heaped them into her arms. I hadn't the faintest clue what she was up to until she carried them into the bedroom and kneeled on the floor.

"Hold the bed up, will you?" she asked.

With a nod, I lifted the foot of the bed while Amy piled the books underneath to create a makeshift leg. "Wow, I never would've thought of that."

Amy shrugged as she stood. "Sometimes I see the solution before I think of it."

Amy was one of the most intriguing people I'd ever met. She was the resident psychic at *Maude* magazine and Josie's best friend, and up until now, I'd always kept my guard up around her.

"It's great to see you again," I said with an uneasy smile. "I'm sorry things got so…messy before."

"It's okay," Amy said, reaching for my hand and enclosing it with her other. "Everything worked out just as it should have."

I stared at my fingers wrapped in hers and opened my palm. I had nothing to hide anymore. "Will you read it?"

"Are you sure?"

With my nod, she studied the subtle lines and creases. "You're going through a huge transformation."

"Please tell me it gets better." It took all my strength not to pull away in fear of her answer.

"It does," she said as her smile grew. "So much better."

My brows lifted. "Details?"

"The details are yours. I only receive glimpses of the bigger picture."

"Which are?"

"Let's just say, someone from your past is about to turn your world upside down." She tilted her head. "Or the right way up, depending on how you look at it."

I rolled my eyes. "Josie told you what happened at her exhibition, didn't she? With Scott?"

Amy's screwed-up face verified her innocence. "Who?"

"Oh, he's just this guy I used to…" I shook my head. "It doesn't matter."

Instead of pushing for more information, Amy squeezed my hand. "Let your heart guide you with this one, okay?"

"Just as long as it's guiding me forward," I said with determination. "The past can fucking stay there."

The truth was, I wasn't ready for a romantic relationship. Although I'd worked through my dependent disorder with my therapist, I remained cautious. Until I was comfortable living alone and supporting myself, men were prohibited. I'd never felt more stable in my life, and I wasn't about to ruin it.

With a sad smile, Amy let go of my hand and turned to the bed. "I'm guessing you've never made a bed before?"

My blush deepened. "Nope."

"Then I'll teach you."

Over the next few weeks, I worked closely with Adrian and Faye, consulting in homes and businesses, as well as planning our monthly exhibition. I managed to secure an upcoming artist, Walt Terrain, who had been gaining traction through social media. He'd never had a show and was genuinely surprised when we offered to host one for him. Once word got out, the RSVPs rolled in, and not once did I have to drop my name to entice the invitees. Everyone knew me as Lanie, and I preferred it that way.

"Are you ready for your first official event?" Adrian asked as he brushed a micron of lint off his suit jacket.

My insides churned, but I remained composed. "More than ever."

Faye sauntered over in a little black dress very similar to mine. It was an AG Galleries rule. Our clothing must never distract from the art.

"This looks fabulous, Lanie," she said, gazing around the gallery. "Is the catering staff ready? Our guests will be arriving at any moment."

Adrian squeezed my elbow. "I'll check. You stay here and soak up the moment."

"Thanks," I said, offering him a half-smile as he walked away. I turned my gaze to the layout of beauty before me and inhaled a sense of inner peace.

"You're proving to be a good fit here," Faye said, watching me curiously. "I can't wait to see the turnout for tonight."

"I'm sorry I couldn't use my socials like I did for Josie. I'm, um…taking a break from it."

"You don't have to explain yourself," Faye said as she straightened my name tag. "The only social media you need to concentrate on is our gallery's."

"Thank you." I hadn't touched my account since I stepped into rehab, and I didn't plan to until I found a healthier use for it. My grid was full of staged photos of a fake life, and I couldn't bear to revisit them.

The artist, Walt Terrain, was the first to arrive, followed by a steady stream of art enthusiasts. The gallery wasn't crammed like it was at Josie's exhibition, but with the pitiful budget and a limited database, I took it as a win.

"You would not believe who just walked through the door," Adrian murmured as he ambled up beside me.

I glanced up from my checklist. "Who?"

"Nicholas Gibbs, the heir of this fine establishment, aka the sexiest man on earth."

My gaze froze on the clean-cut man with perfectly styled obsidian hair shrugging off his coat and offering it to Faye. His familiar arrogance irritated me. "I know who he is."

"So, you've done your homework?"

"Not exactly. We went to Stanford together, and I've been attending AG events since I was a child. So, our paths have crossed…several times."

"Oh, right, the lives of the rich and famous." He chuckled. "Why you left that world, I'll never understand."

Faye slid her arm around Nicholas's elbow, but instead of guiding him through the exhibition, she rotated him in my direction.

"Fuck." I lifted my clipboard over my face and spun around before any eye contact was made.

Adrian's eyes widened at my reaction. "I think your paths have more than crossed," he said as he slid my shield out of my hands. "I'll tend to this while you're tending to that." He acknowledged Nicholas with a nod before disappearing into the crowd.

My throat went dry as I reluctantly turned around. "Nicholas," I said, reaching out to shake his hand with the politest smile I could manage.

"Melanie Warren?" His fingers curled around mine. He placed his other hand on top in an obvious power move….or was it affection? I couldn't tell anymore.

Faye smiled at our familiarity. "This amazing lady is in charge of our exhibition tonight."

"It's been a long time," I said, ignoring his charismatic smile.

His grin widened. "Too long."

"Marvelous, you already know each other," Faye said with a warm smile. "I'll leave you to get reacquainted."

Once Faye disappeared into the sea of prospective buyers, Nicholas eyed my badge—or perhaps the vicinity it was attached to. "You're…*working* here?"

"Just trying something new," I said with a nonchalant shrug. He obviously wasn't aware of my estrangement from my family.

He shook his head with a laugh. "A billionaire heiress working for minimum wage?" His deep-brown eyes tapered. "You've always been a hard girl to figure out."

I gestured to the artwork, hoping to distract him. "Shall I tell you about these amazing pieces?"

"I'd much rather you tell me why you disappeared from my bed all those years ago."

Flames traveled up my neck and scorched my cheeks. "It was college, and I was drunk," I murmured, careful of prying ears.

He smirked. "And you were engaged to American royalty."

"We were on a break," I snapped in a whisper. "And I'd rather not talk about it."

"Grayson wasn't right for you anyway," he said, taking a glass of champagne from a passing waiter. "Why you got engaged so young is still a mystery to me."

I pushed back the familiar dread of my darkest secret. "Well, we were young and stupid, what can I say?"

Nicholas chuckled. "At least you never married. I got hitched straight out of college and divorced last year. No kids, thank God."

"Sorry to hear that," I said, thankful the conversation had shifted to him.

"I'm not. It was the biggest mistake of my life." He pursed his lips as he ran his gaze up my legs before meeting my eyes. "Or perhaps you were."

My mouth dropped. "Pardon?"

"Maybe if I'd been clearer about my intentions, you wouldn't have run back to Grayson."

"I don't know about that," I said, refusing to meet his dark-chocolate gaze. "I was pretty messed up back then."

"A hot mess," Nicholas murmured before taking a sip from his glass.

"Look, I'm sorry I mixed you up in all my drama. I can assure you that is all behind me now. I'm a different person."

"I can see that." Nicholas reread my name tag. "But why change your—"

"You must meet the star of our show," I blurted, signaling the artist over as he ambled by. "Walt, I'd like you to meet Nicholas Gibbs. His family owns AG Galleries." I turned to Nicholas. "Nicholas, this is Walt Terrain."

Walt's face lit up as they shook hands. "Thank you so much for this amazing opportunity."

"You're very welcome, but I hear Mel—" He cleared his throat. "*Lanie* is responsible for all of this."

Walt beamed at me. "Of course. She has been amazing every step of the way."

My heart could have burst. I'd never felt appreciated before, and the unexpected jolt of emotion stole my breath and stung my eyes. "Oh, it looks like Adrian needs my help," I said, pretending to notice something in the distance. "Walt, why don't you give Nicholas the grand tour of your brilliant paintings?"

"I'd be honored," Walt said, motioning Nicholas to follow.

"Perfect." I turned back to Nicholas. "Enjoy the show. We must catch up sometime."

"Perhaps over dinner?" he asked, lowering his mouth to my ear. "Now that I'm overseeing the East Coast galleries, I'll be in town every few weeks."

"Um…sure. I've got some ideas for the gallery I'd love to run past you," I said, trying to keep our conversation professional.

Nicholas's eyes twinkled. "Sure. We can do that too."

My eyebrows rose as he wandered away. I usually knew how to handle forward men, but this one posed a problem. Not only was Nicholas incredibly handsome, but he was also my boss, and whether I refused or accepted his advances, he had the power to jeopardize everything.

Chapter 17

Thankfully, a few weeks passed, and I hadn't seen Nicholas. After Walt's successful exhibition, we were officially off his father's radar, meaning Nicholas had less of a reason to visit the SoHo gallery.

Back in college, I'd stupidly slept with him at a frat party after Grayson had broken off our engagement—the first time. I was so angry and upset I drunk myself into a stupor most nights. Not only had I lost the baby, but I'd also lost my best friend, and I didn't handle it well. It wasn't until I woke up in the hospital with alcohol poisoning that Grayson decided to give me a second chance. I knew his family had forced him into it, but I was willing to take what I could get. I couldn't face life without him.

My cell phone blasted me out of bed.

Adrian: **I need a favor.**

I triple-checked the time and breathed a sigh of relief. I hadn't slept in.

Me: **???**

Adrian: **I'm meant to be at a consultation in Midtown at 8am, but Gaston found my chocolate stash overnight and we're off to the vet. Can you cover?**

Wiping the sleep from my eyes, I reread the message and groaned.

Me: **Sure. I hope Gaston is okay. Who is the client?**

Adrian: **Some rich-ass lawyer. He won't be there, but his housekeeper will let you in to look at the space. I'll send you the address. I owe you!**

As I waited for the details to come through, I quickly showered, applied minimal makeup, and threw on one of Josie's dresses before running out the door to make it to the Midtown address just in time.

The apartment building was a modern and seemingly characterless structure that offended the surrounding architecture. Buildings like these screamed new money, and according to Adrian, that also meant an easy sell. So, thanks to Adrian's French bulldog, I'd soon be a step closer to my goal with a healthy commission coming my way.

The foyer was as pretentious as the exterior, and the doorman reluctantly sent me up to the penthouse where a plump, middle-aged woman was waiting.

"You don't look like a Mr. Santos." Her eastern European accent was thick and harsh.

"Adrian Santos got held up, so I'll be consulting today. My name is Lanie."

With a satisfied nod, she ushered me inside. "The space is in the dining area."

As I followed her down the wide hallway, I was instantly impressed by the quality of artwork on display. Whoever lived here had respectable taste. The décor was streamlined and sleek, and its minimalist vibe made me wonder if anyone resided there full-time. My parents had numerous properties throughout America and Europe that laid vacant most of the year, so it wouldn't have surprised me.

The hallway opened out into a vast living area with floor-to-ceiling windows presenting a panoramic view of the big city. This feature alone made up for the tasteless flaws of the modern building design.

Faint music pulled my attention to the sitting area where a lanky teenager in a school uniform lay sprawled across the stark-white couch, tapping his pencil on a notebook.

His blaring headphones clearly muted my arrival, because when he lifted his gaze, my appearance sent him scrambling to his feet. "Holy shit!"

I flinched at the volume of his voice before offering him a polite wave.

His mouth fell open as he stepped closer. "You're her."

"I'm sorry. Have we met?" He looked familiar, but I couldn't place him.

"You're the chick from the photo," he said, unplugging his ear pods and throwing them on the coffee table beside an empty bowl of cereal.

"I…um…don't know what you're talking about." It had been weeks since anyone had recognized me, which was part of the appeal of moving to Manhattan.

"Come on, I'll show you." He waved me over to the door by the fireplace, which led into a study. "He keeps all his favorites in here."

I glanced back at the housekeeper, who expelled an impatient grunt, then stepped into the room. As I approached the central glass-topped desk, I panned my curious gaze over the walls until my heart plummeted. Positioned amongst tacky motivational quotes and oceanic imagery was…*me*.

It was the portrait Josie had taken for her exhibition last year. The one that was sold to…*fuck*. Fear consumed my mind and paralyzed my body. "Whose apartment is this?" My voice barely reached a whisper. *It couldn't be.*

"Mr. Blackwood's, of course," the housekeeper said, shooing the boy away while muttering something about being late for school. "And he'll be home from his run soon, so I'd like to hurry this up."

She motioned me to follow, but I was frozen. Scott Blackwood lived in the deepest and darkest part of my mind with all the other broken fragments of my soul. If seeing him at Josie's exhibition had sent me spiraling, then seeing him now, in his apartment, would likely destroy me. I had to get out of there.

The housekeeper growled. "Are you coming or not? I'm a very busy lady."

"I'm sorry…but…"

"No buts," she snapped, dragging me back in the living room by my wrist. "This is the space. You measure. I clean bathroom."

As she marched out of the room, I stared at the blank wall. My instincts screamed at me to make a run for it, but my work ethic demanded I stay. All I had to do was measure the space and leave, and Scott would never have to know I was there. He was Adrian's client, after all.

With trembling hands, I pulled out my measuring tape and notepad.

"I can't wait to tell him you were here," the boy said, reappearing at my side with his school bag.

Fuck.

"You wouldn't believe how much he spent on that photograph," he continued with a strangely familiar chuckle. "And he won't even up my allowance."

"Look, I really need to get this done before your..." My voice trailed off as my stomach clenched. How did I not notice the similarities before? His defined jawline, his broad shoulders, the shaggy hair...

"Before what?" he asked, raising his brows as I stared at the features my heart recognized before my head could catch up.

"Before your dad gets home." *What a fucking nightmare.*

The boy shook his head with a snigger. "Oookay then..." He flopped back onto the couch and picked up his notebook and pencil. "Don't mind me."

"Thanks," I muttered, hoping I hadn't sounded too rude. Of course Scott had a family. It had been years since—*wait.* The years didn't add up. My gaze shot to the surly teenager as he scribbled away, and my heart almost burst. He wasn't Scott's son. It was his little brother, Riley, all grown up.

Instead of gushing over the gorgeous boy I once knew, I quickly measured the wall, photographed the space, and reverted to my original plan of getting the fuck out of there. As I gathered up my notes and took one last look at the assigned wall, the distinct sound of keys dropping by the front door pricked my ears.

"Oh, hey, *Dad...*" I could almost hear the smile in Riley's voice.

Squeezing my eyes shut, I kept my back turned, praying I'd be able to maneuver out of the apartment unnoticed.

"Why the fuck are you calling me Dad?" Scott asked as he stepped into the living area. "And why haven't you left for school yet?"

"Watch your language," Riley whispered. "We have company."

My shoulders stiffened the moment I felt their eyes shift in my direction, and my reluctance to show my face only ignited an agonizing silence.

"Lanie?"

I scrunched up my face in an effort not to swear then turned around with the most casual smile I could manage. "Hi."

Scott's mouth parted. "What are you doing here?"

"I work for AG Galleries," I said, quickly breaking eye contact. He was still as beautiful as ever. A little taller perhaps, broader shoulders, and his once flowy coffee-colored hair was now cut short. The boy I knew had become a man. "I'm...um... here for the measure."

"You work for the gallery?" He stepped closer. "Why?"

My eyes snapped to his radiant blue hues. "Why does anyone work?"

Riley sniggered while watching our interaction closely. "Savage."

Scott glared at his brother. "Get to school."

"I don't have any classes this morning," he said, folding his arms in a silent standoff.

"Then go study at the library."

Riley picked up his ear pods and his school bag and stormed out of the apartment, muttering obscenities to himself.

Scott took another cautious step toward me like he was approaching a frightened animal. "Since when does *Melanie Warren* need money?"

As my lips formed a thin white line, I slipped my notebook into my bag and switched to my professional persona. "Well, I have everything I need here, so I should go. My colleague will send you some options in a few days."

When I attempted to move past him, he seized my wrist, firing every unwelcome memory of us through my body in a split second.

"Don't pretend like you still know me," I uttered, keeping my gaze focused on my escape route.

Before he could respond, I tore my arm away and fled through the front door, only stopping to breathe once the elevator doors closed behind me.

I pleaded with Adrian to take back his client, but Faye wouldn't allow it. Once initial contact was made, the company policy stated we had to follow through. Fortunately for me, the rest of the job could be done over email, so there was no need for any face-to-face contact.

Once I reviewed the space through my photographs, I began to search. I tried to stick to the brief and not follow any preconceived ideas of Scott's taste, but I couldn't help it. Within an hour, I'd found the perfect piece in one of our East Coast collections and spent the next three days finding wanting alternatives. It was a tedious task, but it kept me busy. And busy was the only way I could battle the unwanted memory of the incident at Josie's exhibition that had brought me here.

I hadn't seen Scott in eleven years, and the look on his face when he had discovered me snorting coke in the coatroom triggered a complete meltdown and haunted me throughout my rehabilitation. He had no right to look at me that way, and seeing him now only stoked the embers of my misery.

When I couldn't prolong the inevitable any longer, I lifted my chin, opened an email, and typed.

> **Dear Mr. Blackwood,**
>
> **Please find attached five artworks I deem suitable for your dining area. I look forward to hearing your thoughts.**
>
> **Thank you for choosing AG Galleries.**
>
> **Kind regards,**
>
> **L. Warren**

My heartbeat accelerated as I hovered over the send button. With closed eyes, I drew in a deep breath and conclusively opened a direct line of communication with the man who'd sealed it shut eleven years prior.

Moments later, I returned to my desk, nursing an instant coffee I made in our kitchenette. It was cheap and nasty, but its bitterness matched my mood. As I eased back into my desk chair, my gaze struck the email notification at the bottom of my computer screen.

New email from Scott Blackwood.

Coffee spilled over the edges of my cup and scorched my fingers. "Mother fucker," I hissed as I shook the excess liquid from my hand.

"I heard that!" Adrian called out from the next office.

Ignoring him, I opened the email, hoping for a simple read receipt. Surely a hotshot lawyer was too busy to respond so quickly.

I hate them.

I think you'll need to revisit the space.

S.

My internal kettle boiled. "Mother fucker!"

Within seconds, Adrian appeared in my doorway, hand on hip. "Difficult client?"

"The worst," I muttered, peeking up at him. "Thanks, by the way."

"Oh, the lawyer guy?" Adrian winced. "He seemed so lovely when I met him at Josie Spencer's exhibition, not to mention gorgeous." He fanned his face and grinned. "Just think of the commission. That guy bought the most expensive photogra—" Adrian's voice died, but his mouth remained open. "Oh. My. God."

I held up my hand to stop him. "Don't even."

"Are you kidding me?" Adrian's eyes grew wide. "Is he, like, obsessed with you or something?"

"No," I cried. "It's nothing like that."

"Because Faye won't have any of her staff being harassed."

"He's not harassing me, Adrian," I uttered, massaging my temples. "We used to…date."

"What? Pre-Grayson Harlow? Is that even possible?"

"It was high school, and he was my first…"—I swallowed the growing lump in my throat—"well…everything."

"Oh…" Adrian's shoulders lowered. "We all have one of those. Let me guess…it ended badly?"

"You could say that."

"Look, just keep being professional. He enlisted our services before he knew you worked here, so he's not a psycho. Treat him like any other client, and he'll get the hint. It's worked for me numerous times."

"Don't we have rules about dating clients?"

"Dating, yes. But fucking is more of a gray area." With that, Adrian strolled back to his office with a contented smirk.

Once my laughter morphed into a chuckle, I cleared my throat in preparation for my response. I was, after all, a professional now.

Dear Mr. Blackwood,

I don't think a revisit is necessary. I measured the allocated space and took many photos from various angles. I have everything I need.

I'll source some alternative options for you.

Kind regards,

L. Warren

The next day, I sent him a new selection, but none as good as the first.

Nope. S.

He was going to make this difficult, but my determination had me sending another round of possibilities.

Not feeling it. S.

"Argh." I slammed my hand down on the table.

"Everything okay in here?" Faye asked, walking into my office.

"Oh…sorry." I glanced down at the desk. "There was a bug."

Faye peered around my desk with wide eyes. "Did you get rid of it?"

"Not yet," I muttered, glaring at my computer.

Taking a step back, Faye's eyes darted around the room. "Well, I just got a call from Mr. Blackwood's assistant. Apparently, the space you're working on has been altered, and you'll need to go back for a remeasure this afternoon."

My eyes bulged. "What?"

"It's okay. He offered to pay double for wasting your time. Isn't that lovely?"

"Are you sure I'm the right person for the job? He hasn't liked any of my suggestions so far."

"He must have liked something." Faye offered me a warm smile. "Plus, he asked for you specifically."

My teeth ground within my fake smile. "Of course he did."

The door to Scott's apartment was wide open when I stepped out of the elevator, but the housekeeper was nowhere to be seen. As I stepped over the threshold, my gaze panned across the room to note any alterations to the original layout, but unsurprisingly, there were none.

Anger surged through me as I pivoted on my heel to leave, but Scott blocked my exit.

"Please don't run off again," he said, lifting his hands in silent surrender.

A low growl emitted from my throat as I attempted to step around him. "I don't have time for this."

"Please, I just want to—"

"What?" I spat, glaring up at him. "Interrogate me some more?"

"No." His eyes softened. "I'm sorry if it came across that way, but I was in shock. I had no idea you were still in New York, let alone working for the gallery. And to find you in my apartment months after trying to track you down, I—"

"Why would you do that?" I gasped, falling back a few steps.

Scott's brow furrowed. "I've been…concerned about you. You fell off the face of the earth after I saw you at that exhibition."

"Oh, wow," I exclaimed, clasping my chest in mock distress. "You must have been so worried. I mean, four months…" I shook my head before meeting his dangerous eyes dead on. "Try eleven fucking years, you asshole."

He ran his hands up my arms, leaving behind a river of goosebumps. "Lanie…"

"No," I cried, knocking him away. "Don't touch me." Before my tears had a chance to surface, I hurried back to the elevator.

"It's not like it took you long to move on," he called out.

Scott's words pierced my heart and pulled me straight back to where he stood. "I *had* to move on. You were gone."

"But I came back."

I stared into his eyes, but they didn't falter, unlike my voice. "What?"

"I came back for you, just like I said I would…but you were with Grayson. And not just *with* him…" His jaw tightened. "You were *engaged*," he said, tearing his gaze away. "I'd only been gone a few months, and you'd moved on to the one person you promised to not have feelings for." He let out a solemn chuckle as he shook his head. "It made sense, though…more than we ever did."

"What are you talking about?" Confusion clouded my mind. "You never came back. I was alone, and the only person who cared—*really* cared—was Grayson. He was there for me when you weren't, so don't you dare bring him into this."

He didn't seem to be listening. "You know, when I saw him at Hank's wedding…with that photographer…I finally thought you'd broken up for good. But then, just one sneak peek at your socials and—surprise, surprise—you're back together. It's hard to keep up."

My blood boiled. He'd been judging my life through a distorted lens. "Well, pictures can be deceiving…and that photographer is his wife."

"They got married?" His brows rose. "I didn't hear."

"It's not like Grayson's parents were going to put *that* in the papers. Josie isn't exactly who they wanted their son to end up with."

Scott chuckled. "I know how that feels."

"But you know what?" My eyes glazed over as they met his. "They made it anyway."

Chapter 18

I thought it would have been days before I'd hear from Scott again, but when I opened my inbox the very next morning, there he was.

We need to talk.
Are you free for dinner tonight?
S.

The timestamp marked four am. He was either a ridiculously early riser or, just like me, suffered a long sleepless night after our altercation.

Dear Mr. Blackwood,
Let's keep this professional.
Kind regards,
L. Warren

Before I had a chance to make my morning coffee, yet another email materialized in my inbox.

Dear Miss Warren,
I'd appreciate the opportunity to discuss the intended artwork for my apartment, face to face. Unfortunately, I have a very busy schedule, and the only availability I have is this evening. Would you consider meeting with me over dinner?
Yours sincerely,
Scott Blackwood

The corner of my mouth quirked up as I replied.

Dear Mr. Blackwood,

Thank you for your invitation, however, the gallery is hosting an exhibition this evening, and I'm unable to fulfill your request. I'll happily continue conversing with you over email, as I understand how busy you are.

Kind regards,

L. Warren

I tapped my desk, waiting for his response, but nothing came. My heart dipped unexpectedly, but I brushed it off. I had a huge day ahead and no time to play email tag.

After an entire day of preparations, I raced home to shower and change before the big show. I threw on the little black dress I'd bought from Goodwill and ran my gaze over my familiar reflection. I'd rarely worn the same outfit twice.

On my return to the gallery, I was pleased to see everything running smoothly. The catering staff was ready and waiting, the artists had arrived, and Adrian was wearing a huge smile. He was in charge and basking in the glory.

"Where do you want me?" I asked him as I picked up a clipboard.

"Down in the back. With the more..."—he cleared his throat—"challenging pieces. I'm sure your pretty face will successfully divert our guests' attention to their wallets."

I rolled my eyes. "I'll try my best."

There were always a few questionable artworks within our exhibitions, but someone had to sell them.

Within the hour, the gallery was buzzing. I'd already made two sales, and I was determined to make at least two more before the night was over.

"Can you tell me more about this piece?"

I glanced up from my clipboard to greet the prospective buyer, but my smile faded instantly.

"Scott, what are you doing here?" I whipped my eyes around the room, making sure Faye and Adrian weren't nearby.

"As you're aware, I'm in the market for some art. So, I thought I'd come check out this exhibition since my evening freed up."

My gaze tapered. "Since when do you like cubism?" I asked, recalling his uncanny aversion to Picasso.

"Who's pretending to know whom now?" Scott's eyes twinkled as he held back a smile. "Tastes can change over the years…sometimes only months."

I refused to bite. "Fine," I grumbled. "This haunting depicture of a man's inner turmoil is by Oscar Ashford. The bold geometric planes of brilliant hues represent his potential while the sharp interweaving lines cutting through symbolize current day pressures. It's… It's a…"

"It's a goat."

My mouth fell open. "No, it's not."

"Yeah, it is." He chuckled. "Look…head, eyes, horns, tail."

I went silent as he pointed out all the obvious features. It was a goat.

"How much?" he asked, pulling out his wallet.

I ripped it out of his hands and forced it back into his suit jacket. "Don't you dare."

"But this would look great beside my dining table."

"Are you kidding?!" I cried, quickly checking to see if anyone had heard my inappropriate outburst. "It would look terrible."

He brought his mouth dangerously close to my ear. "Are you saying it's ugly?"

"No," I muttered, flicking my gaze away. His dimpled grin weakened my resistance. "I'm just saying it won't suit your décor."

"Then I'll change my décor to suit this masterpiece."

He was trying to fire me up, and it was working. "Fine," I growled. "Just don't tell anyone I recommended it."

"I won't…"—he grinned—"as long as you have dinner with me tomorrow night."

My mouth gaped at the ultimatum. It was a dirty play, and he knew it. Knowing Faye would never forgive me, I scribbled my address on the back of my business card and held it out to him. "Just don't expect me to enjoy myself."

He slipped the card out of my fingers and brought it to his chest as he chortled. "Oh, I would never. I'll pick you up at seven."

I was a moment from moving away when a man's voice filtered through the crowd.

"Blackwood?! Is that you?"

We both turned to find Nicholas Gibbs sauntering toward us.

"How do you know Nicholas?" I asked Scott under my breath.

He threw me a sideways glance. "He's a client."

Nicholas appeared in front of us, champagne in hand. "I hope you're here to spend all that money I paid you last year."

Scott reached out and shook his hand. "I'm toying with the idea," he said, sneaking a peek in my direction. "How's bachelor life treating you?"

"It has its perks." Nicholas ran his gaze over me appreciatively. "It's lovely to see you again, Melanie," he said, leaning forward to kiss my cheek.

Scott's eyes burned into his side but reverted to a simmer once Nicholas stepped back.

"This guy's not hitting on my prettiest staff member, is he?" Nicholas asked, panning his gaze to Scott with a jovial grin.

"Not in the slightest," I muttered quickly. "Mr. Blackwood is a client of the gallery, and I was just showing him some prospective investments."

Scott's charming smile returned as he pointed up at the horrendous artwork before us. "Like this fine piece, for instance."

Nicholas gazed up at the monstrosity. "Wow. That's really something."

While Nicholas contemplated the artwork, I threatened Scott's life with a menacing glare.

"I love it," he continued. "Put it aside for me. It'll look great in my apartment."

"Oh…um…certainly," I stammered, noting his name on the clipboard. I didn't have to peek up at Scott to know he was smiling. "I'll get it shipped to LA immediately."

"Didn't Faye tell you? I'm living in Manhattan now. My new apartment is incredible, but its walls are bare. Perhaps you could offer me your professional advice over dinner sometime. I'm hopeless at these things."

All the humor drained from Scott's face as he waited for my response.

"Oh." I racked my brain for an excuse. "Um—"

"Nicholas, there you are," Faye said, appearing at Nicholas's side. "There's a reporter here who wants to interview you."

"Of course. Lead the way." Nicholas offered Scott a nod before meeting my gaze. "I'll have my assistant call you."

Heat rose to my neck as he wandered away.

"You still have the same effect on men, I see," Scott said, watching me closely.

Irritation festered under my skin. "And you still have the same hang-ups."

"The only hang-up I have these days is which car to drive."

My eyes rolled. He'd turned into one of them. "Is that supposed to impress me?"

"No." He grinned. "I'll leave that for tomorrow night."

I spent the entire day pacing the apartment, almost certain he wouldn't show until a huge bouquet of yellow roses turned up on my doorstep. Moments later, my phone chimed.

Unknown: **See you soon. S**

Throwing the flowers in the kitchen sink, I hunted around for a vase but found nothing. How was that even possible? Surely Grayson bought Josie flowers. Nonetheless, I took it as an omen, because just like the stupid bouquet, there was no place for Scott in my life.

A million excuses danced through my mind but nothing substantial enough to discourage someone like Scott. He'd always been determined, and by the look of his online profile, he still was. Not many lawyers came to own their own firm at such an early age.

Until now, I hadn't dared type his name into any search engine. I'd convinced myself to repress his existence the morning I woke beside Grayson on my eighteenth birthday. It was the only way I could survive the life I'd chosen to lead.

Images scattered across the screen—mostly professional photographs, some at formal events with interchangeable women, and a few seemingly casual. Almost every link sent me back to the Blackwood & Associates website, leaving me frustratingly clueless about his private life. *Had he married? Did he have a string of girlfriends?* All the questions that had consumed me at Josie's exhibition resurfaced. Only, this time, I didn't have drugs to ease my anxiety.

As time ticked down, I rummaged through Josie's closet. Her tastes were different from mine, but she definitely rocked her own style. Amongst the band t-shirts, leather, and denim, I discovered a flowy yellow dress. It was nothing like I used to wear, yet I was drawn to it.

Slipping it over my head, I twirled in front of the mirror. It was a tiny bit loose around the waist, but I enjoyed the freedom it gave. I could take full breaths and eat a little more than was deemed acceptable by my mother. Fortunately, I had heels to match and a cropped denim jacket to keep the chill at bay. The nights were growing cooler, and the last thing I wanted was Scott offering his jacket and encasing me in his delicious scent.

Once I'd applied enough mascara to highlight my feline-shaped eyes, I coated my lips with a faint-pink lip gloss and pressed them together. For some deep psychological reason, I hadn't been able to wear lipstick since my stint in rehab.

My stomach was churning well before he arrived, and when I buzzed him in, I ran for the bathroom to dab a wet washcloth over my neck. I took a few deep breaths to settle my nerves, which only peaked again when a soft knock sounded at the front door.

"Lanie?" his voice traveled through the wooden barrier when I froze in front of it.

"Yep," I croaked, checking the mirror for the hundredth time. I didn't want to care about his reaction, but my racing heartbeat told me otherwise. "Just a second." I collected my bag from the side table and swung open the door.

Scott's eyes widened as his gaze ran over my body. "Wow. You look..."

I stared at his designer suit and grimaced. "Underdressed?"

"Beautiful." His eyes glazed over like he was stuck in a daydream.

"Shall we go?" I said, pointing to the stairs, eager to push past whatever memory he was stuck in.

"Yeah..." Scott cleared his throat. "My car's out front."

"You drove?" I asked, on my descent to the ground floor. "I didn't think anyone drove around here."

"It's not so bad...if you're driving the right car."

My heart skipped as I stepped out of the building. Part of me anticipated his magnificent turquoise Mustang, but I was left sorely disappointed. "So, where are you taking me in the Batmobile?" I asked, unfazed by the black Ferrari parked out front.

Scott poked his tongue around his cheek before answering. "A little place called Lumière. You know it?"

"Everyone knows it," I muttered as I slid into the car. It was one of the fanciest restaurants in Manhattan, and it took months to get a reservation. Scott clearly had contacts in high places. "It's a little upmarket for a business meeting, don't you think?" I asked as we pulled away from the curb.

"Well...I figured since I've already decided on the artwork, we could just...talk?"

My gaze shot to his. "What do you mean you've already decided?!"

"The first painting you chose was perfect, and you know it."

I pressed my lips together to stop myself from cursing.

"Don't be angry," he said, anticipating my reaction. "I just wanted a chance to reconnect with you."

"Why?"

"To be honest, I have no fucking idea." Scott ran his hand down his face and massaged his jawline. "Ever since I bought that damn photograph, I haven't been able to get you out of my mind, and when I found you standing in my living room... well...I took it as a sign."

"A sign for what? Danger ahead?"

He chuckled. "Probably."

"I'm not the same girl I was back then. If you're looking to reconnect with her, I'm sorry, but she's gone."

"Are you sure about that? You're definitely as stubborn as

her." He flashed me a grin. "Prettier maybe, but still a pain in the ass, I bet."

I crossed my arms and turned my gaze through the heavily tinted windows. My head screamed at me not to fall for his charm, but my body conjured an entirely different reaction. "Don't even think about hitting on me," I uttered as my core heated. "I said I'd have dinner with you, and that's it."

Scott pursed his lips. "I'm sorry. Old habits."

As we drove on in silence, I opened the window and let the fresh air cool my inflamed cheeks. My shoulder-length hair whipped around my face, but I didn't care. I was going for the 'messy look' anyway.

"We're here," Scott said, pulling up to the curb.

I glanced through the glass windows of the restaurant, scanning the crowd. I'd never been to Lumière before, but I knew people who frequented often, and I didn't want to be seen.

While Scott handed his keys over to the valet, followed by a healthy tip, I waited on the sidewalk, gazing up at the glistening chandeliers at the entrance of the beautiful restaurant.

A tingling sensation filtered through the soft material of my dress when Scott's hand grazed over my lower back, urging me forward.

To avoid his perilous touch, I quickened my pace as we entered the lavish foyer and stood back while the manager took Scott's name. With a glance in my direction, he motioned Scott over to the side of his lectern and muttered a private word. Perhaps there was something wrong with the booking. *I could only hope.*

Scott returned to my side and gently tugged the edge of my jacket. "No denim, apparently."

I blinked in shock. I'd never failed a dress code. Ever. My blush deepened as I threaded my arms out of the jacket and handed it over to the coatroom attendant. "Well, you didn't exactly tell me there was a dress code."

"I'm sorry, I just assumed you—"

I whipped my head in his direction.

"Never mind." He sighed. "Will you be warm enough?"

I folded my arms. "I'll be fine."

Our host escorted us to our table by the window. "May I get you a drink to start with?" he asked once we were both seated with napkins across our laps.

Scott smiled up at him. "Yes, a bottle of your finest champagne."

His tone, remnant of my high-society days, irked me. "And a glass of sparkling water please," I added, emphasizing my manners.

Scott gaped. "I can't possibly drink a bottle by myself. I'm driving."

"Then I guess you shouldn't have ordered it."

"Fine," he muttered, looking back at the waiter. "Change that to..." He cleared his throat. "A beer...please." As the waiter moved away, Scott's shoulders lowered as his gaze traveled back to mine. "Lanie, will you relax? I want to talk, not fight."

I picked a mini bread roll from the basket and tore a piece off. "Isn't that what lawyers do?"

"Not over dinner, preferably," he said with a smirk. "And not with you."

"What made you become a divorce attorney anyway? Do you have personal experience in that area?" I took a bite, pretending to appear disinterested.

He stared at me for a moment before answering. "I'm a family lawyer, but divorce does bring in most of our revenue. And no, I've never married. My job has made me cynical in that department."

I scoffed. "So has my life."

"Aren't your parents still together?"

I swallowed the bread, wishing I'd coated it with butter for the ride down. "I think so."

"What does that mean?"

"I haven't seen them in a while," I said, carefully adjusting the napkin on my lap.

The V deepened in his forehead. "Is everything ok—"

Before he could pry, I called the waiter over. "We're ready to order," I said before reeling off three random courses in fluent French. I hadn't had a decent meal in weeks.

Scott flustered over the menu before dropping it back on the table. "I'll have what she's having."

With a nod, the waiter disappeared, and I reluctantly turned back to Scott. "What?" I asked when he didn't say anything.

"I knew you spoke Spanish, but French? I'm impressed."

"I'm a little rusty, but you'll be amazed at how much it improves the service."

He gazed around the elaborate dining room. "I doubt you could question the service here."

"My mother could," I muttered.

"Ah, so some things haven't changed."

I refused to meet his searching eyes. "I'd rather not talk about her," I said, cursing myself for bringing her up.

"Okay. What should we talk about?"

I went with the safest topic. "How's Riley?"

"Driving me nuts, but he's a good kid." Scott leaned back in his chair and grinned. "Did you really think he was my son?"

"Only fleetingly." My cheeks burned. "I didn't have time to do the math. Plus, who knows how many kids you have running around by now?"

Scott's head jerked backwards. "I may sleep around some, but I can assure you, there are no children, and I doubt there ever will be. I have enough going on with my brother."

I wasn't sure what stung more—his admission to being a man whore or the fact that he didn't want children. I feared the latter.

"He's still into art, thanks to you," he continued, sipping his beer. "He's actually been attending advanced drawing classes at a studio near your gallery."

For the first time that night, I smiled. "That's so great."

"You should've seen his face when he figured out who you were."

"He remembers me?"

Scott let out a soft chuckle. "You're a hard person to forget, Lanie."

His effort to be sweet only irritated me more. "Unless my father's money is involved."

All the humor in his face died. "Hey, I paid him back *with* interest."

"Oh, wow." My tone oozed sarcasm. "Well done, you."

"Why are you so pissed?" he asked, leaning over the table to keep his voice hushed. "If anyone should be angry here, it's me."

My teeth ground together. "Are you fucking kidding? You. Left. Me." I threw my napkin on the table and stood up. "I can't do this."

Scott shot out of his chair to follow. "But I told you I was coming back."

"I think I would remember that," I retorted, marching toward the coatroom. "Oh, and there's the fact that...*you didn't come back!*"

I grabbed my jacket while Scott rummaged through his wallet to pay for our uneaten food.

He spun me around once I reached the sidewalk. "*Yes*, I did."

"*No*, you didn't," I said, blinking back tears. "You didn't even have the guts to say goodbye."

"Well, no, not in person." His brow shadowed his eyes. "There wasn't any time. That's why I sent you the letter."

I shook my head in frustration and signaled for a cab. "Stop lying."

"I swear to God, Lanie," he said, pulling down my arm. "I wrote to you on my way to Boston. I would've called, but the police took my cell phone for evidence, and I lost all my contacts. The only thing I knew by heart was your address."

"Well, the only snail mail I remember getting was from Stanford, and even then, I didn't get the pleasure of opening it because my parents were so damn contr..." My voice tapered off as their betrayal dawned on me. My stomach roiled, and my head spun as my distorted memories endeavored to find the truth. Had my parents intercepted a letter from Scott?

"I think you need to sit down," Scott uttered, steadying me as he gestured to the valet.

A few moments later, Scott's car appeared in front of us, and he eased me inside. Before I could regain clarity and hail a cab I couldn't afford, Scott buckled me in and jogged around to the driver's side.

"Are you okay?" he asked, running both hands through his hair before pulling out from the curb.

I shook my head while watching the passing traffic, hiding the wells of tears threatening to spill over.

Scott's hands tightened on the steering wheel. "I *knew* something wasn't right," he muttered, throwing me a sideways glance. "I'm so sorry, Lanie. I'm so fucking sorry."

It took all my strength to utter the next words. "What happened to you?"

He drew in a long shaky breath. "After my dad was arrested, my life got really messy. Your father said he'd help me emancipate myself and become Riley's official guardian, but only if I agreed to his terms." His jaw tightened. "I had to take his money and start a new life on the East Coast."

Pain radiated through my chest as he continued.

"I didn't want to, but they were threatening to take Riley away. I figured I'd work out a way for us to be together once everything settled down."

"How much did he give you?"

"Enough to prove to Family Services that I could support Riley until he was eighteen…" He grimaced as the next words left his lips. "And enough to get me through college."

I pursed my lips but said nothing. Of course there was something in it for him too.

"Come on, Lanie. My dad was a criminal, and I had a suspension on my record. I thought my chances of a scholarship were over."

"So, you sold your soul for a college degree?"

"What was I supposed to do?" he growled. "You come from a life of abundance. I was never going to fit into your world if I didn't make something of myself."

"Yet, by trying to fit into my world, you left it completely."

"I know it must've looked that way, but I explained everything in that letter. I never would've intentionally hurt you like that. You've got to know that."

I bent over and massaged my temples. "I don't know anything anymore."

"Well, know that I came back for you. Once Riley's guardianship was final, I flew back to LA, where I stupidly thought you'd be waiting."

My head rose with my anger. "I thought you were gone… *forever.*"

Scott swerved to the side of the road and brought the car to a sudden stop. "It was three months."

"A lot can happen in three months," I bit back.

"Clearly," he grumbled. "I read all about it in some trashy magazine on the flight over."

"You have no idea what I was going through back then."

Scott scoffed. "I highly doubt your problems were bigger than mine."

"My problem was yours!" I cried, curling my hands into tight fists.

"What are you talking about?"

I lowered my glistening eyes. "Just take me home, Scott. I don't want to talk about this anymore."

"Don't you think we owe it to ourselves to hash this out?"

"No…I don't."

"Come on, Lanie." His hand reached for mine. "We need to move past this."

Repelling from his touch, I fumbled over my seatbelt then burst out of the car.

"Hey!" Scott leaped out to follow me. "Where are you going?"

I wiped away my tears while hailing a passing cab. "I can't do this."

"Why not?" Scott asked, ignoring the cab as it pulled up beside us. "What are you afraid of?"

"I'm afraid of you!" Rage replaced my tears. "I just spent three months in rehab, sorting through all my shit, then *you*, the stem of all of it, just walk back into my life and attempt to pick up where we left off…" An infuriated growl left my lips. "I…can't…do this."

He stepped closer, his eyes swirling between pain and confusion. "Lanie, I didn't kn—"

My back collided with the cool metal of the cab. "You broke me, Scott," I said, fumbling for the door handle. "I won't let you near my heart again."

As his jaw slackened, I slid into the cab and slammed the door, not daring to acknowledge the pain behind his glistening eyes as we drove away.

Chapter 19

"Thanks, Amy. I'll pay you back next week," I uttered, shifting my weight from foot to foot once she returned from paying the cab fare back to Greenwich. I stupidly had no cash, nor owned a credit card.

"It really isn't a problem," she said, squeezing my arm. "Happy to help out a friend."

I froze. 'Friend' wasn't a term I was used to. "Well, thanks again," I said before turning for the staircase.

"You want to stay for dinner?" she asked with a sunshine smile. "We have plenty."

"Oh, um…" I gazed up the stairs while my stomach argued with my desire to crawl under my bedsheets. "Thanks, but…I, um…"

Amy's eyes softened. "Just need a good cry?"

I stared at her for a moment then nodded my head. Not much got past Amy and her uncanny senses.

"If you ever need a shoulder, I hear mine is pretty comfortable," she said, offering me a sad smile. "Just ask Josie."

A faint chuckle left my lips. "I'll keep that in mind."

As soon as I shut the door to the apartment, my chest gave way with a sob, followed by a stream of tears. Not wanting to waste costly tissues or toilet paper, I climbed into the shower and let the tears fall with the cascading water. I didn't think it was possible to despise my parents any more than I did, but here I was.

My life could've been different. I could've been happy. My parents had stolen that from me and changed the course of my life. I wanted to yell and scream at them, but for what outcome? My mother and father never apologized for anything, and they weren't about to start now.

Scott *had* tried to contact me. He *had* said goodbye. It may have been in a letter, but it was the only way he knew how. How could I hold my downfall against him now? How could I be angry with him for leaving me pregnant at seventeen when he never knew?

What hurt most of all was the guilt. It was still there, festering away, gnawing at my soul. The horrendous lie I'd told Grayson was the one thing I couldn't forgive myself for, and the universe had rightly punished me for it. Someone like me didn't deserve a child.

Once my tears and body were dry, I slipped on an old t-shirt and shorts and climbed into bed. My head pounded, but I refused to take pain killers. Although my therapist said it wasn't necessary, I was determined to teach my body how to manage discomfort on its own.

As I rested my head against a soft stack of pillows, a flicker of light from the nightstand caught my attention. Messages filled the screen of my phone, which had been set to silent while I showered.

Unknown: **4 missed calls**

Unknown: **Please let me know when you're home safe.**

I didn't want to respond, but I couldn't stop my fingers.

Me: **I'm home.**

My heart quickened when three little dots flashed up on the screen then dipped when they vanished. Why I was disappointed, I didn't understand. I couldn't bring myself to save Scott's name into my phone, let alone converse with him over text.

The vibration of my phone drew my gaze, but the message wasn't from Scott.

Amy: **Check your front door. x**

Leaving the safe confines of my bedsheets, I wandered to the front door, curious to know what she was talking about. I checked the peephole before opening it to find a meal packaged up with a small note.

We can hear your stomach from downstairs. Amy & Reed x

With a melancholy smile, I gathered it up and carried it to the kitchen to reheat. Amy was right, I was starving. I cradled the bowl back to bed and shoveled the delicious mountain of carbs into my mouth until my phone lit up again. Pausing mid-chew, I picked it up and read the message.

Unknown: **I'm sorry for the way we left things. Now and eleven years ago.**

The apology I'd waited years for was sitting in my hands, but it gave me no peace, only an elevated feeling of shame that wasn't going to go away unless he did.

Instead of responding, I placed the phone back on the nightstand, along with the remains of my dinner, and curled up in bed. My head and heart were torn in two. My heart wanted to tell him everything, but my head was full of doubt. Scott wouldn't be able to look at me once he found out about the lies I'd told, so why on earth would I put myself through the inevitable pain?

Back at work on Monday morning, I swiftly arranged for the original artwork I chose to be delivered to Scott's apartment. I needed to finalize his business with us so he'd have no reason to continue contacting me.

Dear Mr. Blackwood,
Thank you for choosing this amazing artwork. I have no doubt it will look perfect in your dining space. I've organized for the piece to be shipped from our Florida gallery and will contact you shortly to arrange a suitable time for installation.
Kind regards,
L. Warren

I hit send without batting an eyelash and waited.

Dear Miss Warren,
Thank you for your email. Due to Mr. Blackwood's heavy workload, I'll be taking care of this assignment moving forward.
Margot Shelton, Assistant to Scott Blackwood.

My jaw dropped. *Margot Shelton?* Jealousy seeped into my bloodstream. A hot, newly graduated assistant, no doubt. I hated her instantly.

I picked up my phone and texted.

Me: **Too important to answer your own emails now?**

Unknown: **You didn't reply to my text.**

Me: **There was no question.**

There was a momentary pause. He was undoubtedly scrolling through his messages to confirm. *Such a lawyer.*

Unknown: **I really think we should talk.**

Me: **Why?**

Unknown: **So it'll be less awkward when we're working together.**

I attempted to tell him our working relationship had come to an end when Faye knocked on my door. I quickly shoved my phone under the pile of folders on my desk, like a teenage boy busted with porn, and smiled up at her.

"You, my dear, just scored a major contract for AG Galleries."

"I...did?"

"Don't pretend like you don't know," she said, wiggling her finger at me. "I mean, selling a couple of paintings here and there is great, but fitting out an entire building with artwork? This is huge!" Her grin covered her entire face. "You must have made quite an impression on Mr. Blackwood."

My jaw dropped. "What?"

"Yes, he wants to give you the grand tour of the building on Thursday morning. So, wrap up anything outstanding, because I want you solely dedicated to this project." With a noticeable bounce to her step, she headed back to her office. "I'm taking everyone out for lunch!"

Adrian cheered from the adjoining room while I rummaged through my paperwork, preparing for battle. Once I fished out my phone, I found another message waiting.

Unknown: **I'm assuming you know by now?**

Me: **Why are you doing this?!**

Unknown: **Getting the best art dealer in Manhattan to fit out my office? I'd say it's because I make smart choices.**

Me: **Well, this isn't one of them. Find someone else.**

Unknown: Not a chance. See you in a few days.

Unknown: And we still need to talk.

My phone blasted out a tune, and it fumbled out of my hand. Without looking to see who was calling, I swiped it off the floor and answered.

"Yes?!" I yelled then immediately grimaced.

"This is Taylor, Mr. Gibbs' assistant." Her ditzy voice showed no offense.

"Oh, hi. How may I help you?"

"Mr. Gibbs will send a car to collect you on Friday evening at seven."

"Is this for the artwork consultation?"

"He didn't give me specific details, but that must be it." A muffled snicker filtered through the speaker. "Have a great day."

The line went dead before I could even mutter a thank you, although I wasn't thankful at all. I had plans Friday night. Yeah, maybe with the couch and multiple episodes of *Gossip Girl*, but they were solid. Now, I had to spend the evening appeasing the owner's son, who possibly wanted to revisit the past, while measuring his apartment for artwork he had no appreciation for. Not ideal, but I wasn't about to jeopardize my job. Without it, I was screwed.

Instead of heading to the gallery Thursday morning, I put on my big-girl boots and took a cab into Midtown. Whether Scott had ulterior motives or not, I was determined to push my personal feelings aside and do my best work. Faye was relying on me, and I was relying on myself.

The address of Scott's office building was only blocks from his apartment, making me question his need for so many cars. For the first time in my entire life, my eyes were open to the unnecessary. Wants and needs were very separate terms in my life now, and I wasn't concerned about closing the gap.

On the outside, the building appeared like any other corporate entity—super modern and flashy. Tall glass windows stretched from floor to ceiling, mirroring the street around me and a dress Scott had already seen me in. I closed my eyes and blew out a long nervous breath, reminding myself that these things didn't matter to normal people, only my mother. Making use of my reflection, I rummaged through my handbag and pulled out my pink gloss, carefully applying it to my lips before pressing them together.

"What are you doing?" Scott asked, marching out of the entrance with two takeaway coffees.

His professional attire threw me into a voiceless stupor. *Damn.*

"You do realize those windows are tinted," he continued.

My mouth fell open as I glanced back at the glass, and heat blasted into my cheeks.

"That's our coffee shop, and if you don't move, I'm going to have to fire half my staff."

"What? Why?"

He stared back at me then shook his head with a chuckle. "Just come inside, will you?"

As I entered the foyer, multiple eyes moved in my direction from the adjoining coffee shop. Scott sent a menacing glare in their direction before handing me one of the coffees then pressed his hand to my lower back to keep me moving.

"Do you think they recognize me?" I asked, ignoring the shivers his fingers induced.

Scott grumbled, "I doubt they can remember their own names right now."

Unsure of his meaning, I warily brought the coffee to my mouth and took a sip. Years of expensive and exotic coffee blends had made me very particular. I closed my eyes as the flavors awoke my dormant taste buds. "You remember how I like my coffee?"

The side of his mouth quirked upward as he took a sip of his own. "I remember a lot of things about you."

My core pulsed as he licked the milk residue from his lips. Perhaps he meant trivial things, like my favorite color or my favorite food, but his eyes suggested something a little more devious, like his tongue running over my earlobe or down my stomach and along my—

"Lanie," Scott called for presumably the second time. He was standing in the elevator, waiting for me to join him.

"Oh, sorry." I stumbled into the small space beside him as blood seared my cheeks.

Scott eyed me curiously while I continued to drink the coffee all the way to the top floor. Once the elevator doors opened, we walked out into a stunning office overlooking the city. But instead of the view, my attention was drawn to the walls.

"You finally own a Jacque Sinclair." I took a step closer to take in the finer detail. "And an original too. Impressive."

Scott sidled up beside me. "This was the first artwork I bought after we started turning a profit."

My brows lifted as I panned my gaze around the other walls. "Business must be booming."

"We're doing alright." Scott shoved his hand into his pocket and sipped his coffee.

"So why do you want *me* to fit out your building? You appear to have good taste, and well, I wasn't very nice to you the last time we spoke."

"History aside, you know what I like, and I'm too busy to do it myself, so it makes sense." He placed the coffee cup onto his desk and began loosening his tie and unbuttoning his shirt.

"What are you doing?!" I blurted, equally horrified and excited.

"Relax," he said with a laugh. "I had a meeting first thing this morning and haven't had time to change for my next appointment." He grabbed a sports bag from his chair and disappeared into another room. "It's not like you haven't seen it all before!"

"Yeah, well, that was a long time ago," I called out, trying to slow my racing heart by focusing my attention on his artwork collection.

Scott re-entered, wearing a casual navy t-shirt and gray shorts. "Come on, I'll give you the grand tour," he said, directing me to the elevator before I had a chance to ask him about the unusual costume change. The suit was nice and all, but the way the cotton sleeves wrapped around his defined biceps made me wish I hadn't stopped him from undressing in front of me.

I tore my eyes away. "If you're busy, I'm sure there's someone else who can show me around."

"I'm not too busy for you," he said, reaching out for my empty cup. Our hands grazed and our eyes met, and for a fleeting moment, I was seventeen again.

Scott's perfect grin knocked me back into the present. "Shall we?"

With a quick nod, I followed him out of the room and back into the elevator.

Scott folded his arms as he leaned back on the rail. "The majority of the top floors house the money-makers. Commercial lawyers, personal injury, IP, the works, really. But the bottom floors are reserved for family law."

"Why the divide?"

Scott grinned. "I'll show you."

The elevator doors opened into an area nothing like the rest of the building. The color scheme was brighter, the furniture had more of a funky edge, and everyone was wearing casual clothes.

"Good morning, Scott," the middle-aged receptionist greeted. Her desk was covered in trinkets and photos of her children. I liked her immediately. "This must be Lanie."

"Lanie, this is my wonderful assistant, Margot."

My cheeks heated. She wasn't the twenty-something-year-old runway model I expected. "Hi, I think we've met over email."

Scott rested his arm on the countertop. "Can you please organize an all-access pass for Lanie? She'll be working here over the next few weeks."

"Roger that." Margot's fingers sprang to life over her keyboard. "Oh, and your midday appointment cancelled. Would you like me to reshuffle your calendar?"

"No," he said, shooting me a glance. "I think I'll take a long lunch today."

"That'll be a first," she mumbled under her breath.

I smiled up at him, not surprised. "Workaholic, huh?"

"Some people say so."

Margot rolled her eyes. "Everyone says so."

While Scott and Margot continued their banter, I wandered over to what appeared to be a waiting room. There were toys scattered across the floor, numerous bean bags instead of chairs, and multiple televisions. The adjoining room catered for a slightly older audience. It had reading nooks in every corner, video game stations, and a foosball table. A teenage paradise.

"What do you think?" Scott asked, appearing beside me in the doorway.

"You don't have a Peter Pan complex, do you?"

Scott chuckled. "Unfortunately, these rooms aren't designed for me. I figured if we're going to financially benefit from fifty percent of marriages ending in divorce, then this would be our redemption. At Blackwood & Associates, we endeavor to make the process as painless as possible for the children and give them a safe place to hang out in while their parents destroy each other upstairs."

Warmth filled my heart. "Scott…this is amazing."

"We also offer a free counseling service and legal advice for any kids stuck in bad family situations."

I gazed up at him in awe. "You've become everything you ever needed."

His Adam's apple bobbed up and down before he took a step back. "Want to see the rest?" Scott asked, his voice hoarse.

My eyes widened in anticipation. "Definitely."

An hour later, I was sitting in front of Scott at the coffee shop on the ground floor, jotting down his vision for Blackwood & Associates. He wanted to brighten up the kids' area, make the teen area 'cooler', and ramp up the sophistication of the corporate offices.

"What's your budget?" I asked, hovering my pen over my notebook.

"Whatever you think is necessary."

"Are you sure?"

His eyes latched onto mine. "I'm always sure."

I sucked in a quick breath before lowering my gaze back to my notes. "Okay…well, maybe I'll start in the kids' area and work from there."

His grin grew wide and utterly adorable. “Perfect.”

I had to get out of there before I climbed over the table and curled up in his lap. “I should get back to the gallery,” I said, gathering up my bag. “I still have a few things I need to finish up.”

“Of course,” he said with a curt nod. “Please know that you’re free to come and go as you choose. I just thought it would be easier for you to consult if you immersed yourself in the space, instead of doing it all from your office.”

“Quicker maybe, but not easier.” Without meeting his eyes, I closed my notebook and stood up. “I’ll get started on the measure tomorrow.”

“Great,” Scott said, matching my move. “Perhaps we can enjoy another coffee together soon.”

I gazed around the bustling coffee shop, biting my lower lip. At least we’d never be alone. “Sure.”

He stuck out his hand as if it made the situation less awkward. “I’m looking forward to seeing what you come up with, Lanie.”

Scott’s fingers devoured mine, and their warmth traveled up my arm and across my chest, threatening to encase my heart. With a sudden jolt, I tore my hand away, grabbed my things, and bolted out of the building. I had no good reason to continue hating Scott Blackwood, and the realization terrified me.

Chapter 20

The next day, I consumed myself with everything Blackwood & Associates. I read their inspiring vision statement, met numerous staff, and listed ideas as I strolled around the family law sector of the building.

Thankfully, Scott's morning schedule kept him away, meaning I could focus on the task at hand. After grabbing a coffee downstairs, I settled into the children's area with my laptop and began brainstorming. The room was huge with a massive blank wall separating it from the teenage area. I couldn't think of an artwork big enough to fill the space, so I had to consider alternative options.

"Excuse me," a tiny voice pulled me away from the screen. A little girl with long blonde hair stared at me with wide, wondering eyes. "Will you play with me?"

"Oh, um…sure," I said, discreetly checking the time. It was almost lunch anyway. "What's your name?"

The girl smiled, but there was no spark behind it. "Lily."

"Pleased to meet you, Lily. My name is Lanie. What would you like to play?"

"Mermaids!"

"Oh…how do we play that?"

"It's easy," she said, rearranging the room into an underwater wonderland. "You just have to pretend you're a mermaid princess trapped by the evil sea witch and her electric eels." She pointed accusingly at the disheveled rag doll sitting in the corner of the room and scowled.

I gasped dramatically. "We can't escape?"

"Not until the handsome prince saves us, silly."

"Surely we can save ourselves."

Lily shook her head while her voice took a more serious tone. "No, we need him."

"Okay," I said with a shrug, happy to play along with her game. Perhaps she was too young to learn the importance of independence.

"The prince will return us to the castle where our father, the king, is waiting." Lily launched herself onto a bean bag. "Quick! Swim up to the rocks. The eels are coming!"

It wasn't long before I was lying across a pile of pillows, legs crossed at my feet, laughing along with Lily's dramatics. She had a vivid imagination.

A throat cleared in the doorway, and I scrambled back onto my feet.

"He's here!" Lily squealed. "Our prince has finally arrived!"

She wrapped her arms around Scott's legs while mine grew weak as he let go of a deep-chested laugh. "Now that I've saved the day, it's time for you to head home."

Lily frowned. "But I want to stay here with Lanie."

Scott's eyes lifted to mine. "That does sound like fun, but your dad did mention something about ice cream, and I'd hate for you to miss out."

"Ice cream!" Lily's eyes bulged. "See ya!"

"Bye, Lily!" I called after her.

Scott shook his head with a chuckle. "Dumped for dessert."

"I would've traded anything for cookies and cream at that age. She has nothing to apologize for." My smile faded as I gazed over the room. "Sorry about the mess. We got a bit carried away."

"Don't worry about it. Lily deserves a little fun."

"Custody dispute?" I asked, picking up a few toys and throwing them into a basket.

"She told you?"

"No, just a guess," I said, gazing over at the black button eyes of the evil sea witch. "I hope she ends up with her father."

Scott shoved his hands into his pockets. "That's the plan."

With a sad smile, I moved back to the laptop to shut it down.

"Are you finished for the day?"

"Um…yeah." I grimaced. "I hope that's okay. I have a few more jobs to hand over to my colleague, but then you'll have my full attention—I mean, your company will have my attention… not…you…" I squeezed my eyes tight. "You know what I mean."

Scott chuckled softly. "It's fine, Lanie. Have you eaten yet?"

"I plan to grab something from the café across the road on my way out."

"May I join you?"

"I…guess, but I really can't stick around." It was a lie. Adrian couldn't care less if I was late.

"Me neither," he said, checking his watch. "I have back-to-back meetings for the rest of the day."

Once I packed away my computer, Scott and I walked to the elevator together.

"I'm just grabbing some lunch," Scott said to Margot as we passed her desk. "I'll be back soon."

A smirk settled on her lips. "No rush."

With a subtle shake of his head, we arrived at the elevator moments before the doors opened. Inside, two gorgeous women dressed in designer power suits stood before us.

Scott offered a small nod as he entered. "Ladies," he said as he swiped his pass and pressed the button for the ground floor.

"Scott!" The taller one smiled while swishing her long chocolate waves off her shoulder. "Are you coming to drinks tonight?"

I averted my gaze to the falling number above the door. *Come on, come on.*

"Maybe," he said, moving closer to my side. "I'll see how my afternoon pans out."

"Your friend can come too, if she wants."

My gaze shot to the women who were watching me curiously. "Thank you, but I have plans tonight."

The blonde narrowed her eyes. "Have we met? You look familiar."

"You've probably seen Lanie around the building," Scott replied, quick to mislead her. "She's fitting out our offices with artwork."

"Oh, wow," the brunette said, clearly not impressed at all. "Speaking of work, were you able to read through those documents I gave you last week? Perhaps we could meet sometime to discuss." There was no denying the flirtation in her voice.

Scott didn't flinch. "Yes, it all looks fine. No need to discuss. I'll have Margot run them up to you today."

Her jaw clenched with her smile. "Okay. Great. Thanks."

Once the elevator doors opened, I burst out while Scott muttered his goodbyes to his adoring audience.

"Whoa, slow down," he said, jogging to catch up.

As we walked through the foyer, everyone was staring—especially the women. "You've got your own fan club these days," I said after an older lady winked as she toddled by.

He bumped my arm. "A little jealous, are we?"

"I'm merely stating a fact," I uttered with an eye roll.

Scott chuckled. "Right."

With a growl, I set off across the street to the café.

"What would you like?" Scott asked as we sidled up to the counter.

"I can buy my own."

"Come on, it's on the company," he said, throwing his credit card on the counter.

I'd grown to hate blatant displays of wealth, yet I couldn't help myself. I reeled off an array of items off the menu and grinned. At least I'd have lunch for the weekend.

Scott's eyebrows rose, but instead of commenting on my appetite, he mimicked my order. "So, how did it go today?" he asked once the man disappeared to prepare our food. "I mean… apart from escaping the clutches of the evil sea witch."

My cheeks heated. "How long were you watching us?"

"Long enough," he said, donning a deep dimpled smile. "I'm pretty sure a certain mermaid princess will feature in my dreams tonight."

"That's disgusting, Scott. She's six years old."

His face dropped. "I didn't mean…"

I smirked. He was still so gullible.

"You're fucking with me." His eyes sparkled with amusement.

"You make it too easy."

As much as Scott troubled my heart, I enjoyed his company. Even with our history and the underlying secret I held tight, there was something about him that settled my soul. Maybe we could be friends. I was capable of that.

While the last sandwich was made, I turned to Scott. "I have an idea for the wall space in the kids' area I want to run past you."

"Go on."

"Would you consider a mural? I could commission an artist to create something great for the kids."

He nodded in silence as he pondered the idea. "I love it. Go for it."

"Really?!" I squeaked, almost bouncing on my feet. "I'll make some calls on Monday."

Scott thanked the server as our lunches were placed on the counter, then he handed me mine once we left the café. The silence between us grew awkward as we prepared to leave in different directions.

"So…" He rubbed the back of his neck. "What *are* your plans for tonight?"

"I just have this dinner thing…" I'd been trying not to think about it all day.

His jaw twitched as he stared down the street. "A date?"

"No, it's work-related…I think."

Scott's eyes shot back to mine and tapered. "With Nicholas Gibbs?"

"He asked me to help choose artwork for his walls. It's not like I'm in a position to refuse."

"Nicholas Gibbs doesn't have dinner with colleagues unless he is fucking them—or wants to fuck them."

I gasped. "Well, that's not my intention."

"Just be careful," he uttered with a sigh. "Your party-girl reputation may catch up with you."

"What's that supposed to mean?"

"You're fresh out of rehab, Lanie." His eyes were full of misplaced worry. "Nicholas Gibbs isn't the type of guy you should be hanging around."

"You don't know what you're talking about."

"I've dealt with addicts befo—"

"I'm not an addict!" I growled. "Of course you'd believe that."

Scott's eyebrows drew together. "I'm sorry. I just assumed..."

"Stop assuming!" I poked him in the chest. "You. Don't. Know. Me." Before he had a chance to respond, I whirled around on my heel and stormed away. Once I finally hailed a cab to take me back to the gallery, I sunk into the faux-leather seat and closed my eyes. Maybe I did still hate Scott Blackwood.

My phone chimed, and I instantly regretted adding his name to my contact list.

Scott: **I'm sorry. I was a jerk.**

I pursed my lips before the phone vibrated a second time.

Scott: **And maybe a little bit jealous.**

His honesty depleted my anger. I didn't hate him. Not even close.

I was picked up from my apartment by Nicholas's driver, who delivered me to a stunning building on the Upper West Side. The doorman directed me to Nicholas's floor, where he was waiting, drink in hand.

"Melanie!" he greeted me with a kiss and ushered me inside. "Welcome to my new home."

"This place is beautiful," I said, gushing over the delicate art deco features.

"You think?" Nicholas screwed up his face. "I would've preferred something more modern, but my father *insisted* on this one."

I smiled. I'd met Alfie Gibbs various times growing up and was in awe of him. "Your dad has impeccable taste. This place exudes character." I panned my gaze around the empty walls and already envisioned the possibilities. "You just need to find the right artwork to complement the building...and your taste, of course."

"Well, I already have one masterpiece," he said, pointing to the ghastly goat painting leaning against the living room wall.

My teeth gnashed. "And hopefully we can find a suitable spot for it." *Like, in a closet.*

"May I offer you a drink?" he asked, wandering over to a trolley full of liquor. He refilled his glass while waiting for my answer.

"Water will be fine."

Nicholas chuckled as he stirred his drink. "You're not on one of those crazy diets, are you?"

"Something like that," I said, smiling tightly.

After a quick tour of the apartment, which seemed way more exciting to me than Nicholas, we settled down for dinner. His personal chef laid our entrées before us, followed by our mains, while I dominated the conversation with ideas for his walls.

"Do you have a preference of art style?" I asked, gazing around the apartment.

After a moment of silence, Nicholas placed his knife and fork onto his plate and leaned back in his chair. "To be honest, I couldn't care less, but my father is visiting in a few weeks, so I just need something to fill the walls before then."

"I wasn't aware there was such a short timeframe on this." Or the fact he had no passion for art. "Would you mind if I hand this project over to Adrian? I'm currently fitting out an entire building in Midtown, and Faye's told me to clear my calendar."

"I heard about that," he said, signaling for his chef to take his plate. "Faye's very impressed with you. I think you've single-handedly brought the SoHo gallery out of the red."

"Adrian and Faye have been working just as hard. It's a team effort."

Nicholas smirked. "Play your cards right, and you'll be running the place one day."

"Oh, I have no intention of..."

My words dissipated when Nicholas stood up. "Let's go sit by the fire."

In a fluster, I trailed after him. "Adrian really would do a fantastic job here," I said, attempting to keep our interaction professional.

Nicholas poured himself another drink then sank into the

lounge chair. "Very well. I didn't want to mix business with pleasure anyway." He tapped the space next to him, signaling for me to sit.

I took the seat opposite. "Excuse me?"

Nicholas exhaled heavily. "Just because I'm the heir to AG Galleries, doesn't mean I want to talk about art all day." He swirled the whiskey glass in his hand. "I was hoping we could spend some time getting to know each other again."

I stared at the raging fire, not wanting to meet his hungry gaze. Scott was right.

"Rumor has it, Grayson got married," he continued, eyeing my reaction.

I had none. "Yes, he did. Josie is great."

"At least you got out of there before he parted ways with Harlow Corp—talk about taking a pay cut."

"I can assure you he's doing fine." I shifted uncomfortably in the chair. "Sometimes you have to break free of your parents."

His grin grew large and too big for his face. "So, that's what you're doing? You're rebelling."

My jaw slackened. "No, I'm not."

"Come on," he jeered. "You can't possibly be enjoying this minimum-wage bullshit. You're a Warren. You can have anything you want."

"But it means nothing."

"I don't have an iota of what you've got, and it means a hell of a lot to me."

"It's different for you," I said, finally meeting his eyes. "At least you get to dabble in your father's business. I'm not even allowed in my dad's office. I'm supposed to sit and wait for the perfect husband to come along to take over the family business while I twiddle my thumbs and attend charity galas like a good little girl." I grumbled. "I don't want that life anymore."

"It can't be that bad. You get all the benefits without having to work."

"But working makes me feel like I'm a part of something. Yeah, my wage isn't great, but why should it be? I have no experience."

"I could get you promoted..."

"What? No," I cried. "I've only been there a couple of months. That doesn't make sense."

"But look what you've done for the business already," he said, rearranging the coffee table. "My father will support my decision. He's always liked you."

"That's sweet, but I'm not interested." I turned my gaze back to the fire. "I'm where I need to be."

"Very well," he said with a nonchalant shrug. "But the offer stands. Even if we decide to sell the company, I'll make sure you're looked after."

My gaze snapped back to his. "What?"

"Relax, Mel," he said with a chuckle. "No decisions have been made as of yet."

"You're selling AG Galleries?"

"If the price is right, yeah, but I highly doubt my father will go through with it. He's been threatening me for years, trying to get me more involved." Nicholas shrugged. "He won't."

"Will Faye and Adrian keep their jobs?"

"Even if they don't, I'm sure they'll find something else. Manhattan's a big place."

I pinched the bridge of my nose. "That place means everything to them."

Nicholas's eyes tapered. "I don't remember you being this caring in college. The opposite, actually."

"I didn't have much to care about back then," I said before clearing my throat. "Well, nothing I couldn't wash away with a bottle of vodka."

Nicholas laughed. "You were definitely a party girl."

I smiled tightly but said nothing.

"Maybe I could offer you a little reminder of the good times?" He pulled out a bag of white powder from his pocket and dumped it on the coffee table between us.

My entire body stiffened. "Actually, I'm super tired. I think I'll call it a night."

Nicholas groaned. "Come on, the night is young."

"I go to bed early these days," I said as I stood.

"I can handle that." His sleazy smile complemented his wink.

With a wince, I picked up my handbag and edged toward the front door. "Goodnight, Nicholas."

His laughter boomed after me. "Poverty's made you boring, Mel."

Gazing back with the politest smile I could manage, I opened the door to leave. "And that's perfectly okay with me."

As he leaned down to snort his first line, I pulled the door closed behind me with no desire to ever reopen it.

Chapter 21

Moments after walking into the apartment, my cell phone rang. I glanced down at my phone with a frown, wondering who'd be calling so late, and my heart lit up.

"Josie!" I cried as the phone collided with my ear.

"Mel, how are you doing?" Her gorgeous Australian accent was like a warm blanket in winter.

I threw my handbag and keys on the kitchen counter and moved to the couch. "I'm okay," I muttered, slumping into it. I was too tired to hide the truth.

"Date didn't go well?"

"It wasn't a date," I grumbled. "Well, it wasn't meant to—wait, how did you know?"

Josie laughed. "I just got off the phone with Amy."

"But how did she kn—oh, forget it."

"Was it with *you know who*?" Josie's whisper was a clear admission that Grayson was nearby.

"If you're referring to Scott, then no. I had dinner with the owner of the gallery."

"Alfie Gibbs?! Isn't he, like, a hundred years old?"

"Gross, Jos," I said, shaking my head to erase the visuals. "No, it's his son, Nicholas Gibbs. We went to college together."

"Nicholas Gibbs," Josie repeated in a muffled whisper.

I heard Grayson say his name in the background, followed by rustling. After an obvious tussle with Josie, his voice burst into my ear. "Nicholas Gibbs?! Are you serious?"

"Don't start." An exasperated sigh left my lips. "You sound exactly like Scott." I winced as soon as his name left my lips.

The line went dead silent. "Please tell me you're not talking about Scott Blackwood."

I bit my bottom lip. I could feel the lecture coming. "He's a client at AG Galleries. I'm doing some work for his company."

"Can't someone else handle him?" he uttered, clearly annoyed. "You don't need this right now."

My temper rose, but I kept my tone level. "Please don't tell me what I need."

"Have you forgotten what happened at Josie's exhibition?"

"No, I haven't forgotten, but we were wrong about him, Gray."

"What are you talking about?"

"Put me on speakerphone. I need you both to hear what really happened eleven years ago."

A rumble of thunder woke me from my Sunday morning slumber, followed by the chime of my phone. I hadn't been sleeping well, and the interruption offended me.

Scott: **What are you doing right now?**

Me: **Sleeping.**

Scott: **It's almost midday.**

Me: **Your point?**

Scott: **I want to take you for a drive.**

Me: **I'm not interested in your fancy cars.**

Scott: **Look out the window.**

Frowning, I crawled out of bed and sidled up to the window in my pajamas. As I gazed down into the tree-lined street, my mouth fell open. Scott's beautiful old Mustang was parked out front with Scott leaning against it.

My phone chimed again.

Scott: **Cute PJs.**

I stepped away from the window in an attempt to hide my smile.

Me: **Wait there.**

In a fluster, I threw on a pair of skinny jeans with a baggy knit sweater and slipped on my narwhal slippers on my way to the bathroom. Once I'd washed my face and tied my hair back, I jogged down the stairs to find Amy returning from walking Luci. Although, it appeared Luci was walking Amy.

"I assume you know that seriously hot guy out there?" Amy asked, sneaking another peek as the entry door closed behind her.

My cheeks warmed. "He's an old friend."

"Someone from your past, huh?"

I rolled my eyes. "They're popping up everywhere."

"Well, have fun," she squeaked as Luci pulled her into their apartment. "Luci clearly wants his lunch."

With a laugh, I pushed open the door and met Scott at the bottom of the stairs. "I can't believe you still have this car," I uttered, passing him to run my hand over the hood.

Scott's arms folded across his chest. "I told you I'd never get rid of her."

I couldn't help but smile. "I remember."

"So, how about it?" he asked, blue eyes twinkling with mischief. "Want to take the old beast out for a spin?"

Panning my gaze back to the car that held so many memories, I grimaced. As much as I wanted to, it was a problematic idea.

"Come on…what else do you have planned today?" Scott said with a slight tilt to his head.

I bit my bottom lip. "Um…I…"

"Nothing!" Amy yelled from their apartment window. "She has nothing planned."

Scott cackled and offered her a friendly wave. "Shall we?" he asked, turning back to me.

I didn't move, but my heart backflipped. "I'm not exactly dressed to go anywhere. I'll have to change."

"Lanie, you could walk the red carpet in those slippers." He smirked at the sight of my ridiculous footwear. "Plus, we don't even have to leave the car. It's just a drive."

"Fine," I muttered, attempting to open the car door. "Argh, it doesn't open from the outside now? Why haven't you fixed this?"

"There's nothing to fix. She's perfect the way she is." Scott bumped the door with his hip and opened it for me. "These days, you just have to give her a little nudge."

Our close proximity made my heart race, so I quickly lowered myself into the passenger seat. The old vinyl smell struck me first, followed by a highlight reel of memories. I may as well have stepped inside Doc's DeLorean and set the clock back a decade.

Slipping into the driver's side, Scott reached for the coffee cups sitting precariously between us and handed one over. His shoulders lowered at the sight of my pale face. "Hey, we don't have to if yo—"

"No, it's fine," I blurted, grasping the coffee in both hands. The heat was a welcomed comfort. "So, where are we off to?"

He rested one hand on the steering wheel and drummed his fingers. "How does a coastal drive sound?"

My eyes lit up. "Really?"

Scott almost appeared lost for words before his smile mimicked mine. "I figured you'd be missing the beach by now."

The car roared to life, and moments later, we were off, zig-zagging through traffic until we reached the outskirts of Manhattan. After an hour of driving through picturesque streets lined with fiery hues, my nerves started to ease. Whether it was the serene landscape or the distance from the city, I didn't know, but it was just what I needed. The rumbling of the engine vibrated through my body and lulled me into a dreamy state of relaxation and then to sleep.

A light tap on my shoulder drew me from my abyss, and my eyes flickered open. "What time is it?" I asked, wiping drool from the corner of my mouth.

Scott threw me a sideways glance and chuckled. "Almost two."

"What? I've been asleep this whole time?" I squinted through the windshield, and my eyes grew wide at the familiar sights of The Hamptons. "I'm so sorry."

"Don't be. The music drowned out your snoring."

I gasped. "I didn't."

Scott laughed. "No, but you did mention my name a couple of times."

"In your dreams," I muttered, giving his shoulder a playful shove.

He flashed me a grin. "In yours too, apparently."

I rolled my eyes in lieu of a comeback. Being a lawyer, he probably had a hidden recording device in his car, so I didn't push it. Instead, I wound down the window and welcomed the salty blast as it circulated through the car. I closed my eyes and took a long, deep breath before exhaling slowly, relishing the scent of the only thing I missed from LA. The beach.

"Are you hungry?" Scott asked, glancing my way. "I know this great place..."

I groaned. "No more fancy restaurants." I wasn't ready to run into any high-society folk, especially in casual attire with questionable footwear.

"They sell burgers, Lanie."

"Oh." My enthusiasm perked up. "I like burgers."

"Well, you'll love these."

Scott maneuvered through the streets like it was his homeland and ventured to a quieter part of town a little farther up the coast.

"Wow, it's beautiful here," I said, peering out the car window at the gorgeous stretch of beach before us.

Scott smiled softly as he parked the car. "Yeah, it's pretty great. Even in summer, the crowds seem to stay away from this spot."

"It sounds like you come here a lot."

"Whenever I get the chance," he said, staring off into the ocean. "Which seems like less and less these days."

"You don't give yourself any time off?"

"Not lately. Too many clients."

"You can't pass them on to someone else?"

"My associates aren't keen to work on the pro-bono cases, so it takes up most of my spare time. I plan to build a special team to help these kids, but to avoid office politics, I've applied for a few grants. If they come through, I'll be able to justify to my entitled colleagues and anal accountants that we won't go bankrupt if we hire a few more people to work exclusively on their cases." He smiled tightly. "*Then*, I'll be able to do *this* more often."

My chest tightened as I gazed up at him. "Those kids are so lucky to have you on their side."

With a nonchalant shrug, Scott grabbed his wallet. "I'll go get us some burgers," he said, opening his door. "Why don't you find us a spot on the beach?"

"Sure." The whole situation felt eerily familiar. Long drives, beach trips, easy conversation. The only thing missing was Riley in the backseat, hollering for ice cream.

Once Scott opened my door, he shot off across the road to the little burger shack while I slipped off my narwhals. I wandered across the parking lot to the narrow opening amongst the sand dunes and entered. The warm sand enveloped my toes with my first step, but the contrasting sea breeze made me shiver. A little farther up the beach, I found shelter between the sandy mounds and settled down, keeping an eye out for my forthcoming lunch. I was starving.

My heart quickened as Scott's dark-brown locks bobbed up and down in the distant dunes. He looked left, then right, and moments before I raised my arm, his eyes found mine.

Once he drew near, he held out a greasy paper bag with a grin. "Enjoy."

"Thanks," I muttered, appreciating the warmth in my hands.

Scott plonked down next to me and tore into his, barely taking a breath before taking a bite.

Neither of us spoke while we demolished our burgers. They reminded me of Nico's. They reminded me of us. The crashing waves filled the silence as we stole sideways glances at each other as we relished the last few bites.

"Do you miss LA?" Scott asked as he scrunched up the leftover paper bag in his hand.

I swallowed my last mouthful and shrugged. "Sometimes."

"How do find living in New York?"

"Hard," I said before turning to him with a half-smile. "But great."

He rested his arms on his knees as he watched the surf. "I never thought you'd leave LA."

"Neither did I."

Scott took the remains of my paper bag and added it to his. "Is that where you did your rehab?"

"Yeah, at a private center in Malibu, along with the usual celebrity misfits."

He grimaced. "I'm sorry for assuming you'd fallen into that world."

"It's okay. Everyone's going to think the same thing once it gets out."

His eyebrows furrowed. "How hasn't this gotten out? Everything you do has always been so public."

"I'm guessing my parents have been paying people off. It's what they do, apparently." I squeezed my eyes shut. "Sorry."

Scott's jaw pulsed, but he didn't bite. "If you don't want to talk about it…"

"It's okay," I said, pushing a few loose strands of hair behind my ear. "I'd rather you hear it from me than the tabloids." My gaze lowered to my twisting hands. "I was being treated for depression and a mild dependent disorder."

He clasped the ball of trash until his fingers grew pale. "I…I had no idea."

"How would you?"

"Yeah," he muttered with a dejected laugh.

"You haven't been in my life for a long time. The pictures you've seen may depict the life of the perfect heiress, but I can assure you, the reality is much darker."

Scott hung his head low for some time before he spoke. "I'm not familiar with dependent disorders."

"It's basically an anxiety disorder where you're terrified to be on your own." I swallowed the growing lump in my throat and continued. "I didn't think I could live without Grayson, and it drove me to do unthinkable things. I used drugs and alcohol to cope with the consequences of my actions, and although I'm not addicted, I definitely went off the rails a few times."

Scott's tormented eyes finally met mine, waiting for me to continue.

"I, um…" My lower lip trembled as I sifted sand through my fingers. "Overdosed last Christmas."

Scott's shoulders slumped, and his voice grew raspy. "Lanie…"

I blinked back tears. "I don't think I meant to, but after a friend told me Grayson had moved on with another woman, I lost it. I took a few pills, then a few more, and I thought, maybe… maybe he'd come back if he saw how much I needed him."

Scott's hand slid through the sand to clasp mine. "Promise me you'll never do that again."

"I'm in a good place now," I said, squeezing his fingers. "I promise. I speak to my therapist weekly, and there have been no signs of a relapse."

With a short nod, he turned his glistening gaze back to the ocean but left his thumb tracing circles over my hand. "Who else knows about this?"

"Just close friends and family." I paused. "And you."

"Do your parents know I'm…we're…" He winced.

"In my life?" I suggested, not knowing how to define us either. "I haven't spoken to them since moving here."

"What?" Scott's head jerked back. "Why?"

I pulled my hand away from his to swipe another stray hair from my face. "They're not in my life anymore."

"They cut you off?!"

"No, I cut them off." I pushed myself off the ground and brushed the sand from my jeans.

"Wow…" Scott blinked numerous times as he absorbed my words. "That's…brave."

With a simple shrug, I turned and wandered closer to the water's edge. I had to keep moving before my emotions caught up with me.

Scott was quick to follow. "I mean it, Lanie. To give that all up…that takes guts."

"I should've done it years ago," I said, dragging my feet through the wet sand. "Before I…" My throat closed up. I wasn't ready to tell him.

"Before what?" he asked, slowing his pace as he faced me.

"Before I screwed everything up with Grayson." It wasn't a lie. It just wasn't the entire truth.

Scott picked up a stone and threw it across the water. It skimmed once, twice, three times before sinking. "You really love him, don't you?"

"I do." I threw him a sideways glance, noting his rigid stature. "But not in the way you think. Our relationship was… complicated. I became too dependent on him."

Scott frowned. "It's perfectly natural to depend on the man you intend to marry."

"Not when your entire relationship is based on a lie."

The lines in Scott's forehead deepened, but he didn't press. Instead, the corner of his mouth quirked upward. "I can't say I'm not happy it didn't work out."

I held back my smile as my heart fluttered away. "So, what about you?" I asked hurriedly, trying to diffuse the warmth traveling up my neck. "I bet there are broken hearts all over New York."

Scott shook his head with a chuckle. "I never let it go that far…plus I don't have time to date."

"So, you just fuck them then?" Adrian's words popped into my head, and I set them free.

"What?!" Scott's eyes widened. "No, that's not…"

I burst out laughing. "I'm just messing with you."

"Fuck, Lanie," he said, letting go of a nervous chuckle.

"What about the women in the elevator the other day? I saw the way they were looking at you."

"I'm their boss. They're either dreaming of a bonus or a promotion. Plus…" He straightened his posture. "I don't date colleagues."

"That's probably a good idea," I said, wondering if I fit into that classification.

"I take my work very seriously."

"I know." I bumped his side with a small smile. "You're the most determined person I've ever met."

We both grew silent as we continued ambling along the beach.

"You've really made something of yourself out here," I said, peeking over at him. "Just like you said you would."

"I guess part of me had something to prove. To my father, to your parents." His eyes met mine. "To you."

"You never had to prove anything to me," I said with a twinge of frustration and sadness. "So, you can take me off that list."

"I did." Scott shoved his hands in the pockets of his rolled-up jeans. "The moment I realized you never received my letter, any residual anger I had felt toward you evaporated." He lowered his gaze. "I was furious for a long time after I found out about you and Grayson. I threw myself into my studies then gambled everything I had on starting my own business. It was a huge, potentially stupid risk, but I guess it paid off."

"You guess?" I laughed. "You're one of the most successful men in Manhattan."

"It came with a price though."

I stared out to sea, loathing the world we lived in. "Everything does."

Scott's hand encircled my left wrist, bringing us to a standstill. "I want you to know…I paid your dad back. For everything. I worked two jobs through college, and with my scholarship to Harvard, I didn't need any of the extra money he gave me."

"I don't doubt you. I'm just sorry he put you in that awful position."

"Don't do that."

"Do what?" I asked, narrowing my gaze.

"Apologize."

"But it's partly my fault. I pleaded with him to help you that night."

He brought his other hand over my right elbow. "My brother would've spent the last eleven years in foster care if it wasn't for you."

"You would've found a way to keep him out," I said, conscious of the effect his simple touch had on my body. "You care about him more than you care about yourself." I folded my arms around my waist, creating an invisible barrier between us. "I can only assume you take after your grandfather, because you're nothing like your dad."

"Yeah," he muttered with a short laugh. "Thank fuck."

"Is he still in prison?"

Scott grimaced. "He went back in a few years ago."

"That must be hard on you and Riley."

"He's not our problem anymore," he uttered with absolute certainty. "We've moved on with our lives."

I was envious of the line he'd drawn. "Maybe you could give me some pointers."

"Easy," he said with a shrug. "Focus on what's good in your life."

"That's it?"

"I haven't perfected it, but I'm trying a little harder these days."

"Well..." I smiled. "It sounds like a decent plan."

As we continued our stroll, I stared at the beach houses that laid beyond the sand dunes. They weren't as extravagant as the properties I grew up in, but they were just as beautiful.

"I like it here." It was the perfect contrast to the bustling city.

Scott studied me as I absorbed the details. "I thought you might." His eyes lingered a fraction too long.

"What?" I asked, examining his unreadable expression.

He cleared his throat. "Nothing," he said, averting his gaze farther down the beach. "We should probably head back if we want to be home before dinner."

"Oh, okay." My heart dipped. I could've walked for miles by his side.

Once we changed course, Scott nudged my side. "Speaking of...how was your dinner with Nicholas on Friday night? Awful, I presume."

I laughed. "It was...uninspiring."

He barely hid his smirk. "Oh?"

"He wants a lot more than I'm ready for."

Scott hummed. "And what is that exactly?"

"Friendship," I stated matter-of-factly. "It's all I can offer anyone right now."

With a curt nod, Scott fell silent while I drifted toward the shoreline, eager to test the water.

Remnants of a wave unexpectedly devoured my bare feet, soaking the bottom of my jeans. "Shit, that's cold," I cried, hopping back to where Scott stood.

He burst out laughing. "Come on, there's a towel in the car."

We spent the next few hours driving home and reminiscing about our adventures with Riley. I hadn't laughed that hard in months, and once we pulled up beside my apartment building, I found myself wanting to prolong the night.

"I…um…have some leftover pizza upstairs, if you want to stay for dinner…"

Scott's jaw tensed as he gazed up at my building. "I…better not. I've got a ton of reading to do before tomorrow."

"Of course." My smile was forced. "No problem."

He hesitated a moment before yanking open his door and climbing out. Once he opened my door, I kept my gaze lowered as I stepped out. "Thanks for the drive," I said once I was safely on the sidewalk. "It was nice to get out of the city."

Scott crossed his arms as he leaned back against the car. "Maybe we can do it again sometime."

My entire body warmed at the thought. "That would be nice." With a small smile, I turned and made my way up the stairs.

"Lanie…" Scott called out.

I paused mid-step, hoping he'd changed his mind about dinner.

"Why did you change your name?"

My mind rummaged through every plausible excuse, but the truth fell from my lips. "It just makes things a little easier," I said, turning to face him. "There are no expectations. No manipulation. I can finally be myself."

"But I thought you hated being called that."

"You know that's not true." I offered him a sad smile while backstepping toward the entrance. "It was the only time I was ever truly happy."

As Scott's mouth parted, I swiftly tapped in the passcode and disappeared into the building, not daring to peek back at the man responsible.

Chapter 22

Over the next few weeks, I managed to coordinate artwork for the majority of the Blackwood & Associates building and was eagerly awaiting delivery and installation. Scott and I enjoyed a coffee together every other day, where I'd update him on the project and chat about trivial things. It was…nice. Too nice.

What concerned me was how much I craved Scott's company. I searched for him in the hallways, hoped to bump into him in the elevator, and every time he sent something funny to my phone, my heart leaped with joy. Perhaps this was what friendship was meant to be like. Apart from Grayson and Josie, the majority of the 'friends' I'd made over the years only used me to boost their status, so I had no idea how the real ones worked.

When I overdosed, my reputation was tainted. My best friend, Staci, hadn't even attempted to call or visit me in hospital, which only solidified my fear of loneliness. I'd tried to talk to her before everything imploded, but she accused me of bringing her down and promptly changed the subject—just like my mother would've done. I was consistently being fooled by narcissistic personalities, and it was a pattern I needed to break.

"Wow."

I spun around to find Scott standing in the doorway of the children's area. I waited for my heart to slow. It didn't. "What do you think?"

Scott stepped closer to examine the magnificent mural spanning the length of the wall. "It's better than I imagined."

I followed his gaze over the underwater scene filled with vibrant coral and friendly sea-creatures and grinned. "See how the sunlight reflects off the scales?" I asked, pointing to the glittering rainbow fish scattered through the image. "Isn't it magical?"

"The kids are going to lose their shit." Scott's eyes darted around the room in fear of violating little ears. "Lily, especially."

My smiled widened. She was my inspiration. I ran my gaze over his aged Batman t-shirt and weathered jeans. "No suit today?"

"They're forbidden down here," he said, crossing his arms as he continued to admire the detail in the artwork. "The kids don't appreciate the power suit as much as my older clients."

I was certain his older clients—especially the female ones—would take whatever they could get. Scott was drop-dead gorgeous, and the years apart did nothing to dull his effect on me.

"So, what do you have planned for the teenage area?" he asked.

My eyes snapped up from his ass. "Oh, um…I can show you"—I motioned to the adjacent room—"if you have a minute."

"I have a minute," he said with a smirk before gliding into the next room.

His distinct, expensive cologne pulled me along like a leash. I was clearly ovulating.

"I'll be with you soon, Ty," Scott said to the lone kid staring intensely at the television in front of him. His bottom lip was swollen and bloody, and I couldn't bear to imagine how it happened.

Ty wrestled with a controller, manipulating the character on screen. "Yeah, cool. I've just gotta beat this sucker." He threw up a glance before doing a double-take. His eyes grew large when they met mine, and the controller fell from his hands. "Who is this fine piece of—"

"Ty." Scott's unyielding tone stopped him dead in his tracks.

Ty held up his hands in surrender, but instead of retreating, he switched his attention to me. "Are you going out with this guy?" he asked with a deviant grin. "Because if you're not…"

Scott cleared his throat. "If you want me to help you, don't speak another word."

Ty slumped back onto the couch. "Sorry, bro…but *damn*."

"Let's talk about this later," Scott said, turning back to me. "I'm all booked up today, but I'll get Margot to organize a time next week."

And just like that, he reminded me of what we really were. Colleagues. Two people using each other for a mutual benefit. I forced the corners of my mouth upward. "Sure."

Scott's eyes fixed on mine, and his brow furrowed.

"Enjoy your day, Ty," I said, averting my gaze to the boy. "You're in good hands."

"Jesus..." Ty grabbed his chest as he stared up at my mouth. "Scott...if you're not tappin'—"

"Let's go, Ty," Scott uttered impatiently, almost dragging him out of the room. "We've got work to do."

Dear Miss Warren,

Due to some unexpected business tonight, Mr. Blackwood can no longer be present for the artwork installation in his apartment. He has requested your attendance in his absence. His brother will be there to let you in. I hope this hasn't caused you any inconvenience and apologies for the short notice.

Margot Shelton, Assistant to Scott Blackwood

Working late on a Friday night? *Bullshit.* I'd heard murmurs about after-work drinks, and he obviously felt his time was better spent sipping martinis with supermodel lawyers than watching our installers hammer nails into his walls. As much as it made total sense, I was miffed.

With a sigh, I sent back a quick response saying I'd be happy to and left the office shortly after. Not bothering to catch a cab, I walked directly to Scott's apartment, needing to work off my irritation.

Riley greeted me at the door. "Hey, Lanie," he murmured with a mouth full of Cheetos. "Scott's not home yet."

"I know, he's working late. His assistant asked me to wait around for the artwork installers. Would you mind if I come in? I doubt they'll be much longer."

"Sure, no problem." He opened the door wide and waved me through. "You can watch *Game of Thrones* with me."

"That works," I said, scared to admit I'd never seen an episode.

I wandered toward the leather couches, noting the pile of art supplies on the coffee table between them.

"Want a soda?" Riley asked on his way to the kitchen.

"Yeah, thanks." I dumped my bag on the floor and settled into the chair.

Riley handed me a soda on his return. "Scott told me you used to date."

"A very long time ago. I think you were about six at the time."

"I think I remember you…at least, the idea of you." He launched onto the couch opposite and opened his can. "I'd thought I'd dreamed you up until Scott brought that photograph home."

"You're still into your art, I see," I said, steering the conversation away from the past.

Riley shrugged. "It keeps me out of trouble."

"Can I see?" I asked, motioning to the sketchbooks.

"Um…sure." He picked one up and passed it over, biting his lower lip.

As I carefully turned the pages over, one by one, my mouth parted. "These are incredible." I peered up at him. "I always thought you were talented as a kid, but now…wow. You've developed into an amazing artist."

Riley's cheeks burned red. "I don't know about that."

"Who taught you these techniques?" They reminded me of something I'd seen before, but I couldn't place the style.

"I've been attending classes at this little studio in SoHo a few nights a week and Saturday mornings. It's a place where kids with…unusual upbringings can go to express themselves through healthier mediums. It's kind of like therapy, I guess. My teacher is amazing. If you like my work, you should see hers."

A wave of exhilaration washed over me. "I'd love to."

"Really?" Riley's face jerked backward. "I've been trying to get Scott down there for months."

"Is he aware of how good you are?"

Riley slumped back into the cushions and took a long sip of his soda. "I don't talk about it with him anymore. He wants me to focus on my grades."

"Well…I'd love to see this place."

"What place?" The approaching voice surprised us both.

"Scott," I uttered, rising to my feet as he appeared in front of us. My heart pounded. "What are you doing here?"

He rested his hands on his hips. "I live here. I was going to ask you the same thing."

"Margot said you were working late and asked me to come here and wait for the installers."

"Of course she did," he grumbled, rubbing the back of his neck.

"Pardon?"

"She must've been confused. I told her the installers had rescheduled to tomorrow morning."

"So, you're not working late?" I screwed up my nose. "Or out for drinks?"

A subtle twinkle appeared in Scott's eyes. "No."

Riley chuckled. "This is awkward."

Drawing in a deep breath, I exhaled slowly. "Okay, well, I'll get out of your hair. I know you've had a big day." I scooped up my bag and headed for the door.

"Stay for dinner," Scott blurted as my fingertips grazed the handle.

"We're having tacos," Riley sang out.

Praying they couldn't hear the growl of my stomach, I slowly turned. "Are you sure? I don't want to impose."

"It's no imposition, Lanie," Scott said, moving closer until we were alone in the hallway. "We're friends, aren't we?"

I winced internally. "Yeah…"

"Well…friends invite friends over for dinner all the time."

"You never invite friends over for dinner," Riley yelled out, clearly eavesdropping.

Scott pursed his lips and strolled back to his brother. "Why don't you go finish your homework in your bedroom while I cook."

"I don't have any." A look passed between them that I wasn't close enough to read. "But I guess I could go revise."

Scott squeezed his brother's shoulder. "Thanks, buddy."

Riley mumbled something under his breath as he stalked off, leaving us alone.

"He's still a great kid," I said, picking up my soda to follow Scott to the kitchen.

He pulled a beer from the fridge and cracked it open. "Yeah, he's alright."

"And so talented." I couldn't help but smile as I took a seat at the island bench. "His artwork is incredible."

"If only he put as much effort into his schoolwork. He'd be a shoo-in for Harvard." Scott took a long swig of his beer then licked the excess from his lips.

"What about art school?" I asked, pulling my eyes away.

"Not if he wants to make a living."

"Money's not everything." I knew all too well.

He scoffed. "Says the heiress."

My teeth gnashed as I pushed my drink aside. "Maybe I shouldn't stay."

"No, no…" Scott rounded the counter with a grimace. "I'm sorry. I shouldn't have said that."

"I'm happier now than I've been in my entire life, and I can barely afford to eat."

Scott leaned back on the island bench and lowered his head. "I just don't want him having the same struggles we grew up with."

"You've given him a pretty good start here," I said, panning my gaze around the apartment that was a billion times better than the house he grew up in. "But he's almost an adult. Let him make his own decisions—and his own mistakes." I reached for his hand and waited until his gaze met mine. "Don't stifle his path…he'll only resent you later."

Scott grew silent before the side of his mouth quirked up. "Since when did you start giving Yoda advice?"

"Patience, you must have," I said, mimicking the little green creature.

Scott burst out laughing. "You finally watched *Star Wars*?"

"Josie's apartment has the world's slowest Internet and an unhealthy selection of sci-fi and horror movies, so yeah, I may have watched it a time or two."

"I always knew it," Scott muttered on his way back to the kitchen.

"Knew what?"

"Under all that beauty"—Scott's dimples deepened—"is just a big-ass nerd."

"Well, thank you." I chuckled. "I'll take that as a compliment."

Scott grabbed all the ingredients from the fridge and dumped them on the counter. "Wait...did you say you're living in Josie's apartment?"

"Only until they get back from their honeymoon. Hopefully, I'll have enough money saved for my own place by then."

Scott pondered me quietly. "You really are starting over, aren't you?"

"Yep, I'm learning all the basics. Paying bills, cleaning, cooking..."

"Do you know how to make tacos?"

"Why do you think I stayed for dinner?" I said with a smirk.

Scott waved me into the kitchen. "Come on, I'll show you."

After easy, lighthearted, and unnervingly familiar conversation around the dinner table, I joined the Blackwood boys in the living room to watch *Game of Thrones*. They were enthralled while I sat there wondering what the fuck was going on. I didn't mind, though. I merely enjoyed the company.

"I should get going," I said when Riley dragged himself to bed at the end of the episode. "It's getting late."

"I'll drive you." Scott rose from the chair to fetch his car keys.

"Don't be silly. The gallery will pay for a cab."

"No friend of mine is catching a cab alone at this time of night."

My heart dipped with his use of the word *friend,* but it eased my apprehension. "Alright," I said, slinging my bag over my shoulder as I followed him into the hallway. "Will Riley be okay on his own?"

"He's almost an adult, remember?" Scott's eyes twinkled back as he grabbed his keys.

With a roll of my eyes, I sauntered past. "Fine, but we're taking the Mustang."

We drove in silence, but my head was full of noise. I shouldn't have been spending so much time with Scott. It was dangerous. My heart was racing, and my neck was perspiring, meaning I was still attracted to him, and by the way he was throwing me sideways glances, I was almost certain the feeling was mutual. Without Riley as a buffer, there was nothing between us but hot, sticky air full of tension and unsaid words.

At least my work at Blackwood & Associates was wrapping up. I'd be able to move on, reprogram, refocus. Scott was bending the rules I was determined to follow. Under no circumstances was I allowed to start another relationship until I had my shit together—and my shit wasn't remotely together.

Relief washed over me with the cool night air when Scott jerked my door open on arrival.

"Thanks for dinner tonight," I said, trying to avoid direct eye contact as I stepped out. "I had fun."

"Maybe we could do it again sometime…on our own?"

My stomach somersaulted. "I'm not sure if that's a good idea."

"That's because it's a *great* idea."

His enthusiasm made me chuckle. "You haven't changed," I muttered with a shake of my head.

"I wore you down last time. I figure I can do it again."

I gazed down the street. "Things are different now, Scott. I'm not the same girl."

He stepped closer until the heat of his breath caressed my neck. "But it feels the same…doesn't it?" His hand slid over mine. "Every time I see you…it's like my first day at Summerhill all over again."

My chest tightened. "But this isn't high school anymore, and I'm not ready to start anything right now."

"Start?" His forehead grazed mine. "We started something eleven years ago that we never finished."

I kept my gaze lowered, knowing if I stared up into his, I'd surely break. "But so much has happened…"

"Is this about Grayson?" Scott asked, taking a step back. "Because if you're still in love with him, I'll walk away."

I should've lied and ended things right there, but I couldn't. As soon as I lifted my eyes to the pain simmering behind his glimmering blue irises, I lost my nerve. "I adore him…but as for love, I haven't felt that since…" *You.*

"Lanie…" Scott's shoulders sank.

"Please don't." I pulled my hand from his. "I spent so many years hating you…trying to forget you…I can't just go back."

"Lanie…" His eyes bored down into mine as he stepped closer.

"No," I cried, pushing against his solid chest. "I won't survive losing you again."

Scott's hands traveled up my arms until they cradled my face, leveling our gazes. "I'm not going anywhere."

With my whimper, his lips grazed mine, soft and gentle and my heart stopped. My mouth parted as I breathed him in, equally petrified and aroused. As his glorious scent penetrated my sinuses, the overwhelming desire to taste him took hold. My lips pressed against his until a low growl rumbled deep within his chest.

"Lanie," he mumbled, drunk with want.

Before we had a chance to deepen the kiss, I jerked back, breathless. "No, I can't…I won't…" Fear riddled my body as my heart threatened to detonate. "I have to go."

So, I ran.

Chapter 23

"That kiss was...spectacular." Amy closed her eyes as she fell back against the front door moments after barging into the apartment with leftover pancakes.

I took the plate before she dropped it mid-orgasm. "Were you spying on me last night?" I asked, cautiously placing the plate on the kitchen counter to avoid a serious syrup incident. The pancakes were swimming.

She pouted. "Why didn't you invite him up?"

"I'm not ready for that," I muttered, rummaging through the cutlery drawer.

"Who says?" Amy plonked her hands on her hips. "Your therapist?"

"One-night stands aren't healthy for me right now."

"This isn't just a random hook-up..." Amy said, approaching with wide, twinkling eyes. "This is *Scott Blackwood*...your dreamboat boyfriend."

My gaze whirled back to hers. "*Ex*-boyfriend...and how did you find out about him?"

"Josie maaay have called last night, and she filled me in," Amy uttered with a guilty wince. "She was a little cagey with the details, though."

I plonked myself onto the kitchen stool and shoveled an extra-large portion of layered goodness into my mouth. "It's complicated," I mumbled, continuing to chew. My mother would've been disgusted.

Amy bounced on her toes. "I could read your palm..."

I clutched the knife and fork a little tighter, not risking

a glimpse. "I don't want to know what the future holds. I'm struggling enough with the present."

"Fair enough. I like surprises too."

It wasn't what I meant, but I let it be. Amy was too adorable to correct, so I changed the subject instead. "Are we still going for a run tomorrow morning?"

She paused for a moment before turning back with a growing smile. "Oh…I think you'll be too busy for that."

"Enlighten me on the amazing plans I have?" I asked in utter confusion. "Because last I checked, there were none…just like every weekend."

"I guess it'll be one of those surprises," Amy said with a wink before turning to leave. "You should get that."

"Get what?" I asked, glancing around the apartment.

Amy conveniently disappeared moments before my cell phone burst into song, so I swiped it off the table and answered. "Very funny," I said, refusing to fall for her prank.

"I'm glad you're amused."

My boss's voice surprised me more than Amy's psychic prediction. "Sorry, Faye, I thought you were someone else."

"Never mind," she puffed, obviously on her morning power walk. "I need you to get to the Blackwood residence pronto. The installers just arrived, and Scott is a no-show. He's not even picking up his cell."

I stared down at my half-eaten pancakes, and my shoulders slumped. At least lunch was sorted. "Sure. I'll be there soon."

"Fantastic! I knew I could rely on you. Ciao."

Faye's abrupt departure didn't surprise me. She was a no-nonsense woman, and I admired her for it. After a quick shower, I threw on the only clean clothes I had left for the week and caught a cab directly to Midtown. My foot tapped incessantly as the elevator rose, and I prayed the installers hadn't already left. Where the hell was Scott anyway?

As the doors slid open, I marched directly into their apartment to find Jeff and Bob, our installers, twiddling their thumbs while Riley prepared his breakfast in the kitchen.

"I told them where to put it, but they don't believe me," Riley said as he covered his cereal with milk.

Jeff grimaced. "Sorry, Lanie, you know our policy. Only you or the homeowner can sign off on this. I'm not making that mistake again."

"That's okay. I'm here now," I said, offering him a reassuring smile. "Let's get this done quickly, shall we?" Preferably before Scott got home and reminded me of everything I wanted but couldn't have.

As I directed and supervised the installation, Riley settled at the island and scooped large mouthfuls of processed sugar into his mouth. I was envious.

"Where's your brother this morning?" I asked, trying to subdue my irritation and be professional. I had an entire Saturday of nothing planned, and Scott was ruining it.

Riley wiped dribbling milk from his chin. "He was all over the place this morning, so he took off for a run to clear his head. He even left his phone here, and he *never* does that."

I guess he was as flustered about the night before as I was. Before I gave it another thought, the sound of the front door flying open and banging against the wall made my heart lurch.

"Sorry, Rils!" Scott appeared in the living room, sliding his fingers through his damp hair. "I totally spaced on th—" He froze when he saw me. "Lanie? You're here?"

"She didn't exactly have a choice, bro. You owe her big time." Riley shook his head. "You should probably take her out for lunch or something."

Panic rammed into my chest. "No, no…it's totally fine," I said, nervously laughing off the suggestion. "We're almost done here anyway."

"How's that, Lanie?" Bob asked, straightening the beautiful piece of art. It complemented the room perfectly.

"Perfect. Thanks." I smiled at the men as they packed up their gear. "You guys have a great weekend."

Once the front door closed behind them, Scott rushed toward me. "I'm so sorry, Lanie. I sprinted all the way back when I remembered."

I ran my gaze over his sweaty body and repressed my desire to taste his salty lips. "I can tell."

"So can I," Riley uttered, waving his hand in front of his nose.

Scott ran his tongue over his bottom lip as he watched me. "Will you wait around until I've had a shower?"

I looked away with a wince. Surely I could muster an excuse or, at the very least, not jump in with him.

"Please?" His fingertips grazed my forearm. "Riley will make you a coffee. He's pretty good at it."

Riley's smile packed a punch. "Pretty great, you mean."

"Alright," I muttered, unable to refuse the Blackwoods' natural charm or my caffeine addiction.

"I won't be long." Scott gave my arm a gentle squeeze before disappearing into what I assumed was his bedroom. The sound of running water followed.

"I've never seen my brother ogle over a girl before." Riley snickered as he prepared the coffee. "Normally, it's the other way around."

Leaning back on the counter, I attempted to exude indifference. "Girls like him, huh?"

Riley shrugged. "I don't know why. I mean, he's super annoying and arrogant...and his smile is entirely too wide." He filled an insulated glass and passed it over. "I'm pretty sure I'm the superior-looking brother," he added with a wink.

After laughing at his corniness, I took a sip. "Well, you definitely make a decent cup of coffee."

Riley proceeded to do a little jig. "I told you, didn't I?"

I chuckled. He was more like his brother than he thought, minus the weight of the world on his shoulders.

While he made another coffee, I studied his profile. His hair was darker than Scott's, and his build was slimmer, but his eyes were replicas of the ones almost every girl fell in love with back in high school. "So, does the superior-looking brother have a girlfriend?"

"Not exactly. There's a girl I like in my art class, but it's a little complicated. Her older sister is my art teacher, and I don't want to cause any trouble. I love that place."

"Do you intend to hurt her?" I asked, crossing my arms.

"No," he gasped. "Of course not."

"Then I don't see any harm in it. Treat her with respect, and I'm sure her sister will sense what type of guy you are."

Riley's mouth tugged up at the sides. "Maybe I will ask her out," he said, placing his empty dish into the sink. "You know, it's kind of nice having a female to talk to around here. My brother gives shitty advice."

"Excuse me?" Scott appeared in the doorway, drying his hair with a towel. His white t-shirt lifted at his waist, giving me a welcome glimpse of the toned body beneath. "My shitty advice paid for this apartment…and your clothes…and your food…"

"Whatever." Riley rolled his eyes as he pushed off the counter. "I need to get to art class."

"Oh." My face lit up. "You're going there today?"

"Yeah, you want to come check it out?"

"I'm sure Lanie has plans, Riley."

"Nope." I grinned at his brother. "You can even hitch a ride in my cab if you like."

Scott's back straightened. "I'll drive you."

I turned my gaze to Scott once Riley disappeared into his bedroom. "You don't have to come."

"Are you kidding? And leave you alone with the superior-looking Blackwood? No fucking way." His dimples intensified with his growing smile.

"You heard all that?"

"I caught a bit," he said, sipping the coffee Riley left for him. "Thanks for giving him some advice on the girl situation. I haven't exactly been a great role model in that department."

"No one serious?"

"There were a couple I had second dates with…but no…not since you." His unwavering gaze penetrated mine, making every hair on my body rise.

Riley burst back into the room, carrying a large folio. "Let's go!"

"Great," I cried, slinging my bag over my shoulder before I slung myself around Scott.

Scott chortled at his brother. "I've never seen you get ready so quick before."

"Well, unlike you, I'm a gentleman. I don't keep people waiting." Riley puffed out his chest and held out his elbow. "Come on, Lanie."

With a laugh, I slipped my arm into Riley's and let him guide me down the hallway with his grumbling brother trailing behind.

Riley's art class was held in a dilapidated building not far from AG Galleries.

"It's beautiful," I gushed as I gazed up at the delicate features of the three-story building that were now worn and ruined from years of neglect.

Riley screwed up his face. "Are we looking at the same building?"

Scott peered up and grinned. "Lanie's always had a knack for seeing the beauty in things."

My body warmed when I peeked over to find him admiring the building also.

"Well, she's obviously not the only one," Riley grumbled as he pointed to the SOLD sign plastered across the window.

"We'll work something out," Scott said, resting his hand on his brother's shoulder.

Before I could probe, Riley entered the building, followed by Scott, who held the door open for me.

"Thank you," I whispered as I edged past his freshly washed body. He smelled so fucking amazing it made me dizzy.

We passed the empty reception desk into a huge room divided by recycled office partitions. Spectacular murals donned every wall while kids worked enthusiastically within separate zones on different mediums. It was a beehive of creativity, and I loved it.

"My teacher's over there," Riley said, motioning us to follow. "Mrs. Freeman!" he called out to the petite brunette woman standing by the washbasins. "I'd like you to meet my brother and his girlfriend. She works at AG Galleries."

"Oh, we're not—" My voice caught when the woman turned around. "Cara?"

Her unforgettable brown eyes bulged. "Melanie?!"

I blinked back tears as I cautiously moved forward. "Is it really you?"

Cara dropped the brushes into the sink and charged toward me. "I can't believe my eyes," she cried, wrapping her arms around me.

I squeezed tight. "It's been so long."

"And Scott? Oh my god," Cara uttered, peering over my shoulder.

Scott grinned as she hugged him. "So, you're the teacher my brother keeps raving about?"

Riley watched the scene unfold, jaw agape. "You all…know each other?"

"We went to school together in LA," I said, unable to wipe the smile from my face.

Cara turned to Riley. "Melanie was actually the person who inspired me to become an artist."

"You were always an artist," I muttered, shaking my head. "Just like Riley."

She smiled at her student. "Well, I won't dispute that."

To ease Riley's embarrassment, Cara turned her focus back to us. "I always wondered what happened to you two," she said, placing her hands on her hips. "I mean, I've followed Melanie on social media for years, but Scott…you fell off the face of the earth after high school."

I frowned. All this time, she had been watching my life unfold, and I knew nothing about her. "Why didn't you reach out?"

Cara grimaced. "Oh, I just figured since you had changed your number and didn't tell me, you weren't keen to keep in touch."

"That's not true." A sharp pain shot straight through my heart. "My parents…they…"

"Maybe that's a story for another time," Scott said, signaling to the pricked ears nearby.

I shook my head. "You're right. Another time."

Cara moved closer, lowering her voice. "And how's Grayson?"

"He's great. Married now."

"Didn't you just break up?"

A laugh burst from my mouth. "We have a lot to catch up on."

"We do," she said with a gleam in her eye.

"So, tell me. How have *you* been? Has life has been good to you since you left LA?"

"I guess it has." An aura of peace radiated through her smile. "I'm married now...with two kids."

My jaw dropped. "Two kids?"

"And my sister helps out here on weekends." She glanced over to the pretty girl on the stepladder, hanging artwork to dry. "Hey, Poppy! Come here a sec."

Riley's blush deepened on her approach, silently admitting his crush.

"These are my old friends, Melanie and Scott. You were probably too young to remember meeting Mel, but we were quite close back in high school."

Poppy's face paled as she stared at me. "You're Melanie Warren. Like...*the* Melanie Warren. You look so different from your photos...I mean...still beautiful, just more...real." Her gaze whirled back to Cara. "Why didn't you tell me you had a famous friend?"

Cara held back her laughter as she peeked my way. "Maybe *this* is why."

"It's lovely to see you again, Poppy," I said, offering her a warm smile.

"Why don't you guys come over for dinner tonight?" Cara asked. "I'd love for you to meet my boys."

My heart burst. "Are you sure?"

"Of course I'm sure! My husband always cooks too much, and Poppy's heading out, so..."

"We'd love to," Scott said, answering like we were a joint unit.

Riley cleared his throat. "I've actually got plans," he said, peering up at Scott. "I'm staying over at Mike's, remember?"

Now it was Poppy's turn to blush. *Interesting.*

"Well, that settles it," Cara said, quickly jotting down her address on a piece of paper. "Is seven pm okay?"

I grinned. "Perfect."

"Now, let me give you a quick tour before class starts."

As the rest of the students dribbled in, Cara explained her vision as she showed us around the studio. She offered art classes to troubled teens from all different walks of life. Some pay, some don't. Her aim was to keep kids off the streets, out of trouble, and protect their mental health by allowing them to express their feelings through art. Unfortunately, the majority of funds were spent on art supplies, meaning the only affordable workspace to rent resided within an almost condemnable building.

While the upper levels laid vacant, the ground floor housed an enormous open-plan art studio with paint-splattered concrete floors, high ceilings, and long narrow windows shooting stunning rays of sunlight inside. Although timeworn, the architecture was beautiful and deserved to be brought back to life.

Once Scott and I uttered our goodbyes, we silently wandered along the sidewalk until a sob expelled my body. I hadn't even realized I'd been holding on to so much emotion.

"Whoa, Lanie. Are you okay?" Scott asked, grasping my shoulder as I hunched over.

"I'm fine." I straightened my back while inhaling a deep breath. "It's just been so long since I've seen her, and part of me has always wondered if she was okay…if she finally got the life she deserved."

Scott's gaze softened as he wiped a tear from my cheek. "I think she has."

"She looked happy, didn't she?" I stared into his eyes, searching. "She wasn't just saying that?"

"Lanie…" His fingers ran along my jawline. "She was glowing."

I exhaled eleven years of relief. "I still can't believe it. I never thought I'd see her again."

"I know the feeling."

My gaze lifted to his, but his eyes lingered on my lips.

"It's funny how the universe has a way of correcting itself," he said, moving closer.

The rising heat between us kickstarted my flight reflex. "I should get home."

"I'll take you."

"No, no…I think I'll walk from here," I said, backstepping out of the danger zone. "I'll see you tonight."

Scott shoved his hands into his pockets. "I'll pick you up on the way. Around six-thirty?"

"Oh, I'll just meet you there," I said, trying my hardest to sound casual. "I don't want them to get the wrong idea."

His hard gaze locked onto mine. "And what idea would that be?"

"That we're…involved."

"Yeah, you're right," he muttered with a humorless chuckle. "Perhaps I should bring a date, just to make it crystal clear."

The hurt in his voice made me wince. "Scott…"

As he stormed off in the opposite direction, I fought every urge to chase after him. Surely it was better this way. The more time we spent together, the more my boundaries blurred. Even if I wanted to tear his clothes off every time I saw him, I refused to give in to desire. There was still so much he didn't know about me, and once he found out, I figured the loss of his friendship would hurt a lot less than the alternative.

Chapter 24

While ambling up to Cara's apartment building, I stewed on the idea of Scott bringing a date. Would he stoop that low? It was hard enough seeing him with a date at Josie's exhibition. Even after eleven years, jealousy had torn through me. I had hidden in the coatroom and indulged myself in the only thing that could mute the pain. Cocaine. The embarrassment of what followed sent me spiraling. I went days without sleeping, without sobering, until it all came to a head the night I sent Josie, my best friend's soulmate, to the hospital. Everything changed that night. I'd hit rock bottom, and it would be the last time I'd ever let Grayson save me. From that day forward, I was on my own.

Shaking off my anxiety, I pressed the buzzer, determined to make the evening about Cara and her family and not my troublesome feelings for Scott. A mouth-watering aroma floated down the stairwell, and I prayed my destination was the source. I hadn't eaten since the measly few bites at breakfast, and I was starving. After years of my mother telling me what I couldn't eat, now it was my bank balance. Although I could afford what I needed to survive, I missed the trimmings—the trimmings I smelled roasting behind Cara's apartment door.

Before I could knock, the door swung open, and a familiar face stared back at me, but it wasn't Cara.

"Zach?" I gasped. "Zach Freeman?!"

He grinned. "Welcome to our home."

"I can't believe it," I cried, throwing my arms around him.

Cara stood back with a giggle before hugging me. "Surprise." She peeked over my shoulder as we parted and frowned. "Where's Scott? You didn't come together?"

I winced. "Oh, we're not..."

"But I thought—"

"We're just friends," I said with an uneasiness I couldn't hide.

"Are you sure? He doesn't look at you like a friend."

"How does he look at me?" I asked, following her into the living room.

She chortled. "Exactly like he did in high school."

"Scott and I only recently reconnected through work," I said, ignoring the heat in my cheeks. "He disappeared from my life not long after you moved, and I, um...didn't take it very well."

Zach excused himself to check on dinner while Cara moved closer. "Is that why you got together with Grayson?"

"Part of the reason," I said, dropping my handbag by the couch.

"I never understood how that happened. Yeah, you and Grayson were close...but you and Scott...hell, I thought you'd get married straight out of high school."

So did I.

"Life got really messy after you left," I said, lowering my gaze. "And has been for some time. I only just got out of rehab a couple of months ago."

Cara's eyes softened. "Poppy said your socials had gone quiet. May I ask what you were being treated for?"

"Depression and a dependent disorder."

Her shoulders lowered, but her gaze was full of understanding. "And how are you doing now?"

"Great, actually. I'm steering clear of my vices, including my parents, and learning how to support myself."

"Wait, so you're living and working in Manhattan now?"

"Yep." I grinned. "And I don't have many friends here...so I think you'll be seeing a lot more of me."

Cara laughed. "I've been here for seven years and feel the same."

Midway through telling Cara about my job and how I came to live in Manhattan, the doorbell rang, and my stomach dropped.

"Sounds like your other *friend* has arrived," Cara said with a chuckle.

As she left to answer the door, I hugged my waist as I wandered around the room, gazing at the photographs on the walls. Graduations, weddings, birthdays, babies… So many milestones and memories. So much love. Their smiles were genuine. Nothing like the images that donned the walls of my family home or the staged selfies of my socials. These were real. This was happiness.

Thankfully, only Scott's voice greeted Cara at the door, and she walked back into the room, holding a bunch of flowers, with Scott trailing behind.

"I'll just go put these in water," Cara said, bringing the gorgeous wildflowers to her nose as she left.

Scott nodded my way, expressionless. "Lanie."

"Where's your date?" I muttered, equally amused and relieved.

"Let's just enjoy ourselves, shall we?"

The bitter edge to his tone surprised me, and I was about to retort when Cara walked back into the room, followed by Zach.

"Holy shit. A Summerhill reunion," Scott uttered, shaking Zach's hand.

"I'm surprised you remember me."

"It's not hard to remember the small list of people Lanie was nice to in high school."

I scowled at Scott while the others laughed. He was deliberately trying to get on my nerves, and fuck, it was working.

A stampede of little legs charged down the hallway and drew my attention, lightening my mood instantly.

"Wow, slow down," Zach said as the two young boys skidded to a halt. "Our company has arrived."

Cara smiled down at them as they hid behind their dad's legs. "Melanie and Scott, I'd like you to meet our sons, Charlie and Oscar."

"Hi there," I said, kneeling for a closer look at their divine faces. "How old are you two?"

"I'm six, and my brother is four," the tallest boy said.

Cara sighed. "Oscar, Charlie can speak for himself."

"Sorry, Mom," he said, pushing his little brother forward.

"I'm four," Charlie whispered.

"Okay, boys," Cara said, clapping her hands. "If you're in your pajamas in five minutes, Dad will set up a movie in your bedroom."

Their lit-up faces went scampering back down the hall with Zach trailing behind them.

"I can't believe you're a mom," I said, returning to my feet.

"Me neither." She laughed. "We didn't intend to get pregnant so quickly after the wedding, but we don't have any regrets."

"Why would you?" I gazed after them. "They're perfect."

"It hasn't been easy, but Poppy helps out a lot. Mom's still in care, so I'm her legal guardian until she turns eighteen in..."—she counted her fingers—"one hundred and eighty-two days."

"I hear you." Scott chuckled. "Teenagers are fun, aren't they?"

While Scott and Cara continued to joke about raising adolescents, I quietly left the room to help Zach arrange platters of roasted meat, vegetables, and gravy on the dinner table.

My mouth salivated on sight. "This looks delicious."

"It should," Cara said, walking into the dining room with Scott. "Zach's an award-winning chef."

Zach's face reddened as he closed his eyes. "Cara..."

"No, I'm allowed to brag." She lifted her chin as we all sat down. "You're amazing, and I get to eat restaurant-quality meals most nights."

"You can relate to that," Scott said to me before taking a sip of his wine.

My teeth clenched within my smile. "Well, I can't wait to try it out," I said, picking up my knife and fork and stabbing the meat on my plate.

"Speaking of amazing food," Cara said, clearly sensing the tension. "You should spend Thanksgiving with us. We don't have any family nearby, and Riley and Poppy seem friendly, so it'll be fun. What do you say?"

"I'd love to," I said almost too quickly. It would be my first Thanksgiving without Grayson, and I was dreading it.

Scott grew silent. "I'll have to get back to you on that one."

"Of course, no pressure," Cara said, throwing me a glance. "I just thought it would be nice to have a few more people around our table this year."

Trying not to dwell on the possibility of not spending the holiday with Scott and his brother, I opted to change the subject. "So, tell me..." I said, gazing at the unexpected couple before me. "How on earth did the two of you end up together?"

Cara peeked up at Zach with a warm smile. "Well, before Zach went off to culinary school, we attended the same college. He'd already been there a year before I started, and let's just say... he was a very attentive tour guide."

Scott chuckled. "I bet."

Zach's freckles disappeared into the heat of his cheeks. "I finally took Mel's advice."

"What advice?" I asked, without a clue.

"Remember in senior year, when we were alone in the AV room..."

"Excuse me?" Scott and Cara blurted in unison.

Zach nudged Cara's side with a chuckle. "It wasn't like that. I was consoling Mel after..." He glanced at Scott and paused. "Well, I can't remember the exact details, but..."

I gasped as the memory came floating back. "I remember! You told me about a girl you liked." My face lit up as the realization washed over me. "That was Cara?"

Zach nodded. "You told me to ask her out, but I was too chicken shit."

"So, you waited until college?!" Cara smacked his arm. "Zach!"

Once our laughter subsided and our plates were empty, we moved to the living room to continue rehashing the last eleven years of our lives. Unfortunately, I didn't have much to offer to the conversation, so I evaded every uncomfortable question with conveniently timed trips to the bathroom.

While Scott boasted about his successful career, his time at college, and raising Riley, resentment started to trickle in. The boy I'd pined for had thrived without me, just like Cara had. While the three of them were battling real-life adult challenges,

I was nothing but a spoiled princess, responsible for nothing. I had no relatable stories or successes to brag about, and I couldn't help but feel envious of their lives.

"I should get going," I said, straightening my skirt as I stood.

Scott frowned up at me. "I'll give you a ride."

"No, no, you stay," I said, holding up my hand to stop him. "You have a full glass." I turned to Cara and Zach with a smile. "Thank you so much for dinner, guys. I can't wait to catch up again soon."

While Scott disappeared into the kitchen, I picked up my handbag and headed for the door.

"You okay?" Cara asked as I stepped outside.

"I'm just tired…and a little overwhelmed, to be honest."

Her brown eyes softened. "I totally understand. Let's have coffee soon. Just us next time." With my nod, she threw her arms around me. "I'm so happy to have you back in my life, Mel."

"No more than me," I uttered, holding on to more emotion than expected.

Once the door closed behind Cara, I made my way down the stairs.

"Lanie, hold up! I said I'll drive you," Scott called out as I reached the foyer. He jogged down each flight while I fished my cell out of my bag.

"We live in opposite directions," I muttered, zipping up my jacket. "Plus, my place is only a fifteen-minute walk from here." According to the map on my phone. "I think."

Scott glared at me. "Don't you dare. It's too dangerous."

"Who do you think you are?" I pushed open the door. "My father?"

He grabbed my wrist and pulled me back. "No, because I actually care about you."

My eyelids fluttered over the moisture in my eyes.

"I'm sorry. I shouldn't have said that." Scott loosened his grasp before letting go to pull out his wallet. "At least let me pay for your cab fare."

"I don't want your money," I growled, storming outside into the cool night air.

"Why?!" he barked. "Is it not old enough for you?"

Anger tore through me as I spun around and marched back. "What is it with you and money?" My heart pounded in my chest as I glared at him. "So you have it now, whoop-de-do. Life clearly worked in your favor after you left."

"Is that what you think?!"

"Look at you!" I cried. "You're everything you aspired to be, and I'm..." My voice grew hoarse. "I'm nothing. Without my family, I'm figuratively and literally worthless."

Scott grabbed my forearms, forcing our eyes to align. "Without your family, you are unstoppable. Not only are you passionate and brave, you're strong-willed and kind, and that's only scratching the surface of what you bring to this world." He lifted his hand to my face, pooling my tears into his palm. "But you're wrong about me. I lost myself after losing you. I threw everything I had into my studies, into my work, thinking it'd get easier, but it never got easier. Every time I stumbled across your face in the paper, I'd drink myself into a stupor, wondering what I did wrong."

Pain tore at my heart as I stared up into his glistening eyes. "You didn't do anything wrong. I loved you completely." My chest contracted. "But I...I..." I wanted to tell him what really happened, but my breaths grew short and strained until I was gasping for air.

Scott pulled me into his arms, encasing my body like a protective shell. "Just breathe, Lanie," he murmured into my hair. "None of it matters anymore." Once my breathing settled and my body relaxed, Scott bundled me into his arms and carried me to his car.

I stared out the window until the streetlights blurred, only returning to the present when Scott's hand gently clasped my knee. Instead of shying away from his touch, I let his fingers linger on my skin, welcoming the warmth and distraction. In that moment, our past slipped away, and the future was irrelevant. All I wanted was now.

As we came to a halt at a stoplight, I studied Scott's profile. His chest rose and fell in quick succession while his jawline remained rigid. My fingers climbed over his and settled upon his hand, drawing his gaze.

Scott's mouth parted but quickly clamped shut when a horn blasted behind us. "Fuck," he muttered, squeezing my leg as he accelerated away.

A tingling sensation shot straight to my core, and my heartbeat quickened. My body craved more, and my head didn't even attempt to stop it. While our fingers interweaved and the air thickened around us, Scott grasped the steering wheel as I inched his hand higher up my thigh. Throbbing with anticipation, his pinkie grazed my underwear, and I closed my eyes.

"Jesus," Scott groaned, shifting uncomfortably in his seat.

I pushed harder against his hand, demanding more, and cried out when he answered. Once I shuddered on release, Scott swerved to the side of the road.

"God damn it, Lanie," he rasped before swinging the wheel to perform a hasty U-turn in the opposite direction.

"Where are you taking me?" I panted, still riding out the waves of ecstasy.

He didn't even glance my way. "To bed."

Scott's lips crashed onto mine the moment we stepped into the elevator of his building. As I scrambled to unbutton his shirt, he hitched my leg around his thigh and pushed his hardness against my pulsating core.

Once we reached the top floor, Scott dragged me toward his apartment, pausing momentarily to press me against the hallway wall, and deepened his kiss.

"Wait," I mumbled, reluctantly forcing Scott's swollen lips away. "Where's Riley?"

"Sleeping at a friend's house," he muttered before closing in on my mouth again. "So, we…can make…as much noise…as we want."

"Don't you think we should go inside first?" I giggled as he drew circles on my neck with his tongue.

A rumble rolled over him as he stepped back, searching for his keys. After a few blundering attempts, the door finally cooperated, sending us stumbling inside where our wrestle continued. A trail of clothes and fragments of a broken lamp was left scattered across the floor while Scott blindly led me to the bedroom.

The moonlight caressed my body as Scott peeled away my remaining attire.

"Fuck," he said, staring at my body like a pubescent boy.

"It's nothing you haven't seen before."

Scott ran his hands over my contours, taking in every dip and curve. "But you're different now…" He exhaled in disbelief. "Better."

"Says you," I said, running a finger down his well-defined chest, in awe of his physique. "Please tell me you work out."

As he stepped closer, I lost my footing and fell onto the bed.

"Some of us have to work at these things," he said, tugging on my ankles before scooping me up and launching me further onto the bed.

I gasped at his strength and giggled nervously as he stalked over my body until I was encased in his arms. Scott's dilated pupils bore down into mine while his chest rose up and down, out of time with his pounding heartbeat. As sadness edged his cerulean gaze, he lowered his trembling lips to find mine waiting.

Our gentle touch soon turned animalistic as eleven years of anger, regret, and sadness surged between our bodies. Our caresses left bruises, he pinched while I pulled, and our bites drew blood as each painful memory resurfaced to be healed by a tender kiss.

When Scott finally thrust himself into me, I cried out, succumbing to years of yearning. He'd always been my benchmark and I'd never let another man come close. I held back, protecting my heart, knowing the cost of loving someone. But now…I couldn't let go. I clawed his back, holding tight as I rode out every orgasm until the past seeped away, and there was nothing left but the present and our wounded souls, desperately trying to save each other.

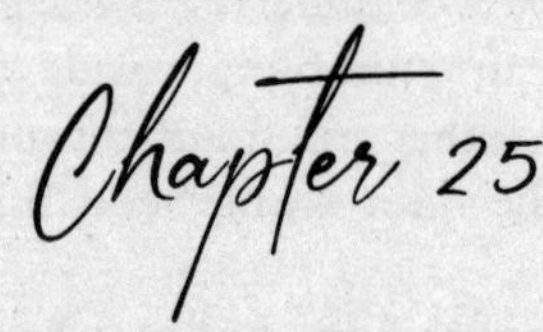

Chapter 25

"Holy shit," Scott uttered as he collapsed beside me, breathless.

A tired laugh floated from my lips after yet another mind-blowing orgasm. "I need time to recover from that one."

Scott rolled onto his side and ran his finger down my arm. "I've never seen you look so…"

"So what?" I asked, gazing up at the ceiling in a daze.

He brought his mouth to the shell of my ear. "Thoroughly fucked."

I nudged him away with a giggle. "You're never going to let me sleep, are you?"

"Unlikely," he said with a chuckle before climbing out of bed and disappearing into the bathroom.

A sliver of sunlight crept up through the curtains, offering a polite reminder.

"I should probably head off," I said, lifting the sheet around my body as I scanned the room for my clothes. "Your brother will be home soon."

Scott reappeared, leaning against the doorframe in his boxer briefs. "I wouldn't worry about Riley."

"Surely he's uncomfortable with girls sleeping over."

"You're not some one-night stand, Lanie," he said, closing the distance between us. "He knows how much you mean to me."

"Yeah, well…I don't want him thinking we're in a relationship." I refused to meet his glare as I slid on my underwear. "I need to get my life in order before I bring someone else into it."

"Well, too fucking late. I'm in it." His sharp tone demanded my attention. "So, label it whatever you like, but I'm not going anywhere."

My chest tightened. "Scott..."

He cradled my face in his palms, pulling my gaze up to meet his. "I'm not...going...anywhere."

Too exhausted to argue, I succumbed with a nod. "I'm sorry I'm such a mess," I uttered in a sigh.

"You're not a mess." Scott tucked a lock of hair behind my ear with a small smile. "You're a beautiful disarray."

"I knew something was going on between you two," Cara said, hiding her smile behind her reusable coffee cup. We'd been meeting in Washington Square Park almost every Saturday morning before her classes for the past month, catching up on each other's lives while her gorgeous boys splashed around the fountain.

"It's not like we're dating. We're just..."

"Sleeping at each other's houses occasionally?"

I winced. "A lot."

"So, who's scared of commitment?" Cara asked, nudging my side. "You or him."

"My therapist warned me about getting involved... I need to be careful."

"That doesn't mean you have to rule it out. Just take it slow."

"I know...but Scott isn't making it easy. He says he's happy to keep things casual and uncomplicated, but his actions say something entirely different."

"It sounds like he'll take whatever he can get from you."

My stomach churned. "That just makes me feel even more guilty."

"Guilty about what?" asked Cara, turning her gaze to study my profile. "I know you don't think you're ready for a serious relationship, but you deserve love, Mel."

"I don't know about that."

"Whatever happened in the past, I'm sure he will understand."

"Maybe," I said with no conviction. "But if he doesn't, I need to be on my own two feet. Relying on others isn't an option for me anymore."

I could sense the questions on her lips, but she didn't utter a single one. The was no judgment there, only comfort. A true friend.

"So, tell me," Cara's voice perked up a notch. "What do you have planned for Scott's birthday tonight?"

"I'm...um...making him dinner."

Her eyes widened in fear. "You're going to cook for him?"

"I've been practicing!"

"Okay, okay!" She laughed.

"But I'm not attempting the cake," I said with absolute certainty. "I've ordered that from Rosie's." Thanks to Josie's recommendation.

"Oooh, I love that place." She rubbed her hands together. "And what about presents? What did you buy him?"

My gut twisted with shame. "I really can't afford anything else right now. I'm still saving for a security deposit."

"Hey...that's okay," Cara uttered, clearly sensing my inner turmoil. "I'm pretty sure he has everything he's ever wanted right now."

Ignoring her smirk, I took a long sip of my coffee. Our label-free, no-complication relationship was sure starting to feel complicated.

"You're not alone, though," she continued. "Our finances are looking pretty dire too. I feel like I'm sitting on a ticking time bomb since the building sold."

"You can't find anywhere else to hold your classes?"

"Not with rent that cheap." Cara's shoulders descended. "Not in Manhattan, anyway."

"Surely they could renovate around you?" I asked, thinking back to the beautiful architecture. "You barely take up any space."

"Nope. They plan to knock it down and build some swanky new office block. I'm expecting an eviction notice any day now."

I gasped. Not only were they destroying a remarkable building, but also Cara's livelihood. "How long will they give you to vacate?"

"I don't know...a few months maybe. I'm dreading telling the students. They've come to rely on my classes."

"Surely there's something we can do. A beautiful building like that deserves to be brought back to life, not turned to rubble. It must have some historical significance we can leverage off."

Cara shook her head. "This isn't your problem, Mel."

"Of course it is." I frowned. "It affects you, and it affects Riley. He adores your classes."

"I think he adores my sister more than the classes." The corner of her mouth twitched. "We'll have to keep an eye on them at Thanksgiving. They're as bad as you and Scott were in high school."

My cheeks warmed at the memory. "Don't tell Scott that. He wants his brother one hundred and ten percent focused on his schoolwork."

"He does realize how exceptional Riley is, doesn't he?"

"I think so, but he's worried about job prospects. With the upbringing they had, he wants to ensure his brother's stability, and I don't think becoming an artist will satisfy Scott's expectations."

"That's understandable. It's a tough gig…but it's also a calling and shouldn't be ignored." Cara grew somber, undoubtedly recalling her childhood.

"But some artists make a good living, right?" I asked, thinking of the talent I dealt with at AG Galleries.

"Some…but unfortunately, most don't. Luckily, there are a lot more career paths for creatives out there now. Riley's bound to succeed in whatever he chooses, as long as he's happy."

"If only I could convince Scott of that. Last time I was over there, he was pressuring Riley to get into accounting."

Cara hung her head back and groaned.

"Tell me about it," I grumbled.

While Cara rounded up her boys, preparing to leave, an idea sprung to mind. "Hey, maybe AG Galleries could help with your predicament. They own a semi-vacant warehouse close by that would totally suit your classes—at least in the short term." Exhilaration rolled over me. "Alfie is always looking for ways to give back to the art community."

Cara peered up at me with a skeptical gaze. "Do you really think they'll want to help us?"

"You never know," I said with a shrug. "I'll run it past the team next week."

Scott's handsome face glowed in the candlelight as Riley and I stood beside him, singing "Happy Birthday". As he blew the candles out with just one breath, I pondered what he'd wished for. For me, it was always happiness—a loophole for uncertain dreams.

As Riley wandered off to adjust the lighting, Scott pulled me down for a kiss, almost bringing me to my knees.

"At least wait till I'm gone," Riley blurted, making a beeline for the front door.

"Be home no later than midnight," Scott hollered, overriding my goodbye.

"Yeah, yeah. I won't forget." Riley grabbed his keys and wallet off the hallway table. "Just like *you* won't forget to accept that invitation."

As the door slammed behind him, I turned to Scott. "What's he talking about? What invitation?"

Scott tugged me onto his lap and slipped his fingers around my nape, dispersing tingles in every direction. "So, there's this event coming up..." he said, running the tip of his nose up and down my neck. "And I was hoping you would come with me."

"What sort of event?" I asked, tilting my neck to invite more contact.

"It's an awards night." His sweet and sensual kisses moved closer to my ear. "You may have heard of it..."

My entire body stiffened in anticipation.

"It's the Warner Philanthropy Awards," he continued, threading his fingers through mine.

Anxiety engulfed every cell in my body as I pulled away. "I can't... I'll know too many people." Including Staci Warner. Heiress of Warner Enterprises. Ex-best friend.

"But you'll have to face them eventually."

"Who says?" I asked, climbing off him. "That world...it isn't mine anymore."

Scott lowered his gaze while kneading his tense jaw. "Then we won't go."

"Just because I can't doesn't mean you shouldn't," I said, my voice riddled with frustration. We weren't a couple, and the more he pushed, the more I pulled away.

"You're right." A despondent chuckle left his lips as he stared at the singed candles on his cake. "Forget I asked."

"I'm sorry," I said, hugging my stomach as the air grew thick with tension. I knew he was angry. It was rolling off him like an avalanche, and I was the trigger. "Should I go?"

After an everlasting moment of silence, Scott's unreadable gaze met mine. "Then who will I share my cake with?"

Although we'd spent most of our free time together leading up to Thanksgiving, something had shifted between us. There was a storm brewing behind Scott's eyes, and I became too fearful to probe. I should have distanced myself, but instead, I grew closer, wanting to lick his unspoken wounds and poke my finger into mine.

"Are you coming over tonight?" Scott asked as he adjusted his tie in the mirror early Monday morning.

I searched the bedroom floor for my other shoe. "Um…no, I have a dinner meeting with Nicholas."

His hands stilled. "Excuse me?"

"I have an idea I want to run past him, and it's the only time he has available before he flies back to LA for Thanksgiving." I slipped my cell phone into my handbag along with the written proposal to temporarily move Cara's studio onto AG Galleries property.

"Will Faye and Adrian be there?"

"No, but they're totally on board with the idea."

"So, you're meeting with Nicholas…by yourself?"

"Yes," I said, irked by his jealousy. "But don't worry. I can handle him."

He ripped the tie from his neck to start again. "I've heard that before."

Blood pooled at my feet. He was undoubtedly referring to Mr. West. "Why would you bring that up?"

"Because I know Nicholas, and I highly doubt he's interested in anything other than your ass."

The knot in my stomach grew tighter. "Cara is about to lose her business, which means Riley's affected too. If I can convince him to—"

His scoff cut off my explanation. "There's only one way you'll convince a guy like that."

"Well, thanks for the advice," I said, seething with rage. "Maybe I'll take it." Fighting back tears, I grasped the door handle as memories of my old teacher's harassment seeped out of my subconscious. I needed to escape before Scott completely split it open.

"Like hell you will," he snapped, stepping between me and the exit.

"Why not?" I planted my hands on my hips with a scowl. "He's had me before."

Scott's jaw pulsed as his gaze bore down on me. "When?"

"Does it matter?"

"Yes, it fucking matters!"

I glared at him, but the anguish behind his eyes broke me. "It was college…" I said, exhaling in defeat. "Just one stupid, drunken night at college."

"Fuck, Lanie." His fingers tore through his hair. "I thought you'd cheated on me."

"How can I cheat on you?!" I threw my hands into the air. "We're not in a relationship, remember?"

Scott's eyes grew dark. "Is that what it feels like when I'm fucking your brains out every night? Like this is some friends-with-benefits situation?"

My teeth ground as I fought a surge of unsettling emotions. "I told you…I'm not ready for anything serious."

Scott expelled a growl. "I'm planning a future with you, Lanie!"

"Then don't throw the past in my face!"

Our eyes battled a silent war before Scott swiped his suit jacket off the bed.

"I'm going to work," he muttered, keeping his gaze lowered as he maneuvered around my stationary frame. "Enjoy your dinner…or whatever the fuck you want to call it."

As the front door slammed, the ache in my chest deepened. I'd hurt him because he hurt me, but instead of easing my pain, I had only amplified it.

Me: **I'm sorry about this morning.**

Me: **Can I come over after dinner?**

Me: **???**

I stared down at my unanswered messages, drumming my fingers on the table.

"You look like you need a drink," Nicholas said, sliding into the chair opposite me.

I hadn't even noticed his arrival. "Nicholas, hi. Thank you for meeting with me." I reached out to shake his hand, making him snigger.

"I think we can drop the formalities," he said while glancing around the room for service. "What's up?"

"I have an idea for AG Galleries."

"Oh yeah?" He clicked at a passing waiter, demanding attention.

I patiently waited until he ordered a drink before sliding the proposal across the table. "There's an old building, not far from our gallery, that houses art classes for troubled kids. Unfortunately, it's going to be knocked down, and they have nowhere else to go. I know AG Galleries owns a warehouse that is currently underutilized close by, and I was wondering if they could run classes out of there—at least until they can find a new venue."

"And what's in it for me?"

"You'll be giving back to the community. Alfie said—"

He chuckled. "My father says a lot of things."

"Could you at least run it past him? It would mean so much to these kids."

"Wow." He chuckled. "Rehab really softened you, didn't it?"

My mouth parted. "How did you find out about that?"

"I ran into an old friend of yours at an event in LA. Staci Warner. She was quite surprised to find out you were living in New York…and working for me."

My stomach clenched. "Well, we haven't spoken in a while."

"I gathered that," he said, sipping his gin. "Sounds like you haven't spoken to your parents either."

"I didn't come here to talk about my parents." I grabbed my proposal and dropped it into my bag. "I'm sorry for wasting your time."

"Alright, I'll show my dad." He leaned back in his chair and exhaled. "You've always been a hard woman to refuse."

"Thank you," I said, smiling in relief.

As I passed over the proposal, Nicholas's hand encased mine. "Hey, if you're not on good terms with your family, why don't you fly back to LA with me and spend Thanksgiving with mine? You could show Dad the proposal yourself."

"I appreciate the offer, but I already have plans."

"With whom?" Nicholas's eyebrow rose. "Scott Blackwood?"

My heart jolted. How did he know? We kept everything private. "With friends…and yes, he will be there."

"So, he's not your boyfriend?" The smirk on his face appeared to think otherwise.

"No," I tried to sound nonchalant, but my voice came out as a rasp. I couldn't even convince myself.

"Faye told me you'd grown quite close." His gaze grazed over my lips. "I figured that's why you and I haven't…you know…"

I almost laughed. "Believe me, there is no correlation between the two."

"So, you're just sleeping together then?"

I pinched the bridge of my nose. "That's none of your business."

"Why so secretive?" His fascinated gaze tilted. "Are you worried Daddy won't approve? Scott's a successful man…but come on, Mel. He's not like us."

Fury simmered just below the surface. "No, he's better."

"Yet you can't admit he's your boyfriend?" Nicholas laughed. "How does Scott feel about that?"

I'd never really thought about it from Scott's perspective. As much as I was protecting myself, I was inadvertently hurting him. While his intentions had always been clear, I was holding him at arm's length, waiting for the proverbial green light. I had no idea when I'd finally have my shit together and be able to support myself, and I didn't even know how having a boyfriend could alter the course of that. It wasn't like we had to move in together or get married. It was just a word. But a word that could give Scott a place in my life. The place he deserved.

"Fuck," I muttered, grabbing my bag. "I have to go."

I pulled my trench coat tighter as the elevator soared up to the top floor. Scott's assistant assured me he was still at the office, so I ran home to change before picking up some dinner on my way into Midtown.

As the doors slid open, I was struck by darkness. Thinking Margot was mistaken about her boss's whereabouts, I almost retreated until a light tapping of fingertips hitting keys caught my attention. I followed the sound toward his open door and discovered his illuminated profile hovering over his laptop. A sea of twinkling city lights danced behind him, framing the man I adored.

"I thought I told you to go home," Scott grumbled without looking up. "That pumpkin pie isn't going to bake itself."

"You know I can't cook."

His fingers froze over the keyboard before lifting his gaze. "I thought you had dinner plans."

"I did," I said, moving closer to his desk.

Scott's gaze traveled to the bag in my hands. "What have you got there?"

"Dinner."

He rubbed his stubbled jaw but said nothing.

"Margot said you were working late, so I thought you might be hungry." I emptied the contents onto the desk in a fluster. "I didn't know what you wanted, so I just got your favorite. I hope that's okay."

His eyes narrowed as he closed his laptop and moved it aside. "I don't have a favorite."

"Yes, you do," I said, sliding the bowl of Thai Green Curry under his nose. "I've seen the way your face changes when you eat this. Your eyes roll back into your head, and you emit this sexy moan each time you take your first bite. It's obvious."

Scott's tongue darted across his lips as I opened the container. "Maybe I react that way to all food."

"Nope. I'd notice," I said, hitching myself onto the desk beside his meal. "Just because you haven't admitted it doesn't stop it from being true."

His eyes softened as he leaned back into his giant office chair. "Go on."

My hands gripped the sides of the desk as emotion swirled inside. "I've been lying to you—and myself—about our situation for months now, because I was scared of becoming dependent on you. That I'd lose myself again." I blinked back tears. "But the truth is…what we have is bigger than my fears, and there is no label in existence that could sum up how I feel about you."

Scott's hand encircled my ankle. "Are you saying what I think you're saying?"

"Yeah, I am," I said, relishing his gentle touch. "I don't want there to be any confusion."

"So, if I, say…tell people you're my girlfriend…you won't get mad?"

My cheeks grew warm. "No."

"And you'll tell any man who comes within ten feet of you that you have a boyfriend?"

I laughed. "Is that what the rule book says?"

"I'm pretty sure it does," he said with a sparkle in his eye. "That, and sex…lots of sex."

With a laugh, I picked up a fork and poked it into his bowl. "Like that was ever going to be a problem," I mumbled with a mouth full of unbelievable flavor.

Scott grew silent as he pondered me. "Listen, about this morning..."

"It's okay," I said quickly, eager to forget. "We both said some shitty things."

He shook his head. "No, what I said about Mr. West...that was uncalled for. I just..."

"Wanted to hurt me? Just like I hurt you? I think we both succeeded."

"I still shouldn't have brought it up. I remember how hard it was for you."

I left my fork in the bowl along with my appetite. "It still is. Ever since that night, I've been petrified of running into him again. In the street, or at work..."

"That's not possible," Scott uttered with absolute confidence.

"Why not? I have no idea where he is now. He could be living next do—"

"He's in jail."

My jaw dropped. "How do you know that?"

"Because I put him there."

His admission rendered me entirely speechless.

"His name came up in a case I was working on a few years back. I tipped off the police and had my firm represent some of the women he assaulted."

Guilt crushed my lungs. "There were others?"

"Hey, hey." Scott leaned forward and placed both hands on my knees. "You aren't to blame."

"But I could've stopped him."

"So could have the girls before you. Do you blame them?"

"No."

"Then you can't blame yourself. He got what was coming to him. I made sure of it."

Tears stung my eyes as I ran my thumb over his fine whiskers. "I'm not worthy of a man like you."

"Lanie..." The intensity of Scott's gaze never wavered. "I'm the man I am *because* of you."

As I dipped my head to kiss him, Scott's hands traveled up my thighs and under my coat. "Lanie..."

"Yes?"

"Where's your underwear?"

"Probably with the rest of my clothes."

Scott fell back into his chair and ran his hand over his mouth. "Please tell me you didn't take the fucking subway."

"Of course not." I sniggered. "But the cab driver got quite a show."

His face dropped, together with his shoulders. "Lanie..."

"I'm fucking with you," I said, nudging his knee with the side of my heel. "It was my backup plan in case my apology wasn't enough."

With a growl, he seized my ankle and rolled his chair closer, settling between my legs. "So, you planned to seduce me into forgiveness?"

"Hey, if you're not interested..." I attempted to hop off the desk, but his grip tightened.

"Don't...fucking...move," Scott said, slowly releasing my legs to toy with the ties of my coat. As he pulled them free and the coat parted, his face lit up. "Fuck...me."

"Oh, I plan to," I said, loving the way he worshiped my naked body. "But don't you think we should eat first?"

"I do," he murmured, but his eyes didn't falter from my core.

When Scott's tongue ran over my seam, my back arched as I fell back on the desk. "Oh god," I cried out, curling my toes until my heels tumbled to the floor. "The windows..." I panted. "They're tinted, aren't they?"

"Not this high," he said, coming up for air. "And I intend to show the entire world you're mine."

Chapter 26

Cara could barely hide her smile when Scott and I entered her apartment, holding hands. The unspoken question radiated through her raised eyebrows and was answered by my flushed cheeks. There was no denying it now. Scott had barely taken his hands off me since we had made our relationship official.

As Poppy and Riley disappeared into her bedroom, Cara called after them. "Door open, please!"

"Okay, *Mom*," Poppy retorted in a sarcastic drawl.

Scott's jaw tightened as he stared down the hallway.

"Relax," I whispered, rubbing his back.

With a grumble, Scott followed Cara and Zach into the living room, dragging me behind.

As we drank and ate the day away, I couldn't help but feel grateful for the life I'd made for myself. I had friends, an amazing boyfriend, a stimulating job, and almost enough saved to rent my own apartment. Life was almost perfect.

"Did Scott tell you about his nomination?" Riley asked, sliding an extra serving of pie onto his plate.

My head snapped to Scott, who was shaking his head at his brother in a desperate attempt to shut him up.

"Since when are you modest?" Riley snickered before addressing the rest of us. "Scott's up for the Warner Philanthropy Award."

As compliments were thrown around the table, I sat there dumbfounded.

It wasn't until Scott's hand slid over mine that I turned to him. "You're a nominee?"

"You didn't tell her?!" Riley smacked his brother in the chest. "What's wrong with you?"

"It's not a big deal," he said, rubbing his torso.

"Yeah…it is." I forced a smile. "Congratulations."

Cara threw her husband a look before gathering up the plates. "Why don't Mel and I clean up while you and Scott take the boys out for a run before the game? Poppy, maybe you and Riley could organize some snacks?"

"Sounds like a plan," I said, letting Scott's hand fall to his side as I stood.

Without looking back, I followed Cara into the kitchen and turned on the faucet. I found washing dishes quite therapeutic and wished I'd discovered it years ago. As the soapy water filled the sink, my irritation waned.

I wasn't angry at Scott, only disheartened that the incredible news hadn't come from him. The Warner Philanthropy Award Night was the biggest event on the high society calendar, and the award was voted on by the most powerful people in America. The Warrens and Harlows were major contributors to the prize money, and up until now, I'd represented my family each year.

"You okay?" Cara asked, picking up a dishtowel.

"Yeah, I will be." Who was I to judge about keeping secrets? Scott's truth barely made a ripple in our relationship compared to the tsunami I was holding on to. "Sorry for putting a damper on the day."

Cara bumped my side with a sad smile. "It wouldn't be Thanksgiving without a little drama."

As we walked into the living room, Scott's hand reached out from the armchair and pulled me into his lap. "I'm sorry," he whispered into my ear.

The noise of the game drowned out our voices. "Why didn't you tell me?"

"I didn't want to pressure you."

"So, you were just going to miss it? For me?"

"Well, there's no way I'm going if you're not going."

"Oh, we're fucking going," I said with a scoff.

"What?" His head jerked back. "Have you forgotten who will be there?"

"No," I said, toying with the top buttons of his shirt. "But I'll be with the only person who matters."

Deep emotion smoldered under Scott's cerulean eyes, stealing my breath. "God, I lo—"

Cheers erupted in the room, ripping our private conversation in two. Someone had scored, but I couldn't care less. I wanted Scott to finish his sentence.

With a nervous laugh, Scott pulled me closer. "We're missing the game," he uttered before pressing his lips to my temple.

"Damn," I muttered quietly, hoping no one would question my aversion to sports.

As Scott's chest bounced up and down, I curled up on his lap and nestled into the crook of his neck. Instead of watching the game, my tired gaze pondered the room. While Cara, Zach, Riley, and Poppy all yelled and cheered at the television, and the boys mucked around on the floor, I closed my eyes and savored every moment. I finally felt the loving comfort of family.

Later that night, on the way back to Scott's apartment, we dropped Riley and Poppy at a friend's party. After a day of hiding their mutual crushes, they deserved a little fun together.

"Remember you have a ton of homework this weekend," Scott said through the car window before they had a chance to escape. "So—"

"Don't stay out too late," Riley said, mimicking his brother's strict persona.

Scott growled. "I can still ground you, you know?"

As Riley prepared a typical teenage comeback, which would most definitely have gotten him grounded, I reached over Scott's lap and wound up the window. "Have fun, guys!" I called out right before it sealed shut.

Scott pursed his lips as I settled back in my seat, but he said nothing.

"Why are you so hard on him?" I asked as he pulled away from the curb.

"Ever since he met that girl, his focus has been wavering."

"That girl is Cara's sister, and she's a good kid."

His hand tightened on the steering wheel. "He's going to screw up his senior year," he muttered, clearly not hearing me.

"So, he's a little distracted right now." I almost laughed at his overreaction. "I seem to remember getting you a little distracted, and you blitzed your way into college."

"Yeah, but I was driven. Riley's..." He winced as he searched for the words.

"Not you?" I asked, frustrated by his inability to see things from another perspective.

Scott's shoulders lowered as he exhaled. The love and concern he had for his younger brother was beautiful, but if he kept pushing like this, he'd drive Riley away, and the mere thought of that hurt my heart.

I squeezed his leg. "Regardless of what he chooses to do, he's got an amazing future ahead of him...because of you."

"I'm just worried he'll do something stupid," Scott said, running his hand through his hair.

"Like what?"

"I don't know. Drinking, drugs...get some poor girl pregnant."

My blood ran cold as I stared at his profile. "That would be stupid," I uttered, turning my gaze out the window as shame tore through my insides. "As long as he checks the expiration dates on his condoms, I'm sure he'll be fine."

Scott expelled an awkward laugh. "I never thought of that... but I'll let him know. Thanks."

A lone tear tracked down my face. "Anytime."

After Thanksgiving, Scott insisted I leave some clothes at his place, but I refused. If we were going to make our relationship work, there had to be boundaries. Plus, sometimes I needed space. Scott and Riley were at each other's throats most days, and it was wearing thin.

Although I didn't agree with Scott's parenting methods at times, I stayed out of it. It wasn't my place, even if they both continually tried to drag me into it.

"Can you talk to him?" Riley asked after Scott left for his run. "He'll listen to you."

Unfortunately, my morning shower did nothing to muffle their argument. "You know how he feels about this," I said, preparing my coffee.

"It's just a ski trip."

"With your girlfriend...without parental supervision." I chortled. "He wasn't born yesterday, Rils."

"It's not like we haven't had sex before," Riley muttered, lowering his eyes as he swirled the milk in his cereal bowl.

I covered my ears with a grimace. "Argh, don't tell me that."

"Come on, I bet you and Scott used to—"

"We're not going there," I said, holding up my hand.

"See! And nothing bad happened, right?"

"Right," I said, clearing the lump in my throat. "But sometimes things do, and he's just trying to protect you."

"He's trying to control me." Riley's jaw pulsed. "Did I tell you he's organized a private tour of Harvard?"

I winced. "What about that art school in Rhode Island I showed you?"

"It's a lost cause. There's no way he'll pay for it."

"Then apply for a scholarship. Maybe that will sway his opinion."

"Maybe..." he said, but he didn't sound convinced.

"I'm sorry I can't help with the ski trip." I'd already tried to ease Scott's aversion to his brother's relationship, but it left my stomach churning.

"It's okay." His shoulders lowered. "I doubt anything will change his mind."

"He is pretty stubborn," I said with a laugh.

"Funny, that's what he says about you."

"Maybe that's why we found each other again. If you want something bad enough, you make it happen."

"Why *did* you break up?" Riley asked, narrowing his gaze. "Scott's always been sketchy on the details."

I poured my coffee, mentally filtering what I should and shouldn't disclose. "Let's just say, my parents weren't exactly supportive of our relationship."

"Are they now?"

"I wouldn't know." My hand trembled as I brought the steaming liquid to my mouth. "I haven't spoken to them in a long time." Nor had they tried to reach out.

"Why not?"

I rested the coffee on the countertop to save myself from third-degree burns. "I stood up to them and refused to let them manipulate me anymore."

"And you walked away from billions of dollars?" Riley whistled. "Geez, it must've been bad."

"It was worth it," I said with a shrug. "It led me back to your brother…and you." And I'd never been happier.

"Well, fuck 'em."

His unexpected cuss was a startling delight. "Whatever happened to that sweet, innocent kid who used to draw me pictures?"

Scott's carbon copy grin flashed back at me. "He grew up to be awesome."

"That he did."

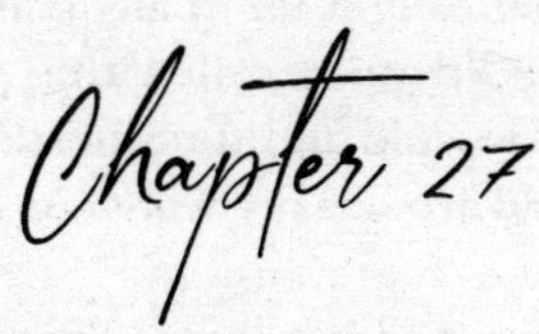

Chapter 27

"Melanie?! No fucking way!"

My entire body stiffened as I bit the inside of my cheek. "Staci, hi."

She grasped her chest as she reviewed my sparkling navy gown. "Where have you been? Your socials have been non-existent since…well…"—she cleared her throat—"you know."

"Well…since leaving *rehab…*" I emphasized the word that was forbidden in her world. "I've started a new life here in New York City."

She panned her gaze to Scott, who was in an in-depth conversation a few feet away. "You don't waste time."

"Actually, I've wasted a lot of time." *With you.*

"He's cute," she said, sipping her champagne with a daring smirk. "But he's no Grayson Harlow."

I caught Scott's eyes and smiled. "No, he's definitely not Grayson Harlow."

"Did he really marry that girl I told you about? The one with the rainbow hair?"

"Yes, he did," I said, willing Scott to save me. "Earlier this year."

"That must have been tough on you. Three broken engagements? No wonder you've been keeping a low profile. Everyone assumed you were hiding out in Europe until I ran into Nicholas Gibbs a few weeks ago."

"Well, you would've known the truth had you ever returned my calls."

"Oh, Melanie, you know how these things work. After that incident at my condo last Christmas, I had to put some distance between us. You clearly had a lot going on, and well, my parents didn't want me getting caught up in any scandals."

I couldn't believe I'd once called this girl my best friend. Had she always been so cold and superficial? My claws retracted when a warm hand slid around my waist. As always, Scott's touch calmed my soul.

Staci's tongue moistened her lips as she ran her gaze over my date. "And you are?"

Scott held out his hand with a genuine smile. "Scott Blackwood."

"My boyfriend," I interjected, peeking up at him. "And one of the nominees tonight."

"Oh, I thought that name sounded familiar. Congratulations."

"Well, we better continue doing the rounds," I said, leaning into Scott while exhibiting my perfected *fuck you* smile. "You know how it is."

Staci's mouth fell open as we meandered away.

"Did you just show me off?" Scott whispered into my ear once we were far enough away.

My smirk grew into a full-fledged smile. "Oh, I totally just showed you off."

"Can I show you off now?" he asked, tickling my side.

I hiccupped with laughter before turning to him. "You can do whatever you want with me."

A low rumble rolled over his chest. "I intend to..." he said, kissing me lightly on the cheek. "But first, I'd like you to meet a few people."

Scott proceeded to introduce me to the individuals who had nominated him. Thankfully, they didn't recognize me, but I knew others had. There were notable whispers as soon as I stepped into the ballroom. Scott assured me they were talking about the divine dress he'd bought me, but I knew better. *Melanie Warren had risen from the dead.*

As if sensing my discomfort, Scott's hand barely left mine as we traveled the room. It felt good being by his side. Natural. Nothing like it did with Grayson. We had attended millions of these events together, and it always felt forced.

As the formalities began, we joined the rest of the nominees around a large circular table adorned with tea lights and white orchids. Scott's hand slid over my leg as Staci made her way onstage and thanked the generous donators who'd made the awards night possible. He squeezed my knee at the mention of Warren Media but kept his eyes glued to the stage, purposely not bringing any extra attention my way.

When the nominations were read, Scott adjusted his collar as his Adam's apple bobbed up and down. He was nervous. I'd been so focused on my reintroduction to high-society life that I'd neglected my role here. I was here to support him, not the other way around.

As Staci opened the envelope, I took his hand and held tight.

"And the winner of the Warner Philanthropy Award and a grant for $250,000 goes to…Scott Blackwood from Blackwood & Associates."

Applause filled the room while Scott hung his head, hiding his growing smile.

Watching him in that moment did something to me. Emotion twisted around my heart like a boa constrictor, and my eyes burned, leaving me scrambling for words to articulate how I felt. As his glistening gaze lifted to mine, I threw my arms around him and let go of my heart. "I'm so in love with you."

"What?" he gasped, jerking back.

I stopped breathing when my brain caught up with my mouth. "I mean…I'm so *proud* of you."

"That's not what you said…"

"Hey, look…" I pointed to the podium. "Speech time!"

"We'll talk about this later," he uttered with a smirk.

As Scott rose, I sunk into my chair, mortified.

The applause continued as he jogged up the stairs to meet Staci onstage. Once she branded his cheek with her burgundy lips, he accepted the award and turned to the crowd while adjusting the microphone.

"Well…that was surprising," he said, staring directly at me with a knowing grin.

My cheeks burned as I held my glass up to hide my face.

"First, I'd like to thank The Warner Foundation for organizing this amazing event. Grants like these can change lives, and I plan to change many. Secondly, I'd like to thank the amazing team at Blackwood & Associates, who live and breathe our values. And finally..." His eyes drew back to mine. "My family. Riley and Lanie. You are my inspiration."

As he stepped off the stage, my heartbeat accelerated. His eyes locked onto mine as he strode toward me, award in hand. While conjuring up a dozen excuses as to why I blurted out the L-word so soon in our relationship, Scott was pulled aside. Staci latched onto his arm and ushered him over to the photo station, where a group of very important guests waited to obtain photographic proof of their generous donation to the cause.

He glanced back apologetically, and I offered him a sad smile. I knew the drill. Winners were required to be at the beck and call of the event organizer, and unfortunately, in this case, that was Staci. Her family was responsible for the entire event, and it was clear to me she'd taken over the reins from her mother. A twinge of jealousy hit me. Not just because her hands were encircled around Scott's biceps like a vise, but because her parents trusted her to fulfill an important role within their business.

A bitter taste occupied my mouth as I gazed around the room, trying to find someone to talk to. People stared back, but nobody approached me. Was I that intimidating? Or had my fall from grace already taken effect? I was no longer a worthy ally.

When the air grew too thick to endure another moment, I glanced back at Scott, who was laughing with Staci and another female, and made my way out of the ballroom. I trusted him, but I couldn't stand there and watch other women fawn over him, especially when everyone was watching me.

Once I reached the lobby, I picked up my pace until I had cleared the hotel doors, hoping to get out undetected. Fresh air welcomed me, but I craved the opposite, and my nose drew me to the smoky haze ahead.

"Do you think you could spare one of those?" I asked the tall dark figure leaning against a broken streetlight. The glow of his cigarette grew brighter, lighting up his face. "Adam?" Grayson's older brother stood before me in all his arrogant glory.

The corner of his mouth lifted. "Hey, Smelly. Fancy seeing you here."

Fear shot through me. "Your parents aren't here, are they?" I asked, glancing back into the foyer.

Adam chuckled as he flipped open his cigarette packet and drew one out for me. "Fortunately for you, it's just me this time."

"I'm assuming they still hate me," I said, twirling the cancer stick in my fingers.

"Quite the opposite. They're now demanding *I* marry you."

I burst out laughing. "What?!"

"It's not funny," he muttered, fishing a lighter from his pocket. "Before Grayson left, I was free to do whatever—and whomever—the fuck I wanted, provided I was growing our portfolio. But now they're on my case 24/7, trying to set me up with every heiress under the sun."

"Well, I hate to disappoint them *again*, but I'm with someone." I took the lighter and lit the cigarette, but its taste didn't satisfy anymore.

"I noticed." Adam blew out a long stream of smoke. "How do your parents feel about that development?"

I scoffed. "They don't even know I'm in New York, let alone who I'm dating."

"I'm sure that will change after tonight." He chortled. "Staci has a big mouth."

"You would know," I shot back with a grin.

"Fuck." Adam hung his head back. "Grayson really tells you everything, doesn't he?"

"We don't have secrets," I said before my smile faltered. "Not anymore, anyway."

"Gray told me what happened. What your parents did was unforgivable."

"What I did was worse," I muttered, tapping unsmoked ash onto the ground.

"Maybe, but you were pretty messed up...and that's on them."

I laughed. "I was pretty messed up, wasn't I?"

"Batshit crazy at times." Adam's chuckle faded. "But if Grayson forgives you, then so do I."

"Thanks," I said, lowering my eyes. "That means a lot."

"So, how did Scott take it? I'm guessing he didn't know about the pregnancy?"

The tightening of my chest made me wince. "I haven't exactly told him yet."

"Mel…" he groaned.

"I'm scared of how he'll react," I said, fighting off tears. "We only just got back together."

Adam wiped my tear away with his knuckle. "I saw the way he was looking at you from onstage, I don't think—"

"Lanie?"

We both jumped when Scott's voice sounded from a few feet away.

Adam's arm dropped to his side while the other brought a cigarette to his mouth.

"What are you doing out here?" he asked, sidling up beside me.

"I just needed some air."

His eyes fell to the cigarette in my hand. "Clearly."

"Oh, I'm not…"

Before I could finish my sentence, Scott lifted his gaze to Adam and held out his hand. "Scott Blackwood."

"Adam Harlow," Adam replied, shaking it.

"This is Grayson's brother," I added, trying to diffuse the tension between us.

"Yeah, I figured."

"Congratulations on the win," Adam said with sincerity. "You had my vote."

"Thank you. I know your company donated a large portion of that grant."

Adam took another drag. "Unfortunately, it may be the last time we do."

"What?" My brow creased. "Why?"

"Since Gray left the company, my father has been pulling all of our usual donations. He isn't the most charitable man."

"Surely you get a say in that?"

Smoke expelled with his short laugh. "Not until he retires."

"And when will that be?"

"When I land something, *or someone,* big enough. He had a lot riding on the Warren-Harlow merger."

I lowered my gaze, knowing my actions had affected him too. "I'm sorry."

"Mel," Adam uttered in a sigh. "You don't have to keep apologizing."

"I just wish I'd done things differently."

"Done what differently?" Scott asked, narrowing his gaze.

Adam and I stared at each other before I stammered a response. "It's, um…complicated."

"Of course it is," he grumbled. "What isn't with you?"

"If you want a simple girlfriend, I'm sure Staci will happily oblige."

A small noise emitted from Adam's throat. "Well, that's me out," he muttered, dropping his cigarette to the ground and stamping on it. "I'll see you around, Smelly." He acknowledged Scott with a nod before disappearing into the hotel.

"What the fuck was that?" Scott said, glaring at me.

I pinched the bridge of my nose. "I'm sorry. I don't know why I said that."

"Something is bothering you. Spit it out."

"No, it's not a good time. This is your night. You need to get back in there."

"Don't tell me what I need," he snapped. "I don't care about those people. I care about you. What's going on?"

"Scott…please. I'll tell you, just not here."

"Then I'll get our coats," he uttered before jogging back into the hotel.

Awaiting his return, I embraced my stomach as I shivered uncontrollably. I was petrified. I had no idea how Scott would react when he found out about the pregnancy and the horrible position I had put Grayson in. Would he hate me? Would I disgust him? How could he possibly understand?

"Here," he said, draping my coat over my shoulders, followed by his. "Our ride will be here soon." His loving gesture gave me hope. Even when Scott was angry, he cared. Maybe I had nothing to worry about. Maybe he would understand. Maybe, one day, we could right my wrong and have a family of our own—the way it should have been.

Silently, he stood beside me, scuffing his shoes on the sidewalk. I could tell he was upset, and I hated being the cause. I loved him. More than he'd ever know. But our relationship felt like a ticking time bomb, and I was moments away from possibly cutting the wrong wire.

Relief flooded my body as we approached Scott's apartment. Music blared from within, meaning Riley was still up and my soul-crushing admission would have to wait.

Once Scott opened the door and threw his keys on the hallway table, I blindly followed until I ran into his stationary frame.

"What the fuck, Riley?!"

Peeking over Scott's shoulder, I discovered Riley's semi-naked body lying over a girl in her underwear. My mouth fell open when Cara's sister, Poppy, yelped and scrambled for her clothes.

I tugged Scott around to give her privacy and found his eyes ablaze.

"You said you wouldn't be home until after midnight," Riley said, yanking on his t-shirt.

"So, you thought you'd bring Poppy here…unsupervised?"

"Scott, calm down," I said, keeping my voice level.

"I'm not going to calm down. He should know better!"

I glared at him, bewildered by how irrational he was. "He's a kid!"

"Exactly," he spat, whirling back around to face his brother. "Do you want your girlfriend to end up pregnant at sixteen, just like our deadbeat mom?" Scott's face reddened with rage. "Everyone knows teenage pregnancy is the quickest way to fuck up your life—and everyone else's. I'm not going to be responsible for another kid, Riley."

A sharp pain penetrated my chest. For years, I'd nursed this idea of an alternate reality. One where I'd never lost the baby, and Scott and I, although young, had made it work. We were happy. Perhaps part of me hoped that it could still happen for us, but reality had just slapped me in the face. It was clear Scott didn't want kids, nor had he ever.

"I'm sorry I'm such a burden on you!" Riley shouted as Poppy cowered beside him. "I bet you can't wait to ship me off to college—oh wait, did I tell you? I'm not applying to your precious Harvard."

Scott faltered. "What are you talking about?"

"I'm going to art school," he said, lifting his chin.

"Since when?"

Riley smirked. "Since Lanie encouraged me to."

Scott's furious gaze spun to mine. "You what?"

My mouth parted, too shocked to speak.

"At least she supports me," Riley said, continuing his war path.

Scott's eyelashes fluttered as he turned to his brother. "I support you. I've always supported you."

"No, you manipulate me. Just like Lanie's parents did to her."

I froze. "Riley, no…that was diff—"

"You compared me to your parents?!"

"No." I shook my head vigorously. "That's not what I—"

"I think you should go," he uttered, barely containing his fury.

"You're not going to let me explain?" I asked, desperate and confused. "Scott?" My heart plummeted when he didn't flinch. He wouldn't even look at me. "Fine," I muttered, biting my lower lip when it dared to quiver. "Come on, Poppy. I'll take you home."

Once Cara's sister waved to me from the apartment window above, I redirected the driver to Greenwich Village. Josie's apartment was my refuge after rehab, and now I needed it more than ever. It was a mistake letting myself get too involved with Scott. It was a fairy tale destined for a Brother's Grimm ending instead of the Disney kind.

Once inside, I tore off my evening gown and jumped into the shower, ignoring my cell phone as it rang persistently. I had no intention of talking to Scott until he'd calmed down. As I flopped down onto the couch in my sweatpants, my cell phone lit up again…then again…and again…until there was a knock on my door.

I warily checked the peephole before opening it. "Amy, what are you doing here so late?"

Her face was pale, almost matching her bleached hair. "It's for you," she said, holding out her phone.

My eyebrows drew together as I warily lifted it to my ear. "Hello?"

"Mel…it's Gray." His voice trembled. "You need to get home. Your father has had a heart attack."

Chapter 28

If it weren't for Grayson and Amy, I never would have made it home to say goodbye. Amy packed my bag while Grayson organized the flight back to LA, making sure there was a cab waiting to take me to the hospital. I arrived only moments before my father took his last breath.

While my mother wept in the corner, I stood over his body, staring down at the man who never returned my love. In death, he was just as in life. Cold. The only time he showed any affection toward me was when I was with Grayson, the son he never had. I was merely the daughter he never wanted.

I loved him for innate reasons, just like I loved my mother. They'd brought me into this world, only failed to nurture me through it. So many times I'd turned to my father to save me from my mother's vicious ways, but he just looked the other way and enabled her behavior. Grayson was the savior of my childhood. He taught me about the good in the world, that things would one day get better. He loved me like a best friend and cared for me like family. My parents were strangers to me now, and in some ways, I'd already mourned the loss of them.

"I'll need help going through your father's things," my mother said, dabbing her eyes with a handkerchief.

I moistened my dry lips. "Sure. I'll come by tomorrow." For the first time ever, my mother looked broken. "I'm sorry for your loss," I muttered quietly, not knowing what else to say.

Her bloodshot eyes grew hard. "Are you?"

Refusing to bite, I offered her a sad smile before walking away. I didn't have the energy to fight. It wasn't until I reached the waiting room that the tears began to fall.

Strong arms wrapped around me within seconds, encasing me with the familiar scent of my childhood. "I'm so sorry, Mel," Grayson murmured into my ear.

"You're here," I whimpered into his shoulder. My best friend. "Wait." I pushed him back. "How are you here?"

"We were in Hawaii when my mom called. Our plane arrived just after yours."

I panned my gaze around the empty room. "Where's Josie?"

"Getting coffee," he said, glancing behind me. "Where's Scott? He didn't come with you?"

My chest tightened. "It all happened so fast. I didn't get a chance to tell him."

"You want me to call him?" Grayson asked, pulling out his cell. "I'll get him on the next flight."

"No, no." I held my hand over his phone. "I'll do it when I get to a hotel."

Grayson's eyes softened. "Please stay with us. Adam has plenty of room and has already extended the invitation. We don't want you to be alone right now—or worse...with your mother."

"Thanks, Gray," I said, too tired to argue or actually find a hotel. "That would be great."

"We'll leave whenever you're ready."

"Oh. I'm ready," I said, wanting to disappear before my mother resurfaced. "Please get me out of here."

With a nod, Grayson texted Josie to meet us at the car, and within moments, we were on our way to Adam's beach house. Josie held my hand the entire way as I drifted in and out of consciousness and guided me into the guest bedroom on arrival. I'd barely slept in twenty-four hours, and I was physically and emotionally exhausted.

As soon as my head hit the pillow, I passed out, not stirring until the afternoon sun filled the bedroom. I was momentarily disoriented until the crushing memory of the previous night slammed into my chest. Needing air, I dragged myself out of bed and pulled open the French doors facing the blazing sun. I stood there for quite some time, relishing the salty breeze as it caressed my face. I'd missed California, but it didn't feel like my home anymore.

Banging doors echoed through the house, followed by whispers, and my ears immediately pricked up. With puffy eyes, I shuffled down the hall to find Josie and Grayson rummaging through the kitchen cupboards.

"Are you sure Adam lives here?" Josie asked, glaring into the fridge.

"He stays in his apartment in the city most of the time, so I don't think you'll find much food around. This is his…retreat, I guess."

"No wonder the cupboards are bare," Josie muttered. "Adam never takes a break."

"Want me to order some pizza?"

Josie's smile grew. "Yes please!" she said, rising on her tiptoes to kiss her husband. "You know what I like."

"I sure do," he murmured, sliding his hand over her ass.

"Gross, guys," I said, wandering into the room. "Save your dirty talk for the bedroom."

"Mel, you're awake!" Josie cried, rushing toward me. "We're going to get some pizza. Want some?"

"Definitely." My stomach rumbled at the thought. "I'm starving."

Grayson pondered me with a grin, saying nothing.

"What?"

"You just remind me of a girl I used to know, that's all. I haven't seen her in a while."

"Well, she's back," I said, resting my hands on my hips. "And she's hungry."

After polishing off three pizzas between us, I returned to my bedroom to shower and change. There was no point in prolonging the inevitable.

"Gray?" I asked, returning to the living room to find Josie napping in his arms as he watched an old movie. "Oh, I'm sorry… never mind." I pivoted on my heel, not wanting to disturb her.

"Hey, come back," Grayson whispered. "What is it?"

I warily returned, careful not to raise my voice. "I was just wondering if you could give me a ride to see Mom. I promised I'd help her with some stuff today, but I can get a cab."

"Not a chance," Josie murmured as she stirred awake. "We're going to see Grayson's parents this afternoon anyway, so we'll drop you on the way."

Grayson rubbed his temples. "We are?"

"Yes, we are," she said, pulling him off the couch. "They must be devastated right now."

"Fine," he grumbled. "But we're not staying long."

Josie narrowed her gaze. "As soon as Melanie calls us to come and get her, we'll leave…no earlier."

"She'll have to turn her phone on for that," Grayson said, pressing his lips together as he faced me. "I got a call from Amy this morning. She said Scott came around looking for you because you weren't returning his calls. She gave him my number."

My face dropped. "He called you?"

"He's worried sick, Mel."

I lowered my gaze. I didn't want to think about him right now. "He shouldn't be."

Josie and Grayson grew silent, but I sensed their silent language.

"Why don't we go for a walk on the beach while Gray calls his parents," Josie said, handing him his cell phone. "You know they don't like surprises."

With a nod, Josie took my hand and led me to the beach. Once my feet hit the warm sand and the waves crashed onto the shore, I opened my heart and bled out my fears the moment Josie uttered the words, "What's up?"

With wide eyes, Josie stared up at the mansion I used to call home. "Are you sure you'll be okay on your own?"

"I'll be fine," I said, but my racing heartbeat believed otherwise. "She can't hurt me anymore."

"Call me when you're ready to go," Grayson said, encasing my bony elbow in his giant hand. "Anytime…" He glanced at Josie. "The sooner the better, preferably."

Josie punched his arm. "Your parents won't be that bad…" Her smile faltered. "I don't think."

Grayson's eyes widened as they twinkled into mine, sharing a mutual understanding of the dangers ahead. "Take all the time you need, Mel," he said, giving my arm a squeeze. "We're not far away."

Wearing my bravest mask, I waved goodbye as they sped down the elongated driveway. The moment they disappeared through the gates, my smile faded. I never wanted to come back here.

As I approached the front door, I took in the details I'd overlooked as a child. Perfectly manicured gardens, the long stately stairway framed by outlandish columns, and a shiny black door big enough to fit a giant through.

Like a mouse approaching a lion, I edged closer, ignoring my instinct to run. Instead, I drew in a shaky breath and did something I'd never done before: I knocked on the door of the house I grew up in.

The door creaked open. "I wondered when you were going to show."

My mother's face startled me. "Since when do you greet visitors?"

"I sent the staff home."

"Even Miguel?" I couldn't help myself.

"We have a new driver now," she said, sauntering back into the house, leaving me standing alone on the front porch.

"Lucky him," I muttered, panning my gaze around the majestic foyer as I stepped over the threshold. Everything looked the same. Lavish, luxurious, and lonely.

"Are you coming?" my mother called out impatiently.

I flinched at her demanding tone. "Um, sure," I said, shadowing her down the hallway. "Do you need help planning the funeral?"

"No. Your father sorted that out years ago." She paused in front of his study and turned to me. "He didn't want my input… like most things."

I narrowed my gaze. "So, what did you need me for?"

Her jaw grew rigid as she drew open the heavy doors and entered the room that had always been forbidden to me. This was my father's world, where my mother and I didn't exist.

"I need you to find a copy of your father's will, and it's somewhere in this pigsty."

"Won't his lawyers sort that out?" I asked, frozen in the doorway.

"I want to prepare for the extent of my responsibilities," she said, dragging her finger over the desk and scowling at the divided dust particles.

"Fine," I uttered in a sigh. "Where should I start?"

"Wherever you like," she muttered, clearly disinterested. "I have calls to make."

I rolled my eyes as she breezed past. My mother had always been a master delegator. Everyone else was simply a minion, including myself. The moment I had gone through with her outrageous plan to trick Grayson, she owned my soul. I became the perfect daughter, never faltering, until Grayson met Josie. I tried to hold on, desperate for his love and my parents' approval, but I failed. He loved her.

Along with my parents' dreams, my life unraveled. I was a failure. A disgrace. Pathetic. Worthless. My parents used every suicide-inducing adjective to motivate me to fix what I'd broken. *Well done, Melanie. You've ruined Christmas.*

My stomach churned at the memory. There wasn't enough alcohol to take away the deep-seated ache in my heart, so I took some painkillers, followed by a few more, until I felt nothing at all.

The aroma of expensive cigars hit me as I stepped into the room. Whether it was impregnated into the furniture or my father's ghost reminding me I wasn't welcome, I didn't know, and I also didn't care. I was going to touch every last object in that room until he was rolling in his grave.

Circling the room like I was sizing up my prey, I absorbed the aesthetic. A heavy mahogany desk laid dead center while carefully alphabetized bookshelves donned every wall. It wasn't a mess as my mother implied, but it wasn't picture perfect either. Files were scattered across the desk, and the trash bin overflowed, but nothing else appeared out of order.

As the drink cart in the corner beckoned me, I averted my eyes to the antique filing cabinets behind my father's desk.

I pulled them open, one by one, flicking through the files until I came across a drawer that wouldn't budge.

I rummaged through my father's desk, hunting for the key, but stumbled across his deep dark secret instead—a mountain of snack bars hidden beneath an empty file marked *Finance Report*. Genius. My mother would never touch that.

Ripping one open, I took a bite and wandered over to the bookshelves as I chewed. In the midst of first edition classics and expensive antiques was a photograph of Grayson and me, framed with crystal. It was the night of my parents' annual Christmas party. We were seemingly the perfect couple, grinning for the camera, but little did my father know that, that night, my smile belonged to someone else.

As I picked up the frame for a closer look, something clattered onto the floor. A key. Adrenaline soared through my body as I whisked it up and raced over to the locked cabinet. Without resistance, it slid right in, offering a satisfying click before the drawer rolled open.

Hoping to uncover some covert operation that explained his absence from my life, I was underwhelmed to discover more boring files. With a sigh, I pulled them out of the drawer and dumped them on the desk, suspecting my father's will to be somewhere inside.

Sinking into the oversized office chair, I flipped open the first file. *Jackpot.* My father's will. Job done. Without hesitation, I whipped out my cell phone, switched it on, and messaged Grayson to collect me. I didn't want to be in the house a moment longer than needed.

While standing up, I brushed past the remaining files, scattering their contents onto the floor. "Fuck," I muttered, angry at myself for prolonging the nightmare.

As I kneeled to gather up the mess, a grainy photograph caught my attention, and my hands stilled. It captured my mother and Miguel in an intimate embrace, seemingly unaware they were being photographed. The attached report, written by a private investigator, suggested their affair dated back several years, which made me laugh. I could have told him that.

Unfazed by my father's ability to turn the other cheek, I flicked to the next document, curious to know what else he'd been hiding. My amusement evaporated the moment I recognized Scott's adolescent face alongside mine. The palpable love between us was so beautiful I would've framed the photograph had it not come from such a deviant source.

His brother, father, and a woman—presumably his mother—all featured in the investigation, and my heart dipped. Not only did the report detail Scott's academic records and dire living situation, it delved into his father's sordid criminal history. No stone had been left unturned. There was more than enough ammunition enclosed to manipulate Scott's future, and my father had used it all.

The next document proved my parents had known of my whereabouts since leaving rehabilitation. Monthly reports had been sent back to my father, detailing where I was living and my job at AG Galleries, along with photos of me in various locations throughout Manhattan. Perhaps they did care, in a twisted way, or they were simply gathering intel for their next attack. Knowing my father, the latter seemed more likely.

As my blood boiled and my stomach churned, I tore up every page until only a yellowed envelope remained, previously hidden amongst the betrayal. The handwriting of the address was heartbreakingly familiar.

With a racing heart, I unfolded the truth.

Lanie,

I'm so sorry. Everything happened so fast there was no time to say goodbye. You need to know that I wouldn't have left had I seen another way out.

After my dad's arrest, your father's lawyers were able to keep Riley out of the foster system and fast track my custody of him, as long as I agreed to his terms. He wants me out of your life.

He has organized temporary accommodation on the East Coast, where I'll attend a local high school and graduate there. He's also given me enough money for college, which I have no intention of using and will return it as soon as Family Services are off my back.

Once Riley's guardianship is final, I will find a job, a place for us to live, and come back for you in a few months. I know I can't offer you much, but we'll be together. I love you, Lanie, and already miss you more than you know.

Love, Scott x

My teeth gnashed as I paced the room, trying to remain calm, but no mantra would simmer my fury. With a growl, I ripped the picture frame off the bookshelf and threw it across the room, exploding glass all over the floor.

This letter would have changed the course of my life. The tears, the heartache, the lies never would have followed had I just read those words. The words my parents stole from me.

"What on earth was that?!" my mother cried out as she raced into the room.

I glared at her as I held up the letter. "Did you know about this?"

She stared at the envelope then down at the unlocked filing cabinet in disgust. "I told him to burn it."

All the air left my lungs. "You knew I was pregnant with Scott's child and deliberately kept him from me. How could you?"

Mom lifted her nose. "I stopped you from making a terrible mistake."

"Grayson was the mistake, Mom!"

"No, you were!" she growled, mirroring my scowl. "Because of you, I couldn't bear any more children, and your father had to go without a son." Her eyes morphed into slits as she moved closer. "I promised him you'd marry Grayson to carry on his legacy, but no, you had to ruin that also. You have no idea of the burden you've been on this family. The shame you've caused. And when your father found out you were back with *him*..." She shook her head in revulsion. "Well...his heart couldn't take your betrayal any longer."

"Betrayal?" I scoffed. "Are you fucking kidding me? You filled my head with lies then preyed on my vulnerability. You robbed me of so much happiness...so much love." Tears peeked out my eyes, but I batted them away.

"Oh, don't be so dramatic."

I'd grown up hearing those words every time I experienced a valid emotion, and this was the final straw. Hoping to ground myself and recede my anger, I clasped the bookshelf and focused on the antique vase my mother had given my father on their anniversary. I took deep breaths as I ran my finger over its delicate design, trying to regain control.

"Don't touch that," my mother hissed. "It's priceless."

I lifted it from its protected position. "This ol' thing?" I asked, tossing it from one hand to the other.

"Stop that immediately. You'll break it."

A small laugh floated from my lips. "Oh, but I thought you enjoyed watching pretty things break?"

"Melanie…" Panic flickered across her face. "Put…it…down."

Consumed with resentment, I parted my hands and let the fragile vase fall to the floor, bursting it into a million pieces. Tiny shards of porcelain splashed up against my ankles, slicing through the skin, but I felt no pain. "Whoops."

"You…bitch!" my mother cried, lifting her fiery gaze to mine.

My smirk only fueled her wrath. "I learned from the best."

"Get out!" she screamed, pointing to the door as her face burned bright red.

"Or what?" I chuckled. "You're going to call the police? Make a scene?" I smiled at her. "I dare you."

"You've lost your mind!"

"On the contrary, I've most recently found it," I said, gathering up my things. "And I'll be damned if I ever let you near it again."

As I stormed out of the house, fumbling for my cell phone in a furious haze, I slammed into a solid mass at the bottom of the stairs.

I lifted my gaze as strong muscular arms wrapped around my body. "Scott?"

His soft smile beckoned my lips. "You'd think, after all these years, they'd change the passcode."

Without another breath, I threw my arms around his neck and brought his mouth down to mine. As our kiss intensified, my anger diffused until I crumbled into him, submitting to his love and protection. I was safe.

Chapter 29

"Hold still."

"Okay, okay!" I cried, grimacing as Scott sprayed antiseptic over my insignificant wounds. I averted my gaze to the setting sun before turning back to a prettier sight: my bare legs draped over Scott's lap in the backseat of his rental car.

I needed to calm down before heading back to the beach house, so Scott kept driving until we ended up at our old make-out spot overlooking the city.

"I think you'll survive," Scott said, applying a bandage from the basic first aid kit he'd found in the trunk. He ran his hands up and down my legs, inspecting his handiwork. "I'll have to give you regular check-ups, of course."

The corner of my mouth twitched. "Of course."

Scott pressed his thumb into the sole of my foot, moving it in a circular motion. "I wish you'd called me. I would've come with you."

"I didn't even know if we were still together."

"Lanie, just because I got angry at you doesn't mean I wanted to end things." His shoulders lowered as he spoke. "After you left, Riley and I had a long talk. He made me realize how much of a jerk I was being—to him and to you." He lifted his eyes to mine, full of shame. "I never should've spoken to you that way. I'm sorry."

"You were trying to protect your brother. I get it. I shouldn't have interfered."

Scott reached for my hand. "But I want you to interfere. I want you to tell me when I'm wrong or if I've hurt you. I don't want there to be anything unsaid between us."

I entwined my fingers in his, savoring our perfect fit. "Neither do I," I said, knowing someday soon I'd have to divulge my darkest secret.

"So, tell me…"

My gut twisted. *Not yet.*

"Why were you running out of that house so fast?"

Another surge of rage flowed through me. "I found your letter."

Scott's jaw slackened. "It did make it," he said in a whisper.

"Yeah, just not to me." My eyes burned under the threat of tears.

Within an instant, Scott shifted closer until I was almost sitting on him. "Hey, we found each other again, and that's all that matters now."

"But all these years…" I lowered my gaze as the trauma resurfaced. "I thought…"

"Stop thinking and look at me," he said, tipping up my chin. "I love you, Lanie. I loved you then, and I love you now." His eyes gleamed into mine. "What happened in between…it doesn't matter anymore. We have to focus on our future, and with you, Lanie…it's fucking bright."

Tears ran down my face as I climbed onto his lap and kissed him, deep and wanting. "I love you, too," I murmured over his supple lips. "I've always loved you." And I hoped, when the time came to say what remained unsaid, he'd remember that.

A week later, Scott held my hand through my father's funeral. He'd taken time off work and left Riley to fend for himself, refusing to leave my side.

After the congested church service full of business associates, we returned to my parents' house for the wake. My mother was in her element and barely noticed my arrival until she saw who was by my side.

"How dare you bring him here," she hissed, grasping my wrist as I returned from the restroom.

Instead of answering, I tore my arm away and kept walking. I refused to fuel her hatred or let her perpetual disappointment seep into my subconscious any longer. In my haste to escape, I swiped someone's shoulder as they turned from the bar, spilling their drink.

"Oh, shit," I muttered, searching for a napkin to clean up the mess. "I wasn't watching where I was going." Once I finally located a dishcloth, I turned to find one of the staff already mopping it up and sighed.

"Melanie, are you okay?" A gentle hand grasped my elbow.

I peered up to discover Adam's furrowed gaze. "Sorry, Adam, I'm not myself," I said, glancing back at my mother who'd already switched back to her perfect persona.

"It's fine," Adam said as a waiter handed him a new whiskey. "I've been meaning to tell you how sorry I am for your loss. Your father was a remarkable man."

"Was he?" I expelled a humorless chuckle. "I guess you and Gray knew him better than I ever did."

Adam eyed the room. "Well, he was popular."

"That he was." I followed his gaze through the mass of strangers before catching sight of William and Caroline Harlow. "How are your parents dealing with it?"

"They're pretty rattled."

"That's understandable," I said with a solemn smile. "They've been friends for a long time."

With a quiet nod, Adam took a sip of his whiskey, seemingly hesitant to move on.

"Growing tired of it yet?" I asked, curious to pick the brain of the most ambitious man I knew.

"Of what?"

"This world? The networking? The insincerity?"

"Me?" He scoffed. "Never." But something in his eyes suggested something deeper.

"Why don't you change it up a bit? Come and spend a few days with us at *your* beach house. We still have a few days left until we have to get back."

Adam grimaced. "Sounds fun, but I'm about to start a new project, and it needs my full attention right now."

I placed my hands on my hips, growing impatient. "When are you going to give yourself a break?"

"And do what exactly?"

"I don't know," I said, throwing up my hands. "Relax? Hangout at the beach? Travel the world…"

"Seems like a waste of time to me."

"That's because you don't have anyone to do it with."

Adam chortled. "Oh, I've got plenty of girls to *do it* with."

I rolled my eyes. He'd been like this since we were kids. "Don't you ever plan on settling down?"

"I'm entirely too much for one woman. Plus…" He ran his hands down his suit jacket. "It wouldn't be fair to the rest of them."

I burst out laughing, drawing scowls from every direction. "You don't fool me, Adam," I said, lowering my voice. "I've seen the way you watch Gray and Josie."

A wrinkle materialized between his eyebrows. "And what way is that?"

"The way I used to," I said, sneaking a peek out the window to find Scott furiously texting while Josie and Grayson chatted by the pool.

"Well, you're clearly back on the booze," he muttered, downing the last of his whiskey. "Speaking of, where are they?"

"Hiding," I said, tugging his arm as I passed. "Come on."

With our parents close by, we opted to stay out of their way and let them grieve with their friends and colleagues. By now, everyone was aware of the strained relationships within our families, but their curious glances told me they didn't know the complete truth.

Scott slipped his phone into his pocket as we approached and shook Adam's hand.

"Thought you'd be inside, trying to acquire new business," Grayson said, undoubtedly trying to stir up his brother. "Didn't Dad once tell us funerals were great networking opportunities?"

Adam poked his tongue into his cheek. "Even I won't stoop that low."

"Has my brother grown a conscious?"

"Quit it, Gray," Josie said, nudging his side.

Adam snickered. "Yeah, listen to your wife, douchebag," he muttered, signaling to the waiter for another drink. "I did overhear some interesting news, though. Something I think Melanie should know about." His light-blue eyes turned to mine. "Shortly before your father's death, Warren Media acquired a new company."

"And this affects me how?"

"Mel..." He sighed. "It's AG Galleries."

My stomach plummeted. "No..."

Scott glared at Adam. "Where did you hear that?"

"The man himself." Adam tilted his head toward the house. "Alfie Gibbs."

"He's here?" I asked, darting my gaze through the windows. Surely I could convince him to change his mind.

Grayson ran his hand through his hair with a grumble. "I'll go speak to him."

"No," I bit, irritated by his impulse to save me. "I'll do it myself." With a deep breath, I marched back into the house, determined to find the man who'd unknowingly sold my freedom. My job at the gallery let me live a life away from my family name. It gave me the space to find myself, to become independent, to trust my own decisions. And most importantly, it had led me back to the man I loved. Without it, my future was uncertain.

"Hey, slow down," Scott said, appearing at my side.

"I can fight my own battles," I muttered in annoyance.

"I know that." He pulled me to a halt so our eyes could meet. "I'm here to support you."

Embarrassment filled my cheeks as my heart swelled. "Oh."

"And you walked straight past him. He's over by the mantel."

Diverting my gaze, I discovered Alfie standing alone by the fireplace, admiring the elaborate Christmas tree as he sipped his tea. He was older than I remembered. More fragile.

"Alfie," I said, approaching slowly, not wanting to give him a start.

He lifted his tired gaze and smiled. "Oh, Melanie." His cup shook as he placed it back on the saucer. "I'm so very sorry for your loss."

"Please tell me you didn't sell your company to Warren Media," I said, not interested in his condolences.

"Your father made an offer too good to refuse. I hope you understand. I need to slow down, and Nicholas...well, he isn't very enthusiastic about the business."

"But surely the sale can't go ahead now that my father is..." My voice cracked unexpectedly. "Gone."

"I'm sorry, Melanie, but the papers were finalized weeks ago. The announcement is planned for the new year. I did pass on your brilliant proposal, though. I'm sure Warren Media will be able to help your friend."

"I doubt that," I said as fear trickled down my spine. "So, what happens next?"

Alfie's grimace didn't comfort me in the slightest. "I guess that's up to Warren Media, but I would hope..."

"We're shutting it down and liquidating all the assets." My mother's voice cut through our conversation like a serrated knife. "Of course, we'll make sure everyone gets their severance pay—if they've worked there long enough." Her venomous gaze met mine, knowing very well I hadn't.

Although I desperately wanted to claw her eyes out, I remained eerily calm. "Are you really going to destroy a profitable business just to prove a point?"

She rolled her eyes, seemingly exhausted by our conversation. "And what point would that be, Melanie?"

"That I need you."

"I don't know what you're talking about," she muttered, screwing up her plastic nose.

"You have no control over me anymore, so you thought you'd buy your way back in."

"Don't be ridiculous."

"Well, guess what, Mom. I don't need you anymore. I don't need your money. I don't need your approval. And most importantly, I don't need your love."

Her face grew red as she scowled. "You're nothing without your family."

"No," I said, full of poise. "I'm everything without you." As my mother's lips parted, I stepped forward, observing the subtle sheen over her eyes. "I'm sorry for your loss, Mom, but I'm not sorry for mine."

Without a backwards glance, I whirled around and walked out of the nightmare I grew up in.

Anxiety riddled my soul as I succumbed to my father's final blow. "What am I going to do?" I muttered, pacing the tiled floor of Adam's beach house. "I'm going to be unemployed within months, and once I've exhausted my savings, I won't be able to buy food or pay bills, let alone rent my own place."

"We're hardly going to throw you out, Mel," Grayson said, handing Josie a steaming cup of ginger tea as she settled onto the couch.

Her eyes answered his unspoken question. "That's right. Even if we come back a little earlier than expected, we'll make room for you."

"There is no way I'm living with newlyweds. Plus, I refuse to sponge off you any more than I already have."

"You've been housesitting. It's hardly sponging," Grayson uttered, standing in front of me with his hands rested on his hips.

I matched his stance. "People would pay good money to housesit an apartment like that, and you know it."

"Then..." He shook his head with a grumble. "Move in with Scott."

"She won't," Scott said, walking back into the room after making some calls. "I've tried."

Grayson turned my way. "Why not? Amy says you stay there most nights anyway."

"That's true," Scott muttered, falling onto the couch behind me.

"You know why, Gray." I welcomed Scott's hands as they guided me onto his lap. "I moved to New York to become independent. To not have to rely on anyone. If I move in with Scott now, I'll never know if I can do it on my own." I peered up at Scott as he tucked me under his arm.

"Everything will work out, Mel," Josie said, sipping her tea with an unusual grimace. "There are plenty of galleries in Manhattan that will be thrilled to have you."

"I hope so…for Faye and Adrian too. They're going to be shattered when they find out."

Scott's fingers interwove through my hair. "Are you going to tell them?"

"I have to." Surely they'd want to know. "Don't I?"

"From my experience, no one wants this sort of news before the holidays," Grayson said, sitting down beside Josie. "Christmas is hard enough."

"Good point." I rubbed my aching eyes. "I'm too tired to think straight."

Scott pressed his soft lips to my temple. "Why don't you sleep on it? It's been a day."

"That it has," Grayson murmured, turning on the television to find a movie to occupy the gloomy afternoon.

I curled my legs under my body and snuggled closer to Scott. "Everything okay at home?" I asked, taking comfort in the steady beat of his heart. "You've been on the phone a while."

"Um, yeah. Everything's fine." Scott's heartbeat fluctuated under his forced nonchalance.

I lifted my head to question his hesitation, but my cell phone rang, breaking my curiosity. "That's probably Cara," I said with a grimace. AG Galleries was no longer in a position to help her situation, and it pained me to admit that the proposal I'd worked hours on had failed to save her studio. Now I had to break the news.

"Hello?" I answered warily, not recognizing the number on the screen. Perhaps she was calling from Zach's phone.

"Am I speaking with Melanie Warren?"

The deep authoritative voice sharpened my attention. "Yes…"

"My name is Derek Green. You may not remember me, but I was your father's attorney and now the executor of his will."

"I remember you," I said. *And the part he played in my father's plan eleven years ago.*

There was a subtle pause before he continued. "Great. Well, I'm meeting with your mother tomorrow morning to go over your father's affairs. I'd like to extend the invitation to you."

"I'm sure my mother will suffice," I said, shifting myself off Scott. "I really need to get back to New York." I hadn't booked my return flight, but it made for a good excuse.

"I understand, but in order to proceed, I'll need to speak with you before you leave."

My jaw tightened. I had no intention of seeing my mother again, but it seemed the universe had other plans. "Very well," I grumbled. "Send me the address."

"I'll have my assistant do so immediately. Thank you, Melanie…and I'm very sorry for your loss."

"What was that about?" Scott asked, watching me inquisitively as I hung up the phone.

"More formalities," I said with a heavy sigh. "My father's lawyer wants to go through some stuff with me and my mom. No doubt she wants to rub her inheritance in my face."

Scott pulled his cell phone from his pocket and stood up. "I'll call Riley and let him know I'll be staying a few more days."

My heart dipped. "But aren't you visiting that art school with him this weekend?"

"I don't think my opinion is the one he's after."

Scott didn't know how wrong he was. "Tell him we'll go next weekend…and I'll buy him an ice cream."

"He's not six anymore, Lanie."

"So…" I shrugged. "He still likes ice cream."

Scott pursed his lips, but his eyes twinkled in amusement. "See…this is why he's always liked you more than me."

"One of the many reasons," I muttered loud enough for him to hear.

He shot back a dirty look on his way back to our bedroom, making me laugh.

"Look at you, all loved up," Grayson teased as Scott closed the door.

I poked out my tongue. "Says the man rubbing his wife's feet."

Grayson's hands froze.

"Don't stop," Josie cried, nudging him with her foot. "If we're having lunch with your parents tomorrow, I need to be well and truly relaxed."

"I can think of some other ways to relax you," Grayson said, completely abandoning our sibling-like banter to flirt with his wife.

Josie's cheeks grew pink as she gazed lovingly into Grayson's eyes. "Oh yeah?"

"Come on, guys," I groaned. "I thought we were watching a movie?"

Grayson took Josie's hand and pulled her off the couch. "Sorry, Mel," he said, throwing me the television remote. "It's all yours."

The sound of their muffled laughter through the wall brought a smile to my face. Grayson had found happiness with Josie, and she was everything he deserved. Caring, funny, talented, and most of all, she loved him back with the same ferocity.

Grayson and I had never experienced that kind of love. Ours was laced with resentment, knowing the choice was not ours. Our parents were like impatient children, forcing mismatched puzzle pieces together until they fit. Never mind the damage done or the disjointed picture. In their minds, it was complete.

"Where did everyone go?" Scott asked, dropping back onto the couch.

A squeal echoed through the house, followed by a loud thud.

"Oh…This is awkward."

I laughed. "They really can't keep their hands off each other."

Scott's hand crept across the couch, grazing my thigh. "I know the feeling."

My entire body warmed at his delicate touch. "Maybe we should make it awkward for them," I said, turning to him with a smirk.

His grin grew irresistibly large. "Maybe we should."

Wanting to dive into his dimples, I climbed on top of him and kissed the hollows that framed his perfect smile. First left, then right, until Josie's cry reverberated through the house. "Nope," I muttered over Scott's parted lips. "Too awkward."

His laughter filled the room as he lifted me off the couch, cradling my ass in his large hands. "Come on, we're going for a drive."

"What?" Mom barked. "Is this some sort of joke?"

My father's lawyer winced. "Unfortunately, the copy you found is outdated, and the latest version clearly states that Warren Media will be passed down to the child of Kenneth Warren."

"But that was written when she was engaged to Grayson. Melanie isn't capable of running the company."

"Then she'll have to learn fast," Derek said, ignoring my mother's concerns. "Everything else, aside from the company, is yours to do with as you please."

Her face reddened with rage. "That's it?!"

"I'm sure you'll live very comfortably."

"This is ridiculous! You'll be speaking with my lawyer—my new lawyer!"

"Of course," Derek said, not even flinching as my mother stormed out of the office.

The whole scene unfolded in a haze. I was too shocked to absorb the reality of the situation until Derek waved his hand in front of my face. "Melanie, are you okay?"

I cleared the growing lump in my throat. "Yeah, yep, yes. I'm fine." I was not.

"I'll give you some paperwork to read over, but once signed, you will become the sole owner of Warren Media. As you're already listed within the company documents, the transfer will take immediate effect."

"And if I don't sign?"

Derek frowned. "I don't understand."

"Never mind," I muttered, wishing I hadn't left Scott in the car. I was clearly out of my depth.

"I know it's a little overwhelming right now, but I'm here to help in any way I can. My firm has worked with your father for many years, so if you require further legal representation, I—"

"I have my own lawyer," I blurted, not interested in his obvious sales pitch. "His name is Scott Blackwood. You may remember him."

Derek's smile faded. "Very well then," he said, adjusting his tie. "I wish you all the best."

With a tight smile, I grabbed the paperwork and left his office, escaping down three flights of stairs and out the front door before promptly vomiting into a manicured garden bed beside the building.

"Whoa, are you okay?" Scott asked, wrapping his arm around my shoulders as I heaved.

"I need to sit down."

Scott guided me to a park bench nearby. "That bad?" he asked, handing me an old-fashioned handkerchief with his grandfather's initials embroidered in the corner.

I wiped the corners of my mouth as the nausea settled. "Yep."

"Please don't worry," he said, filling the space beside me. "Not only will you find a new job and get your own place, but you're surrounded by people who love you. You have everything you need for a good life, Lanie. Don't let them convince you otherwise."

With a trembling hand, I dumped the paperwork onto his lap. "Then what should I do with this?"

Chapter 30

Scott sauntered into the living area where Josie, Grayson, and I were playing poker with M&Ms. "Well, I've read all the paperwork, and if my calculations are correct—and they always are—you're about to become the wealthiest woman under thirty-five in America."

My stomach churned.

"Get a bucket," Grayson called out.

"No, I'm fine," I muttered, dumping my royal flush on the dining table. "I just don't know what to do. Mom's right. I have no idea how to run a company."

"Your Mom has no idea what you're capable of, Mel," Grayson said, throwing his cards down in defeat.

"But I don't want this. I've never wanted this."

"So, sell it," Grayson said with a shrug.

Scott chuckled as he sat down beside me. "To whom? Have you seen how much it's worth?"

Grayson pursed his lips. "You're right. Even Harlow Corp can't afford their portfolio." He crossed his arms as he leaned back in the chair. "And you can count me out. The thought of taking on anything to do with Warren Media makes my skin crawl."

"I know the feeling," I moaned, massaging my temples. "What a disaster."

"Or an opportunity," Josie said with a warm smile. "Money can be a gift or a curse. At least you get to choose this time."

Grayson slid his arms around his wife's waist and kissed her cheek before turning his softened gaze to me. "Do what makes you happy, Mel. Life's too short."

Scott squeezed my hand under the table. "I'll support whatever decision you make."

While I contemplated their thoughtful words, my cell phone sprang to life. "It's Cara," I said when her name flashed across the screen. "I'll take it outside." Sliding out of my chair, I wandered through the doors leading onto the grand terrace overlooking the beach. I had so much to tell her but didn't know where to begin.

"Hey, Cara," I said, turning my back to the warm setting sun. The heat surrounded me like a supportive embrace.

"Hey, sorry I didn't call yesterday, it's, um…been a little crazy here."

"What's going on?" I asked, picking up on the stress in her voice.

There was a long pause. "I thought Scott would've told you."

"Told me what?" I met Scott's pained expression through the glass doors and tapered my gaze.

"The owners of the building have decided to speed up the project. Demolition starts Monday."

"But that's only days away! They can't do that!"

"Unfortunately, my reduced rent was based on the provision that I'm able to exit within seventy-two hours. I just never thought they'd request such a thing."

I ran my hand down my face. "What are you going to do?"

"I don't know. I told the kids it's only temporary and we'll find a new place, but I don't even believe myself. Zach and Poppy have been here all day helping me pack, and Scott's arranged some temporary storage, but after that, I have no idea what the future holds."

"Surely we can buy you a little more time," I said, disgusted at the unreasonable timeframe thrust upon them by some ruthless corporate enterprise. "I'll call them and plead your case. Who owns the building?"

"Lanie…" Cara sighed. "It's Harlow Corp."

"Harlow Corp?!" Anger outweighed my shock. "Harlow Corp is trying to kick you out and destroy that beautiful building?" My fingers curled into a tiny ball of fury. "Fuck that."

Cara lowered her voice in apprehension. "Lanie…"

"Give me twenty-four of those seventy-two hours," I said as the ideas started trickling in.

"To do what exactly?"

"I'm going to negotiate new terms."

After I ended the call, Scott's eyes trailed after me as I marched across the living room. "Shit," he muttered, chasing after me.

Grayson and Josie raised their eyebrows simultaneously but didn't utter a word.

"I'm sorry I didn't tell you." Scott burst into the bedroom behind me. "You just had so much going on with your father's funeral, and I didn't want to—"

"I'm not angry, Scott," I said, opening my laptop.

"You're…not?"

"Well, I can't say I'm not a little miffed, but it's nothing you won't make up for over the next few hours," I said, grinning up at him.

Scott's pupils dilated before he tore off his top. "That I can do."

"Put that back on!" I cried through my laughter. "I won't be able to concentrate with you looking like that."

The glimmer in Scott's eyes dulled. "We're not having sex?"

"No!" I ran my gaze down his muscular chest. "Not yet, anyway. I've got an idea that will potentially solve everything."

"Lanie…" He pulled his top back on with a sigh. "I've had my team look into Cara's situation, and it's a lost cause. Harlow Corp doesn't leave loopholes in their contracts."

The corner of my mouth lifted as I met his gaze. "Then you're going to help me create one."

The next morning, while Grayson and Josie enjoyed sleeping in, Scott drove me to the epicenter of Harlow Corp. With help from Scott's firm, we'd spent the entire night working out the finer details of my plan, and now it was time for action.

"Do you have an appointment?" the receptionist asked, not even glancing my way.

"I don't need one."

Her eyes shot upward. "Oh, Miss Warren, please forgive me." She fumbled over the keyboard with a tight, ultra-white smile. "Go right up."

"That's what I thought," I said as I continued to the elevator. I'd always been treated like royalty at Harlow Corp, and Adam's refusal to answer my early-morning calls forced me to abuse my privileges.

Scott placed his hand on my lower back as he guided me inside. "Are you sure you want to do this?"

"No," I said, moistening my dry lips and straightening my outfit. "But I'm doing it anyway."

As the elevator rose, so did my heart rate. I hadn't visited Harlow Corp in over a year, and I'd forgotten how much I despised it. Hierarchy meant everything to people like William Harlow, and their headquarters reflected their ideals. Each level of the building determined an employee's importance to the company. The higher you were, the more power you reigned. While the entire top story belonged to William Harlow, Adam occupied the floor underneath, counting the hours until his father's retirement and the ultimate promotion.

Before Grayson left the company, William Harlow would play his sons against each other, promising their ascension if they followed his absurd rules. While Adam had always been the clearer candidate, his father was blinded by Grayson's relationship with me. The Warren name was equally as powerful, and our parents had agreed that, together, we'd be an unstoppable force.

Once the doors to Adam's floor slid open, Scott stood back and let me take the lead. I passed the attractive receptionist with a curt nod and continued down the hall toward Adam's office.

"Melanie," he greeted from his desk, unfazed by my sudden appearance. "Twice in a week. People will start talking."

Scott emitted a low growl while I panned my gaze around the room. It was cold and stark with not a personal item in sight. I almost felt sorry for him until I remembered who I was dealing with: William Harlow's protégé.

"I'm here to talk business," I said, knowing how much Adam loathed small talk.

"I'm not in the market for any art, but thanks."

"That's a shame," I muttered, eyeing his lifeless walls. "But that's not why I'm here. I want to talk about the building in Manhattan you're about to demolish."

"You mean the site of our East Coast headquarters? What of it?"

"I want you to give it to me."

He expelled a deep-chested laugh. "Why on earth would I do that?"

"Because of what I can give you in return."

Adam tilted his head with a smirk. "Your hand in marriage?"

I pressed my hand against Scott's puffed out chest as he stepped forward. "He's kidding."

Chuckling in amusement, Adam leaned back in his chair. "Unfortunately, there's not much else my father would want in return."

"I don't care what your father wants. I'm here to make a deal with you."

His left brow rose. "And what could you possibly offer me?"

"Warren Media."

Adam grew very still before narrowing his gaze. "You're fucking with me."

"I fuck you not. As of yesterday, much to my mother's dismay, I'm the new owner."

"No shit," he said, rubbing his jawline. "That's…unexpected."

I wandered around the room. "As you know, I have no desire to build my father's business or relish in its success. I'd rather burn Warren Media to the ground than make it another dollar. Unfortunately, I care about the people who work there. I don't want them to be collateral damage in my pursuit to shatter my parents' legacy. So, with Scott's help, I've come up with a plan." A small smile played upon my lips. "One that could benefit both of us."

"Go on," Adam said, interweaving his fingers.

I met his gaze and didn't falter. "I'm willing to transfer the entire Warren Media portfolio, minus AG Galleries, to Harlow

Corp, on the following conditions." I took a deep breath and continued. "First, your father retires. I will deal with you and only you. Second, you must reinstate all the grants Grayson created and maybe even implement some of your own. I know you have a heart hidden somewhere beneath that emotionless businessman facade. And last, the ownership of that beautiful building in Manhattan is to be transferred to me immediately."

"That's it?" The line deepened between Adam's eyes. "You've barely had the company a day, and you're willing to give it all away for next to nothing?"

"What you consider nothing means everything to me and the people I love. I don't want to waste my existence acquiring wealth and status. I want to bask in the beauty of life, and this plan will enable me to help others do the same."

Adam's lips pursed while he pondered me.

"There's no one else with the ability to take this on, Adam," I added, fearing he'd decline the offer.

"Oh, I know that." He chortled. "May I read the contract?"

Scott stepped forward and placed the detailed document on the desk in front of him. "I had my associates review this overnight. Everything should be in order."

Adam drummed his fingers as he perused the pages, one by one. The deal was straightforward. No tricks. No hidden clauses. I wanted the nightmare over as soon as possible. Once he reached the final page, he stared at the dotted line, expressionless.

"Well…?" I asked.

With a paling face, Adam pressed the internal intercom on his desk. "Jacinta. Set up a meeting with my father before he goes to lunch. Tell him it's important."

A wave of exhilaration washed over me. "So, it's a deal?"

Adam stood up and sauntered toward me, his smile growing with each step. "I'll sign it as soon as my father makes the announcement." As I reached for his hand, Adam bumped it aside and wrapped his arms around me. "You have no idea how long I've waited for this."

"You deserve it," I said, momentarily shocked by Adam's warmth. "Just don't get too full of yourself."

"It's too late for that, Smelly," he uttered with a chuckle.

"Can you quit calling me that?!" The nickname he had given me as a child wore thin more than twenty years ago. "I'm a grown woman now."

"But it's my duty to tease you. You're like the little sister I never had." His playful glint disappeared when Scott laughed. "Which reminds me…" he said, averting his gaze to my boyfriend. "If you hurt her, Grayson won't be the only one hunting you down."

Scott's back straightened as he nodded. "Noted."

"I mean it. If you leave her in that state again…"

Panic surged through me. "Right, well, we're going now," I said, ushering Scott out the door and down the hallway. "I… um…don't want to be here when William arrives."

With a sigh, Adam shoved his hands into his pockets and followed. "You'll have to face him eventually, Melanie," he sang out as we entered the elevator.

"And I will," I said, meeting Adam's concerned gaze moments before the doors closed. "Just not today."

Chapter 31

Although I desperately wanted to tell Grayson and Josie the prospective news, I was thankful to return to an empty house. William Harlow still had to step down from Harlow Corp for my plan to eventuate, and I wouldn't know the outcome for hours.

"Are you okay?" Scott asked as I stared out the living room window. "You look a little pale."

The crashing waves churned the shoreline, mimicking my stomach. "I'm just overwhelmed…and tired, and excited, and nervous…" I continued to ramble on until Scott took my hand, silencing my frantic mind.

"You've got this, Lanie," he said, sliding his hand around my nape as I turned to him. "And I've got you."

Any lingering doubt of his love slipped away as I gazed into his deep blue eyes. "Thank you."

"You just need a little distraction until Adam calls," he said, trailing his finger down the curve of my neck and across my collarbone.

Shivers rolled over my body at the seductive suggestion. "Got any bright ideas?"

He stalled on the first button of my blouse, grazing his knuckles against my pert breast. "We could watch a movie…"

I pretended to yawn while my nipple peeked out of the sheer silk, demanding attention.

With an alluring smirk, his fingertip orbited the rise. "A walk on the beach, perhaps?"

"Uh-uh." I barely found my voice.

His finger continued its downward journey, swirling closer to the ache below. "How about a swim?"

"No." I was already wet.

"Or..." His deep voice caressed my ear as his hand dipped between my thighs, cupping my pulsing core. "I could fuck you into oblivion?"

Almost losing control as Scott stroked my center, he grabbed my trembling legs and carried me to the couch. His muscular body engulfed my slender frame while he rocked his hardness against my soaked core, pushing me closer to the edge. When the friction became too much to bear, he hooked his finger over my panties and tore them off, casting them to the floor. And with one feverish thrust, my eyes rolled back as I cried out, surrendering to his love.

The distinct sound of rattling keys in the front door stirred me out of my orgasm-induced slumber. "Shit," I muttered, half-naked, with Scott's heavy arm draped over me. "They're back!"

Scott's eyes snapped open. "I thought you said they were out for lunch," he whispered, climbing off the couch to fasten his pants.

"They were! Maybe it went badly." I scrambled to my feet and patted down my skirt, wincing at the creases.

Scott caught sight of my thong moments before our company revealed themselves and swiped it off the floor.

"Adam?" My eyelashes fluttered in surprise.

Adam's gaze locked onto my flushed cheeks, and the corner of his mouth rose. "Looks like the celebration has started without me."

"We fell asleep," I blurted, running my fingers through my tousled hair.

He placed two bottles of champagne on the kitchen counter. "Then why is Scott holding women's lingerie?"

My eyes grew wide as I spun around, snatching my thong out of Scott's hand. "Excuse me," I muttered, storming out of the room to change. While I slipped on clean underwear and gathered my senses, Adam's greeting made contact with my brain. "Wait..." I scurried back into the room. "William agreed?!"

Adam's grin matched Scott's. "He's breaking the news to Grayson at lunch, and the official announcement will come out later today. Oh, and I called off the bulldozers, so that dilapidated building is yours. I think I'm going to have my work cut out for me on the West Coast anyway."

I lurched forward, throwing my arms around him. "Thank you!"

"I think I should be the one thanking you," Adam said as we parted. "At least now I won't have to woo some ugly heiress I don't want to fuck, let alone marry, to earn my place at the top."

I placed my hands on my hips, ignoring his emotional detachment. "You may even be allowed to marry for love now."

Adam recoiled in disgust. "Not an issue I'll need to address."

"Of course. I forgot. You're blessed with an impenetrable heart." I rolled my eyes back to Scott. "Adam doesn't believe in marriage…or love…or romance."

Scott's eyebrows rose. "And what do you believe in?"

"Money." His grin widened. "And sex."

With a groan, I squeezed Scott's arm. "While Adam divulges his philosophy on life, I'm going to call Cara and tell her to stop packing."

Scott leaned forward to kiss my lips. "Enjoy."

"I will."

Informing Cara she no longer needed to vacate her studio was one of the happiest moments of my life. She thanked me profusely through a torrent of tears and didn't pry into the how's or why's. She trusted me.

A flurry of voices entering the house drew me back to the living room.

"You fucking did it, man," Grayson called out as he ambled up the hall toward his brother.

Adam welcomed a hug from Josie. "It wouldn't have happened without Smelly here."

Grayson averted his gaze to me with a bemused grin. "I can't believe you gave him the company."

"I didn't give him all of it," I said, crossing my arms. I had my own plans for AG Galleries.

"Clearly enough to convince my father to retire."

"I didn't want this agreement to feed our parents' egos. I want whatever happens now to be our legacy, not theirs."

"Such a bad-arse," Josie said with a glint in her eye.

With a chuckle, Grayson pulled his brother in for a hug. "Congrats, bro. You'll kill it."

"Thanks," Adam muttered before shoving his brother away. "Enough with the mush. Can we drink now?"

While Adam popped open the champagne, I found five crystal flutes in the kitchen cabinet and placed them on the counter. I hadn't had an alcoholic drink in months, fearing my reasoning. Before rehab, I drank to forget, to dull the pain, but now, the darkness was fading. I could finally see the light and celebrate my future.

As I handed them out, one by one, I savored the smiles of my best friends. The only one to falter was Josie.

"Why aren't you drinking the champagne?" Adam asked her. "It's a five-hundred-dollar bottle."

"I...um..." She peeked up at Grayson with a grimace.

"What?" Adam snickered. "Are you pregnant or something?"

Grayson massaged Josie's nape as she paled. "Well...we were hoping to wait a few more weeks before..."

All the air expelled from my lungs. "You're pregnant?"

"Surprise," Josie said with a wince.

Adam gulped the rest of his champagne. "Holy fucking shit."

"Congrats, guys." Scott stepped forward to shake Grayson's hand and hug Josie. "That's amazing news."

"Looks like we have multiple reasons to celebrate tonight," Adam said, following Scott's lead.

Everyone turned my way as I stared at them, frozen in disbelief. I thought my envy had subsided, but there it was again, wanting something that would never be mine. Something I almost had. "Congratulations," I rasped as my caving chest threatened to crush my heart.

Grayson stepped forward as tears crept into my eyes while Scott reached out, understandably perplexed.

I jerked back from both of them. "I'm just surprised, is all," I said, forcing my facial muscles to form a smile.

As Josie's hazel eyes softened in understanding, my resilience crumbled.

"Excuse me," I muttered, making a beeline for the terrace. I desperately needed air.

While a muffled argument erupted in my wake, I jogged down the wooden steps to the sand, welcoming the cool sea breeze. Closing my eyes, I focused on the sound of the waves and the grainy sand between my toes, desperate to calm the demons that had haunted me for eleven years.

"I'm sorry, Mel." Grayson's voice drew me out of my inner torment as he sidled up beside me, hands in pockets. "We planned to tell you in private."

My eyes glazed over. "I don't want you walking on eggshells around me, Gray. This is wonderful news." I hooked my arm around his elbow. "It may not look like it right now, but I'm so happy for you guys."

"I know," he said, nudging me softly with his shoulder. "But Scott is pretty confused right now. You haven't told him yet, have you?"

I released my grip. "It's not something that just comes up in conversation."

Grayson exhaled heavily as he faced me. "Not if you don't bring it up, Mel."

"But what I did was so awful. You may have forgiven me, but it doesn't mean he will." Tears flooded my eyes as I yielded to my deepest fear. "What if he leaves me?"

"Why would I leave you?"

My heart plummeted as Scott's desperate voice sounded behind us.

"Exactly," Grayson whispered before laying a gentle kiss on my forehead. "I'll give you guys some privacy." After patting Scott on the shoulder, he retreated to the house, leaving the two of us alone on the beach.

"Lanie…What's going on?" Scott seemed hesitant to approach. "Why are you so upset about their news? Do you not want them to have a baby?"

The heartbreaking burden of my secret grew too much to

bear. "I'm not upset about their baby, Scott… I'm upset about ours."

"What are you talking about? We've never even spoken about hav—"

"I was pregnant." The admission stole my breath. "I found out a few weeks after my father sent you away."

Scott's mouth parted as he drew in air. "But we were so careful."

"Not always," I said, gazing out to sea. "Not enough."

"What happened to the baby?" The quiver in his voice surprised me.

I swallowed the lump in my throat as I grasped my stomach. "I lost it," I said, remembering the morning I woke covered in blood. "Just like I lost everything else back then."

"Lanie…I'm so sorry," he said, closing the distance between us. "Had I known, I never would've left you. I would've looked after you. Supported you."

A storm rolled over me as I met his angst-filled gaze. "But you weren't there. No one was there. I had to make decisions that affected my future. Our baby's future."

Scott stilled. "You were going to keep it?"

"That baby was my proof that love existed. That you weren't just a figment of my imagination. That what we had was real." I recoiled from his touch, knowing my next words could change the way he felt about me. "But, like everything in my life, it came with a cost. When I refused to have an abortion, my mother gave me an ultimatum. I had to convince Grayson the baby was his… or I was on my own."

Rage swelled behind Scott's eyes. "She did what?"

"She slipped something into Grayson's drink at my eighteenth birthday party, and all I had to do was make sure he fell into my bed. He woke up the next morning, thinking we'd slept together."

Scott ran his hands through his hair as he paced the beach. "So that's why you got engaged?"

I nodded. "My mother knew his parents would pressure him to do the right thing."

"I thought you'd moved on." His shoulders lowered. "I thought you were happier with him."

"That's what I wanted everyone to think. For years I've been flooding my socials with perfection. My hair, my makeup, the clothes, the lifestyle…but it was all a facade. Every photo was staged. Every smile was fake. Pretending was the only way I could live with what I'd done."

Scott closed the distance between us and grasped my biceps, forcing me to meet his gaze. "You were just a kid, Lanie. I don't blame you for this. You shouldn't blame yourself for this. What your mother did… Fuck!" He tore his arms away and kicked the sand. "I shouldn't have left you with them. I should've taken you with me. We could have…"

"What?" I scoffed. "Started a family? If you don't want kids now, you definitely wouldn't have wanted one back then."

Scott shook his head. "What are you talking about?"

"I heard what you said to Riley when you caught him with Poppy. You don't want to be responsible for another baby."

"Jesus, Lanie…" He hung back his head. "I meant another kid that wasn't *mine*."

"So…you *want* kids?"

"Not unless they're with you," he muttered, anger lacing his words.

My stomach somersaulted. "Oh."

Tugging me back into his arms, Scott ran his hand down my hair, directing the loose strands behind my ear. "Lanie, you're the reason why I've never settled down or gotten serious with anyone. I've never wanted any woman the way I want you. Until I saw you standing in my living room, I'd given up on love or any plans of a family."

I drew in a shaky breath. "And now?"

Scott encircled my hand and brought it to his chest. "Now I can't see a future without you, and I'm praying to God you feel the same."

"I didn't think you believed in God…"

Scott smirked. "Then, I'm praying to whatever divine entity that is responsible for creating you."

A small smile played on my lips. "Well, you know how I feel about you."

"I know you're *proud* of me…" he said with a twinkle in his eye.

Heat traveled up my neck as I recalled my blundering admission at the awards night. "So proud."

With a dimpled smile, he pressed his forehead against mine. "I love you, Lanie."

"I love you too."

Scott's lips grazed my cheek, seizing the tear tracing down my face. The ocean mist and his intoxicating aroma filled my senses with bittersweet memories of our lives so far until I captured his lips, desperate to make new ones.

We returned to the house as the sun dipped into the horizon to find Josie and Grayson snuggled up on the couch.

"Where's Adam?" I asked, panning my gaze around the living room.

Josie smiled at our interlocked hands. "He left to party elsewhere."

"In some unsuspecting woman's bed, no doubt," Grayson added with a chuckle. "You know he doesn't deal with emotion well."

I grimaced. "Sorry to ruin the celebration."

"Hey, I can't drink anyway." Josie let out a longwinded sigh before Grayson kissed her cheek. "It's going to be a long nine months."

I beamed down at them. "You two are going to make the best parents."

"Thanks, Mel," she said, rubbing her non-existent bump. "I think you guys will too—someday, I mean."

My cheeks warmed as I peeked up at Scott. "Oh, we haven't discussed that far ahead."

Scott's warm breath over my shoulder sent tingles straight to my core. "Just say when," he whispered with a seductive kiss under my earlobe.

My eyes widened as I cleared my throat. "Excuse me," I said before pulling Scott toward the bedroom. The moment the door closed, muting Grayson and Josie's laughter, I whirled around to face him. "What are you talking about? We're not ready for that."

Scott tugged me closer with a shrug. "Maybe not, but it wouldn't hurt to practice a little."

"And what exactly are we practicing?"

"You know…" He kissed my neck as he caressed my hips. "The art of baby-making."

I gasped. "You're fucking with me, right?"

His grin widened. "I'm pretty sure that's one of the steps."

"Scott!" I cried, stumbling backwards.

"Well, I'm a traditional guy," he said, throwing up his hands. "I want to get married before starting a family."

A surge of panic rippled through me, stealing my breath.

"And before you freak out, this isn't me asking…" He folded his arms across his chest. "Not yet, anyway."

"Well…good," I muttered in a fluster. "There's so much I need to do first…" My mind frantically summoned up every reason. "I have to find an apartment…"

"Lanie…"

"I need to concentrate on the galleries…"

"Lanie…"

"I want to get my driver's license, and a cat…"

"Lanie!"

His raised voice caught me off guard. "What?!"

"Stop overthinking and get undressed."

"But I haven't finished," I grumbled, placing my hands on my hips.

With a growl, Scott picked me up and threw me onto the bed. "You're still a pain in the ass, you know that?"

I lifted myself onto my elbows, relishing the desire in Scott's eyes. "Someone once told me all good women are," I said, curving my lips ever so slowly.

He grabbed one leg and then the other and dragged me down until his denim bulge collided with my core. "Then you, Lanie Warren, must be the best damn woman there is."

Epilogue

Scott

After every self-imposed milestone Lanie had achieved over the last six months, I proposed. Instead of giving me a solid answer, she'd change the subject, pretend she didn't hear me, or reel off a list of excuses that were fading fast. Most guys would've walked away broken-hearted by now, but she only made me more determined. I was going to marry that girl.

Her resistance wasn't because she didn't love me or believe in our happily ever after. Lanie needed to know, in her heart, that she'd be okay on her own. That she could rely on herself in the most trying of times. I knew she was ready. I just had to wait for her to realize it.

Even before her inheritance, Lanie had proven herself. After years of people underestimating her, she rose like a phoenix, stronger and brighter than ever, ready to show the world how incredibly intelligent, kind-hearted, and brave she was. There was no need to pretend anymore or live under the curse of her family name. Lanie could finally uncover her true self, and she was a fucking masterpiece.

Giving Warren Media to Adam Harlow, while confusing at first, was a brilliant idea. Lanie wasn't hungry for money and power, so she leveraged off William Harlow's unrelenting greed to get something she did want. Now, without much effort at all, she earned more money than she'd ever need and has put it toward something truly remarkable.

Finding Beauty opened its doors just three months after the planned demise of Cara's art studio. The center, managed by Cara, offered free art classes for troubled children and teens, with an in-house counseling service. While each level was dedicated to a particular technique, the entire ground floor housed a magnificent gallery of the students' work, and tonight was their first exhibition.

"Scott!" a young boy yelled from across the gallery moments after my late arrival.

I smiled at my client's son, the casualty of a messy custody battle. "Hey, Andy. Great to see you."

"Come and see my painting," he said, grabbing my hand. "It's over here." His tiny grasp brought back bittersweet memories of my little brother, who had left for art school at the beginning of the year. While my life was full with Lanie and the firm, I couldn't help but miss him, even if he did come home every other weekend.

As Andy pulled me through the crowd, I scanned the room for my girlfriend, acknowledging our friends and her colleagues as I passed. I hadn't seen Lanie since I had left her apartment that morning, and she hadn't returned my calls all day. She'd been so nervous about the opening of the gallery that she'd barely slept and vomited twice before breakfast. This night meant everything to her.

"What do you think?" Andy asked with a huge grin.

I turned my gaze to the artwork mounted on the wall before me. "Wow!" I said, clutching my chest. "It's so lifelike. I thought it was real for a moment."

Andy cackled with laughter. "Lanie says I have potential."

"Well, if that's the case, I'll have to buy it for my office. It could make quite the investment someday."

"Really?!" His eyes grew large. "I have to tell Mom!"

As he sped off, I gazed back up at the painting and smiled.

"Don't you just love the bold lines and dramatic way the artist uses negative space to draw your attention," an alluring voice said behind me. "The chaotic emerald splashes symbolize the subconscious fears of man's inner child."

I tilted my head. "I thought it was a dinosaur," I said, turning to the most exquisite woman I'd ever met.

Lanie's playful smirk confessed her bullshit. "That too."

"Oh, you're good." I stepped forward to kiss her cheek while breathing in her captivating scent. "And you look fucking amazing."

The long golden dress draped off her body like a goddess, complementing the feature mural at the entrance of the building. The artwork, based on an original painting by Cara, inspired the name of the center and its philosophy. To find beauty within the darkness.

"You look devastatingly handsome, as always," she said, brushing my shoulder. "Even with Claude's fur all over you."

"Dammit," I cried, tearing off my jacket. "Why couldn't you get one of those hairless cats?" With a roll of her pretty blue eyes, I couldn't help but reach out and draw her closer. "I'm sorry I'm late. One of my pro-bono cases just got a little more complicated, and I couldn't leave."

"Hey," she whispered, running her soft palm down my coarse jawline. "If one of those kids needs you, I want you to be there for them." Her eyes didn't leave mine. "You don't have to explain yourself to me."

I tucked her body into mine. A perfect fit. "You're incredible, Lanie," I said, running my hand over her subtle curves covered in silk. As my pants tightened, I quickly stepped back and distracted myself with the amazing artwork around us. "*This* is incredible."

Lanie grinned knowingly until an elderly man took her hand, stealing her attention. "Melanie, this place is wonderful," Alfie Gibbs said, oblivious to my presence. "Thank you so much for inviting me. After all the improvements you've made to AG Galleries, I'm surprised you've had time for this. I must say, you're quite the businesswoman—unlike my son, who is gallivanting all over Europe right now."

"Thank you, Alfie." Her smile radiated warmth. "Your support means the world to me."

"But I think it's time for a name change. AG Galleries is your legacy now, not mine."

"Oh, I have one in mind." Lanie's twinkling gaze struck mine before resuming focus on Alfie. "I just need to sign a few more documents to make it official."

My eyebrows pulled together as I tried to catch up. New name? Documents? Since when? She hadn't run anything past me, and I was her lawyer.

"Fabulous," Alfie said, squeezing her hand before letting go. "I look forward to seeing what you come up with."

As he strolled away, a platter of food was thrust between us, stifling any chance of interrogation.

"Hors d'oeuvres?" The waiter said, mispronouncing the word like my brother enjoyed doing.

My head snapped up. "Riley?"

Riley grinned under his dark locks. "Lanie begged me to help out tonight. She's a hard woman to refuse."

"Like you're not really here to see Poppy," Lanie said, crossing her arms.

As his cheeks burned a brighter shade of red, I reached for the last appetizer.

"Don't you dare!" A hand launched between us, swiping the sole shrimp cocktail off the platter. "I've been chasing these around all night."

As Riley wandered away, chuckling, I turned to find Josie scarfing it down while Grayson stared at her with wide eyes.

"I thought you were avoiding shellfish," Grayson said while Amy and Reed sidled up beside them.

"She was." Amy chuckled. "Until she found out Zach Freeman was catering."

Josie narrowed her eyes at her husband. "I'm a week overdue, Gray," she mumbled. "If this baby isn't going to follow the rules, then neither am I."

"Well, I'm happy Baby Harlow is stalling," Lanie said, stepping forward to place her hands on either side of Josie's protruding belly. "But after tonight, I'm expecting aunt status immediately."

Until Lanie's admission, I had no idea she wanted kids. I had no idea *I* wanted kids until I found out we almost had one twelve years ago. Now, I couldn't stop thinking about it. Every time I saw Lanie giving advice to my brother or supporting the kids at the center, I wanted to drop to one knee and get the ball rolling. Her innate strength extinguished the lingering damage caused by her mother and created a nurturing and compassionate deity destined for motherhood. She deserved a second chance. We both did.

"The sooner this baby comes, the better," Josie grumbled, shifting uncomfortably in her sapphire gown. "I feel like Violet Beauregarde in this dress."

"I do love blueberries," Grayson said, sliding his arms around her.

"Wow!" Adam's voice boomed into our conversation. "What a difference a few months make," he said, gaping at his sister-in-law's stomach.

Josie's eyes turned into slits while Grayson laughed, resulting in an elbow to the ribcage.

"You made it!" Lanie hugged Adam, knowing very well it made him uncomfortable. "I thought you were stuck in LA."

Adam glared at his brother. "Well, *someone* has been pestering me to visit Grandpa, so I thought I'd kill two birds while I'm here."

Lanie's shoulders sank as she zigzagged her gaze between the Harlow brothers. "How's he doing?"

"Not great," Grayson said, rubbing the back of his neck. "Cancer's spreading. Mom and Dad flew over a couple of days ago to organize his care."

"I need a cigarette," Adam muttered, spinning on his heel before disappearing into the crowd.

Grayson threw Josie a concerned glance but said nothing.

"Did they like my sister?" Amy asked, breaking the awkward silence. "She just texted and said the interview was grueling."

"I'm sure it was." Grayson chuckled. "I haven't spoken to them yet, but I know Grandpa loved her."

Amy smiled, seemingly relieved. "Ultimately, it's up to him, right?"

"Yeah...but I don't think my parents will approve."

"Caroline and William don't take kindly to outsiders," Josie uttered, rubbing her stomach with a grimace. "Just like that prawn hasn't taken kindly to my stomach." A moan escaped her lips as she buckled over. "Oh my god, the baby is punishing me!"

Lanie gasped. "Was that a contraction?"

"No..." She chortled. "It can't be." Her humor faded as she turned to Grayson. "Can it?"

"I...I don't know..." Grayson paled, clearly perturbed.

Panic filled Lanie's eyes. "If you need to go to the hosp—"

"No! We're here to celebrate your big night." Josie grasped her husband's hand and forced a smile. "We're not going anywhere."

Grayson winced as his fingers turned white. "Well, maybe just until the speeches."

"You better do them now then," Amy said, shooting Lanie an all-knowing look.

With wide eyes, Lanie raced off while I fetched Josie a chair.

"Thanks, Scott," Grayson said, attempting to sit down.

Josie waved him off with her hands. "It's for me, dipshit."

My laughter tapered off when the clinking of champagne glasses drew everyone's attention to the center of the gallery. While the children and their parents moved closer, I stood back as Lanie sauntered into the circle, swaying her hips like a dancing flame in the middle of a birthday cake.

"Good evening, everyone!" she called out, panning her gaze around the crowded gallery. "I'd like to thank all of you for coming tonight and being a part of something that truly means the world to me. It's been an epic six months here at Finding Beauty, and I'm incredibly proud of all the teachers and students for filling these walls with so much heart. The talent uncovered here is immense, and I hope, in one way or another, we're brightening people's lives."

There were a few cheers and whistles before she continued.

"To the amazing woman who really runs the show here..." Lanie spotted Cara shying away from the limelight and pointed her out. "Cara Freeman...thank you for being an absolute superstar. Cara gave birth to this idea, and I'm incredibly honored to help it grow. And if you haven't seen her extraordinary artwork yet, head over to LB Galleries in SoHo. You're in for a treat."

LB Galleries?

"To all my staff, whom I love dearly, I really appreciate your help tonight. And Zach Freeman, our guest chef...your delicious appetizers are an art in themselves." Lanie grew silent before clearing her throat. "And finally…" Her eyes tracked through the crowd. "Where's my man?"

As warmth traveled up my neck, Amy grabbed my arm and shoved me forward, catching Lanie's attention.

"Scott…" Her smile grew when our eyes collided. "*You* are my inspiration. Your support has been unwavering, your love unconditional, and your patience…untiring. So, instead of wishing you'd ask again, just one last time…I'm going to ask you." Lanie took slow purposeful steps until she was standing before me in all her unmeasurable beauty. "Scott Blackwood…will you marry me?"

I wiped my hand down my face, trying to mute my smile, but it wasn't going anywhere. "Well, this is awkward," I muttered, pulling the little blue box from my pocket that had been taunting me all day. "I planned to ask you the same question."

Lanie gasped as I kneeled before her, revealing the diamond ring nestled within.

"Hell yes, I'll marry you," I said before she could muster a response.

"You just stole my answer."

"You stole my proposal."

The corners of her mouth rose as she blinked back tears. "I guess we're getting married."

"Finally!" I exclaimed, angling my gaze heavenward.

While applause erupted through the crowd, I slipped the ring on her trembling finger and rose to my feet. "You okay?" I asked, anxious about my ring choice. "If you don't like it, we can—"

"No, no, it's perfect," she said, laying her hand upon my thumping chest. "It just hit me, that's all." Her voice cracked with emotion.

"What did?"

Her oceanic eyes peered up at me, deep and glistening. "How happy I am."

"I'm pretty damn happy too," I said, wiping a lone tear from the apple of her cheek. With a surge of adoration, I lifted her into my arms and surrendered to the pull of her enticing lips. Our mouths barely touched before giggles echoed around us.

"Keep it PG, will you," Adrian said, shielding us from our curious onlookers. "There are kids around."

With a chuckle, I redirected my mouth to Lanie's ear. "We'll continue this at the beach house."

"I'm looking forward to it," she said with a smile that almost brought me to my knees again.

After a hectic few months, I'd organized a weekend at my beach house to give us a much-needed break from the firm and the galleries. Only, it wasn't my sole motivation. I planned to propose. Only this time, I had a ring and was determined to get an answer. But in true Lanie fashion, she turned the tables and did the unexpected.

As the crowd dispersed, Cara flung her arms around us. "I'm so happy for you guys," she cried, grabbing Lanie's hand and gaping at the ring. "Go and celebrate. I'll take over from here."

Lanie frowned. "Are you sure?"

"It's almost the end of the night. Between Faye, Adrian, and me, I think we've got it handled."

With one last hug, Cara took control of the event while we accepted a string of blessings from friends and guests before they left.

"Does this mean I'm going to have the apartment to myself tonight?" Riley asked immediately after congratulating us.

"I guess so," I grumbled, still not entirely comfortable with Poppy's 'sleepovers'. "We're spending the weekend at the beach."

Lanie ran her fingers over my nape, calming me as Riley waltzed over to his girlfriend and whispered something presumably inappropriate in her ear. "You'll have other things on your mind," she said, kissing my cheek. "Trust me."

The familiar twitch below had no doubt.

As if sensing our rising heat, Grayson cleared his throat on approach. "So, you finally wore her down," he said, patting my shoulder. "Just like in high school."

With a soft chuckle, I drew Lanie into my side as she beamed up at me. "I'm stubborn like that."

"Sounds familiar." Grayson diverted his gaze to Lanie with a smirk.

"Shut up," she muttered, attempting to punch his arm, only to be caught mid-swing.

His eyes softened as he let go. "I'm proud of you, Warren."

"Thanks, Harlow." Lanie's smile grew melancholy as they hugged, undoubtedly reminiscing about their lives together and the growth they've made since. "Now, get your wife to the hospital before her water breaks all over my gallery floor."

Adam almost spat out his champagne as he passed. "The baby's coming?"

"She's adamant it's nothing," Grayson said, stepping back to observe his grimacing wife from afar.

Lanie placed her hands on her hips. "Well, Amy says otherwise. Who are you going to believe?"

"I'll get the car," Adam uttered without hesitation. He pecked Lanie's cheek and offered me a firm 'you better fucking look after her' handshake before dumping a freshly filled glass on a nearby table. "Grayson, I'll see you outside in five."

All of our mouths dropped when Adam marched out of the gallery.

"Anyone would think he's excited to become an uncle," I said, bemused. Perhaps he had a heart, after all.

Lanie and Grayson threw each other a sideways glance. "Nah," they said in unison before snorting with laughter.

"Adam is petrified of kids," Grayson continued.

"And commitment," Lanie added.

I crossed my arms, pondering. "Has he ever had a girlfriend?"

"Many." Grayson sniggered. "But nothing serious."

"Yet he came alone tonight." The lawyer in me was eternally curious. I always had a knack for seeing more truth than people were willing to share.

"Huh," Lanie mused. "He was alone at the Warner Philanthropy Awards night too. That is strange. Perhaps he isn't as popular on the East Coast."

Grayson laughed. "He does just fine over here, believe me."

A horn blasted outside, breaking our thoughtful daze and startling some guests.

“I better get Josie before Adam completely loses his mind,” Grayson muttered on his way back to his wife.

With Amy’s support, Josie stood up as we approached. “Congratulations, you two,” she said, kissing our cheeks. “My psychic friend had an inkling something exciting was going to happen tonight.”

Amy’s eyes widened as she hugged us. “Not what I had in mind,” she said with a nervous laugh. “But it was a lovely surprise, nonetheless. Congratulations.”

Another horn ricocheted off the building.

“Who is doing that?” Josie asked, squinting through the narrow windows. “Is that Adam’s car? Why is he flashing his headlights?”

“Because he’s taking us to the hospital,” Grayson said, rubbing Josie’s back.

“But I’m fi…uuck,” Josie grasped her stomach.

“I’ll get her coat,” Reed said, racing off to the coatroom.

Josie breathed in and out in quick succession before latching onto Grayson’s arm. “I’m not ready for this.”

“Yes, you are,” he said, growing serious as he cupped her face in his palms. “And you’re going to make a great mother.”

In their private moment, I lowered my gaze to find Amy squeezing Lanie’s hand before whispering something in her ear.

Lanie’s cheeks grew pink as she attempted to hide her smile. Before I could decipher the moment they’d shared, Amy picked up Josie’s handbag and chased after the anxious couple.

“You have that look again,” I said, watching Lanie’s eyes glaze over as her friends left the gallery.

She shook herself out of the daze. “I’m just so happy for them.”

“I can tell.” I slipped my arms around her waist, hoping to absorb a fragment of her radiance. “I could bask in that glow forever.”

With a sharp intake of breath, Lanie glanced around the room. “I should help clean up.”

“Sure.” My eyes tapered. “Where do you want me?” Her desire to jump straight back into work screamed avoidance. There was something she wasn’t telling me.

"Why don't you see if Zach needs help in the kitchen."

With a curt nod, I joined the bustle of worker bees while Lanie farewelled the remaining guests. I knew better than to push. Lanie needed to do things in her own time, in her own way, and from the moment she had stepped back into my life, I was willing to wait forever.

As staff numbers dwindled, Lanie went to her office to change her clothes while I slipped outside to move my car to the front of the gallery. My Mustang was packed up and ready to take us to our favorite hideaway.

I'd bought the beach house years ago to give me space from the big city and a chance to reflect on the girl who'd unknowingly broken me. Instead of picking up a bottle every time I caught a glimpse of her in the paper or a photo in a magazine, I'd get in my car and hightail it to the beach. The hum of the engine, the long drive, and the sand beneath my feet evoked memories of our entwined past. That the love we'd shared wasn't a figment of my imagination or some spoiled-princess rebellion. It was real.

Exhilaration washed over me as I leaned against the car, spying Lanie through the window, activating the security alarm. Even without the makeup and the perfectly styled hair, her beauty prevailed. It ran deep, coursing through her veins, saturating her aura. She grew up in the shade, never able to truly blossom until she found the sun, and now there was no stopping her.

Once Lanie locked the door and checked it twice, she lifted her gaze to mine.

I couldn't help but grin, knowing my dimples drove her crazy. "Ready to go?"

Her face brightened at the sight of the beast. "We're taking the Mustang?"

"I wanted tonight to be special." I ran my hand over the turquoise duco. "Washed her and everything."

"She's going to make a beautiful wedding car," she said, shuffling across the sidewalk in her ridiculous narwhal slippers.

My chest swelled at the thought. "I can picture it now. White ribbon across the hood. Tin cans rattling off the back."

The corner of her enticing mouth hitched up. "I may even have to find you a matching tie."

"Always the planner." I chuckled, reaching out to take her bag.

"Not always." She puffed out a laugh. "But it's one of the better traits I inherited from my mother."

The fleeting sadness in Lanie's eyes had me dangling my car keys in front of her. "Want to drive?" I asked, distracting her thoughts away from her callous mother.

"Really?" Her eyes widened. "But I only just got my license."

"I trust you'll look after her."

With a squeal, she tore the keys out of my hand and ran around to the driver's side. I nudged open the passenger door and slipped inside, making a mental note to have it fixed before the wedding.

As Lanie turned the key and the car rumbled to life, her entire face lit up. I'd been giving her lessons all year in my later model cars (the ones with airbags), so this was an entirely different experience for her...and me. I'd never let anyone else drive this car since high school.

While she maneuvered through the streets of Manhattan, my gaze fell to the ring on her finger. The streetlights glittered off the diamond like a miniature disco ball.

"Whoa," I cried as the car abruptly veered to the left.

"Sorry, sorry!" Lanie lifted her hand with a wince. "It's the ring. It's so sparkly...and beautiful...and super distracting."

"Then take it off." I laughed.

Lanie flashed me a scowl. "I'm never taking it off."

"Do you want me to drive?"

"That will probably be safer," she said, biting her lower lip. As Lanie searched for a place to pull over, her phone chimed within her handbag, creating yet another distraction. "Can you get that? It might be the security company."

Like Mary Poppins, I rummaged through her seemingly bottomless bag until I found the phone and opened the new message. "It's from Grayson."

Grayson: **I know it's late, but I couldn't wait to tell you. It's a boy!**

"Oh my god!" She swerved into the curb, knocking over a trash bin as she came to a halt.

"Lanie!"

Her eyes squeezed shut with her grimace. "Sorry!"

"Call him," I muttered, handing over the phone. "I'll assess the damage."

Grasping the phone, Lanie frantically dialed while I stepped out of the car. Thankfully, there was nothing more than a small mark that buffed out with the rub of my sleeve. *Thank fuck.* My grandfather believed every mark, dent, and scratch told a story and should never be repaired. As long as her motor was running, the details didn't matter. I valued his ideals, but the thought of anything happening to my car, no matter how superficial, hurt like a motherfucker.

As Lanie's excited murmurs filled the interior, I waited outside while she shared a private moment with her best friend. Although she never admitted it, it had been hard for her watching Grayson and Josie prepare for their baby. The joy she witnessed was a solemn reminder of what could have been, and everything we had lost all those years ago. But lately, something had shifted. Her smile was no longer laced with sadness, her words matched her expression, and her laughter was full. She was lighter than I'd ever seen.

"Is she okay?" Lanie asked, circling the car after the call ended. She knew how much I loved my Mustang, and the guilt was written all over her face.

"She'll live," I said, leaning against the car as she moved closer. I slipped my hand beneath Lanie's hair, cradling her cheek. "Are you okay?"

Her eyes twinkled in the moonlight. "I'm great."

"So, what's his name?" We'd been taking bets on whether they'd follow the family tradition.

"Harrison *William* Harlow." The corners of her eyes welled. "They named him after Josie's dad."

I wiped away a falling tear with my thumb. "And how are the new parents?"

"Exhausted. Josie was asleep, so I'll call again tomorrow."

"About that..." I said, disregarding my relentless desire to have Lanie all to myself. "I know we've been planning our little getaway for a while now, but why don't we push it out a few weeks? The beach house isn't going anywhere, and I suspect you're dying to visit the little guy."

"Oh, Scott..." Lanie threw her arms around me with a sob. "Thank you," she cried, raining kisses down my face. "He's the closest thing I have to a nephew. That is, until Rile—"

"Do *not* finish that sentence."

Lanie's mouth snapped shut, but her eyes continued to sparkle. "We're going to be spending a lot of time at the beach house soon anyway."

"We are?"

"Of course," she said with utmost certainty. "We only have a few months to get it ready for the wedding."

I drew back. "A few months? At the beach house? Are you sure?" My eyebrows drew together. "We still need to make a guest list, find caterers, a celebrant, book a honeymoon, not to mention your dress. Surely you'll want to try on a million dresses to find the perfect one."

"Perfection is overrated. Plus, I doubt the perfect dress will even fit by then."

I rolled my eyes. "You've barely put on a pound since the day we met."

"Well, I'm predicting a lot more."

My laughter faded as she guided my hand to her stomach.

"If you want to get married before starting a family, we will need to do it soon."

All the air expelled out of my chest as I lifted my gaze to hers. "Are you messing with me?"

The corners of her mouth rose as she shook her head. "Not this time."

"You're pregnant?"

"Almost ten weeks."

I blinked back tears as I combatted a surge of emotion. "Lanie..." I drew her into my arms and buried my face into her hair. "I can't believe it."

"Me neither."

"Wait," I said, pulling back. "Ten weeks? How long have you known?"

"A few weeks," she replied sheepishly. "I didn't make it past eight weeks last time and was afraid I'd jinx it." The quiver in her voice shot straight through my heart.

"Afraid?" I pressed my forehead to hers. "I would've supported you every step of the way, regardless of the outcome," I said, tucking a stray hair behind her ear.

Her smile resurfaced. "For better or for worse?"

"Forever," I said as warmth filled my entire body. "I didn't think this day could get any better."

"Oh, I reckon it could…" she said, tugging the collar of my shirt.

All my blood rushed south. "Oh yeah?"

"Get back in the car, and I'll show you."

Without hesitation, I flung open the door to usher her inside.

"Wait," Lanie said, narrowing her eyes at the problematic door. "How did you get out of the car before?"

Her question threw me. "I…I don't know." The passenger door hadn't opened from the inside since my grandfather had bought it, nor the outside in years. I'd been so preoccupied I hadn't even noticed.

"You fixed her?" The accusation in Lanie's voice was evident and mildly amusing. My grandfather would've loved her.

"No…I didn't," I said, shutting the door and reopening it three times with ease.

Lanie folded her arms. "Are you saying she fixed herself?"

"I guess she did," I said, shaking my head in disbelief.

Her beautiful smile grew as she gazed over the vehicle. "I knew I liked this car."

I circled my arms around her waist to spoon her body into mine. "She is pretty amazing." Shivers rolled over her body as my lips touched the delicate skin of her neck.

"Mmm…" she moaned, rolling her head back onto my shoulder.

My pants tightened at the alluring sound. "We need to go," I said, guiding her into the car. "Before I take you up against this door and break it again."

"I wouldn't mind."

"Lanie…" I growled.

"Alright." She laughed, clearly knowing the effect she had on me.

"But you're in trouble when we get home," I murmured over her lips before kissing her.

As I jogged back to the driver's side, I paused before stepping inside, needing to take a moment. A girl like Lanie could have any man she desired, yet she chose me. Twice. And now she was going to be my wife and the mother of my child. I couldn't fucking believe it.

"You okay?" Lanie asked, threading her fingers through mine as we drove to her apartment.

I drew in a deep breath. "I've just…never felt like this before."

"Happy?"

"Always with you," I said, squeezing her hand. "But this is something else. Something I can't put into words."

Her eyes softened as she tilted her head. "Maybe you could draw me a picture."

"Unfortunately, I don't possess the artistic skills of my brother."

"Then you'll have to show me," she said with a seductive smile.

I ran my finger up and down her arm, creating goosebumps in my wake. "That I can do."

As her laughter filled the car, the heaviness that had haunted me since childhood floated away. It wasn't only love and happiness flowing through my veins…this was peace. My life was finally as it should be.

Up until my first day at Summerhill, I'd lived in a world full of torment. My brother and I didn't stand much of a chance with a non-existent mother and a drug-dealing father, but I was determined to break the cycle. All I had to do was study my ass off, work hard, and not get distracted by pretty things. But pretty didn't come close to describing the girl I had locked eyes on within my first few minutes at Summerhill. Fuck the guys who told me she was an ice queen and the girls who said she was a bitch. I had to know her, and once I did, I was entranced. She gave me something to aspire to, to live for, and each day I was with her, my future grew brighter.

Although we were torn apart in the chaos of our adolescent lives, our roots remained entangled, laying dormant underground. Those feelings I'd spent years repressing resurfaced the instant I discovered her stunning portrait at Josie's photography exhibition. Her tear-streaked face tore at my soul, and when I stumbled across her hiding in the coatroom that very night, it was clear our connection ran deeper than any teenage fling. It was in her eyes. The pain, the heartache, the fear...all simmering below her perfect facade. It was from that moment that I knew it wasn't over between us, and the day she turned up at my apartment, my sun rose again.

The universe had given us a second chance. To untangle the lies, to mend our fractured hearts and to unearth the path we were destined to walk together. We found the love that was stolen from us, the love we deserved, and the love we created, and goddammit, it was beautiful.

THE END

EXCLUSIVE PAPERBACK CONTENT

Reed

"You okay, Pix?"

Amy wiped her eyes as she hung up the phone. "I'm fine." She swallowed. "That was Grayson from the hospital. Josie just had the baby."

"Wow, that didn't take long." I placed my hands on her delicate shoulders, willing her blue eyes to meet mine. "Is it a boy or girl?"

"A boy." Her lower lip quivered as she peered up into my eyes. "His name is Harrison."

"And mom and baby are okay? Healthy?" She was definitely upset about something.

"They're great." Amy's smile was genuine, but tears welled regardless. "I'm so happy for them."

I tucked a wisp of blonde hair behind her ear. "Are *you* okay?" My girlfriend was hard to read at times. She held a lot of emotion beneath the surface, never wanting to be an issue for anyone, not even me.

"I'm just tired. It's been a long night." Amy lowered her head as she pulled away. "I'm going to take a bath."

Before I could respond, she slipped away. I wanted to join her, but I also needed to respect her space. Between Melanie and Scott's surprise engagement and Josie and Grayson having a baby, it had been an emotional night, and it was clearly taking its toll.

While most people considered Amy to be the life of the party, it had become evident to me that it was mostly a mask.

She concealed her emotions to protect others, and although she could see visions of the future, not all of them were positive, and she had to live with that every day of her life.

After pacing the apartment for what felt like an hour, I popped my head into the bathroom. "Ames?"

Her sniffles drew me in, and when I spotted Amy's puffy, bloodshot eyes, I grabbed a towel and pulled her out of the cold water, swaddling her petite frame.

"What's going on?" I asked, carefully laying her down on our bed and pulling the covers over her trembling body. When she didn't respond, I stripped off my clothes and slid in beside her, spooning her petite body perfectly into mine.

"I'm too exhausted to talk," Amy croaked, wiping her face against the pillow.

"That's okay." I kissed the back of her head and pulled her closer. "I've got you."

As Amy's body melted into mine, her shivers slowly morphed into long deep breaths until she finally fell asleep.

Fuck, I was out of my league here. The most beautiful woman I'd ever met was curled up in my bed, verging on despair, and there was nothing I could do or say to make her feel better. Amy was usually so happy, always smiling and up for a laugh, but something had shifted. The twinkle in her eyes had dulled, and I needed to know why.

Perhaps, with all the life-altering moments tonight, she was having second thoughts about our future. We did move in together quite soon after we met, but there was no way I was going to let her live in that mold-ridden, shoebox apartment. She deserved more.

Amy was reluctant at first, but since she'd been spending most nights at my place anyway, it made sense to stay. Josie *may* have helped my case by asking her to keep an eye on Melanie during her stay, but it had worked in my favor. I loved her living in my apartment, and I'd assumed she felt the same—until tonight. Tonight, her faraway gaze told me she was re-evaluating everything, and that scared the shit out of me. *She was my everything.*

———

The next morning, I awoke to her usual bubbly self, making breakfast, with Luci lurking around the kitchen for leftovers.

"Ames." I leaned on the kitchen counter with crossed arms. "About last night."

"I know! Josie and Gray had a baby. I still can't believe it." She grinned at the frying eggs. "I can't wait to meet him."

"Amy, I'm not talking about the baby."

Her attention switched to making coffee. "There's nothing else to talk about, Reed."

I tilted my head. "Ames."

"Last night was a lot to take in," she uttered, still not meeting my gaze. "I just had a moment, that's all."

That was one hell of a moment. "And you'd tell me if there was something else?"

Amy blew the steam off her coffee before taking a sip. "Of course."

She was lying, but I knew better than to accuse her of it.

"So, when should we visit the doting new parents?" I asked while she handed me a mug of our favorite brew with a noticeable tremor.

Amy left her coffee on the kitchen counter. "Maybe we should wait until they get home."

"Josie will want to see you. You're like a sister to her."

She bit her lower lip. "I know."

Amy hated hospitals. She'd already had to deal with so much loss in her life. First her mom, then her grandmother, then supporting her sister through her husband's illness and untimely passing. She'd never experienced a happy memory in a hospital, nor believed she could.

"Just focus on your best friend." I placed my coffee next to hers and stroked her upper arm. "No one else matters."

"That's easy for you to say," Amy muttered, gazing out our floor-to-ceiling windows. "You can't see what I can see in those places."

My hand trailed down to her fingers. "I know, but I'll be with you, Pix. You can hold my hand the entire time if you need."

With a faint smile, Amy reluctantly nodded before turning off the frying pan and throwing the burnt eggs to Luci. "Then we should go before I change my mind."

———

Taking the lead, I pulled Amy into the hospital elevator that took us to the maternity ward and didn't let go until we entered Josie's room.

Josie peered up from her sleeping baby. "Hey…" Her tired smile grew at the sight of her best friend. "Come and meet Harry."

Amy edged closer, eyeing the bundle in Josie's arms. "Hi, Harry Harlow," Amy whispered before pressing her lips to her friend's forehead. "I'm so proud of you, Jos."

I peeked over Amy's shoulder. "Hey, little guy."

"Hey, Reed." Josie grinned up at me. "Meet your newest neighbor."

"He's so tiny." It took every manly inch of me not to gush.

"But his feet are huge." Grayson strolled in with a to-go coffee. "You know what that means?"

Josie rolled her eyes. "Big socks."

"Starting the bad dad jokes already, huh?" Amy nudged Grayson's arm before hugging him.

"I have license now," Grayson uttered with a chuckle.

Josie lifted Harrison out to Amy. "Would you like to hold him?"

"Oh, um…" Amy's eyes widened and struck mine, pleading for help.

"I'd love to," I intercepted, distracting Josie from Amy's panic. I scooped up Harrison with ease and brought him closer to Amy, expecting her to soften into it.

"Wow, Reed." Josie cooed. "You're a natural."

"I helped my parents out a lot when my younger siblings were babies."

Josie shook her head. "I can't believe your mom did this six times." She proceeded to glare up at her husband. "Don't even think about it, Gray."

Grayson snorted. "We'll see."

As I ambled around the room with Harrison snuggled in my arms, I caught sight of Amy, paling and edging toward the door.

"I'm going to get a coffee," she said, pointing to Grayson's beverage. "Can you show me where you got yours?"

With a nod, Grayson ushered Amy out of the room while I lowered myself onto the armchair beside Josie's bed.

"Is Amy okay?" Josie asked, clearly surprised by her friend's sudden departure. "I know hospitals make her uncomfortable, but—"

"It's more than that," we uttered simultaneously. At least I wasn't imagining it.

Josie frowned. "Do you want me to talk to her?"

"No, you have enough going on right now. I'll try again tonight."

After a while, Harrison started to fuss, so I relocated him to my shoulder.

"You really are a natural at that."

"Like I said, lots of practice."

"Do you want your own kids someday?"

"Oh yeah, I'd love one or two." As the words departed my lips, my gaze struck Amy's fear-laced expression in the doorway.

"Do you want to hold him, Ames?" Josie asked, realizing she'd returned with Grayson.

Amy shook off whatever caught her by surprise then ambled into the room, sipping her coffee. "Oh no, he looks comfortable there. Plus, I'm in desperate need of caffeine."

Josie's gaze passed between us before Grayson interrupted. "Did you guys hear Mel's exciting news?"

"I'm sure Amy already knows." Josie sniggered as Grayson kissed the top of her head.

"Oh, Mel's pregnant?" Amy giggled. "Yeah, I know."

Josie smiled up at her husband. "See."

"You didn't tell me," I said as another wave of uneasiness struck.

"It wasn't for me to tell, and I only had the vision before Josie left for the hospital."

Her best friend yawned. "That was a very eventful night."

"You should get some sleep, Jos," Amy said, squeezing her friend's hand as she motioned me to pass Harrison back to Grayson.

"Thanks for visiting, guys," Grayson said before walking us out. "We'll see you at home in a few days."

Josie chuckled sleepily. "Where the real fun begins."

"I think we rushed into this, Reed," Amy said after an agonizingly quiet drive back to our apartment building. She'd spent the entire time frantically text messaging her sister.

I scrunched up my nose as I unlocked the front door. "Rushed into what?"

She sheepishly followed me inside. "Moving in together."

"Maybe." I shrugged. "But I don't regret it."

"Not yet," she murmured, closing the apartment door behind her.

I spun to Amy's lowered gaze. "What does that mean?"

She averted her attention to Luci, who'd come to greet us. "We've never talked about the future."

"Because you refuse to talk about it." I threw my wallet and keys onto the kitchen counter before grabbing Luci's leash, who was in desperate need of a walk.

"Because I think, deep down, we want different things."

Fuck. Here it comes. "Like what?"

"Like…having children."

My stomach twisted. "You don't want kids?"

"I… I don't think so." Amy's voice grew hoarse. "No."

This was it. The reason she'd been acting so strangely. "Then we won't," I said, without giving it a second thought. I couldn't lose her.

"Reed."

I sensed her gaze burning into my profile as I attached the leash to Luci's collar. "What?"

"I saw how good you were with Harrison." She exhaled a

shaky breath. "And I've been having reoccurring visions of you since last night...with children."

"So?" I shrugged off her comment. "I have heaps of nieces and nephews."

"They were *your* children, Reed."

I rolled my eyes. "And you're most likely their mom."

"No." She shook her head vigorously. "That can't be possible."

"Ames... This isn't fair. You can't make decisions based on something that hasn't happened yet."

"What isn't fair is me holding you back from fatherhood."

"Well, maybe you'll change your mind. Have you looked into your future?"

"I won't." The determination in her glare was as mighty as a stomping foot. "I've never wanted children, and I'm not going to risk what I'll see by looking into my future to confirm it."

Irritation flooded my veins. "Because you're scared."

"Of course I'm scared," she cried. "I'm scared of losing you when I can't give you what you want."

"Pix..." I dropped the leash to take her hand. "All I want is you."

"And when that's not enough?" She slipped her fingers out of mine. "You'll find someone else."

"Is that what you saw in your vision?"

"Well, no." Amy turned away. "But it makes sense. If I refuse to have kids, then you'll find someone who will."

"So, you're ending things based on this fucked-up assumption?" Rage swelled in my chest. "This is bullshit," I uttered, snatching Luci's leash from the floor. I had to get out of there before I completely lost it. "Can we finish this conversation later?"

"Cass is about to head back upstate, so I'm going with her." Amy grimaced. "I won't be here when you get back."

My blood ran cold. "What?"

"I need some time to think things through."

Hopelessness wrapped its dirty hands around my heart. "Please don't go, Pix. I love you."

"And I love you, but I need to get out of here. There's been so much going on lately, perhaps my visions are muddled. I need my sister's help to figure them out."

"And if they're not muddled?"

Amy sighed. "Then I'll pack the rest of my stuff while you're visiting your parents next weekend."

I closed my eyes. *Fuck, my mom's birthday weekend.* "Mom was really excited to finally meet you, Ames."

"It's best I don't meet your family. Not until I'm sure."

"And what about your family?" I'd already met Amy's sister and dad and had grown close to her nephew over the past year.

"I'm so sorry, Reed."

I tugged Luci out the door. "Me fucking too."

My days and nights rolled into each other over the following week. Fueled by energy drinks and no sleep, I played more than ever and didn't record any of it. I completely sucked and lost most games, but I kept going. Anything to avoid sleeping in that damn bed alone. Even Luci had gone back to Josie and Grayson's apartment.

I'd messaged Amy multiple times, checking on her, but she didn't offer anything more than confirmation that she was okay.

On the Friday afternoon before heading to my parents' house, I logged into *Aetherheart* one last time. I'd decided to take a break from screens for the rest of the weekend, so this was my last-ditch effort to run into my favorite avatar.

BigTed: **Hey, @EchoWisp**

EchoWisp: **Hey. Where's @RippleVex?**

BigTed: **Ditched us for a new crew, but I've convinced @SharkFinn to join us**

EchoWisp: **Your aunt know about this, @SharkFinn?**

SharkFinn: **Yeah. She's okay with it.**

Hope stirred in my chest.

EchoWisp: **Does she want to join our game?**

SharkFinn: **No. She's packing.**

EchoWisp: **When is she leaving?**

SharkFinn: **Soon, I think. She told my mom that she's waiting for you to leave first.**

My stomach plummeted. She was moving out of my apartment while I was gone, just like she'd said. It was over.

BigTed: **I guess it's just the three of us, then.**

EchoWisp: **Make that two. I gotta go.**

Once logged off, I threw the controller across the desk. "Dammit!" I roared before grabbing my packed bag. I couldn't stand to be in the apartment a moment longer, knowing I'd never see her in it again.

"I told you she didn't exist!" my youngest brother blurted as he opened the front door of my family home, along with my two younger sisters.

"Where is she?" Ivy asked, shoving my brother out of the doorway.

"Something came up."

Aria gasped. "Did you guys break up?"

"I don't want to talk about it," I snapped, pushing through my younger siblings into the hallway.

"Reed, is that you?" my mother called out from the kitchen.

I dropped my bag and walked into the kitchen where my mom was sliding out a tray of cookies from the oven. "Happy Birthday, Mom."

She dropped the tray on the stove and threw her arms around me. "Oh, Reed. I've missed you." She grabbed my cheeks with her mitt-covered hands. "How are you more handsome than the last time I saw you?"

"Genetics." My father chuckled, ambling inside with my older brother.

I shook my brother's hand before my father wrapped me in a bear hug.

"We've missed you, son."

"So, where's this girlfriend of yours?" Rusty asked, peering behind me. "Scare her off already?"

"Don't start on him." My older sister appeared behind my mother. "He just got here."

"We're having a rough patch, okay?" I averted my gaze from Violet's sympathetic eyes. "She's not coming."

Mom's face fell. "So, we're not going to meet her?"

"Apparently not." I turned for my bag. "I'm going to go unpack."

Murmurs erupted as soon as I left the room. This was why I had to move to the city. Too many people with too many opinions on my life. Although my parents were devoted Catholics, they rarely interfered with our life choices. They were happy if we were happy, but not without a whiff of judgment in the air—just ask any of my siblings.

When they discovered I had a girlfriend, thanks to my younger sister's online prying, they assumed an engagement was on the horizon. Hell, maybe it was. They'd been begging to meet her, but I'd successfully evaded it, knowing how overwhelming it would be for Amy and, to be honest, me.

My family rarely visited the city, and the few times we'd driven upstate, we'd stayed at Amy's dad's house instead. Not because I didn't love my family. I just needed more space, physically and mentally. I banked my energy for the bigger, unavoidable events, like today. My mother's sixtieth birthday, and she'd wanted everyone to be there, including Amy.

"Want to talk about it?" Violet asked while the others were outside preparing a barbeque feast.

"Not really," I muttered, scarfing down another one of my mother's chocolate chip cookies.

"Come on. What happened?"

I exhaled, knowing she wouldn't give up. "She doesn't want kids."

Violet's mouth fell open before she snapped it back up. "And you do?"

"I don't know. I hadn't even thought about it until last week.

She got all weird after our friends had a baby and just left. I haven't seen or spoken to her since."

Violet rubbed my back. "Maybe it's her way of protecting you."

"I told her if she doesn't want kids, then we wouldn't have any."

My sister frowned. "And you're okay with that?"

"Yes," I replied, but I couldn't even convince myself.

Violet gazed out the window at her son chasing my other nephew around the backyard. She'd had it tough since her soon-to-be ex-husband left her. "That's a lot to give up for love. Personally, I think you'd make a great dad. Better than most."

"And Amy would make a great mom."

"Did Amy have a great mom?" Violet asked, pondering me curiously.

"Not exactly. She died when she was very young."

"Perhaps that's one of her reasons." Violet's psychology degree was clearly at work.

"Fuck." I hadn't even considered that. Amy had had a traumatic start to life. No wonder she was anxious at the thought of becoming a mother.

"Maybe she just needs some time to process her feelings."

"That's what I hoped she'd do, but she's moving out this weekend."

"Are you sure about that?" Violet asked as the doorbell rang. "Hey, can you get that? I need to get the salads out of the fridge."

"Sure." I swallowed the last of my cookie and made my way to the front door, wondering how many more people were invited to Mom's birthday party.

I swung open the door and inhaled sharply. "Pix?! What are you doing here?"

Amy's glistening blue eyes peered up at me. "I'm hoping I'm still invited to your mom's birthday."

"Of...of course." I struggled to find my voice. "How did you find the house?"

She smirked over my shoulder at Violet. "I had a little help."

"Lovely to finally meet you, Amy." Violet's smile was full of warmth while she discreetly squeezed my arm. "Invite her in, dumbass. I'll go rummage up the family."

"Shit, sorry." I moved out of the way to let Amy inside. While she was instantly captivated by the family photos on the hallway walls, I took her suitcase and left it by the stairs. "Are you sure you're ready for this?"

She took my hand and held tight. "With you, I'm ready for anything."

"The famous Pix!" Ivy squealed as we stepped out into the backyard where a huge decorated table was set up on my father's perfect checkerboard lawn.

"I knew she was real." Aria punched my brother's arm. "Dick."

Asher rubbed his bicep, pretending to be hurt. "Well, fuck."

"Watch your language, Asher." My mom scowled as she stood. "We don't speak like that in this house."

"I can't wait for college," he muttered while my mom approached Amy, who was giggling at the altercation between my siblings.

"Amy!" Mom held out her arms and enveloped her. "We're so happy you could make it."

"Happy Birthday, Mrs. Jenson." Amy handed her a striking bunch of pink flowers. "Thanks for having me."

"Oh please, call me Sandy, and you didn't have to get me—" She paused as she eyed the flowers. "Peonies?!" My mother gasped. "My favorite!"

"How did you know that?" Violet's eyes widened. "Reed wouldn't even know that."

"And they're her favorite color," Ivy added.

"Lucky guess, I suppose," Amy said, sneaking a wink in my direction before turning back to my mom. "I'm so sorry I'm late."

"Not at all. You're just in time for dinner." Mom hooked her arm around Amy's elbow. "Come sit with me."

While my family monopolized Amy's attention over dinner, I watched in disbelief. She hadn't gone home to move out. She'd come here. To my family home. To meet *everyone*.

"How are you doing?" I whispered into Amy's ear as I cleared the plates.

"Great." Her eyes sparkled up at me. "I love your family."

"They clearly love you too."

She latched onto my hand. "Can we go somewhere and talk? Just the two of us?"

Without hesitating, I addressed the entire family. "I'm giving Amy a tour of the house."

"And the bedroom, I bet." Asher chortled from across the table.

"Asher!" Dad threw a carrot at my brother. "Mind your manners."

"Go on, you two," Mom said, nodding her head toward the house. "But don't miss the cake. The girls have been working on it all day."

"Oh, I would never miss cake." Amy grinned at my little sisters. She already had them wrapped around her little finger.

I guided Amy back into the house, giving her a quick tour before entering the bedroom I'd once shared with my brothers.

"Wow," Amy explored my space, donned with old sci-fi posters and collectable action figures. "I'm guessing you were really popular in high school?"

Amy may have been teasing, but she was right. I was a total nerd in high school. "Let's just say I was a late bloomer."

Her gaze rolled over me. "I bet those cheerleaders are kicking themselves now."

"Cheerleaders were never my type."

"Oh yeah?" She leaned against the desk. "What was your type, then?"

"Beautiful, quirky gamers with uncanny psychic abilities."

Amy laughed wholeheartedly as blush filled her cheeks. "Not many of them around!"

"Like finding a needle in a haystack."

Her eyes softened. "I know the feeling." Before I could respond, her shoulders slumped as she moved toward me. "I'm so sorry for running out on you like that, Reed."

I drew a deep breath and pulled her to sit on the edge of my bed. "If I somehow pressured you… I'm sorry too."

"You never pressured me. Far from it." She ran her soft fingers down the side of my face. "You've been incredible, and patient, and so grounding..." She inhaled deeply. "You're so damn perfect for me it hurts."

"And that scares you?"

"So much." Tears flooded her eyes. "I've never let myself get too involved with anyone, especially romantically. I see too much. I know too much." A single tear slid down her cheek. "I saw Cassidy lose her husband before anyone knew he was sick. Do you know how hard that was?"

"Oh, Ames." I pressed my forehead to hers as I caressed the nape of her neck. "That's devastating."

"My heart can only take so much, Reed. And the more people I let in, the more I have to lose."

"Then just let me in. I don't care if we have kids or not."

"But I do." Her eyes squeezed tight. "I lied when I told you I didn't want them. I do want them. I'm just petrified of what I might see in their futures—or worse...that they're just like me."

"Like you?" My brow furrowed. "Incredibly kind and caring with a beautiful soul?"

She shook her head. "These gifts Cassidy and I have...they're hard to tame. My own mother tapped out of the challenge."

"You're not your mother, Amy. She didn't know how to handle her ability. But you do. You'll be able to guide your children and embrace whatever beautiful gift comes their way from the very beginning."

Her oceanic eyes glazed over as she stared into mine until tears spilled down her cheeks.

"Did I say the wrong thing?"

"Not at all," her voice rasped out in a whisper. "I just allowed myself to see a glimpse of my future."

"And..."

"You were right." She drew a deep breath. "Those kids of yours...in my vision..."

My chest pounded.

She smiled through her tears. "Are mine too."

My throat tightened as I forced back the brewing emotion. "I never had any doubt."

"But let's not rush into that phase of our lives," she added quickly, poking my chest. "I want to see the world first."

I grasped her sweet face in the palms of my hands before kissing her tear-soaked lips. "Then I'll show you the world."

If Melanie and Scott's story captured your heart, you won't want to miss what comes next. Discover Cassidy and Adam's unforgettable love story in *Saving Soul*, the powerful conclusion to the Love, Beauty & Soul series. Keep reading for a sneak peek.

Chapter 1

Cassidy

He saw the ring.

I knew he did.

The lingering gaze on my hand was his irrefutable admission. So, why was he still approaching me?

My wedding ring was my shield against every man who took a second glance. Only, this guy's eyes didn't waver. If anything, his pupils dilated. From the moment he walked into that Midtown Manhattan bar, his piercing gaze caught mine and refused to budge.

Sitting at the far side of the bar, I tilted my head enough to let my golden beach waves tumble over my face to hide the heat in my cheeks. I wasn't used to attention. Marrying my first love at eighteen meant I never had to venture into the wilderness to find a mate. While all my friends were off clubbing and having epic one-night stands, I'd had other priorities.

Shifting uncomfortably on the barstool, I peeked through my hair, praying his gaze had moved to his next option, but alas, there he was. Staring…pondering…smirking. *Dang.*

The mere upward tilt of his lips shot straight to my core. *Hello there, stranger.* It had been years since my body reacted in such a way—and never so instantaneously. This man was a magician… and incredibly sexy, standing well over six feet tall with alluring broad shoulders that belonged in a swimming pool. His striking stubbled jawline and scruffy blond hair were a total contradiction to his immaculately tailored business suit, making me wonder if, perhaps, his day had been as shitty as mine.

My heart lurched as he lifted his drink from the counter and sauntered through the bar in my direction. He oozed confidence, unlike myself with beads of sweat winding down my neck to where I toyed with the crystal dangling between my breasts. This was the sort of guy who knew what he wanted and took it, and the sheer thought had my heart pounding and my core pulsing below.

While my friends were only now settling down and having kids, me? I was a seasoned pro. But this? *Fuck.* I was in over my head. This wasn't me. I wasn't this girl. What would Dominic think? *Fuck.* Why did that even matter anymore? It had been four years.

Maybe this was a good thing. No one but my sister knew me in Manhattan, so there was no harm in pretending to be someone else for one night. With sleep off the cards, a man like him would make the perfect distraction while I waited for the outcome of my interview.

After the day I'd had, I didn't fancy returning to Amy's miniscule apartment, so this made for a tempting solution. If I didn't get that damn job, the almost windowless abode would directly reflect the claustrophobic situation I was in, and it was sure to break me.

I glanced down at my embarrassingly old cell phone resting on the bar and blew out an irritated sigh before pouring the remains of my bank balance down my throat. I needed that job. It was our ticket home and they had assured me they would make a decision by the end of the day.

With only minutes remaining, the weight of my reality crashed down with my empty glass. While my interviewers tucked themselves into their thousand-thread-count sheets, completely oblivious to the impact of their indecision, I had to endure another sleepless night scheming up plan B, or C, or whatever fucking letter was up next.

It wasn't that I didn't like living in upstate New York; it was that I *loved* living in Los Angeles. I craved the sun, and the beach, and holding the memories of my grandmother close. After my mother died, my sister and I were sent to live with Grams in

Venice Beach while our father struggled to come to terms with the death of his wife. She provided us with a safe space to grieve, then nurtured us through our child and teen years, when our father couldn't.

Grams taught Amy and me to embrace the gifts, that would've otherwise been ignored. While Amy was gifted at capturing glimpses of the future, I was an empath. Not only did I know what other people were feeling, I could feel it too. It was a gift and a curse at the same time.

Swirling his neat whiskey, the sexiest man alive parted the crowd like fucking Moses and dropped onto the barstool beside me. "Hey," he uttered with an arrogant nod before taking a sip.

My eyebrows lifted, more out of amusement than interest. "Hey..." With the first glimpse of his eyes up close, my breath caught. No human could have eyes that blue.

"A beautiful woman like you really shouldn't be drinking alone." His voice was as smooth as his expensive silk tie.

"I'm not alone..."—the apples of my cheeks lifted with my smile— "...anymore." *Damn girl, who are you?*

His eyebrows lifted, seemingly surprised. Perhaps I had him fooled.

I purposely used my ring-bearing left hand to raise my empty glass, waiting for the penny to drop, but still no reaction. If anything, my subtle attempt to deter him only made the corner of his mouth rise. *Fuck, that's hot.*

"Looks like you need a refill," he said, lifting his finger to the barman before peeking back at my glass. "Gin and tonic?" With my nod, he signaled another round before leaning closer. "Celebrating or commiserating?"

My smile grew tight. "Commiserating...I think."

His eyes narrowed. "You think?"

"I had a job interview today." I tapped my cell. "They said they'd let me know by tonight, and well, it's almost tomorrow."

The gorgeous man leaned back in his chair, watching me. "How do you think it went?"

"Terribly. The interviewer was a complete bitch."

"And you still want the job?"

My stomach roiled. "I *need* the job."

With a slow nod, he took another sip of his drink.

"What about you?" I asked as another gin materialized in front of me. "Celebrating or commiserating?"

A small smile played on his lips. "Celebrating."

"That's great. Are you meeting with friends?" I panned my gaze through the bar, searching for others like him, but I doubted there were.

His panty-dropping grin faulted. "No."

"Oh." My brow furrowed, sensing something I had no business sensing.

"My brother just had a baby," he added quickly. "I thought I'd have a quick celebratory drink before I head to bed." His gaze penetrated mine. "My apartment is across the street."

"Well, congratulations," I said, ignoring the seduction in his mesmerising eyes. "First-time uncle?"

"Yep." He gulped down another mouthful.

A surge of happiness rolled through me, clearly his, but he didn't show it. "Niece or nephew?"

"Nephew."

My heart lit up, but I refrained from elaborating about how great kids were, especially of the boy variety. My son, for instance, was an absolute legend and he'd only been in existence ten years. I could talk about him all day, but much to my heart's utter discontent, today I had to pretend like he didn't exist.

The three-month live-in position I interviewed for left no room for family. My sister told me they were looking for someone without external commitments, so my son would've been a massive barrier. So, in desperation, I manipulated my application just enough to hopefully get the job that was going to resurrect our old lives.

My phone vibrated across the table and I snatched it up, worried something had happened to Finn. I'd become accustomed to bad news, and my heart dropped every time my phone chimed after 10 p.m.

Unknown: **Apologies for the delay. Please call my assistant tomorrow to make arrangements. I'll see you at Harlow Manor in four weeks.**

"Holy shit." I covered my mouth as hope and dread churned through my body.

"What's wrong?"

I stared at the screen. Numb. "I got it."

"But that's a good thing, right?"

"Yeah..." My heart screamed no. "Yes...of course...it's a great opportunity."

The blue-eyed stranger's brow furrowed, but he didn't press. He didn't care. Why would he? He hadn't even asked my name.

"Now we're both celebrating tonight," he said, shifting closer.

I pushed past the guilt already gnawing at my heart. "I guess we are."

He lifted his hand to the perky brunette behind the bar. "A bottle of your most expensive champagne."

Her cheeks burst with color as her eyes bulged. She appeared starstruck, but how could you not be spellbound by this man? Men like this didn't exist in my world. They featured in magazines and movies, or at the very least, some charity ball with a supermodel on their arm. Not here. Not with me. And not staring at me like I was his next meal.

Maybe my luck was changing. First the job, now this. Perhaps the universe was throwing me a bone (quite literally). I needed this. A night off. No worries. No stress. Just me and some handsome stranger clearly craving the same anonymous release. We didn't need to know each other's names. We knew what this was, and damn straight I was going to enjoy every second of it.

"Are you trying to get me drunk?" I asked my new friend as he summoned over another bottle of champagne.

"Why would I want you drunk?"

"To loosen me up." I giggled openly, embracing the buzz. I hadn't felt this free in years.

His fingers brushed against my thigh. "Do you need loosening?"

My chest constricted as a surge of electricity rushed straight to my core. *Wow.* I glanced around the bar for prying eyes, but it was far too dark and crowded for anyone to notice his hand's deviant adventures.

He rotated his stool until my side was encased by his large frame. "Because I can help with that," he whispered into my ear as he rested his right arm across the back of my chair.

"I—" my voice caught as his left hand slid over my bare leg.

He grasped my thigh as his gaze locked on mine. "You can stop me anytime. Just say the word."

Not daring to say any word that may hinder his movements, I tipped more champagne into my mouth.

His eyes trailed after my tongue, as it glided across my lips, before falling to my chest. "You've got *spectacular* tits."

I hiccupped at his abrupt remark. "Thank you…I guess."

"Are they real?"

Laughter burst from my mouth. "Of course they are!"

His gaze narrowed as if analyzing the situation. "Bullshit."

"If I had the money, I'd get them reduced, not enhanced."

"Don't you dare," he hissed. "They're fucking perfection."

I shook my head, trying to hide my smile. His forwardness was refreshing.

"I still don't believe you." He rubbed his stubbled jawline. "You're going to have to prove it."

"How could I possibly prov—oooh." I walked right into that one. "You want me to show you my boobs."

"I'd have to feel them to *really* know."

Heat swirled through my body. "Then I guess you'll never know." *Lie.*

"Never?" His hand inched up my thigh.

"Yes," was all I could muster as the hem of my dress rose.

"Yes?" His finger grazed my panties. "Or never?"

I sucked in my breath. "Oh, God."

"Easy, Tiger." He curled one of my blonde waves around his finger before grazing his nose across my neck. "I've barely even touched you."

My chest rose up and down, fighting the building tension, while his finger circled my clit.

He smirked as I squirmed. "Jesus, you're sensitive." *He had no idea.*

Not only was I drowning in desire, I was absorbing his lust. It was all-encompassing, and the pull of our bodies was incredible.

"I think you should come back to my apartment before you scream the place down," he said into the shell of my ear as he increased the pressure below.

"Surely the restroom will suffice." There was no going back now. I was clearly a closet slut.

"No fucking way am I taking you in there." His tongue grazed my earlobe before nipping. "But I'll be taking you every fucking way in my bed."

ACKNOWLEDGMENTS

Firstly, to my boys—Small, Medium and Large, I hope this will one day be worth all the hours spent away from you. Thank you for supporting my dreams.

To my friends and complete strangers who reach out to tell me they love my books…it really means the world to me. If you have promoted my books via word of mouth, social media, or left a precious Amazon review…Thank you! I'm still doing this because of you.

To my beta readers, Mal, Sarah, Fleur & Jenn, and my proofreaders, Kath and Shae, please know how grateful I am for your help, encouragement and support!

To my amazing editor, Jenn, thank you for being so easy to work with and translating my Aussie jargon to American.

Finally, to the team at Keeperton / Arndell, thank you for believing in me and my stories, and launching them out into the world.

A x

ABOUT THE AUTHOR

Ann Penny is a contemporary romance author from Melbourne, Australia, known for her emotionally rich storytelling that resonates with readers drawn to tales of passion, resilience, and hope. A two-time finalist for the prestigious Romance Writers of Australia (RWA) Romance Book of the Year Award, Ann Penny is quickly gaining recognition in the romance genre for the exceptional depth and heart in her stories.

Her journey into writing began in childhood, where she often found herself lost in daydreams instead of completing schoolwork—a trait that was later understood to be connected to undiagnosed neurodivergence. These early experiences, where she would immerse herself in imagined worlds and scenarios, ultimately became the foundation for her writing career. Her ability to weave intricate plots and create layered, interconnected stories is a direct result of her imaginative mind and her unique perspective on the world.

Her stories delve into themes of self-discovery, healing from past trauma, and the transformative power of love. Beyond romance, they offer readers tales of post-traumatic growth and personal empowerment, all delivered with a unique voice and a touch of quirky humour.

When Ann Penny isn't writing, she enjoys having a laugh with her husband and sons, cuddling her fur babies, and immersing herself in anything creative. Penny is always striving to craft something beautiful and unexpected while endeavouring to harness her hyperactive mind.

With deep emotional insight, and a huge backlog of untold stories in her head, Ann Penny will continue to embrace her storytelling skills to captivate readers with relatable characters and heartfelt stories—where love and personal growth go hand in hand.